Wasted Time

Also by David Baldwin:

Wildheath Crags

A Burning Matter of Completion

The Last Thing You See Before You Die

Wasted Time

David Baldwin

Published by Davroba Publishing

A CIP catalogue record for this book is available from the British Library.

ISBN 978-1-7396404-4-6

Book layout and cover design by Clare Brayshaw

Cover images | Dreamstime.com

Prepared and printed by:

York Publishing Services Ltd
64 Hallfield Road
Layerthorpe
York YO31 7ZQ

Tel: 01904 431213

Website: www.yps-publishing.co.uk

Acknowledgements

Thanks to Gill Alderson, John Baldwin, Mike Conboy, Brian Horton, Stuart Lund, Peter Snow and Georgina Wright for their invaluable support and advice in reading and editing parts of this novel.

Part 1

CHAPTER 1

12 April 2005: Early Morning

It was gradually getting lighter as a large, dark car drove speedily into the college's expansive but almost deserted car park. There were only two cars present at that time of day and the dark car came carefully to a halt at the far side of the vehicle nearest to the adjacent buildings. Anyone observing this would have thought it an extremely strange thing to do unless, that is, someone didn't wish the car to be seen by inquisitive eyes. Although fairly confident that no one was watching, but, as if trying to become invisible, the driver ducked down out of sight behind the steering wheel. In a few minutes a fourth car would arrive and that would be the signal to put into action the final stage of a deadly plan.

About half a mile away in the town centre, a middle-aged bank employee was sitting in the back of a slightly smaller car with a sawn-off shotgun pressed firmly against his ribcage. He was whimpering softly. He was fretting about his wife who was lying, bound and gagged, at home on the kitchen floor but he was worrying more about the three other passengers in the car, each of whom had a nylon stocking over his head.

It was going to be a busy time for the local police force, which was already stretched to the limit. As bad luck would have it, their most experienced detectives were going to be dispatched at quarter to nine to deal with a bank robbery.

* * *

Ariadne Hopwood awoke with a start. Her alarm clock was telling her it was time to end the power sleeping for another night. She threw back the black duvet on her silver-framed bed and in one swift movement launched herself upright to stand in front of the full-length mirror of the white, fitted wardrobe. As she scanned herself from head to toe, she saw that her striking face had no wrinkles and her dark, shoulder-length hair was perfectly cut, layered close to the sides of her cheeks. She observed that her breasts were still shapely and her stomach was flat. Turning round to admire the rear view, she was satisfied that there was still only the faintest traces of cellulite on her buttocks and upper thighs.

"That's what the exercises are for," she grinned, "Give me five," and she immediately dropped down to the blue-carpeted floor to assume the press-up position.

"One – two – threeeeee – foooooouuuurr …fiiiiiiiiive."

She jumped up, breathing slightly more heavily.

"Shower next," she gasped, as she staggered off to the en-suite bathroom.

Of course, Ariadne's eyes had impeccable, twenty-twenty, airbrush vision, and five were more than enough press-ups for a woman who was forty four years old.

Her day invariably began this way, give or take five minutes. When the mirror, press-ups and shower phases had been completed she sat in her dressing gown at a white, silver-inlaid dressing table to pluck her eyebrows, one rogue hair at a time, after which she applied creams of various viscosities and aromas to her face and neck. A few minutes later she removed her improvised towel-turban and dried her hair, not with a hand-held dryer but with a fan heater placed on her bed, a method she'd used since childhood; she crouched in front of it so that both her hands were free to mould and brush the style she required, and this meant re-wetting her hair and re-drying it until it was perfect. Next she applied brown eye shadow to her eyelids and mascara to her eyelashes, and finally she put on flame red lipstick, which she would replenish when she reached her office so that it always appeared immaculate. She selected her clothes with the utmost care, including her foundation garments, choosing every day to wear something tasteful and expensive. This morning she decided on a white jacket, a burgundy blouse, a black skirt and black tights with a matching Gucci handbag. As often as not she wore high heels for, at five feet six in her shoeless feet, she had to appear several inches taller to fulfil her role as chief executive, especially in a workplace that, in spite of her nefarious intentions, still contained men.

After the lightest of breakfasts, she set out for work at five to seven precisely. She paused for a moment to check that everything in her carefully furnished and organised one bedroom, luxury flat was where it should be, after which she hastily made her way outside to her six months old, silver Porsche sports car. It was getting lighter as she pulled out of the paved courtyard and turned left onto the main road. She drove for about half a mile then swung right into the driveway leading to her personal parking space outside the building that formed the shell of her tightly controlled empire, Storbury College, which she ruled with a rod of iron. She didn't pay any attention to the other cars that were already there; she didn't need to in any case because she knew they belonged to the estate technicians, the only people who would be on site at this time of day. Two minutes later she was inside, waiting in the foyer to be let in to her sumptuous, silver-themed, state-of-the-art Principal's office.

"Morning, ma'am," said a tall, shaven-headed, thick-set man as he tapped numbers into an electronic security lock. "You look radiant today. Are you doing anything interesting this morning?"

"Oh yes," she replied. "It takes me back to my schooldays. I've been looking forward to it."

She paused and looked quizzically up at the man, whom she regarded as nothing more than an oafish flunkey. Then she tossed her head back.

"I presume you're referring to my meeting," she continued self-importantly. "It's going to be an extra special one. Thank you for asking."

The man held the door open for her and touched his forehead obsequiously with his right index finger.

"I expect you'll enjoy yourself," he said cheerfully, as she hurried past him and walked quickly down the dimly lit corridor to unlock the door to her office. Once inside she switched on her reading lamp, hung up her jacket and placed her handbag on the floor by her desk.

"Ah," she whispered, consulting her personal planner. "Time for a treat before I prepare my address to the senior management team. I can hardly wait. Today will be a very important day in the history of this institution."

She picked up her notebook, wrote a few words in it and smiled.

"How terribly unhappy I've been without you all these years, Mort, you handsome, intelligent, miserable, weak man." she said aloud to herself. "So many contradictions. You don't know what you've been missing. That's why I had to make you despise me."

She opened one of her desk drawers and rummaged inside.

"Let me see…this one, I think."

She switched off the lamp and walked to the window to close the curtains, not fully but leaving about six or seven inches through which the early light would allow her to see what she was doing. On returning to her chair, she sat down gently and took a deep breath, unaware that there were two other people nearby, neither of whom knew of the other's presence. One was outside, cautiously watching through the crack in the curtains, but the other was inside, standing only a few feet away on the other side of her unlocked, office door. A low-pitched beeping noise sounded but Ariadne didn't appear to hear it, and the first figure slunk away, frustrated by this unwelcome interruption. More ominously, a few minutes later, she didn't hear the door open, nor did she feel the swift point of a needle lightly pierce the skin on her neck followed almost immediately by a second, more forceful jab into her exposed right arm, after which her rhythmic breathing slowed and she became still.

As her energy dissipated her body became rigid and she could no longer move at all. Soon she saw a black-clad figure lean over her and cover her mouth with one gloved hand, squeezing her nose with the other, but she felt no pain even as the downward pressure increased. Then slowly her life ebbed away. Everything turned black and she was dead. It didn't really matter in the general order of things, for in around another thirty years or so she would have died anyway. She lay there ghoulishly frozen, her head hanging over the back of her chair, her eyes still open, her tongue lolling out of the corner of her mouth…where had this milestone been in her action plan for early morning delight?

* * *

"One, two, three, four." Pause. "Five."

The leaving ritual was always the same.

"One, two, three, four, five, six."

He looked to his right.

"Seven."

He looked to his left.

"Eight."

He closed the kitchen door and moved on to look in the living room after which he closed this door as well.

"Nine."

"Ten" was out of kilter and required a dash upstairs, followed by the whole recount. Next came the burglar alarm, and, on leaving the house, the door was locked using three different keys. Finally there was only the matter of waiting for thirty seconds to make sure the alarm had set and didn't go off whilst he was away from home.

It was quarter past eight and Mortimer Todd was finally ready for his hour's drive to Storbury where he worked at the further education college. This included roughly the same idiosyncratic behaviour as the leaving procedure, involving a set of carefully computed times according to distance so that he could calculate at various points on the journey whether (and by how much) he was going to be early, all being well, or, more frequently, whether (and by how much) he was going to be late. Now in his fifties, he'd been like this ever since he could remember whenever he left home; only the extent of the domestic checks had changed.

The numbering system denoted the separate stages in ensuring that the large, inner-city, Victorian semi where he lived alone was as burglar-proof and as safe from burning down as he could make it. All had to be correct and in sequence before he could leave the house. There were four keys required to lock the back door and outhouses and if they were all in the drawer nearest the kitchen door, he could be reasonably sure those doors were locked. Steps 'five' to 'nine' indicated that the electric cooker (and its six control knobs), the toaster, the portable radio and the TV were each switched off. 'Ten' was the immersion heater in the bathroom, hence the gallop upstairs to confirm that it was also switched off…and, since the whole process had to begin again at 'one', this was followed by a return to the kitchen…the final count from one to ten, burglar alarm, exit and thirty seconds listening on the doorstep.

As a result of this obsessive behaviour, a timeworn procedure rooted in countless superstitions passed on to him by his mother and his childhood Sunday school teachers, he was already way behind the clock on his twenty five mile run to Storbury. In spite of this recurrent delay, he rarely managed to get up earlier or to start getting ready sooner. Nor had he ever considered moving closer to work and all attempts to look for a job nearer home had ended in failure. To make matters worse, his schedule was greatly hampered each morning by the number of cars, vans and lorries inexcusably and deliberately going out of their way to hold him up by moving slowly and erratically in front of him – and this morning it would be worse than ever because he'd set off even later than usual.

The journey, which he'd undertaken many, many times before, started in the city's suburbs, passed through a small town and ended in the outskirts of Storbury. In between there were two stretches of flat, sweeping countryside each about ten miles long. This entailed crawling, in his old but large and powerful, black Mercedes, through three lengthy queues of vehicles in the built-up areas with theoretically two fast runs in the middle. So the initial part of his drive was repeatedly taken up with worrying about whether he would be following the long-wheelbase, articulated lorry, which had just drawn up in front of him at the first set of traffic lights, for most of the next four or five miles...yet again.

Mort (he preferred this to Mortimer) didn't look like someone who worried much about anything. Although he was now fifty two he'd worn quite well and he could easily have passed for a much younger man. Just above average height, he had a full head of thick, light brown hair and he still wore it longish. He'd always had it stylishly cut, and he'd kept it like this, more from predisposition than by intent, so that it looked something like a youthful lion's mane. He also wore a younger man's clothes: jeans, black pullover and shirt complemented by a black, leather jacket – no dull, conservative suits for him – but this was mainly because he felt more comfortable this way rather than any conscious attempt at looking cool. He'd tried to take care of himself over the years judging from his slight but wiry frame and he was regarded as handsome by many women, his deep-set, piercing blue eyes the most striking of his winsome features.

* * *

Helen Armstrong slammed the door without any ritual preoccupations or special preparations and strode purposefully straight out of the small terraced house and down the street, there being no garden. She didn't care that she hadn't drawn back the curtains or made her bed. She was also oblivious to the raucous blare from her music centre but that would stop as soon as the CD had finished. She'd left all the lights on and the iron in the kitchen too, but it was thermostatically controlled and probably wouldn't burn the house down. She hadn't realised yet that she'd forgotten her key, but when she got back that evening her next door neighbours would be at home, and they would let her in with the one she'd given them, as this happened two or three times each week.

She had perhaps fifteen minutes to walk to the local college, about a half a mile from Storbury town centre, through an adjacent, bijou housing estate, the only distractions to her journey being the rows of identical, newly-built, semi-detached houses and the puerile jibes of young schoolboys on the rare occasion that any were up and about so early. Around half way through her journey, she met her first schoolboy but he didn't look at her as he trudged wearily past, weighed down by the size of his bulging rucksack. He might have been going mountaineering and if he was, he wasn't looking forward to the prospect. Normally the boys shouted something like "Look, it's the wicked, old witch", but only if they were in a gang because they knew there was safety in numbers. Helen didn't understand why they even noticed her, never mind the witch bit. She'd often looked in a mirror to see if she could see the reason. No hooked nose, no upturned chin, no warts, no pointed hat and unquestionably no broomstick or black cape. More to the point, she was too young, going on twenty five. She was in fact small and chubby with shoulder length, curly black hair. In addition, her plain, round face was only noteworthy, if that, for the smallness of her nose on which a pair of round–framed glasses perched above a fleshy, if slightly twisted mouth so that when she spoke or smiled her teeth could be seen on the left side protruding between her lips. She didn't even dress in black – she usually dressed in a brightly coloured jumper and grey, cotton trousers. It can't just have been her teeth; it must have been something else.

"Look out, it's the wicked, old witch! It's Griselda!" came a shout from across the road as she turned a corner at half past seven and walked past a small group of three scruffy schoolboys lighting up a communal first cigarette of the day.

"Piss off, knobheads," she hissed as she walked by, and the boys dissolved into feigned, raucous laughter, waving their arms in the air and slapping their thighs in mock frivolity.

However they were soon more concerned with retrieving the cigarette that the tallest of the three had dropped in a puddle on the shiny, wet pavement as his hands went down for the third time.

"She's cast a spell," he shouted, "Oh sod it, the fag's wet through and this is the only one I managed to nick from my mum…"

They began to squabble and they immediately forgot about Griselda as she strode on under the darkening skies. The rest of her walk was uneventful except when she paused to admire a large, dark-coloured car. It hurtled past her going in the opposite direction down the college's long driveway and away from the block of buildings for which she was heading, where she was employed as an administrative assistant. She would, as ever, be one of the first to arrive.

"Someone's in a hurry," she muttered as she watched the car rapidly disappear from view.

* * *

Mort was anxious to make up time as the lorry pulled away from the traffic lights and signaled to go left but no smile of relief passed his lips. It went straight on ahead of him, as if the driver knew who was behind and was playing some sort of childish game. He drummed his fingers on the steering wheel in frustration at not being able to enjoy a journey he'd made much more speedily during the night. He'd had a lot on his mind, so he'd driven out into countryside through the dark, wet streets to try to figure out for the umpteenth time why the woman who had once confessed her love for him had treated him so heartlessly. He'd showed her nothing but kindness and, had he known her true feelings for him sooner, things might have been very different. But she'd have to be got rid of now, he was sure of that. She was no longer the same and this time she'd gone much too far. The roads were eerily empty and he became engrossed in his conflicting thoughts, so much so that he lost track of time and where he was. Suddenly, as if waking from a nightmare, he found he was outside the college in Storbury and the sky had changed from cobalt blue to gunmetal grey. He didn't know how he'd got there but he was breathing heavily and it made him feel confused and angry. His anger intensified when he realised that he'd have to drive all the way home and then come straight back again – and he'd have to hurry. Then he began to fret that he hadn't checked everything properly before he left his house…he was a stupid fool. What had made him do it?

At least this morning it was light and, although chilly and cloudy, there was absolutely no chance of snow and he hated driving in snow. The roads he took passed through beautiful countryside, green and tree-lined all the way, with gloriously thatched cottages, country pubs, tall-steepled churches and fields filled with budding cereals or sheep with their new-born lambs. Spring is a period of renewal but it didn't seem so for him today and he rarely noticed them as he had to concentrate hard on his driving, his sphere of vision relentlessly blocked by the lorry ahead of him. All kinds of birds flew overhead and occasionally across his path in death-defying but geometrically accurate and perfectly timed swoops. He only noticed the magpies: one for sorrow, two for joy. As a rule he saw them in ones and he called them off in wonderfully superstitious fashion: "Good morning Captain Magpie. Have a nice day," and as he said these words he had to smile to ward off the sorrow that would soon come into his life, especially at work, if he didn't. The thought of what unpleasantness might be skulking in his in-tray and/or email always followed immediately, and made his stomach churn, but it took his mind off the lorry ahead which had gradually increased its speed to nearly thirty five miles per hour.

The road widened and he tried to pass the lorry but he was thwarted at every attempt by oncoming cavalcades of cars driving at snail-paced speeds. He glanced in his rearview mirror and saw that a procession had formed behind him with the nearest car, a BMW, right on his tail, weaving in and out in many spectacularly unsuccessful attempts to pass both his car and the lorry. The convoy slowed a little for a thirty mile an hour speed limit and at last the lorry indicated left and slowed to a crawl to turn into a lay-by. And, *as usual*, just as the surprised but relieved Mort pressed his foot on the accelerator to speed away, a small car driven by an elderly man came out of the next junction, narrowly avoiding a collision, and replaced the lorry's tempo, albeit slightly more slowly.

"Why, oh, why?" he sighed. "Not again. No, no, no, no, no."

The little car trundled on, its aged driver wrestling with the steering wheel along the winding stretch of country road at all of twenty miles per hour.

"I'm one of the main targets of the Countryside Vigilantes," he told anyone who would listen whenever he tried to explain why he was regularly late for work. "They're a group of top-secret, undercover agents and their clandestine operations involve the discreet surveillance of everyone driving around their locality. They use a huge fleet of cars, trucks, wagons, tractors and assorted white vans on their collective mission. Only they don't follow people, or tap phones, or spy on them from behind lace curtains. They don't even keep dossiers. They simply drive in front of all of them…very slowly. In perfect synchronisation after one operative turns off, he or she is immediately replaced by another. On the rare occasions this doesn't happen, I find myself at a spot on my journey where there's a restricted speed limit and I have to take my foot off anyway. 'Victor one. Mission accomplished'. That's the subliminal signal to the next Vigilante who's already in place and waiting for the convoy to approach, exactly where the road's dead straight and there's a higher speed limit. It takes extremely precise planning to co-ordinate this vehicle with other Vigilantes so that if any foolish optimists try to overtake it, they're met by a long, dawdling procession coming in the opposite direction. Interestingly, the car owning Vigilantes buy the last model of a range that a garage can't sell, because it's going cheap and they get it at rock bottom price – the lemon-coloured one, the lime green one, or the one whose engine power slightly exceeds that of a pedal cycle. And their cars are without exception very small."

"Are you sure they're not just a figment of your frustration at being late every day?" was the customary, alarmed reply from anyone who hadn't heard his passionate declamation before. "Sounds a bit paranoid to me."

"Someone must know who I am and where I live" Mort whined on regardless. "They know about my journey and they want me to be late, therefore I will be late. I will be late because of them. There must be lots of them therefore I will be late."

For some people their glass is half full; for others it is half empty. For Mort it had, for a great deal of his existence at any rate, seemed totally empty, by all accounts ever since he was a boy. Born into a working class home in Leeds, he was very much overawed by the mysterious world and mores of the boys' grammar school he attended where, despite showing considerable promise, he'd consistently underperformed in examinations due to anxiety. Shy and nervous by nature, and because of these early setbacks, he soon lacked self-confidence as well. Something would hold him back or go wrong when he least wanted it to, so he had to be continually on his guard. He did manage to get into a university, though it was via the clearing house, onto a course in English he didn't really want to take, but he toiled conscientiously and left with a lower second class degree when he hoped he might have got a first. After a couple of brief attempts at establishing a career in the civil service, then as an copy writer for a small advertising company, both of which he found mind-numbingly dull with definitely no short-term prospects at all, he decided to try teaching. It took him a year to qualify, and, to his astonishment, he became a lecturer in English at a large, inner city technical college. Apparently he'd impressed the head of department on his teaching practice there. To his further surprise, within a few months he was asked to be section leader with a team in the region of twenty five if you counted the part-time teachers. Things certainly seemed to be looking up and a lighter, more relaxed side to his character was able to blossom for a while until he moved, three years later, to a small, rural college of further education. On this gloomy, early spring, Tuesday morning in 2005 he was still making the same long, frustrating trek there that he'd made for the last twenty years.

CHAPTER 2

25 May 1984: 10am–6pm

Mort never forgot the time, almost twenty one years ago, when he went for interview for the post of Senior Lecturer in English and Liberal Arts at Storbury College of Further Education. He hadn't minded the long drive that day for summer was approaching, and he travelled across that 'beautiful countryside, green and tree lined all the way, with gloriously thatched cottages, country pubs, tall-steepled churches'…and he drank it all in, marveling at the sheer, verdant luxuriance that he was passing through. The 'selection process', his letter of invitation informed him, 'was to commence at ten o'clock', so he didn't have to plod through the rush hour, he saw magpies in pairs and the Vigilantes didn't exist.

He actually enjoyed the journey, confirming that he'd developed a more cheerful outlook since he became a teacher and his glass was more than half full on many occasions. He'd grown to be more sanguine and easy-going and he was capable of being sharply witty. This endeared him to many of his colleagues, even though occasionally he could be savagely scornful, more than ever after a few drinks. Nevertheless, in view of his largely unimpressive, chequered past, he was serious-minded and conscientious, preferring the safe option to the consequences of any foolish or imprudent actions. He still worried a lot, mainly about what people thought of him and, most of all, about his job, and this made him manifestly tentative and indecisive at times when others would have been more confident in their own judgement. He persuaded himself that it was because he was evenhanded and that he could always see both sides of a story or another person's point of view, when in fact he was dithering, seeking the correct outcome that wouldn't upset anyone. Oddly, these many contradictions had produced in him a steadfast durability and a resolute sense of duty, and he was a man to be relied on as long as he hadn't to make too many hasty decisions. Teaching was the ideal career for a man with such qualities.

In his early thirties, then, there was a lot for him to be positive about. He was looking his best; his well-groomed, longish, dark hair and his stubbly beard gave him an air of relaxed flamboyance complemented by a more formal, dark suit and tie. Yet there was one thing constantly on his mind. At the technical college there was little chance of advancement in the foreseeable future. He wasn't particularly ambitious but he wanted to make a go of something for once; he didn't think he'd be able to make any progress when the senior lecturers were all as young as he was and he started looking round for other posts. He may have travelled to Storbury that late spring day in a spirit of optimistic, high adventure but his deep-rooted misgivings about his lot in life were also there with him, lurking furtively inside.

When he arrived at the College, ten minutes early, he couldn't find anywhere to leave his car in the miniscule and heavily congested car park, so he pulled up outside what looked like the main building. As he was about to get out to check that he'd left enough room for other vehicles to pass, a short, plump, round-faced, latish middle aged woman in a grey twin set and pearls ran out of the building, shouting angrily.

"You can't park there, you can't park there!" she thundered. "Can't you see the double yellow lines?"

He hadn't.

"You'll have to move…now…without delay!"

"I'm here for interview and there are no parking spots left," he told her politely. "You'll know where I am, and you can come and fetch me to move my car if I'm causing an obstruction…"

"You what?" she screamed "Didn't you hear what I said?"

Her eyes widened manically and her voice rose a few more decibels, startling passers-by and doubtless rattling all the nearby windows.

"Get this car off the premises…*now*!" she cried, swinging her arms up and down so rapidly that she looked like a panicking hen flapping its wings. "This is a busy car park and your car's not registered on the College lists. No one seems to want to take responsibility for keeping the traffic moving. If it wasn't for me there'd be chaos. Go on, clear off."

He asked her again quietly where she thought he could leave his car safely.

"I don't give a damn," she shrieked. "What do you think all those streets out there are for?"

He was thirteen minutes late for the interview.

It got worse. As the candidates – five including Mort – took their seats for the initial meeting with Simon Junkin, the Head of Humanities, Mort asked if he could smoke.

"No you bloody well can't, young man," roared the Head, a fanatical anti-smoker even in those days. "It's a filthy habit and if I had my way, the whole campus would be a no-smoking area. In fact, I'd go so far as to say that cigarettes should be made illegal."

From this Mort assumed he was doomed and, with no chance of getting the job, he decided to go along with the flow, keep his mouth shut and make the best of what was likely to be a chastening experience. After the briefing Junkin led a guided tour of the two external buildings housing the Engineering workshops, two antiquated training kitchens and eating area, and the Art studios. There was also a dilapidated, wooden hut which, judging from the books and other paper resources on view, appeared to be a library and study area. The excursion didn't last long and he was astounded by the smallness of the main block. Leading off to the right of the foyer as you entered were three floors of classrooms with offices at the stairs end and small staff rooms at the other. Leading off to the left were two more floors of classrooms below which was the Executive suite; this housed the Principal's office, the meetings room in which the interviews were being held and a few small offices for administrative staff. At the far end was a refectory with separate areas for staff and students. He reckoned that the whole lot, including the tiny car park, would easily fit into the technical college's cathedral-like entrance hall and he was beginning to get very cold feet. A tinpot, rural college where you're screamed at when you arrive – what was he letting himself in for?

The words of Stan Collins, his best friend at the technical college, rang in his ears.

"It's a bloody weird, little place, matey-boy," he'd said the day before. "It's known as 'Sleepy Hollow' by the few poor sods that are aware of its existence. It's what's called a white shire county college and the number of students and lecturers from ethnic minorities rarely approaches double figures, which means that they can happily ignore any multicultural *issues*. From a teachers' perspective, it's a place you retire to whether you like it or not, and in living memory, you can count the number of staff who've moved on to promotion on the fingers of one of your hands."

"Hang on," said Mort, looking puzzled. "Why are you telling me now?"

"Shut up and listen," replied Stan, annoyed at being interrupted in full flow. "You see, Storbury's seen by most as a rustic idyll. The lecturers don't need to push for the extra pay or responsibility that promotion brings. Of course, most of them go there and stay a long time because of this. The student population's fairly constant, largely middle class and well-mannered so there's little pressure for anyone to work outside their comfort zones. Lucky for you, there aren't many problems with student discipline unless you include the odd fight between the young lads on the lower level courses or the occasional, high-spirited antics and precocious lippiness of the spoilt, little rich kids. It is, to put it succinctly, an isolated, rural college and, it's unbelievably arrogant in its isolation – despite what Thatcher and her cronies are trying to do. The Art teachers have their own studios, the Hospitality lecturers run their own restaurants or small hotels, and many other hippy types dabble in holistic therapies, oriental massage and magic crystals. Even the Engineers provide a cheap car servicing facility if you want to risk having your vehicle tinkered with by thick-fingered apprentices. Storbury's an affluent town, populated with people who've easily enough disposable income to dine out regularly, buy authentic objets d'art and play at being spiritual."

"How do you know all this?" enquired Mort, taken aback by the comprehensiveness of Stan's description.

"I went out with a woman who'd worked there for a couple of months. She jacked it in because it was so old-fashioned. Just like the nineteen fifties, she said."

"You could've told me before I applied," returned Mort despondently.

"It should be a doddle of a place to work in for someone as talented as you," laughed Stan impishly. "You'll walk the interview. There's something else to bear in mind as well: the local yokels. They'll all be droll-uns so you're bound to be Principal in a couple of years if you keep your distance…"

"That's really convinced me. What else do you know that you've not told me?"

"Only that we want rid of you. Then we can get someone half competent to run this section, someone who'll cut us some slack instead of incessantly worrying about our results and teaching methods…a busty blonde, for instance."

Mort's interview in the middle of the afternoon did go well, however. Junkin, accompanied by another Head of

Department and two governors – the Principal was at an education authority meeting that day – led the questioning. Mort coped with everything they threw at him with ease including what he supposed were the tie-breakers. How did he deal with recalcitrant staff? What was his policy on covering for absent lecturers? What would he do if a lecturer refused to teach evening classes...and so on, and, buoyed by this unexpected surge of self-belief, Mort's feet were thawing a little. None of his answers involved screaming and shouting, but he could see where they were coming from. It looked like they wanted someone to do some radical sorting out to take the pressure off themselves, but he wasn't sure if he was the right man for the post.

There were also the other four candidates to consider. All were male and Mort felt typically intimidated enough by them to believe that each one might be more suited to the College than he was. Three were 'externals'; they were enormously self-confident and eloquent, and they worked in similar small, rural colleges within the same educational district as Storbury. Mort was the true outsider and he suspected that he was probably a make-weight to show that the College did look further afield than a few miles past the end of its gatepost. The other one was already employed in the Humanities department, therefore, Mort logically concluded, he had to be the favourite. He was Paul Honor, the very well dressed and articulate section leader in English, with a face like a rotten apple. He'd poked it around the nearby waiting room door to introduce himself to the other interviewees after the guided tour, which he hadn't bothered to take part in.

"I can't understand why you've all turned up," he'd added swaggeringly. "I'm going to get the job – you might as well go back home now."

So Mort relaxed, sensing that he wasn't the kind of middle manager they were looking for and the decision about taking the job wouldn't be his to make. His feet were getting back to somewhere near their normal temperature.

As he sat there in an administrative office that had been made into a make-shift anteroom waiting for the other interviews to finish, he, like his feet, warmed to the idea of more pay and increased status and he considered things from a new, opposite perspective. It was the next rung of the ladder, after all, and he might only have to stay for a short while before he was ready to move on somewhere else and eventually run his own department. The journey to work would be longer each day but it had been picturesque and relaxing so he could easily put up with it. He started to believe he *would* be able to change things, remembering Charlton Heston's sardonic comment in the film *Planet of the Apes* when he first saw the primitive humanoids on what he believed was a new world far away in outer space. He smiled to himself as he paraphrased it.

"Look on the bright side. If this is the best they've got around here, in six months *I'll* be running this place."

Did he really suppose he could though? He was feeling happier but his feet were cooling down again. He couldn't make up his mind what to do if he *were* offered the job. He'd have to take it, wouldn't he? This was why he'd applied, wasn't it?

"You've got to accept it," he heard his wife, Cassandra, saying. "Consider me for once. All you think about is you, you, you. Besides the gang back at the technical college will be jealous as hell. Do it for me, Mort."

Despite all his previous doubts and, to some extent, his own uncertainty about whether he would like the job or be able to do it, he decided he'd accept. Or would he?

He felt the unfamiliar thrill of intense excitement and elation about an hour later when his name was called out. He'd gained another promotion and he'd be able to have a proper say about how things were run, even if it was at a second-rate establishment like this. When it was offered to him by a beaming Junkin, he suddenly wavered as his earlier reservations and Stan's trenchant warning about the place and its peculiar people welled up inside him, and he had to spend the next few minutes explaining his hesitancy as extreme surprise (which it actually was). He astonished himself further when he fixed the start date which was to be after the summer holidays in September. He also agreed enthusiastically that he would move to Storbury in due course (to be part of the local community) when he knew he had absolutely no intention of doing so even if they were to pay his expenses (which they wouldn't). Before he knew it he was being congratulated by the other members of the panel and welcomed as an 'integral part of an innovative and proactive ethos at Storbury College,' which he hoped didn't require him to kick backsides and shout a lot. In need of a cigarette and anxious to be alone to collect his many conflicting thoughts, he rose to leave and was about to say his goodbyes when Junkin asked him to wait so that he could 'have a word or two' about the new appointment.

This 'word or two' lasted well over an hour. They moved up to Junkin's second floor office, a large, well-appointed, brightly painted room with original watercolours on each plum-hued wall and many ornaments arranged tastefully on his desk, on bookshelves and on the window sill. Anti-smoking leaflets of various sizes were fanned out on a coffee table next to the desk – undoubtedly explaining his outburst at the pre-interview briefing. Junkin, a tall, thin, unattractive man in his mid-fifties wearing an ill-fitting, dreary suit, settled into his high-backed chair and beckoned Mort to sit opposite him.

"Well, young man," he began. "You stood out as the candidate who gave by far the best answers but you're lucky you got the job, because you were deemed a tad abrasive by the selection panel."

Mort squirmed at the very sound of such a phrase. He'd never been described in such a way before and he wasn't too sure what it meant anyway. He imagined how they'd all laugh back at the technical college when he got to this part of the account of all the ludicrous and wonderfully weird events that had taken place in what was fast becoming one of the most ridiculous days of his life.

"We're not looking for someone to stir up a hornet's nest," Junkin continued imperiously. "We need someone to steady the ship, to provide a calming influence, and, above all, to change the culture of Liberal Arts teaching at Storbury."

So don't cause too much trouble, thought Mort. No shouting needed. Junkin then changed the subject.

"However there are more important and pressing matters to concern us," he added, no longer looking at Mort but sitting back in his chair, arms folded and gazing up at the ceiling.

He was clearly taking great pleasure in playing the role of well-informed expert on all things educational, more than ever when he considered he had some privileged information to impart and a new subordinate to harangue.

"There has been a recent, highly significant change of national government strategy," he said with considerable authority. "It's much more than a straw in the wind, let me tell you. A more austere, centrally-managed approach to further education is on the horizon. In short, rationalisation and strict regulation are on the way, and the good, old days of laissez-faire and spend, spend, spend are numbered. This is where you come in. Your role will be to ensure that your teaching teams do their jobs properly and become accountable for their conduct and achievements."

Mort's head was spinning. He'd never heard so much gobbledegook in such a short time before and he presumed that somehow it was his responsibility alone to bring the College into the *twentieth* century or there'd be trouble. His suspicions were soon confirmed.

"You have, by far, the worst lot of teachers at this College," Junkin hissed officiously, continuing to lie back in his chair but now staring directly at Mort who sat cringing, his hands pressed tightly between his knees. "Your section leader in Art is rarely present at his classes – the ones he doesn't cancel, that is. He has an art gallery outside town and spends far too much time there, but we can't touch him as he has friends in high places in the education world. Indeed most of them are among his best customers. He's also very clever. He sets 'projects' for most of his students which nearly always involve their doing something in the town centre…if you follow me. Trouble is, he gets good exam results. But that's Art, isn't it? 'Art is what I say it is', the 'hanging gallery' and all that. I suspect that all the examiners are probably customers of his too. That's all going to change. I want him sorted."

Mort's feet were getting colder again and the temporary euphoria of gaining promotion was ebbing rapidly away. He looked intently at Junkin's face, the man who was to be his boss for the immediate future. It was egg-shaped and bony with small, effeminate features highlighted by a bristly moustache and topped off by a full head of greasy light brown hair, greying at the temples and parted, arrow straight, on the right. A large, protruding Adam's apple completed his rather nineteen forties, army officer appearance. Mort imagined that in days gone by a clean shaven Junkin would have been considered a dandy in a powdered wig and he certainly sounded like one, but he was soon brought back to reality.

"Then there's the English lot," Junkin continued, leaning back in his chair again and staring at the ceiling, his hands behind his head. "They're all frustrated university lecturers and most of what they teach goes right over their students' heads. Well, apart from two of the buggers, who are alcoholics, er…well I mean, they like a tipple at lunch time. It's a bit of a risk giving them any classes in the afternoon. Last year a few of them couldn't produce any marked papers for a scheduled visit by an external moderator in English Language. But they managed the night before, extremely hastily but no doubt plausibly, to present a complete set of records showing all the students had passed their course work.

They told the moderator that they thought it demeaning to give grades, to make comments, including positive ones, or to point out errors and cover all the essays in red ink – which is why they hadn't. It was a controlled experiment and, as the moderator could plainly see, it had produced remarkable results. The moderator, a pretentious old goat himself, fell for it hook, line and sinker and was highly impressed – so much so that he even went on to write a paper for the exam board recommending this approach in future."

Junkin continued in this vein for three quarters of an hour, going through the personnel of each of Mort's sections and pointing out the "frightfulness" of each one. He was keen to see what sort of reaction he was eliciting, but Mort merely sat there quietly feeling the chill in his feet spreading higher and higher up his legs until he felt frozen from the neck down as the catalogue of indifference, incompetence and, more worryingly, behaviour bordering on lunacy increased.

"Why wasn't some of this mentioned at the interview?" Mort asked politely when he summoned up enough courage to interrupt Junkin's diatribe.

"It's your responsibility, as a serious candidate, to ask the right sort of questions," Junkin retorted slyly with a puckish smirk.

"You haven't mentioned the previous Senior Lecturer," said Mort, unable to disguise the iciness in his voice as his whole body was now rigid. "Why wasn't she at the interview?"

"Oh her," snapped Junkin. "She retired last term which is why she wasn't here today. Paul Honor's been in charge temporarily so he'll be a bit miffed about not getting the job. She's probably been here since the place was built and has been, if you want my honest opinion, totally senile for ages – and this is why your sections are in such a mess. They've got away with anything and everything for too long. It's the old Storbury way, you see. Don't make waves, don't rock the boat and, above all, don't get found out."

Mort thought about his next question carefully, trying not to sound at all 'abrasive'.

"Why are you telling me this and why haven't you done anything about it?"

"Not my remit, my lad," Junkin thundered, slamming his fist down on the top of his desk. "My God, as if I haven't got enough to do running this department! This is why you've been appointed – but tread carefully. They're clever bastards when it comes to wriggling out of things, and I don't want a revolution on my hands."

At this point, Junkin looked at his watch. It was gone six o'clock. He jumped up suddenly and a nervous tension unexpectedly came into his voice so that he spoke much more quickly and less coherently.

"Is that the time? I've got my hens and geese to feed – I have a small holding and the dogs will be howling for a walk…shit, the caretakers will have gone home as there are no evening classes tonight. Don't forget to ring me as soon as you know when you can come for a preliminary visit during the summer holidays…By the way I like your suit…Oh and one other thing. I thought your letter of application was superb, plainly tailored to the job description. That's what got you it."

And with that he motioned Mort to leave. They made their way hastily out of the building, whereupon Junkin took out a bunch of keys from his jacket pocket and locked the main doors of the entrance to the College. The car park was totally deserted apart from a gleaming, grey-green Jaguar that looked like a small island in the middle of an ocean of tarmac. With a curt goodbye and a token jerk of his arm he left Mort standing spellbound like a forlorn castaway, desperate for a smoke and trying to remember where he'd abandoned his car.

CHAPTER 3

12 April 2005: 8.30–9.25am

Half an hour after yet another hold-up due to roadworks, Mort approached Storbury. He'd made up some time and he was hoping that he might pass speedily through the suburb of Mallory, the final logjam caused every term-time day by the plethora of cars driven by overprotective parents on the High School run. It was made much worse if it was raining, but today it was fine, if overcast, although it had poured down overnight. As he neared this last section of his fraught journey, about half a mile from his destination, he could calculate, almost to the nanosecond, how long it would take, depending on his position in the queue, to the first set of obstacles: cars seeking access to Mallory Lane where the school was situated. They had to turn right against the traffic, and, more frustratingly for him, push back into the ever increasing line of cars as they sought to rejoin the main road. He'd made up a childish poem over the years as he'd sat and waited to judge how long it would take: 'Past the pub, past the gallery, past the scrub, let's wait for Mallory'.

This morning he got as far as the pub, a run-down looking place on the left with nothing at all to entice any gridlocked driver. What had the brewers known to call it 'The Barred Gate'? Then he inched his way past a row of houses on both sides of the road, on the left hand side of which was situated Mallory Art Gallery, a large, in-fill, sprawling bungalow set further back from the road from the five or six adjacent semis, with a small drive on which an old and battered but surprisingly bright, white Rolls Royce was parked. Next to this, and totally out of context, was a small barren tract of weed-filled wasteland – about an acre in area. Here he sat and pondered (he'd had several hours to do this over the years) why such prime building land had remained an overgrown eyesore, especially as the right hand side was fully occupied with large, modern houses, but he never came to any conclusion, other than it was a speculative investment by profiteering builders, as the vehicles ahead often surged on, soon to be brought to a full stop again for minutes on end at the school junction. He couldn't remember how many times he'd considered overtaking the tailback recklessly, but he never did. He'd invented another little aphorism to excuse his cautiousness: 'It's better to be late than *the late*? It only takes a second to die'. Unfortunately it took hundreds of seconds to get to the College from there and live.

* * *

Stan Collins was spot-on. Storbury was a 'rustic idyll'. At the dawn of the twenty first century it was an out-of-the-way but fussy, dormer town in one of the more rural parts of the Midlands region of England in between two motorways. It was situated in an ancient, glaciated valley which had, over the millennia, developed into promising sheep-farming land surrounded by expansive forests and steep hills. Even the industrial revolution had only left a small scar on the town, mainly of lead and coal for which it was once briefly famous, and 'Storbury Gold' is still a locally-used expression for something ridiculous and worthless after several false claims were registered in the seventeenth century. These days, however, the old mining industry had long since vanished and most of the wool factories that replaced it had been demolished. The few that survived had been converted into quaint, expensive flats for those who commuted to well-paid jobs in the city about twenty miles due east, or into large, spacious crafts studios for the thriving local artisan community. There were still a few farms, an operational textile mill or two and small manufacturers of various kinds such as light engineering companies, but the focal point of business lay in service industries such as banks, restaurants, hairdressers and a large variety of retail outlets. Up in the hills there was, oddly, an alpaca ranch owned by the local Member of Parliament who had an interest in wool farming. In the 1990s, when he was a local councillor, he'd developed a strong attraction to South America and he'd persuaded the powers that be to twin Storbury with Piura in northern Peru.

* * *

Hundreds of seconds after being stationary at Mallory, Mort finally arrived at the College and managed to find one of the last car parking spaces. It had started to drizzle. He dashed into the main building and ran up four flights of stairs, but he stopped for a moment outside the modest office he shared with three others on the second floor. He drew a deep breath and opened the door. He was late again, this time by twelve minutes. As he entered they were all there silently staring at their computer screens. Nearest the door sat Helen, the departmental secretary, and on each side of the room, were two middle-aged men both sitting with their backs to each other and facing the wall. Without looking up Helen greeted him in her customary manner.

"Afternoon boss, pretend-Vigilantes out in force, traffic jam at Mallory again or was it the artic all the way from your drive? Did you sleep in or have you been up to something dastardly you're not going to tell us about?"

He ignored her. It had been much the same every morning for the last year or so as he made his Reginald Perrin entrance, except that the explanation for lateness unfailingly came from his colleagues as they'd heard every detail of all the delays in his journey many times before. But the 'something dastardly' bit was new. What made her think he'd been up to something? How could *she* know that he'd had a disturbingly extraordinary night? Had someone seen him driving away from the College? Had she seen him?

"What made you say...?" he countered, but he bit his tongue.

It would be best to say nothing and wait for her to elucidate in her brashly aggressive way – as she doubtless would if she knew he'd been in Storbury.

The other two paid no attention to him as he stood there thinking about the last few unsettling hours; they were more intent on what they were reading on the Internet. He hurried past them to his desk at the far end of the room, put down his bulging hold-all and switched on his own computer. This had once been Simon Junkin's office, and now, as the recently appointed Head of Humanities, it was his, but there was little trace of its former appearance and decoration. In the 1990s the College had reluctantly been forced to change in the face of complex, new legislation which had made all further education institutions independent corporations. A new breed of Principal had taken charge, intent on transforming 'Sleepy Hollow' into an ever-expanding, financially buoyant, 'world class organisation' and an extensive rebuilding and rebranding programme had been undertaken which had irrevocably put an end to the College's free and easy existence.

The College itself was situated on the eastern outskirts of Storbury in several acres of ever-shrinking, grassy fields and now consisted of five modern, purpose-built buildings. The largest, three storeys high, still housed the management and administrative offices, the executive suite and several large, well-furnished, general-purpose classrooms, but it had been extended to accommodate a modern training kitchen, a brand-new refectory and a small, rarely used prayer area. Another three buildings, which were single storey and took up much more ground space, comprised an Engineering and IT block (extended to include computer rooms in 1996), the Art, Hair and Beauty studios (completed in 1997) and the learning and resources centre (the refurbished library). About half way along the college drive, the fifth building had recently been erected in front of all others facing east, ostensibly for newly planned science courses; previously the ground had been used as football and rugby pitches in winter and a cricket pitch in summer. The car park had trebled in size but so had the number of cars using it.

There were now four occupants of what had once been the nucleus of Junkin's domain, each with a desk, computer and filing cabinets. The piles of anti-smoking literature had long since been consigned to the waste bin, for they were largely unnecessary in a no-smoking zone and the plum-coloured walls had been repainted beige, part of the College's new 'corporate identity'. The many pictures that had tastefully adorned the walls had been replaced with all kinds of educational paraphernalia – posters, promotional leaflets, graphs and charts showing the department's performance, lists of names of staff and contacts, and so on. The whole room epitomised the change in ideology and attitude to further education in the twenty first century.

After a few seconds Mort's computer booted into second gear and allowed him access to his emails. Most were, typically, from people wanting something urgently yesterday. He hated emails. He wanted to be philosophical about this hatred and come up with some earth-shattering insight into why they were turning everyone into obsessive typists, quite a novel experience, well, for everyone except typists, right up the hierarchy to the chief executive. He also hated the high degree of illiteracy that had resulted from allowing every Tom, Dick or Harry…Tracey, Debby or Hayley…constant access to instant communication with anyone anywhere as long as they had an address. How much further could it go, he often speculated?

"Did you get the email I sent you last night, Mort?" Helen asked impatiently from across the room.

"I'm looking, I'm looking," replied Mort equally impatiently, at the same thinking "Christ, she sits ten feet away. Why can't she just *tell* me?"

He found the email:

"hi mort, the senior management meeting will start at 9.30 prompt helen."

It had been sent that morning, reminding him mockingly of both the earliness of her arrival at the office and her keenness to impress him. And the fact that she'd lied to him. Obviously her talents didn't appear to run to using the shift key but he knew it was affectation…stating implicitly that she was a busy, and *very hip* and *in-your-face, young* woman…who interestingly also told lies.

"Why can't you lean over and tell me?" he asked, interrupting the inner invective.

"Because you're late every day and I'm a very busy girl, *sweetheart!*" came the mildly sarcastic but definitely disrespectful, *in-your-face* reply.

"Well, if I'm always late, how did you know I'd read the email?"

"That's your problem, *sunshine*. My duty's done. I sent it."

"But the meeting always kicks off at nine thirty…why did you need to send it at all?"

"Just doing my job, *ladyboy*. You'd better get a move on."

Luckily for Helen, Mort had had no involvement in her appointment as his secretary. Her interview a year or so earlier had been short and perfunctory, such was its relative importance in 2004. She'd applied for it from London where she'd been living for two years after leaving University there with a third class degree in English Literature. She had however been born and raised in Storbury and she was anxious to return since she'd found it impossible to find anything at all in the capital except for serving behind the counter in fast food outlets. No matter what kind of employment she applied for befitting a graduate, she never received a reply. This was most likely because she had important weaknesses to which she was totally blind. She had since early childhood been very aggressive both in attitude and comportment which immediately put most people off. She was also a very stubborn, young woman which in turn made her more belligerent…and so she'd chosen to live alone in a dingy bed-sit in Camden. Her mother, who was very concerned that her daughter was struggling to survive in what she considered to be dismal poverty in a dangerous city, had seen the advert for an administrative assistant in the local paper and urged her daughter to apply for it so that she could come home. Helen was at first reluctant as she didn't want to admit defeat in her quest for independence and agreed to go back on condition that she didn't have to live with her parents for longer than it took to find her own place, and her mother readily agreed. Within two weeks, Helen packed her things, left her job, her few acquaintances and her pokey, little flat and travelled back the day before the interview. She was the standout candidate. She was massively overqualified to begin with but what impressed the panel of female interviewers was her forceful self-assurance which they all agreed would stand her in good stead in dealing with the three incumbents of one of the last bastions of male dominance they were trying to rid themselves of.

Mort gave up and scanned his screen again. He scrolled around the emails impatiently, counting the new arrivals.

"Ladyboy? Ladyboy?" he murmured. "My God, she's going too far. Fifty two emails…fifty two since last night…"

"Sssh"…"Sssh" came out from the backs of the heads of the two other men who preferred browsing the Internet to dealing with their emails.

"It's going to rain this morning," shouted the black hair belonging to middle-aged Gordon Moss (the Social Sciences Manager) to the white hair belonging to even older Barry Roberts (the Liberal Arts Manager). "I've left my umbrella in my car. Do you think I should go and get it?"

The white head grunted its customary animalistic reply signifying 'I couldn't care less', and the first-thing-in-the-morning-silence was restored briefly. The others weren't aware that Barry, a Mancunian, was at that precise instant playing football for Manchester United. At the age of fifty three, but looking a little younger in spite of his totally white hair, he'd made the team for the Cup Final. They were one down with ten minutes left to play. Barry, a late substitute, ran on to the pitch. Within seconds he won control of the ball and in a mesmerising run beating opponent after opponent, he scored with a thunderous volley. Then a corner. The ball came over in a perfect arc just right for him to head the equaliser. He rose, like a salmon…

"I said it's going to rain this morning," the back of Gordon Moss's head stated again, only louder. "I've left my umbrella in my car. Do you think I should go and get it?"

Barry's daydream exploded all over the room but he'd score the winning goal again, safely tucked up in bed and able to concentrate on the most important match of his life… for possibly the thousandth time. As Gordon was grumbling about his umbrella, Barry was bowling for England who needed five wickets to win the Ashes… but inexplicably rain suddenly stopped play.

"It's bucketing down," shouted Helen triumphantly. "You can go and get your umbrella now… ha ha ha ha har!"

Gordon wasn't amused. He hated getting his hair wet. He hailed from the Lake District where, he often complained, huge raindrops could fall from a cloudless sky.

"Oh hell, what am I going to do?" he screamed. "The rain's due to be set in for the day according to the weather forecast – Barry, please do me a favour, will you…?"

"Go get it yourself. Anyway it's bound to stop soon…"

"Stop putting up that bloody umbrella in the office to dry it off," shouted Mort. "It'll bring bad luck…"

"Now, now, now, boys," interjected Helen mercilessly, her wicked tone protected by the spirit of the age. "You're going to get your bottoms smacked if you don't stop your childish arguing. And you'll be late for whatever it is you do at nine thirty on Tuesdays."

The three 'boys' stood up as one, picked up their bundles of paper and trudged off, each muttering as he went – Barry because he hadn't yet scored that winning goal, Gordon because he had no umbrella, and Mort because he was wondering what the reference to 'lady boy' was all about as well as why Helen had used the word 'dastardly'. It wasn't like this every day…well yes it was. Helen came in very early followed by Barry and Gordon, equally early, with Barry arriving five minutes later than Gordon, and Mort always the last. Barry and Gordon occasionally got on each other's nerves but Mort tolerated them because, fortunately for him, they were very good at their jobs despite what he had to put up with.

CHAPTER 4

3 September 1984: Early Morning

Mort woke up blearily to the sound of the radio downstairs. It was the day he was to take up his new post. He'd been dreading this moment for three months, ever since he got the job at Storbury, but nonetheless there would be two weeks to familiarise himself and get things organised before the teaching term kicked in. Predictably, however, he'd developed an embarrassing nervous illness shortly after it fully dawned on him that he was going to have to stay there for at least two or three years before he could move on, but it had mercifully cleared itself up so that he wouldn't have to call in sick on his first day. The 'illness' which made it painful whenever Mort passed water was, the doctor had concluded, probably psychosomatic – the mind's way of dealing with a highly emotional reaction to something deeply perturbing, he explained carefully – since he couldn't find anything physically wrong. He was right but he still prescribed some tablets which had a surprising side effect: they turned Mort's pee green. This made it difficult for him to use public urinals, principally in crowded places like pubs, where they were usually all in a row and urine flowed down the gutter or a trough to an outlet at one end. He tried to use a cubicle whenever he could but when this wasn't possible he soon learned to occupy a position in the line with someone next to him, so that when other users saw a stream of green liquid flowing past their feet and looked to see who it was coming from, he would also turn and look at this unsuspecting man. He'd then raise his eyebrows and smile back at the other mesmerised onlookers down the line.

His wife Cassandra was already up which was unusual as it was just past seven o'clock. Normally she slept until about ten since she had no job to go to. She was very happy with this since she had each weekday to herself and complete freedom to do as she pleased with few, if any, financial worries. He could hear her singing to herself in the kitchen, so he got out of bed and very slowly made his way downstairs to make his breakfast. To his further amazement when he walked in she was naked. She grinned at his reaction to the unbelievable absurdity of this spectacle and beckoned him to sit down at the table where a plate of bacon and eggs was waiting for him. On the worktop behind him were a packet of sandwiches and a flask of coffee for his lunch.

"I want you to remember this day for the rest of your life," she beamed.

She was very happy that he'd got a new job because there was a substantial pay rise and, unknown to him, she was already planning how to spend it.

"Oh I will, I will, dear," he replied, sitting down obediently. "For a few more reasons than I expected."

As he sat and ate this unforeseen and absolutely unwanted treat he looked at her as she stood with her back to him washing up at the sink. He'd always thought she was very remarkable, but this morning, of all mornings, she looked strikingly alluring against the bright light of the sun-drenched, early autumn day. She had long, golden-brown hair, which reached far down her back, and a slim waist which made her bottom look larger than it actually was. Her legs were long and slender and when she turned round and he looked at her full on, he saw her two small breasts and her pubic hair as if for the first time. He shifted his gaze to her face and drank in once again her delicate lips and her dark, slightly slanted eyes, but he wished she'd taken her glasses off so that he could see the wonderful angularity of all of her features combined.

"Do you want a quick one before you go?" she teased.

"I don't think so," he said with his mouth half full. "Not after I've eaten this lovely, big meal you've made me. I've still got the terrible sinking feeling in my tummy as well so I'd probably throw it all up in mid-thrill. Sorry."

"I'm going back to bed anyway," she replied in the slightly disappointed tone she used on the rare occasions he rejected her advances. "If you change your mind you know where to find me."

And with that she left the room and ran upstairs, leaving him to the breakfast he didn't really want and an intensification of the ache in his gut he didn't want either.

As Cassandra was in the house, albeit in bed, he only needed to do a few checks before leaving the house (back doors locked, cooker, radio, toaster, TV and immersion all turned off) and he was able to set off well before eight. He assumed the journey would take about forty minutes to do the twenty odd miles to Storbury as it had taken him that long when he went for his interview. So he was quite surprised when the first part of his journey was much slower than he expected as he had to follow a large articulated lorry (which had just drawn up in front of him at the first set of traffic lights) for the first few miles. He arrived at the College at about quarter past nine. Luckily, he spotted a space towards the back of the car park into which he carefully reversed his blue Vauxhall Astra, just managing to avoid embedding its boot in the overgrown bushes which served as a boundary. He hurried into the main building and reported in at the empty reception area, where he was greeted warmly by an extremely pleasant, young woman who directed him to Simon Junkin's office on the second floor. He hoped this was a good omen and that the misgivings formed at his interview were to be unfounded. Sadly he was wrong as he discovered when he reached Junkin's office.

"Glad you could make it today, Mr Todd," he bellowed sarcastically, as he beckoned Mort to sit down, while he remained standing.

He was again wearing the ill-fitting, grey suit.

"I thought I made it clear to you at your interview that as a senior lecturer I expect you to set an example to your staff. They will all have noticed your lateness already – and your jeans and leather jacket – and they'll assume you're a fellow traveller dressed like that. So you must decide right away whose side you're on – theirs or mine. As a manager I expect you know what I think. That goes for your appearance as well. I thought you'd have put a smart outfit on."

"I'm ever so sorry, Mr Junkin," said Mort timidly, not sure which part of Junkin's admonishment he was apologising for. "I'm afraid I miscalculated how long it would take me to get here and the amount of traffic that would hold me up, especially where I reckoned I could put my foot down…"

"Well now you know," interrupted Junkin sharply. "If you'd come in to see me in the holidays once or twice, as you said you would, you'd have realised how long it would take you."

Mort decided it wasn't the most suitable occasion to tell him that he'd not been well for most of the time and judged it best simply to sit there and take the reprimand. In fact he'd had no genuine intention of going to the College if he could avoid it with some credible excuse or other, and he'd had a lot of time to think of at least two. Cassandra had arranged a month's holiday driving round Europe and that meant a very worrying week getting ready to go and another week recovering afterwards. That – and his 'illness' – had taken up most of the summer break. Yet deep down he'd been dreadfully depressed at leaving the technical college and his many friends. To him it was heartbreaking and immensely daunting – like leaving home for the first time. In the last week of term there, when all the classes had finished, he had his farewell party which all of the department attended. Some of his closest friends also arranged a farewell wake which lasted three days and nights during which he didn't go home, sleeping on the settee at the house two of them shared near the technical college. They only went in at lunchtime in any case since there wasn't much to do when the students had all finished their exams and no senior member of staff would be checking on them. Besides they were well aware that if they were seen at lunchtime the head of department would assume they'd been in all morning and they'd be still there in the afternoon. He couldn't remember much about any of it except that he seemed to be permanently drunk, and it was the only time in his life that he was sick at work. This was the early eighties, after all. Colleges enjoyed long holidays, eight or nine weeks in the summer, when lecturers weren't expected to attend. Many went away for the whole period, reappearing at the start of the autumn term, batteries recharged, well rested and splendidly sun-tanned. Yet it wasn't going to last. Junkin had been right. A new era was dawning as Margaret Thatcher's government was asserting itself on the country's workforce in the name of increased efficiency and it was about to have a long look at further education. A more austere approach was on the horizon and rationalisation was already under way. Somehow it hadn't quite reached Storbury yet which continued to carry on as usual.

Mort was feeling even more uncomfortable as Junkin began to go on again about the awfulness of some of the teachers in the department; he was sitting facing the window through which that bright morning's sunshine was also streaming and he felt blinded. The room was exactly the same as it had been when he'd been summoned there after his interview except that Junkin's desk was covered in what looked like teachers' timetables. He could hear a bird chirping loudly and rhythmically somewhere outside in the College grounds and the incessantly repeated notes were distracting him from what Junkin was saying. It didn't bother him though as he'd heard it all before. He preferred to run through some of the tactics he'd devised during the holidays to get off on the right foot with everyone. He'd decided to call a team meeting as soon as he could and hear what their version of events was, although he knew from his own experiences as a lecturer what it was likely to be. He was fully expecting them to blame Junkin for being a tyrant and a bully, out of touch with their needs as teachers, because this is exactly what he would have said, and he'd thought much the same ever since the interview. His musing was interrupted by Junkin dismissing him.

"You may go," he said. "You'll find all your predecessor's things in a cardboard box on your desk. It's in the departmental staff room down the corridor."

"Er…could you show me where my desk is please?" asked Mort ruefully, his face contorted with discomfort, and he found himself wringing his hands in genuine anguish.

"Well, that's how to impress me with your initiative and confidence, isn't it, lad?" snorted Junkin, obviously enjoying Mort's display of obsequiousness. "Come along then."

He ushered Mort out and led him down the corridor to the staff room and left him standing by a large, wide desk nearest the door, the one allocated to the Senior Lecturer in English and Liberal Arts. Mort looked round at the gathering of teachers, most of whom were standing and chatting in little groups among the desks which were arranged around each wall with another row along the centre, piled high with files, books and paper documents. They didn't seem to notice him or perhaps they were acting as if they hadn't, but no one acknowledged his presence, nor, for that matter, Junkin's. He was able to determine, however, from a brief glance round the room, that most of them were middle aged or older with neither gender in preponderance. He stood there, momentarily transfixed, when a balding, white-haired man with a hawk-like face wearing a grey cardigan and brown corduroy trousers, approached him hurriedly, as if eager to introduce himself. Mort smiled politely and held out his hand in grateful anticipation of at least one genial greeting but the gesture was unsmilingly ignored.

"You can't have all of this desk, young fellow-my-lad," the old man said aggressively. "See that socket? That's where the kettle goes so remember that when you unpack your things. Even though you're a senior lecturer you're not entitled to a desk that's larger than all the others. Alice never trespassed on our side."

He returned to his own desk (which Mort observed was about half the size of the one that he'd been allocated), took a large, silver kettle from behind a pile of papers and then walked briskly back whereupon he banged it down on one side of Mort's desk and plugged it into the wall socket nearby.

"That's where *our* kettle goes," he said and he smirked contemptuously, turned round and strode purposefully away.

Mort continued to stare after him as if hypnotised, involuntarily putting his right hand into his jacket pocket and feeling for his car keys. He shook his head in total disbelief and looked around to see what the reaction of the others might be but no one seemed to have noticed this peculiar occurrence, although he thought he saw a couple of them looking out of the corner of their eyes and sniggering.

He decided to see what 'Alice' had left him in the cardboard box which, as Junkin had said, was standing alone on the side of the desk it appeared he was permitted to use. He forced open the flaps at the top and pulled out half a dozen or so crumpled pieces of paper. He peered inside. Empty. What other unpleasant surprises were in store, he wondered? He studied the pieces of paper; the first was a set of minutes from a full-team meeting which had been held in November 1982 and included a list of names that might be useful for his first meeting although most of them were listed under 'Apologies'. The next four appeared to be guidelines for a three term course in English for Craft Students or it might have been a syllabus, but he didn't recognise any of the subject matter. The final one was the first page of an unmarked essay entitled 'Explore the ways in which the poems of John Donne present the differences between men and women.' He read it slowly, mouthing each word as he did so.

'Consistently throughout the works of metaphysical poet John Donne, the difference in roles of men and women is very apparent. Donne, whose presentation of contrasting genders is often not atypical of the seventeenth century, frequently wrote about sexuality and subsequently the two sexes in that context.'

He laughed for the first time that day, thankful that one of the students seemed to care about things. He looked for further evidence of his predecessor and wondered what might be in the two small drawers at the right hand side of the desk's leg space. The top one was empty save for a few pieces of fluff and two small fragments of unused blotting paper. Clearly she hadn't taken *everything* with her. The other one contained four old ballpoint pens and the stale remains of some sort of sandwich which were stiff and black with mould, perhaps part of one last snack? He took a tissue out of his trouser pocket and scooped up the mess, depositing it in the waste paper bin near the door, looking round cautiously to see if anyone was going to warn him that he wasn't allowed to use it. The pens and the blotting paper followed when he thought the coast was clear again.

It was getting on for ten o'clock and he leaned over his desk to peer out of the window which overlooked a lush, unmowed, green field forming part of the College's western border. In the distance, to his left, he could see a road on which many cars were speedily making their way in both directions, one of which led back to Mort's home and Cassandra. He was missing her more than usual, and the image of her standing naked in the kitchen a few hours before swept away some of the confusion and dejection which was now consuming him entirely. He wished he'd had that 'quick one' she offered but his distraction was immediately cut short when the entire room behind him began to empty, and several amorphous bodies filed past silently behind him. It was the morning coffee break and he was left alone in the room, standing disconsolately looking out of the window.

"No one's bloody well invited me, the bastards," he said aloud, hoping that no one was still in there, hidden behind their walls of textbooks and paper.

This had never happened at the technical college, where his crowd went down to the staff common room together. What's more, Stan Collins would make a point of going up to a newcomer (particularly if it was a woman) and introduce himself and the gang before inviting him or her to join them. Mort chuckled ruefully as he remembered how Stan used to introduce him.

"This is Todd" he would say. "He hates everything and everyone, especially the fairer sex."

He was missing Stan and as he thought of them drinking coffee and laughing and joking without him from now on, he took the flask that Cassandra had made for him out of the hold-all that served as his briefcase. In a mood of hopeless disappointment and desolation, he left the staff room and spent the morning break sitting in his car smoking and sipping the boiling coffee, wanting more than ever to burst into tears. But he didn't have time. All of a sudden he heard a tapping on the half-open side window and as he turned to see who or what had made it, he saw first a green, low cut cotton dress, then a charming, smiling, young woman's face flanked by shoulder-length, black hair which was perfectly cut, short and close at each side. Two pendant earrings were swaying slowly from side to side as she stooped and her flame-red lips were moving slowly and sensuously.

"Hi, I'm Ariadne Hopwood," said a husky voice as he wound down the window, "But most people call me Annie. I'm a lecturer in English. I've come to tell you that the Principal's meeting starts in five minutes in the library and I don't think he'd like you to miss it."

CHAPTER 5

12 April 2005: 9.28am

Quietly the College senior managers filed into the meetings room. Mort normally tried to be the first to arrive so that he could find a place furthest away from the 'chair', who for senior managers' meetings was without exception the Principal – known unaffectionately as 'Lady Ariadne', a pejorative nickname he'd conjured up for her very soon after her return to the College. The room was spartan, to say the least. Large, uncurtained, full length windows formed the outside aspect of the room and there were no pictures on the three beige-coloured, inner walls. The only item of furniture of note was the large, very old and deeply varnished, oak table, a relic of better times, but most of the chairs surrounding it were plastic and grey. Needless to say the chair reserved for 'Lady Ariadne', referred to as the 'throne', was large and comfortably well upholstered. Mort always tried to sit with his back to the windows so that he never had to squint against the light if he was ever asked a question or he had to make a presentation. He also felt more comfortable when back-lit, photogenically speaking. He preferred to be as far away as possible from the 'throne' so that he could make humorous asides to his best friend, Maureen King, the Head of Student Services. She'd been at Storbury for as long as he had, having been appointed as Youth Training Co-ordinator two years before he arrived there. She was small and full-figured, with strikingly large blue eyes and short-cropped hair which, once dark, was turning grey although she had, like Mort, only recently turned fifty. She'd been very pretty as a young woman but she'd let herself go a bit lately, being very content in a happy marriage and for this reason she never used hair dye. Without a doubt she would have regarded this as frivolous vanity and for the same reason she never wore ostentatious make-up or ear rings. She didn't need to, because she was still considered very good-looking by most male members of staff who jokingly tried to seduce her even though they knew they didn't stand a chance. She wasn't at all interested in being found attractive.

As he entered he saw that she was already sitting in the far corner nearest the windows and, to show she'd saved him his favourite seat, she beckoned him over histrionically. The other managers were mostly female and came in a group of three and two respectively. The threesome, as well as Maureen, wore black trouser suits, *de rigueur* for the younger ones who wished to think of themselves as upwardly mobile. The two older women, both of whom had been at the College since they left school, dressed more conventionally in jumpers and skirts. The men on the management team, one of whom was much older than the others and left over from preceding regimes, were formally dressed in dark suits also, a token of convention as well as their career aspirations, which for the older man were in reality non-existent. The two other men were newer, younger, keener and very ambitious. Mort, also a relatively newcomer to this group, usually wore his pullover and casual trousers or jeans; he was totally unaware that, because of this, no one ever took him seriously or indeed listened to him on the rare occasions that he spoke. It was 2005 and he didn't look like a senior manager.

They all sat waiting patiently. The younger women whispered among themselves, occasionally smiling or laughing girlishly at some little pleasantry or other. The three men (who had each come alone) either stared into space or doodled on their papers or note pads (or both) and everyone completely ignored Mort and Maureen who were whispering cynical comments about the agenda, trying childishly to outdo each other's fatuous wisecracking.

"I bet *any other business* will be the longest item," giggled Maureen.

"It was *matters arising* last week," replied Mort despairingly. "I don't know why she bothers with a list of topics anyway."

Maureen waved her hand casually in the direction of the rest of the assembly.

"Look at their faces. They're crapping themselves about item three: *Restructuring of the Senior Management Team*. Who's for the chop then?"

"You're safe along with the three witches and the two old hags. You're all women, so the dinosaur's probably first on her list, followed by me. I don't care if I'm only the one who goes anyway."

"She won't give you the push, you silly sod. You've got history…"

"Oh yes, I have, haven't I? A lot of good that'll do. She doesn't act as though she knows me, does she? It was the worst day of my life when she came back here."

"You're so negative. Here come the long bouts of introspection and self-analysis again. You're too neurotic…"

He looked around apprehensively, pointing an accusatory finger at her.

"Keep your voice down. I'm serious. You know very well that I'm destined to suffer. Things always go wrong for me…"

"You *expect* things to go wrong, and you worry too much about what other people think of you…"

"I'm trying not to…I'm trying not to. I'd love to be able to smile at the world and not give a toss about anyone else. Then I'd calmly kill the first person who annoyed me."

"Like the Lady Ariadne?"

"Yes, she'd be one of the first on my list, but there are plenty of others."

Maureen shook her head and smiled. She didn't wish to prolong a conversation she'd had many times before and she turned away to glance through a report on student counselling she'd been asked to give to the meeting. Mort began slowly to survey the other managers as they waited for Ariadne. Sometimes he liked to imagine each one as they might have been as a child. He'd developed this as a defence mechanism whenever he felt overawed by people he didn't know and felt might be 'formidable' in meetings or at interviews. It was his own invention, much as those ingenious individuals who, when feeling similarly intimidated, gain their equanimity and poise from visualising their adversaries sitting on the lavatory.

The group of three female managers, sitting opposite, caught his eye first. Two had come to power, like most of the others, from relatively junior positions at the College. Both were, unlike Maureen, blonde and of similar age, somewhere in their early to late thirties, and extremely slim to the point of looking undernourished. No need at all to imagine them as children. The first, Lucy Carlton, was tall and actually looked like a young boy, intensified by her flat chest and short, curly hair.

"She looks a lot like Millais' painting of the boy blowing bubbles," said Mort when he and Maureen had first clapped eyes on her nearly ten years ago.

"Except that she's black," Maureen had replied. "What's more, her hair's bleached and she always wears heavy make-up and bright purple lipstick."

"There's something about her I find fascinating," he added, not noticing Maureen's wry smile and shake of the head.

The other, Penny Castle, was shorter and unquestionably more curvaceous, her long face curtained at both sides by even longer straight hair which she had the habit of twirling slowly with either hand whenever she was listening, particularly in male company. She had a long, thin, Modigliani nose above which two small eyes were situated, both highlighted starkly by very blue eye shadow. She also wore purple lipstick (perhaps she shared it with Lucy Carlton) which completed the impression that the whole effect had been carefully managed to appear greater than the sum of its individual parts. However, her greatest asset, which brought her many admirers, was definitely the size of her bust.

"They've both used their sexuality to rise horizontally through the ranks," Mort often irreverently blustered to Maureen. "This always happens when there are still enough men in senior positions to fall for girly coquettishness and I despise these men for their weakness to it. Well, they couldn't really help it, could they? Unattractive men...who'd sweated bullets to get where they were...married to the only women they'd ever kissed who, equally plain and monogamous, are no longer interested in any kind of sexual contact after they'd delivered their two point four children...where was I? Oh yes...these unattractive men are no match for the simpering sensuality, theatrical hair flicking and exaggerated leg crossing of these ruthless, young harridans. How could they really believe that they were *actually* attractive to these women? Flattery gets you everywhere if it's from a leggy blonde."

Mort's opinion, however, was a little biased and based on past disappointment.

"It's because they won't succumb to your flawless chat-up technique and get into to bed with you," Maureen reminded him sardonically each time he went on about them.

He wouldn't want to sleep with either of them these days, even if it had been offered on a plate, yet at that moment he wasn't seeing one of them as a child; he was undressing her as a sexually provocative woman...slowly and lustfully. She'd changed his sex life fleetingly a long time ago, possibly permanently; it was the two most prominent parts of her body that had done the trick. He pulled himself together and turned his attention to the third member of this trio. She didn't fit into his paradigm, although she had blonde hair and was also in her late thirties. Harriet O'Reilly was chubby, she was no oil painting, and she wore thick glasses.

"Now Harriet's very intelligent, but I don't fancy her in the slightest," he told Maureen a few days after she was appointed to her senior position by Ariadne, having previously been at a college in Birmingham, and this added even more weight to his ranting about the other two. "I respect everything about her and I try to laugh whenever she says something vaguely funny or tries to make a joke. Unfortunately she's as dull as dishwater."

He didn't need to see her as a child simply because she still looked like a schoolgirl. He wondered whether she wore baggy, blue knickers and he shuddered at the thought. These were Mort's three black-suited witches: Penny, the Head of Business Studies, Lucy, the Head of Life Sciences, and Harriet, the Adult Education Manager.

Mort moved on. Sitting to the left of the coven, on the 'throne' side of the table, were respectively Iris Baxter, formidable, long-serving and newly promoted Head of Finance and Educational Support, and Bernadette Arden who was there to take the minutes. Bernadette, junior to Iris but well into her late fifties, had recently replaced her as the Principal's secretary; she didn't like Mort and because of this he didn't like her. On the first day in her new post she'd asked him who he was, despite having known him for over twelve years, when he put his head round her office door to ask if he could see Ariadne without a written appointment. She never acknowledged him if they met by chance anywhere in the building, she rarely answered his emails, she was perfunctory on the telephone and she was very uncooperative if he ever asked her directly for help or information. A few years ago she'd tried, when very tipsy, to have her wicked way with him at a staff party but Mort, equally well-oiled, had declined – rather unchivalrously according to office gossip, although characteristically he couldn't remember anything about it. He'd got his eyes on someone else, one of the three witches who was then a brand new, exotic face at the College, and he wasn't in the slightest bit attracted to a woman who was short and fat with a sagging face and much older than him. Even blind drunk he wouldn't have touched her with a bargepole.

Iris was similar. Now in her early sixties, she'd started at Storbury as an office junior aged sixteen and, after many years of diligent service, had become the Principal's secretary, loyally serving two of Ariadne's predecessors, both of whom had been male. She'd been Ariadne's first senior appointment eighteen months earlier since she knew exactly what Iris was like and she wanted to use her to keep the other managers in line. Ripples of disapproval ran through the College when the new post was created for her on the retirement of the previous Finance Manager, since she had no qualifications or experience in financial or estate matters, and many assumed that this would be exploited. Yet she was regarded as single-mindedly officious and domineering and would therefore maintain discipline ruthlessly – so this was all Ariadne really needed from her. This generosity wasn't reciprocated. Iris disliked Ariadne for many reasons, primarily because she was a female Principal.

"I love this College but I can't stand that dreadful woman," she confided to Maureen one day in the ladies toilets. "I firmly believe that women should know their place and look after their menfolk. This new job's not really what I wanted, although I'm not complaining about the salary. It's mainly because I can't get away with half as much – like leaving early to go shopping or to pick up my grandchildren from school…or to get my hair done. Ariadne works me hard and, infuriatingly, there are no surprise presents on top of my desk and, even more infuriatingly, I don't enjoy all-expenses-paid, leisurely weekends assisting at conferences any longer."

She held herself to be better than anyone else and she detested everyone equally except a male boss. She was obnoxious to all the staff therefore but they had to put up with it because of her position. She was, like Bernadette, short and plumpish with an equally fleshy face. Mort called them "Pea One and Pea Two as they came out of the same Pod." He also held a special grudge against both of them: against Bernadette because of the incident at the party all those years ago, and against Iris for many things beginning when she shouted at him so imperiously after he'd parked his car outside the main building on the day of his interview twenty years go. They disliked him too for much the same reasons. Hard as he tried though, he could never visualise them in any other way than they were, and he certainly could never bring himself even to attempt to imagine them sitting on a lavatory.

Mort moved on again to the three male managers. They always sat together facing the 'throne' but they never spoke much to each other. In the middle was Mike Smith, in his early forties with a Classics degree, so he was Head of Marketing. He was tall, fat, bespectacled and balding and there wasn't much more to say about him, other than that he appeared to be on top of his job. For the last four years he'd produced the right amount of advertising to attract thousands of customers, he'd carried out all the necessary market research and surveys and he'd gained most of the business kite marks going. He also mixed in the right networking circles without ever calling anyone 'darling'.

"He's the last person I'd have chosen to publicise anything," said Mort suddenly to Maureen. "Or…in today's parlance, to analyse and meet the needs and wants of the local community."

"He's not a man to be trusted either," said Maureen, looking up from her papers and seeing Mort staring at Mike and scowling. "Rumour has it that he's having an affair. He's a married man with children, the dirty…"

"That's ridiculous," interrupted Mort irritably. "Who'd want to have it off with him on the blind side unless he was paying for it?"

Had she told him who his mistress was, he'd have laughed in her face.

The second chap, sitting to Mike's right, looked equally sinister but, in reality, he was quite harmless. He was also tall but thin with a wispy beard showing many traces of grey and white. No one really knew where he'd come from as he predated anyone in the room, except possibly Iris. This was Mort's 'dinosaur'. As Head of Engineering and Computing he produced what was required and no more. Richard Head seemed to be very straightforward. Unfortunately as his name implied, he was not. Everyone wondered how his mother and father could have given him that Christian name. He'd been bullied at school because of this lack of parental forethought and he'd retreated into his own world at any early age. Secretly all his life he'd wanted to be a rock star, so he was lucky that he never made it. If Mort and Maureen had known, they've have named his band Dick Head and the Willies – or something much more cruel. Even as time rolled on and he got older, he never lost interest in this fantasy world. At home, where he lived alone, he could mime to all his favourite songs and he played air guitar perfectly. In truth he couldn't sing or play any musical instruments, although recently he'd managed to master the air drums to add to his vicarious enjoyment.

The third, slightly younger man in his late thirties was the Head of Information, responsible for the College's many kinds of data, principally for keeping a count of student numbers and their progress and achievement records which brought in most of the money. Like Mike Smith, Hugh Jones had been highly successful for the two years he'd been in post but he'd gained a reputation (of which he was mostly unaware) for being slippery, arrogant, overbearing and largely unapproachable, and yet, as everyone needed his assistance in the current managerial obsession with all kinds of statistical information and figures, they all tolerated him and hung on his every word and pontification. He was tall but blubbery, particularly around the waist, he had a bulbous nose, bags under his bloodshot eyes and thick lips, which made his face look like a mask that would scare children. He had very yellow teeth from smoking fifty a day and it was best to keep upwind of him if he ever came close, because he had breath that could strip paint at two hundred yards. Somehow he was married with three young children but he had a weakness for women, especially blondes, and he tried to sit near the three witches at meetings so that he could banter with them flirtatiously. Little did he know how deeply they each loathed him but in keeping with their aspirations they went along with him, as he was Ariadne's Deputy Principal and so senior to them. Mort and Maureen had no opinion of Hugh, preferring simply to treat him as nothing more than a source of facts and figures to complete their termly audits on time.

It was exactly 9.35 and still Lady Ariadne hadn't appeared. Iris, who used to take the minutes when she was the Principal's secretary and knew she could organise things better, looked at Bernadette meaningfully.

"Where is she?" she whispered. "Did you remind her that she wants us all here at nine thirty sharp?"

"I haven't seen her this morning," replied Bernadette nervously biting her lip. "It was ever so quiet in her office. I thought she was busy and you know she doesn't like to be interrupted…"

"Well, go and see," Iris spat back. "Chop-chop. As Principal's secretary it's your task to get things going."

Bernadette coughed and banged her pen on the table to get the managers' attention.

"Ladies and gentlemen, I'll go and see why the Principal is late, er, not here yet. Please excuse me."

A minute later the meeting heard a scream from down the corridor. It was Bernadette's scream. She'd discovered the Lady Ariadne's dead body and she'd absolutely no idea what to do or how to tell the others what she'd found.

CHAPTER 6

3 September 1984: Mid-Morning

Mort was grateful that he'd met someone who didn't seem to despise him. It was also good to be told what first day meetings he had to attend and at last he was to be conducted to where one was being held. No one had so far told him anything and he hadn't received a letter or even a telephone call from the College during the summer except for his official confirmation of appointment. He'd expected some communication or other but he knew it was really his fault as he hadn't contacted Junkin either – and Junkin was expecting him to spend a day or two there during the holidays. He'd have found out all he needed then. He remembered too that he got most of his information about what was going on at the technical college on the grapevine from his colleagues in the department, so he couldn't expect that sort of service on his first day among strangers. In truth he hoped that he wouldn't have to go to Storbury at all which is why he hadn't done anything. He could hardly believe what he'd done. It had all been like some sort of bad dream. He hadn't even seen the advertisement for the vacancy – it had been read out to him in the staff room one wet Friday afternoon by Stan who was in a mischievously playful mood that day.

"Come and look at this, bud," he said. "There's a fabulous job going that's right up your street. A Senior Lecturer's post in a college about twenty miles away. Easy commute, good money. You'll have to put in a few more hours at the coalface but think what Cassandra will say if you get it."

"Give me the title of the job, the closing date for applications and the college's address," replied Mort, who was in a particularly bad temper for some reason he couldn't recall.

A couple of days or so after all the forms, specifications and details came he typed out his usual letter of application outlining his experiences, changing only the title of the post for which he was applying and posted it off. He frowned many times afterwards when he thought of Junkin's comment that it was that letter that earned him the appointment. He'd gone off to the interview with little or no research, not really expecting to get the job but hoping mainly to gain some valuable experience for when he saw one he wanted more. Now he'd got this one, he wanted it less and less each day during that summer, but he couldn't think of a way to get himself out of his dilemma other than by writing to inform Junkin he'd changed his mind. He couldn't do that though. It was against his principles.

Ariadne only had enough time to introduce herself more formally and say how much she was looking forward to working with him as she took him the short distance to the library which the Principal made use of at this early stage in the academic calendar, to give the staff his annual morale boosting sermon on what lay ahead for them in the next three terms. Although wooden in structure and in need of refurbishment, the library contained the biggest room in the College and could accommodate well over a hundred people when the book stacks were pushed back against the walls and replaced by chairs in tight rows. It was light and airy being bordered on one side by large glass windows, most of which were open to make it more comfortable on warm days like this. The place was filling up as they went in and already most of the chairs at the back had been taken. He invited her to choose where they sat and was somewhat taken aback when she chose two seats on the empty front row. As they squeezed down the aisle between the chairs and the stacks, he noticed that everyone seemed to be looking at him and smiling – or were they smirking? He soon found out. The same short, plumpish, ghastly, piggy-faced, middle aged woman who had shouted at him so rudely when he'd arrived for interview, clapped her hands at the back of the room and asked for silence. Then she said as loudly as she could manage, trying to suppress her obvious annoyance:

"I'm afraid the Principal is going to be a little late as someone has parked their car in his space and currently he's waiting for the owner to go and move it. It's a light blue Vauxhall Astra, registration number J645NFA."

Mort stood up slowly, flushed with embarrassment as the assembled body of people laughed out loud at him.

"Delusions of grandeur already, eh?" someone shouted from the back row. "He's only been here five minutes and he's promoted himself to Principal."

He recognised the voice and realised immediately that it belonged to Paul Honor, the man who'd boasted so confidently he would get Mort's job a few months ago.

"I didn't know it was *his* space," Mort groaned to Ariadne as he pushed his way back up the cramped passageway.

She gave him a sympathetic look but he didn't notice it as his back was already turned.

"Didn't you see the sign with the Principal's name on it at the back by the hedge?" said piggy face, with both hands on her hips trying to look even fiercer – and succeeding. "It's clearly marked for all those who can read."

Mort rushed out to the car park and saw the Principal pacing about impatiently in front of the Astra. He was a short, stout, bald man with glasses wearing an almost threadbare, brown suit. He had the careworn look of a man who'd had enough of the responsibilities of leadership and was waiting for retirement.

"About bloody time," he shouted, red-faced with anger. "I presume this is *your* car. Didn't you see my sign?"

"I'm very sorry, I didn't," replied Mort timorously as he went behind the car to look for it.

It was there all right, but it was partially obscured by the overgrown hawthorn bushes and unless you knew of its existence, you wouldn't have seen it. As he parted the branches, he looked round to offer this an excuse but the Principal had disappeared, presumably to bring his own car. Once again Mort was faced with having nowhere to park except in the nearby streets. He climbed into his car and wanted to settle himself into the driving seat but he found himself hunched over the steering wheel, gripping it tightly.

"That's it," he sighed. "I've had enough. I'm not staying here."

Slowly he moved his car out of the space he'd mistaken as his own for the day, drove carefully out of the College and headed for home.

CHAPTER 7

12 April 2005: 9.45am

When a tearful Bernadette came back into the meetings room and broke the totally unexpected and dreadful news that Ariadne was dead, there was a long silence as there always is when something like this happens. Mort and Maureen looked at each other, the three witches looked at each other and the three men stopped doodling, looked up and searched around the room for someone to gape at to express their dismay visibly. It was Iris who spoke first. She was taking charge, albeit temporarily. She gestured across the table to Hugh.

"Right, you deal with the police," she barked in her usual dictatorial way. "It's your responsibility as Ariadne's deputy."

"Don't you mean *liaise*?" Hugh replied sharply, suddenly feeling very important and wanting to exert his authority straightaway.

Iris scowled at what she deemed to be a pointless remark and moved on.

"Call it what you will," she acknowledged grudgingly. "Mike, as Marketing Manager your role is to handle the media. Be careful what you say, you know the drill. Tell them there's been an accident, no an *incident*, which the police are investigating. You'd better start making a few notes."

Mike nodded. He knew what to do. Keep it short and vague and let the police answer all the difficult questions.

"Do I refer to them as 'cops' or the 'fuzz'," he grinned, hoping to relieve the tension a little.

"No," said Iris dismissively, and then looked at Bernadette who was wiping her eyes with a small, cotton handkerchief she kept up her sleeve. "Pull yourself together, dear. I appreciate it's horrid and, dare I say it, very frightening but we, as managers, have to keep calm and get the College through this. Right, was her door locked?"

Bernadette nodded.

"Did you lock the door behind you before you came here?"

Bernadette shook her head vigorously, her handkerchief now in her mouth. Iris picked up her large, brown leather handbag and stood up.

"Give me your key. The rest of you get on with the tasks I've given you," she proclaimed. "I'll go and ring the police. You'd better all stay here for the time being. We don't want this getting any further than this room if we can help it, do we? So keep calm, all of you. I'll be back as soon as I can."

After another long silence Hugh stood up.

"So I'm in charge, am I?" he said scornfully, staring round the table at the others. "Doesn't sound like it, does it?"

"You know what she's like, Hugh," said Penny, anxious to get the next word in and appear calm, as Iris had instructed. "She'll do all the running around and organising whoever she thinks is in charge. All she wants you to do is to deal with, I mean *liaise with*, the police so that everything appears normal."

She looked at Mike and winked.

"You know what the first thing the cops will ask, don't you?"

She was about to imitate the voice of the stereotypical old-fashioned bobby but she was beaten to it.

"*Who's in charge 'ere then?*" shouted Lucy placing each of her thumbs inside the lapels of her black suit jacket.

She laughed as she said it, but Penny wasn't amused, nor for that matter was anyone else. Lucy looked down at the table.

"Sorry," she whispered eventually. "Ever so sorry."

Mort stifled a yawn. His lack of sleep the night before was catching up with him.

"I don't want to appear disrespectful," he said, looking at Lucy sympathetically. "But all we're aware of is that she's dead and I expect she was murdered. Bernadette, can you possibly tell us what's happened?"

Bernadette had moved her chair away from the large table and was sitting in the corner of the room at the opposite side to the windows. She was still blubbering into her handkerchief.

"No, no I can't," she said in between sniffs. "It was too awful."

"Why do you *expect* she was murdered, Mort?" said Maureen, narrowing her eyes.

She'd remembered what he said about killing Ariadne a few minutes ago.

He shrugged his shoulders.

"We all know she had it coming," he said, yawning again.

No one appeared to want to challenge him and Richard even murmured his agreement. Bernadette howled.

"Well, as we're all in the dark about what's happened or how it happened, Bernadette, we can't prepare our alibis, can we?" Maureen added insensitively.

"I know where I was," exclaimed Harriet, sitting up suddenly like a frightened animal.

It was as if each member of the meeting was taking turns to contribute something to the discussion.

"I was at home and then I dropped my children off at the nursery. I didn't get here till gone nine because of the traffic at Mallory."

"Was it worse than usual today, Harriet?" asked Maureen, nudging Mort.

She leaned back and tapped her mouth twice with her right hand and pretended to look bored. Richard, who had followed the conversation by noting down what each person had said as if he were taking the minutes, wanted to speak next but he couldn't think of anything useful or humorous to say. It didn't matter because just then Iris came back into the room.

"Righto," she said as she reassumed her seat at the table. "I've called the police and they're on their way. Before they get here I suppose you want me to explain what's going on."

"Yeees," came the unanimous reply.

They sounded like a bunch of primary school children. Richard, who hadn't joined in, seized his opportunity.

"It would be very useful. Bernadette's obviously too upset to tell us anything at all," he said trying to sound as insightful as possible.

"Well then," said Iris running her tongue round the inside of her mouth. "I've been in the room. The Principal's dead – murdered by the look of it. I won't go into detail…"

"Oh go on, pretty please!"

It was Lucy who had cut in at the wrong moment again, trying to maintain the kindergarten atmosphere. No one laughed and once again she looked down at the table in contrition.

"Thank you Lucy," frowned Iris without looking at her. "The position of the body suggests that she was murdered. Either that or there's been a very embarrassing, dare I say it, highly tragic accident. That's all I'm going to say at present. If anyone here knows any more than that, they'd better… That's all I'm going to say – except that I've locked the room so that no one can go in. Here's your key back, Bernadette."

"You can't leave it like that," said Mike, reflecting everyone's obvious disappointment. "What am I supposed to say to the press?"

"You said *they*, Iris." inquired Mort slightly quizzically, before she could answer. "Are you implying that there may be more than one murderer, er, *person* who knows something?"

"You're correcting my grammar," snapped Iris. "I expect you're being facetious, Mr Todd."

Mort had no time to reply. There was a knock at the door and a tall, thin, uniformed police officer entered, his cap under his arm.

"Who's in charge here?" he inquired very brusquely but he was dismayed when most of the people he was looking at in the room appeared to be trying to suppress their laughter.

"Is this another of your stupid hoaxes?" he asked suspiciously, and he was about to give them a harsh dressing down when Iris raised her hand.

"No officer it's very serious," she said gravely. "There's a dead body in a room along the corridor. I think you should call a senior officer to investigate this matter."

"You what?" he exclaimed, looking shocked.

He wasn't expecting anything so earth-shattering, and he was frantically trying to work out what to do next.

"Right!" was all he could think of to say.

Then after a short pause during which he stared straight ahead of him, out of the widow over the fields and into outer space, he lowered his head robotically and spoke into his shoulder radio. He was calling for reinforcements.

"Everybody, stay here, please," he ordered as he left the room.

CHAPTER 8

4 September 1984: Mid-Afternoon

Mort called his first team meeting on the second day at his new College, or rather, Junkin had arranged it for him during the summer holidays. He'd found out about it from Ariadne the afternoon before, after he got back from his inadvertently extended morning coffee break. He hadn't gone home as his heart had decreed; he'd stopped about a mile from the College and quietly thought it through. He told himself that he wasn't the sort of man who ran away from difficult situations. On the contrary it was his *duty* to return to that awful place and tough it out. After all he *had* parked in the Principal's spot and that tired looking, old man needed it more than he did, regardless of status. The teachers in the staff room had presumably liked Alice and resented her being replaced by an unknown element from a large, inner-city technical college. Everything would be fine after he'd got to know them better. It was also going to be useful to have a kettle on his desk. Cassandra would be cross too if he walked out on his new job on the first day. But what clinched it for him was that he knew he'd be blacklisted if he didn't go back.

When he eventually arrived at the car park, it was a lot emptier than it had been an hour before, so he guessed the Principal's meeting had finished. He unpacked some his teaching notes and materials from the boot of his car and carried them resignedly up to the staff room where he found a meetings' schedule waiting for him on his desk. Clipped to the top left hand corner was a note. It said simply, in heavy italic script, 'Ani' below which there was a very large 'X'. He was feeling better. He had a friend. And he knew how to spell her name.

When he found the classroom allocated for his meeting on that second afternoon, he decided straightaway that it would be a good idea to rearrange the desks, which were predictably set out in single rows, into a square in the centre of the room. It would be easier for everyone that way, he thought. They'll see right away that I'm not going to be autocratic. He was lifting a chair when the first group of people arrived.

"What do you think you're doing?" said a familiar voice from the doorway. "The caretakers won't like this, young man."

It was the elderly, hawk-faced chap who Mort had already dubbed 'Kettleman'. He liked to give nicknames to people who perturbed him so that they'd seem comical, even ludicrous figures to him in times of stress.

"Hello, I'm Mort Todd," replied Mort as cheerily as he could, mindful of their first encounter the day before.

"Yes I know who you are," Kettleman said frostily, ignoring Mort's outstretched hand once again as he sauntered over to the impromptu meeting table. "Sit anywhere can we?"

Shortly after two thirty the rest of Mort's new team filed in two or three at a time, talking and laughing as they entered and chose their seats. Ariadne came with Paul Honor and they too were talking and laughing. He observed that she was dressed differently, in jeans and a blue, cotton jumper, and he was surprised to see Honor pat her on her bottom twice just before they sat down. She and Honor were also the only people in attendance who seemed to be under fifty. The other eight were casually dressed in summer wear and they all looked in good shape and healthy for their age. He was about to pass round the formal agenda he'd devised the evening before, when Honor began shouting, slightly more aggressively than he intended:

"Didn't see you at yesterday's union meeting. Were you still looking for a parking space?"

Everyone found this very funny including Ariadne who was chuckling along with the crowd. Great start, Mort thought, but it seems I've had my mind made up for me about whose side I'm on, and I don't think 'Diss' Honor likes me very much.

"I was in a timetabling meeting with Mr Junkin" retorted Mort calmly, his tone of voice in no way betraying his irritation. "I'll be issuing you with your timetables soon, item five on the agenda. However, I want to take a roll call?"

He took out the set of minutes he'd found in Alice's box, entirely oblivious that his audience were looking at each other in amazement. He read out the first name on it.

"Gary Owen – English."

"Left a year ago," someone said, followed instantly by mocking laughter.

"Mike Collins – Art."

"Apologies," another voice replied, and the collective mirth suddenly subsided.

"Anyone know where he is?"

This time there was no answer.

"Geraldine Jackson – English."

"Part-timer. Left ages ago – pregnant."

"Barbara Brown – Art."

"Died six months ago."

"Wouldn't it be easier if we signed our names on a piece of paper?" suggested Ariadne, before Mort could go on. "Afterwards you can check it against your staff lists. I think the one you've got is a bit out of date."

Mort blushed, realising that he wasn't making the impression of leadership he was hoping for.

"OK," he said, sounding grateful for a sensible idea and he passed around one of the blank sheets of paper he'd brought on which to make notes. "Will anyone volunteer to take the minutes?"

He looked around the room but predictably one and all were looking anywhere but at him as they each silently signed their names in turn. He picked up his agenda.

"As we've covered item one, let's move on to item two, apologies."

"You can check against your staff list," Ariadne piped up again, this time more impatiently.

Mort ignored her, aware that, despite his best intentions and his careful planning, things were going wrong again when he least wanted them to.

"Item three, matters arising."

"Arising from what? We've no minutes."

It was Honor again.

"Ah yes, I was coming to that," said Mort earnestly. "I couldn't find any among Alice's things. I was wondering if you had any."

"She never called any meetings," Honor chimed in. "I called all the English meetings and Roy called all the Art meetings. I think Maureen King calls the youth training meetings but they're mostly cross-college anyway."

At least he's being helpful for once, thought Mort.

"Thank you" he replied, looking down at his notes. "Is, er, Roy here?"

"Apologies!" said a middle-aged man, with long greying hair, glasses and a Santa Claus beard. More raucous hilarity.

"Where is he?"

"You'd better ask him. He might be in tomorrow."

"He's the section leader for Art. He should be here."

He looked around for some response but none was forthcoming. Foolishly he'd forgotten one of the unwritten rules of the shop floor, and he was desperate not to make any further slip-ups.

"Item four, introductions," he said as the list of the names of those present was unexpectedly pushed in front of him by the last signatory. "I think this is where I should have started."

He listened intently, smiling and nodding, as one by one the six men and four women all gave their names, what they taught (either English or Art subjects) and how long they'd worked there. He jotted down the main details as each person spoke to remind him who they were until he found out more about them. He also wanted to build a profile of his new teams, keen to match the names of those who'd attended the meeting against those who were absent if and when he received an up-to-date staff list from Junkin. He noted that Honor hadn't been the English section leader for very long – two years, it transpired – and that might have been why he didn't get the Senior Lecturer's job. He was also surprised to find that Ariadne had only been there for three terms and it was her first post since finishing university and teacher training. And he was flabbergasted when he heard 'Kettleman' describe himself as "a lecturer in social and life skills".

"Thank you," he said after the introductions were complete. "Let's move on to item five, timetables."

He felt that things were getting a little better now that he'd broken the ice, and he was beginning to feel more relaxed when Ariadne put her hand up again.

"Aren't you going to introduce yourself?" she asked coyly, her head slightly tilted to one side, her brown eyes open wide. "I'm sure everyone would like to learn a bit more about you."

Mort stared back at her for a split second too long, he concluded afterwards when he carried out an inconclusive review of the meeting on his way home, and he apologised for his oversight. Everyone was looking intently at him as if they were waiting for him to tell them an anecdote or a joke.

"I'm terribly sorry," he said, looking round the room. "I've been teaching English Language and a bit of Literature for the last four years. For the last three I've been section head, doing roughly the same job as Paul, I suppose, except in a much larger college..."

"The only difference between a small college and a large one is the number of staff and students."

It was Honor yet again, butting in for a third time.

"Here we have one course, one teacher. There you have larger numbers of the same course and consequently have to have more teachers to cover them. Here I have five full-time English teachers and a four or five part-timers. They cover the whole range from A Level to servicing."

"That's not strictly true," asserted Mort, not wishing to get into an argument. "I think you may be implying that I'm coming on with 'the big college man act', but nothing could be further from the truth. I think we'll move on to timetables."

He didn't think it wise to mention the size of his team at the technical college.

Honor sat back in his chair, folded his arms and scowled sullenly. He was wearing the same suit that he'd worn to his unsuccessful interview and he looked out of place among the rest of the casually turned out lecturers. Mort, in the jeans and leather bomber jacket he usually wore to work, felt he also might look inappropriately dressed. He wondered if senior staff were expected to wear suits and, if so, this is why they were all being so boorish. He picked up the pile of timetables, expecting them to form the basis of some discussion about the year ahead.

"Please pass these round," he said, more confidently than before. "Please find the one with your name on it."

There were a few sighs and groans but he ignored them.

"We've already got these," said Honor melodramatically throwing his own up in the air when he'd taken it from the pile. "We got them at the end of last term. Anyway they're bound to be changed after enrolment so at present they're provisional."

He suddenly stopped speaking and hastily picked up the timetable, scanning its content quickly.

"You haven't changed anything, have you?" he shouted petulantly.

"Why?" asked Mort, sensing he had the upper hand, but the others were now looking more closely at their own copies.

"Well, have you?"

"Some changes were made to the timetables by Mr Junkin during the holidays, I believe."

"You'd better not have changed mine. *I'm* responsible for English."

The rest of the teachers continued to look suspiciously at their timetables.

"I can't do Monday mornings or Friday afternoons," growled Kettleman angrily.

Mort sat and watched as most of the previously amused teachers started shouting all at once, waving their timetables in the air as though they were stock market traders. He clapped his hands.

"Quiet please. I'm not sure I understand what's going on," he announced, as gradually a kind of strained hush was restored. "I haven't done anything to them. I haven't even looked at them other than to check that the hours are correct, and I've discovered that most of them aren't. That's mainly what I wanted to talk to you about. I want to speak to you in your separate teams about them so that I hope we can resolve this amicably. You'll see on the schedule when we're due to meet. Until then, as Paul said earlier, please treat them as temporary. Any more questions?"

No one spoke.

"Any other business?"

He looked round at the collection of surly, annoyed faces, all frowning except for one. It was Ariadne and she was smiling back at him as a doting mother might do when her son has just accomplished something wonderful. Nevertheless, he wasn't feeling successful at all. He'd had his first taste of Junkin's shortcomings, and his allegiance had shifted slightly to the other side despite all the hostility he'd encountered in this meeting. On top of everything else, he'd been shouted at again.

Part 2

CHAPTER 9

12 April 2005: 10.25am

"Bloody hell, lad, don't let anyone in here without my say-so," said the Detective Inspector, as he unlocked the door to Ariadne's office and pushed it open.

He hadn't expected anything like this. He'd seen a few dead bodies before and he hadn't batted an eyelid, but this one was different. He turned away, took out his handkerchief and blew his nose noisily.

"Who's seen the corpse then?" he asked the other detective as he wiped his nostrils, his voice sounding oddly comical.

"Dunno yet, guv," came the reply. "I haven't had a chance to ask."

"Well, bloody well go and ask that lot in the room up the corridor," said the Detective Inspector, at a loss himself where to start. "Three or four are wearing suits so one of them must be in charge. Find out who they all are and get them to write something on paper – names, job titles and so on. While you're there, ask the woman who made the 999 call why she didn't report a *murder*. And let the control room know what's happened. While you're at it, request some back-up and get a uniformed chap from the car park to guard this door. No one comes near here till I give the word, OK?"

"Right, sir, er, which one shall I do first?" stammered the other detective.

He looked about seventeen, although he had to be much older.

"Hell's bells, lad. Call for forensic and SOCO first. Then, tell the person in charge to stop anyone leaving the College for the next hour or two. Oh and by the way, notify that caretaker chap that I'll keep his key for the time being."

The young detective nodded, slowly backed away, searching his pockets frantically for his notebook and mobile phone, and closed the murder scene door.

John Harrison hadn't been a Detective Inspector for very long and it was the first serious crime he'd had to deal with but he knew roughly what he had to do in a suspected murder case. Things hadn't gone exactly by the book so far. For a start the emergency telephone operator had only dispatched a patrol car to respond to the 999 call, thinking it was yet another juvenile prank from the College. They received quite a few each year, frequently from hooligans fooling around but sometimes from malicious students who held a grudge, usually against a lecturer, and worst of all, from those who were scared of failing an exam. That always involved the fire brigade too. Besides the caller had reported 'an incident' and that could have meant anything. So it was well after ten o'clock when he was summoned by the responding officer to attend the crime scene, although at this point in his investigation he wasn't exactly sure where it was. He was also aware that a bank robbery had taken place in the town centre a little after eight thirty and that the control room had prioritised this, so he was more or less on his own.

As senior investigating officer he knew he had to secure the site, but how was he going to be able to do so in such a large place with so few officers at his disposal? He'd decided to start with the gates at the end of the College drive, conscious that it was really a cosmetic gesture since the murderer, if there were one, would doubtless be miles away by now, escaping over the fields in any of the four points of the compass and off over the boundary fencing. He'd be long gone, assuming that the murderer was male. There was no need to call for a helicopter; it would be too late and it was probably raining too heavily. He shook his head. He hadn't established the time of death yet either so he hadn't much to go on. Then there was the problem of what to do with the hundreds of people on the premises – how could they all help him with his enquiries?

He'd never been to the College before so he wanted to work out where he was. He took out his notebook and started to draw a rough sketch of the layout of this part of the building which he assumed to be the administrative block. He'd been shown in by a receptionist who had taken him through a door to the left of the small foyer, protected from unauthorised entry by an electronic lock, although it had been opened before he arrived so that he could move freely about the place. He'd then entered a short hallway which opened out, on turning right, into a long, narrow corridor, off which were a series of rooms along the left. In the first room he'd seen a group of about a dozen people sitting round a heavy, old fashioned, wooden table. The second room, in an alcove, looked like a secretary's office, and the third, across from this, was where the body had been found. At the end was a small open area in which there were four or five easy chairs arranged around a coffee table covered in magazines and newspapers, which he deduced was a waiting area. There were two doors on the right of the corridor and when he tried the handles they were both locked – possibly store rooms of some kind. He added a note to his drawing to the effect that the walls were painted beige on which were hung a few photographs of the College and what looked like some of its past principals.

He took off his damp car coat, threw it onto a chair in the waiting area and stood in the corridor pondering where to begin. He'd already spoken to that frightening woman, whatsername. He flicked through his notebook and found it. Iris Baxter. But she hadn't found the body. She'd made the 999 call. It was a Bernadette Arden, his notebook told him again, and as far he knew no one else had seen the body until he and his detective constable had arrived. He went into to Ariadne's office and walked carefully round the room taking care not to disturb anything. In front of him he saw a large, gleaming, metal desk on his left at right angles to the door and facing the window where the curtains were not quite fully drawn. Slumped backwards in the chair was the body of a smartly dressed woman. He couldn't help but be drawn to the body every time he looked in its direction and he was considerably uneasy about how to describe the position in which it had been left. What a way to go, he thought, and to be found like this. What sick, evil bastard had done this to such a good-looking woman? She wasn't looking too lovely at the moment though what with her wide-open, slightly bulging eyes, lolling tongue and the rest of the grotesque tableau. He wished he could at least cover her head because he felt somehow she was looking at him and judging him. He knew what she'd looked like when she was alive as her picture was regularly in the local newspaper and this led him to wonder if she might ever have found him attractive in return. He was forty three, he still had all his hair and teeth and he wore sharp suits. He kept himself fit so he had a good physique but she probably wouldn't have given his face a second glance, sadly, because he looked, in a good light, like a bloodhound; in a bad light his features looked as if they were made of wax and had partially melted.

He remembered that it was procedure to check the floor area first but what was he looking for? There was no sign of a forced entry or exit, the door was unmarked and the windows looking out on to the field were locked. Only the smaller, top half of each window opened and they opened outwards so it would be virtually impossible to climb in or out. He walked round and round slowly but saw nothing remotely suspicious on the light blue carpet and surmised that the cleaners had probably been in recently. He took out his notebook again, this time to make an inventory of the room as it was at 1025 hours, since nothing had changed since he arrived ten minutes ago.

It was much smaller than he expected for a chief executive's office but then it was a smallish College and previous principals had presumably found it big enough and ostentatious enough for most of their modest needs. On the beige walls were a number of photographs of the deceased with prominent people, many of whom he didn't recognise. For some reason he couldn't fathom why he was strangely intrigued by one with the local MP, one with a group of smiling men and women in suits taken in what looked like the grounds of a hotel, and another, taken some time ago, with a long-haired man, almost certainly a rock star, but he didn't recognise him either. There was also a collection of colourful, abstract paintings that he took to be modern art or something similar; he wasn't sure but he wasn't really interested in that sort of thing. As he scanned the highly polished desk's surface on which Ariadne's lifeless ankles rested, he felt ashamed that he found the whole morbid scene somehow luridly fascinating, even erotic. What would he tell his wife he'd been doing at work today? On top of the desk also were a flat screen computer, not switched on, a small vase of wilting, red roses, a hardback exercise book and an expensive, silver ballpoint pen. He couldn't see any fingerprints anywhere (the cleaners *had been* thorough) and, apart from a large, stainless steel filing cabinet and matching bookcase, that was it. No clues. He put his cotton gloves on and opened each of the filing cabinet's drawers but nothing suspicious caught his eye, merely a lot of papers, and the bookcase, as he anticipated, was filled with educational works and reports. Everything seemed to be very clean and shiny.

There *was* nothing at all to go on, except for the corpse itself and the unnatural position in which it had been discovered, but his instincts were telling him that he was missing something obvious. He didn't believe himself to be the brightest of men but he was methodical and careful in his approach if on occasion somewhat unorthodox. He'd joined the police force upon leaving school and had risen slowly through the ranks to his current level by virtue of seniority rather than outstanding talent, earning himself the nickname PC Plod because he believed that thorough, old-fashioned police work was the best way to solve a crime; he didn't like the rapidly increasing use of modern technology which he regarded as far too complex, and he considered new-fangled methods such as psychological profiling were no more than hammy gimmicks. It was rumoured that he'd been very lucky to make Detective Inspector because, at his promotion board, no one else wanted the vacancy at Storbury, and the first two who were offered it had turned it down, even though it meant they had to remain as sergeants. He ran his fingers through his hair, wondering what to do next, when a well-built, uniformed patrol car officer pushed the slightly open door.

"Where do you want me to stand, sir?" he asked resignedly, fully aware that he was in for a long vigil that day.

CHAPTER 10

4 September 1984: Early Evening

Mort arrived home at about five o'clock still thinking about the unproductive, if not wholly disastrous staff meeting earlier that afternoon. He'd played it out in his mind over and over again on the journey in an attempt to analyse where his careful preparations the previous evening had gone wrong. He decided finally that his crucial error was to use those ancient minutes he'd found in Alice's box. That's what started them all laughing at him and he'd have to work very hard to regain their respect. He wanted to talk it through with Cassandra but once again she wasn't there. 'Out with the girls' her note on the hall table said. There were three kisses under the 'C' she'd written, as usual, as her signature. He walked into the kitchen where, only yesterday, with no clothes on, she'd made him breakfast and a packed lunch. She hadn't even bothered to get up to see him off this morning and he hadn't seen much of her (he smiled at the double meaning) the previous night. She'd got in late, very tipsy, and had gone straight to bed, leaving him alone with his planning.

He sat down at the kitchen table in the centre of the room and, resting his elbows on its surface, he put his head in his hands.

"OK," he said aloud. "Let's see where we're up to. But first a cup of coffee."

He went over to the worktop where the kettle was standing and then to the sink to put enough water in for one cup.

After he'd turned off the tap, he looked out of the window at the small garden surrounded by trees and shrubs which hid all the other houses from view and most of the sunlight too, especially in the evenings. The tall, summer flowers in the beds bordering the bushes were almost finished and he could see that Cassandra had been dead-heading most of them earlier in the day, judging by the piles of leaves and petals strewn all over the smallish, moss-infested lawn in the middle. As he surveyed the scene his eye was caught by the slightly open door to his right.

"She hasn't locked up properly *again*," he sighed. "Probably in too much of a hurry to get out and enjoy herself."

He closed the door gently, locked it and, picking up the kettle on his way back, plugged it into the wall socket. He stood with his back to the hissing water and looked round to see if anything else was not as it should be when the house was empty. The two keys should be in the drawer over there, he thought, and taking them from their respective keyholes, he carefully placed them in the top drawer of the unit nearest the door. The keys to the outhouse doors were there also, so he didn't have to worry; she'd clearly locked them after putting her gardening tools away. Or had she? He re-opened the door and went out to check that they were locked. When he was sure that they were both shut tight, he remembered the kettle and rushed back inside, vowing once again to get round to buying one which switched itself off.

The kitchen was the one room in the house that looked modern. It was roughly square with brown oak units on all four sides, spaces left only for the central heating radiator and the inner and outer entrance doors at opposite ends. Above these were wall-mounted cabinets, some with glass doors but the majority were wooden. In the centre stood a large, round table and four tall-backed dining chairs which matched the units. The rest of the house was a shrine to all things Victorian and had been painstakingly restored to its original condition.

There was a sitting room filled to bursting with pictures in abundance on every wall, and small tables filled with all kinds of ornaments, stuffed animals in bell jars and assorted brick-a-brac, all bought fairly cheaply, like most of the fixtures and fittings in the rest of the house, at various auctions, junk shops and the odd posh antique shop when Mort and Cassandra could afford it. The vintage three piece suite, the backs of which were prosaically covered in plain white lace antimacassars, had also been obtained second-hand, and even the TV was hidden inside a specially designed box resembling a wooden sideboard. The third room on the ground floor, the dining room, was similarly furnished except that a large mahogany table and matching chairs replaced the TV, settee and armchairs. It was also where they kept their extensive library, mostly paper backs, housed along one wall in a series of large, elaborately carved bookcases reaching all the way up to the ceiling. Both of these rooms had refurbished Victorian fireplaces – white marble in the sitting room, black and tiled in the dining room.

Upstairs was a capacious bathroom extended from its original size by knocking down the walls of an adjacent bedroom, containing a cast iron bath and two white slab sinks – his and hers. The toilet was also a vintage one, flushed by a chain attached to a cistern several feet above it. The two bedrooms, one for them and the other for guests (usually Cassandra's friends) were decorated in the same style as the downstairs rooms and contained wide, brass beds and free-standing, rosewood wardrobes and dressing tables surrounded by innumerable framed prints of rural scenes, stately houses and portraits of long dead, anonymous people. Most of this was of Mort's choosing which is why he had to concede the kitchen to Cassandra and its modern-day fitted accoutrements. They'd put a deposit on the house when he embarked on his teacher training course with the money they'd saved from his two previous jobs, so he felt he was entitled to have the major say in how it was fitted out.

Besides, he prided himself on being a practical, working class man and he liked DIY.

Taking his cup of coffee with him, he trudged into the sitting room and stretched out on the sofa; he preferred to lie down when he had things on his mind. He closed his eyes and went over the meeting yet again trying to itemise the positive and negative outcomes. It hadn't been a pleasant experience – of that there was no doubt – but he was a manager now and had to take the animosity of his subordinates in his stride. He couldn't please everyone and he realised that his new position had made him some sort of go-between, with Junkin on one side and the teachers on the other, and he'd have to take flak from both parties. What a motley bunch they all were, especially Honor, Junkin and Kettleman – but he *had* chanced upon an ally in Ariadne, or was it she who had sought him out? Whatever, she'd shown him kindness and made some sensible proposals when all the others had merely been hostile. They were all trying to bend him to their respective wills and he had to discover what it was they all really wanted. Yet he did know what his new boss required of him – he'd been up front with him all along. It was just that he didn't want to be that person or rather, he *couldn't* be.

He lay there searching for a meaningful solution, fully aware that he'd brought it all on himself by taking the job in the first place, when all of a sudden Cassandra marched into the room. He'd been so deeply lost in his brooding that he hadn't heard her open the front door. She looked flushed as though she'd been running.

"You're home early," she snarled, standing over him, noticeably agitated for some reason. "What are you doing lying about in here?"

"I made a bit of a mess of my first team meeting this afternoon, so I decided to leave early to think it through," Mort replied meekly as he got to his feet and stood facing her.

"Well I don't want to hear about it. It's getting on for six and I can't be bothered to cook, so let's go for a curry."

She hurried out of the room and Mort moved off after her.

"I wanted to tell you what happened so you could let me know me where I went wrong," he said as he followed. "I spent most of last night planning it, for God's sake. I'd like a fresh mind on it."

"Look, Mort, you spent most of the summer moping about and you almost ruined our holiday," she snapped, turning round as she entered the kitchen. "It's only bloody *work*, get on with it and stop worrying. I mean, you're making a mountain out of a molehill."

He walked up to her and was about to embrace her but her body stiffened.

"Yes, yes, but why, no matter how hard I try, does everything seem to go wrong? It's like the worst happens when I least want…"

She cut him off and turned away again to look out of the window.

"That's because you think too much about things," she said, not able to disguise the annoyance in her voice. "You spend too much time working out what could go wrong and trying to compensate in advance instead of getting on with *doing* things. I think you like being miserable and you will unpleasant things to happen to you just so you can suffer."

She whirled round and looked him straight in the eye.

"I mean it's not as if they're going to be your *pals*, is it? You don't have too many of them as it is because you aren't aware of how much you put people off with your negativity. I bet those bloody teachers aren't thinking about you right now. They'll be getting on with the rest of their lives."

He stared back at her dolefully, appreciating she was right.

"But I've got to find some way to make them respect me," he pleaded. "I don't know how to do it."

She moved closer to him as if she were about to give him a hug but, to his disappointment, she placed her right index finger on his lips. It was a more tender gesture and he sensed that he was being too self-indulgent – he hadn't even said hello or asked her where she'd been. Before he could say anything else she burst out laughing.

"Come on, get your jacket. Let's go out. I want another holiday and I want to go to Egypt. I want to tell you all about it while we eat. Now shut up about that bloody place and get a move on!"

* * *

Cassandra and Mort silently perused their menus at a table in a dark corner of the small Indian restaurant a few streets away from their house. It was much the same as any other with tables in two rows by five deep mainly set for four diners, except that at one end there was a grandiose banqueting area, apparently very popular at Christmas. It was empty as usual in the early evening, most of its customers traditionally eating late after closing time at the nearby pubs. Sitting face to face, they would have looked the perfect couple to any observer but inside they were very different people. Cassandra was extremely gregarious by nature whereas Mort had always been something of a lone wolf. Perceived as attractive when younger, ironically by all but himself, he'd had a few girlfriends, although nothing permanent had developed because he didn't exhibit the kind of reckless spirit of adventure demanded by many young women in the nineteen seventies, and the relationships simply petered out.

Cassandra had come to the conclusion that this was exactly what kind of man she wanted six years ago after a wayward and wild time at university getting a lot of things out of her system, and, as more than one wag put it, *into* it. She'd left, like Mort, with a lower second but she couldn't even think of the kind of career she could just walk into with a degree in Geography. She needed some stability, her parents had said, but they were stunned when she told them she'd got engaged to 'a working class boy from Leeds'. They even told him that, although they knew their daughter was fond of him, the last thing they had in mind was marriage – which, in spite of this warning, took place two weeks before he embarked on his teacher training course. To her, however, not only was he good-looking and dependable, he was sensible and hard-working, something of an investment she hoped, and, most of all, he never appeared threatening, least of all to her.

This is what many women found most attractive about him. They wanted to mother him. Cassandra, however, needed more than anything to marry him because he was the most considerate lover she'd had and she'd had more than a few by then. They were reasonably happy until he started teaching and had to spend too much time getting ready for the many different classes he taught. She was however by far the more contented as he didn't seem to care whether she had a job or not, and she was having the best of both worlds: time to herself to do as she pleased during the day and someone to take her out and entertain her in the evening – and later when they went to bed. She also liked the steady income he provided. He hadn't taken much convincing that he'd be far more cheerful if he had a clean and tidy house to come home to and a hot dinner on the table, but lately she hadn't been doing too much housework or cooking. She was changing, she could feel it. She wanted more people and excitement in her life and she was getting extremely restless.

"Look, Mort," she began, after they'd chosen their meals, "You've made your own bed, now you've got to lie in it. All you've done for the last few months – ever since you got that damn job – is worry and grumble. Look on the bright side. You've got a better post with a bigger salary. You're on your way up. Two promotions in next to no time. You don't have to be Mister Perfect. Things are bound to go wrong at first, then they'll get better, I know they will, like after you left the advertising agency and started the teacher training course. You've got to tough it out and set your own agenda. Stop trying to tackle them as a group. You'll never win them over. The only way to do that is to meet them one by one."

Mort took a sip of his beer which he'd ordered as soon as they'd sat down.

"I can't help thinking…" he said, pausing to take another mouthful, but before he could continue he was interrupted again.

"You do far too much of that," she scowled, as if to emphasise her point.

"I miss the lads at the tech and I'm going to miss the students as well," he went on. "There are so few courses at Storbury and I've already had to allocate myself classes I don't like the sound of. It's a college of further education and quite a few of the students are under eighteen. I haven't taught that age group much, not since my first year anyway, and you know I prefer them older. They're more interesting, more streetwise. I mean most of the courses I taught were at higher levels as well so that meant they were more intelligent, more of a challenge…"

"Yes, and they were mostly female, from what I remember."

She'd cut him short again but she was trying to cheer him up. He frowned at her, finished his beer and ordered another, a pint this time.

"I can't help reminiscing about the technical college," he moaned. "I'd do anything to go back there. What am I going to do, Cassandra? I hate Storbury already."

She leaned towards him and gently touched his arm.

"Funny you should say that. I bumped into Stan this afternoon in town. He asked how you were getting on and he told me to tell you that you're an arsehole, no one's missing you and, best of all, you've been replaced by a busty, blonde nympho."

"Har har har," said Mort feigning amusement and nodding his head.

He smiled self-consciously when he realised what Stan had actually said.

"He didn't say that, did he?"

"No, I'm joking," she lied, looking at him intently and

trying to be more serious. "He asked how you were getting on and wants to know why you haven't rung him."

"He told me he was going to Majorca over the summer. I bet he's just got back. Did he look brown?"

"Yes, all over. He showed me his chest and said he'd been doing some nude sunbathing. He's a handsome guy and he looks great – he has a sportsman's body. He found a small, secluded beach in the back of beyond and spent most of his holiday camping in a little village on the east coast. I told him a bit about our summer expedition – we ended up going to a pub in South Street – and I told him about your, er, illness and what brought it on. He laughed his head off and that's when he called you an arsehole. He said you never appreciate how lucky you are. He's still a basic lecturer at forty five and he'd cut off his right arm to order people around. I think you should phone him. That'd definitely make you see things from another perspective. By the way why do you call him 'Old' Stan?"

"Because he knows everything. He's like Methuselah. He's probably a million years old."

"That's scary. If he is, he doesn't look it, and he certainly doesn't act like an old man."

Mort was feeling better, what with the news of a fine friend and the effects of the alcohol on his empty stomach. They were sitting more closely now, their heads almost touching. He took both her hands in his and gazed directly into her dark, slightly slanted green eyes.

"Thank you," he said, "You're cheering me up. To hell with that dump."

He paused, drew his body back a little and continued to contemplate her face.

"Do me a favour, will you?" he cooed. "Take your glasses off. Then you can tell me all about why you want to go to Egypt – as if I can't guess!"

Before she had a chance to say another word, the waiter arrived with a trolley and slowly served their food. In between mouthfuls, she recounted how Stan had given her the idea, because he 'fancied seeing the pyramids and all that ancient history' before he died. He was, she said, weighing up whether he'd rather go there in spring or save his money for 'another summer shagging in Majorca'. Mort wasn't listening. He was thinking how lucky he was to have a beautiful wife who could always lift his spirits, and a very good mate in 'Old' Stan.

CHAPTER 11

12 April 2005: 10.40am

Harrison knew he couldn't keep the College closed for long because the Chief Constable had just telephoned to notify him that he didn't want to read the headline *Murder at college – police say a thousand people helping with their enquiries*. 'Digits will be extracted or feet will not touch,' were something like his final, plagiarised words from the BBC sitcom Porridge. He also said, not very sensitively, that he couldn't spare anyone else at the moment because most of his plain clothes officers were still dealing with the bank raid. The robbers had taken the bank manager hostage and one of their accomplices was holding his wife at home. It was very complicated and concerned the living, he'd said insensitively, not the dead.

"Bloody terrible, isn't it, Tim?" said Harrison after he ended the call.

The young detective was staring open-mouthed at Ariadne's legs. He hadn't taken everything in the first time he'd seen the body.

"Have you found out who's in charge yet?"

Tim nodded.

"Go and fetch whoever's it is and ask him or her to find me a room where I can talk to people. Then tell whoever it is I want a meeting. See what you can find out from the others but be careful. Don't *tell* them anything – ask a few questions about who they are and make sure you get all their names and addresses."

A few minutes later Harrison was finishing his notes with a sketch of the room when the uniformed officer sent to guard the crime scene knocked on the door and pointed across the corridor.

"They've found you a room, sir," he whispered. "Best they can do at such short notice what with all the other rooms being full and that. A Mrs Baxter suggested you use it."

"Why are you whispering, Naylor?" Harrison frowned, puzzled by this odd behaviour from someone as scrub-haired and thickset as the constable – who usually sounded like a foghorn and was aptly nicknamed the Incredible Hulk back at the station.

"Out of respect for the dead, sir," he replied, still speaking softly, "And I don't want to let anyone hear what we're saying."

Harrison walked out of Ariadne's office and slowly followed the constable towards the room he'd been allocated, then he stopped to reflect on the last remark he'd heard. He was about to turn round to finish this short exchange with some sarcastic remark, when the constable slammed the murder scene door and stood rigidly to attention outside it, his arms behind his back.

"Is that all, sir?" he barked, normal service resumed, but Harrison didn't hear him – he'd just seen the size of his operations room.

He was shaking his head in disbelief when Acting Principal Hugh Jones appeared suddenly behind him and nearly knocked him over. The detective was leaning inside the doorway and there was barely enough room for both of them to stand up.

"I understand you want to see me, officer," said Hugh. "I'm temporarily in charge of the College."

"Sit down, please and shut the door," Harrison ordered brusquely. "I'll stand."

Hugh didn't obey immediately. He had to move the chair out of the room, walk past it and bring it back in again behind him to comply. The door remained half open.

"My name is *Detective Inspector* John Harrison and I'm investigating the death…in very suspicious circumstances I have to inform you…of a woman who I assume is Ariadne Hopwood, the Principal of this College. Can you verify that that is her name?"

As Hugh signaled his confirmation, Harrison's irritation got the better of him. He was seething with anger that his preliminary investigations would have to be carried out in a windowless room which could accommodate no more than one desk and one chair, and he wasn't even able to sit on the desk as several piles of dusty files were tottering precariously all over its surface. He could also still see the Hulk smirking stupidly.

"What's this room used for?" he inquired suspiciously.

"I'm not really sure. I think it was used for typing or something," Hugh said, hoping that the questions weren't going to get much harder. "Come on, we'll move these files onto the floor under the desk. I don't think they're very important. Nothing confidential I hope…"

As they both bent down, their heads almost knocked together.

"This is getting bloody farcical," muttered Harrison as they crouched down face to face. "Blimey!"

He recoiled as though he'd smelled something nasty.

"Are you all right?" Hugh asked. "I don't think our heads touched – at least I didn't feel anything."

"No, no…it's not that," Harrison groaned. "I think I'll go outside while you clear the desk as best you can."

He stood up and swayed past the still crouching Acting Principal, kicked the chair away, and rushed out into the corridor taking out his handkerchief as he ran.

"Is everything in order, sir?" asked the Hulk cautiously, as he saw Harrison stumble out of the room clutching his nose.

"No…I mean yes…" Harrison grimaced. "Can't you smell his breath? Bloody Nora, it's like a sewer in there and I haven't even started yet."

The Hulk was beaming from ear to ear. He was having the time of his life. There he was standing guard over a dead body in a state of mild arousal, and he was currently watching two grown men that looked like bizarre dummies from the chamber of horrors knocking each other about in a room not much bigger than a matchbox. All in the name of police work. He was wondering what other fantastic tales he'd be recounting in the pub that evening – unless he'd have to do a double shift.

When Harrison edged his way back into the storeroom that would have to suffice as his office until he had any suspects, he saw that enough space had been made for him to sit down on the desk. He had to squeeze once again past Hugh, who'd managed to manoeuvre the chair into position, to do so. But he still couldn't close the door.

"Phew," he said, breathing heavily and trying hard not to inhale much as the foul smell was getting worse.

He put his handkerchief to his nose again and pretended to wipe it, pinching his nostrils as he spoke.

"Have you any idea what's happened?"

"None, *Detective Inspector*," Hugh replied. "We're all totally surprised and shocked by what we've been told. To be honest no one's seen the body, except for Bernadette, the Principal's secretary, who said she'd found it ...but she's not here now – your detective constable told her to go round the College and order everyone to stay where they are. Incidentally these files, they're old student records from the nineteen eighties. They've probably come out of the archive. I don't know why they're in here but it's of no consequence. The students will be long gone."

As he spoke, the stench was getting even worse, as was Harrison's mood. His temporary HQ was no better than a broom cupboard, and his only witness was running errands when she should have been the next person to speak to.

"That's bloody typical," he said. "I've been here for nearly three quarters of an hour and I've got nowhere."

Then he stopped and thought for a second.

"Perhaps it's for the best though. I can't possibly interview a woman in here. You've got to find me a more suitable room. Go and turf someone out of a bigger one, will you. What about your office?"

"I don't have an office as such," Hugh replied awkwardly. "I share a big room with my staff. It's the way Ariadne wants…wanted to run things. Iris, er, Mrs Baxter has an office though. You could use that but it's at the other side of the building on the first floor, so it's not near the, er, scene of the, er, crime, if that's what you call it these days?"

Harrison raised his left index finger. Someone was talking to the Hulk.

"Who's that?" he shouted across the corridor.

"The doc," the Hulk replied, pointing to somewhere behind him. "I mean the forensic pathologist, sir. He's already in there and he's not suited up."

"At last we're getting somewhere. Ask him to have a look at the body, will you. I'll be there in a minute."

He was relieved that he'd be able to get some fresh air again, so he turned to Hugh as he pushed his way past him.

"That'll be all for now. Don't say anything to the others yet. In fact, please stay here."

He beckoned to the Hulk.

"Constable, please ensure that Mr Jones doesn't leave this room until I get back."

When he went into Ariadne's office, he saw that the doctor was busy examining her lifeless body. The Hulk was right, he wasn't wearing his blue overalls. At that very moment he was bending over with his back to the detective and looking up her skirt.

"Morning Charlie," said Harrison, pleased it was Charles Edwards who'd been around for years and who was highly regarded for both the accuracy and speed of his crime scene post-mortems. "Can you tell me anything?"

"Just a tick, John," said Charles reassuringly, not at all concerned at what he must have looked like.

If he hadn't bothered to change into a sterile suit, thought Harrison contentedly, it wouldn't be long before he had the physical details of the death. He watched as the elderly, white-haired man began to look closely at the corpse's face. He was wearing a fawn and brown checked suit and if he'd had a moustache, Harrison supposed he could have easily passed for Doctor Watson. Dead ringer, in fact. On the other hand Charles had met Harrison several times before and knew that PC Plod was no renowned private investigator. He turned round and smacked his lips.

"I know the cause of death," he said, smiling confidently. "It's murder, I'm afraid. It looks like she's been burked."

"You what?" said Harrison, wondering what kind of sexual perversion Charles was about to describe.

"Burked, asphyxiated," continued Charles, smiling at the startled detective's face. "Comes from Burke and Hare. They sold dead bodies to a Doctor Knox in Edinburgh about two hundred years ago, the 1820s I believe, so that he could dissect them for medical research. Highly illegal in those days. What's most interesting is the way they did it so the bodies weren't disfigured or contorted."

He sat on the edge of the silver desk; he enjoyed telling a good yarn.

"In those days doctors wanted fresh cadavers and the body snatchers, as they were called, would sometimes follow funerals and return to dig up the bodies the following night. But often the corpses were too old or there were too many health risks if they hadn't died of natural causes. So Burke and Hare hit upon a plan. They got their victims, mostly young women interestingly, so drunk that they passed out. Then they went about their business. One would sit on the victim's chest to stop any struggling and hold the jaw shut while the other would cover the mouth and pinch the nose to stop the breathing. Something like that. Didn't take long and the body, although nearly pickled on the inside, was undamaged. Only Burke got hanged though."

"Do you mean there were two people involved in this?" said Harrison, having heard enough of the macabre history and warming up for a debate which he knew was likely to be pointless as Charles usually had all the answers.

"Possibly."

"But there's no sign of a struggle."

"Ah yes, well spotted, John," said Charles, trying not to sound condescending. "I was coming to that. Unless I'm highly mistaken, she probably didn't see or even hear her murderer or murderers come into the room."

"But her eyes are open."

"Yes, yes. I haven't finished yet. This is the clever bit. The murderer – or murderers – didn't kill her *while* she was going about her business. When he…let's leave it at that for now… came in, her eyes were probably closed. I think she was drugged *before* she was killed. That's why her eyes are open. She probably opened them as she became less and less able to move and later saw the whole thing."

Harrison felt a shiver run down his spine.

"So," he said. "The killer…

"Or killers."

He ignored this. He was getting somewhere.

"So when the killer comes into the room, her eyes will have been closed. Then as he drugs her, she opens her eyes. Then he waits for her to fall asleep…"

"Ah, no John – he waits till *the drug takes effect*…"

"And then he throttles her!"

"Something like that, yes."

Charles was beaming. He was going to have the last word as he usually did.

"Except for three things, old boy. One – I'll have to do an autopsy to find what drug, if any, was used. I think I have an idea. It could be tetrodotoxin but that would probably take too long to act quickly. Might be a little *fishy* but I suppose that joke's going over your head, John. Two – I never said the killer was a man, and three – there may have been more than one of them."

Harrison smiled weakly. He had to show him he could do some detective work of his own.

"One more thing. You haven't told me the time of death yet," he asked, sensing Charles might have missed something after all.

Charles scratched his head. Harrison kept going, sensing for once he might have the doctor on the ropes. He looked at his watch. It was just gone eleven.

"She can't have been here all night," he said excitedly. "This place must be locked up and alarmed at night so the caretakers must be the last ones out after making sure all the buildings are empty. All we have to do is ask them what time they opened up this morning and assume she came in afterwards. We can be very accurate on this one, Charlie! I'd say she's been dead for about two to three hours tops."

"The autopsy will inform us more precisely. I think you're about right, though. There are some signs of rigor mortis in her face and neck, her clothing's clean on – that's what I was looking at when you came in – and her make-up looks fresh although the lipstick's smudged. At least we know someone's had their – *his or her* – hands on her mouth. There are also some faint red marks on her nostrils and there might even be traces of DNA, although I suspect thick gloves will have been used. I've taken her body temperature and I might be able to calculate fairly precisely when I've correlated everything else."

It looked like he'd got the last word again.

"OK John, I'll get the forensic team to come and take her away, if that's OK with you. I've nothing on this afternoon so I'll be able to do a preliminary report for you by about four – that is unless there's another murder! I also want some pictures and tell anyone who takes the photographs that I'll have their balls if I find them anywhere else but in the file…"

"I think you mean *his or her nether regions*, don't you Charles, old son?"

Harrison laughed. He'd had the last word this time.

CHAPTER 12

5-7 September 1984

Mort took Cassandra's advice. He began to concentrate on what he had to do to get the timetables arranged for the new term. He ignored the other teachers and their eccentricities, their moaning and groaning and the ploys some of them used to get their own way. He was well aware that this was how they could wangle the cushiest teaching programmes possible so that they could devote more time to their outside interests or personal affairs. He also knew that when the teaching term started he wouldn't see as much of them as they'd be scattered around the College doing whatever they did in class. He cancelled the scheduled section meetings and met them one by one, instead of combatting the many-headed hydra and he found out that some weren't too bad after all when he got them on their own. He confronted the absentees from his team meeting and when he'd heard their feeble excuses, he advised them as sternly as he dared that he wasn't going to put up with it. Alice was gone and he was now their Senior Lecturer. He told them he had lots of ideas to discuss with them, but he wasn't going to change things overnight, so they needn't worry that he intended to impose anything radical.

He reminded Paul Honor that he wouldn't interfere in the day to day running of English and instructed him in no uncertain terms what he expected of him – good teaching, good exam results and no more unconventional marking schemes. He also met Roy Jolly and gave him roughly the same speech that he'd given Honor but, since he wasn't as sure of himself about Art, he let Jolly make most of the running. Gradually he won a few of the lecturers over as he sorted out their workloads more reasonably, which meant that some of the longer serving members of staff lost the least demanding groups of students they'd been accustomed to teach year after year. This considerably upset Honor and Jolly as they'd benefited most from Alice's slackness in allowing them to have control and thereby have first choice of which courses they taught, and he would ensure that he kept a close eye on them. He even managed to get Kettleman off his back by allowing him his long weekend. The old grouch needed the Friday afternoons and Monday mornings to visit his long-term sick son every Saturday and Sunday in a special hospital near Oxford, and the two extra half days gave him more travelling time. In return he volunteered to teach three evenings a week, when he was required to teach no more than two – but that was as far as their mutual reciprocity went.

What pleased him most, however, was that he'd been right all along about Junkin. The teachers *did* see him as a tyrant and bully who used his rank and status as a means of control, and they despaired at his incompetence. He soon discovered that Junkin didn't seem to understand the mechanics of running a department, judging from the incomprehensible timetables he'd had to present to the team meeting on his second day at Storbury. There were clashes with rooms, often two or three courses having been allocated the same one, and there were several classes that had been omitted altogether and were therefore uncovered by teachers. These could have been mistakes anyone could have made after a first attempt but Junkin had altered the timetables already drawn up and checked by the section leaders, and some of his changes had been spitefully as well as carelessly made. There was no doubt at all he had something against Kettleman. No one had a good word for their Head of Department and some often used several bad ones incautiously when confronting him over some injustice or other they believed he'd perpetrated against them. Mort saw him chiefly as an inept charlatan, who loved to sound important and omniscient when there wasn't any substance to him at all. In other words, he talked a good game.

Mort knew his man when, during that first week at the College, he received a letter from the education authority inviting him to a training day for new senior lecturers, and he asked Junkin straightaway if he could attend. The next day he was summoned at lunchtime to be briefed about an important new development. Junkin, in familiar pose leaning back in his chair with his hands behind his head, told him that the senior lecturers in the county were a ragbag and there was going to be some training or other soon; if Mort played his cards right, he would recommend that he should be involved. Mort could hardly believe his ears when less than twenty four hours before he'd shown him his personal letter of invitation.

He also got to know Ariadne better. As they shared the same staffroom, she came to sit with him once or twice. Her desk was at the opposite end of the room, well out sight because of all the books teachers used and the volume of paper they generated, which made the room even darker on the windowless side. It was all very businesslike; he called her over when he had to discuss any adjustments to her timetable or she'd stroll across and ask for advice on something – in what order to teach set texts, for instance. She was very accommodating when it came to changing which classes she taught and when, and she volunteered to take on Kettleman's Monday morning class when previously she'd been free. She smiled and joked a great deal and this cheered him up no end in the midst of all the pre-term turmoil. Occasionally she tapped him gently on the thigh if he said something funny, and sometimes he felt she was sitting too close on the rare occasion they were sharing some small confidence together. She was ever eager to talk about herself. He was very surprised to learn that she was, like him, from Yorkshire, near York she said, because her voice betrayed no trace of any regional accent. He did exasperate her occasionally when, for instance, he didn't react after she hinted that she was single and had no steady boyfriend. She wanted to be the first person in the staff room to glean some personal detail about him, and she desperately wanted to find out if he was in a regular relationship or married. However he never talked about himself much, and when he did it was always about some irksome problem he was having with Paul Honor or Roy Jolly, and he frequently complained about the slowness of the traffic he encountered on his way to Storbury, particularly about wagons and slow cars driven by little, old men. If he *had* volunteered anything he'd have told her that he was extremely happily married to a woman he adored and who understood him more than anyone he'd ever met – and neither woman would have wished him to say anything like that. One thing they did have in common, although it hadn't occurred to either of them at the time, was a burning desire to get away from Storbury and its ghastly little college – but for entirely different reasons. She also disliked his smoking.

He finally met Jeff Shaw, or more accurately *overheard* the other senior lecturer in the department in charge of something called Social Anthropology, which he hadn't come across at the technical college. It turned out to consist of History, Geography, Sociology and Psychology, a few modern languages and something called General Studies. There were about six of them altogether and they all congregated at the other end of the staff room, near where Ariadne sat. He hadn't had much to do with them, but he often listened to them discussing weighty matters from behind their enclave in the far corner. He thought they all sounded extremely pretentious from the brief snippets of conversation he gleaned from time to time when he was taking a short break from preparing for the first week of the teaching term. They were all dedicated union members and the only 'outsider' who regularly joined in their lunchtime debates was Paul Honor. They liked to discuss politics, from a left wing perspective of course, and he often wondered what the 'working man' they championed would have made of them. The only time they quarreled and complained was when Shaw asked for volunteers to teach General Studies. It transpired, from what Mort could gather, that this meant teaching the Engineering and Catering students, something none of them clearly relished.

"There's no way I'm teaching any of that bunch of semiliterate no-hopers." Mort caught one afternoon from over the ramparts. "They're all 'whip and chair jobs' anyway. No one wants to learn anything. All they want to do is mess about or go home. Get the part-timers in again, Jeff. They need the money. They'll teach that rubbish to anyone."

"No can do, old man," Shaw's disembodied but resonantly impeccable accent replied. "You're all light on your timetables and Simon will have a fit if I do that."

Another voice, this time female, floated across the room. "He's never bothered before."

"Yes, but this year he's been *ordered* to get timetables up to hours," intoned Shaw. "There's a squeeze on the budget and they're trying to keep part-time hours down to a minimum. That new chap, Todd, he's been sorting out the English and Art lot and they're not best pleased."

"Well, what about Bunty and Tilly?" the first voice shouted, sounding quite angry. "They'll be out on their arses. That's compulsory redundancy and perhaps anti-feminist to boot. Call a Union meeting, Jeff. We need to nail the management on this one."

It was at the very end of the first week, on the Friday before the start of the enrolment period, that he met Shaw face to face in a late afternoon meeting in Junkin's office to finalise all the arrangements. He realised he'd often seen him about the place but he'd never *seen* him speak. It came as quite a surprise when he finally connected the two together. There sat a huge man, so generously proportioned that he looked like an enormous, glossily coloured balloon with a face painted on it. He was almost bald, the few strands of dark hair that remained straggling long and limp down to his shoulders and he had an unkempt, bushy, ginger beard. He wore round-framed, national health glasses, a fawn, cheesecloth shirt and brown corduroy trousers and boots, and he would have looked like an orang-utan had his white, flabby face been the colour of his clothing. Mort invented a nickname instantly: the venerable Doctor Zaius, from *Planet of the Apes*, although he wasn't sure if Shaw was that old.

The meeting was short, but Mort had enough time to ascertain that the other two got on very well together. They were chatting and laughing as he came into the room. Junkin, wearing his ill-fitting, grey suit as usual, was describing in his plummy voice some amusing incident or other that had had taken place the night before on his small holding involving his hens which had seen off a young fox before it could do much damage. Shaw had responded in typical fashion by likening it to the power of trade union movement, and they'd have sounded like two effete country squires had not one been siding with the peasantry.

"Now, now, Jeff," said Junkin like a father talking to his favourite son. "You always have to go there, don't you? I think it's more like feminism, myself. The sisterhood was ganging up on the ravenous male."

"Put like that," Shaw drawled in acknowledgement, "I must agree with you but it's still the power of the many defeating the grasping few."

"Yes, yes, I know where you're coming from," said Junkin, his lightheartedness rapidly disappearing. "But I can't have incomplete timetables. You can call all the union meetings you want and call me all the names under the sun, but they've got to be up to hours. You know what's imminent don't you? Well, let me tell you…"

He broke off when he saw Mort standing in the doorway.

"Come in, Mr Todd," he said, maintaining his stern tone. "Have you got anything that Jeff's full-timers can have to fill up their timetables? An O level English class or something?"

Shaw also turned to face Mort, fixing him with a menacing stare.

"Not really," said Mort, uncomfortable at being interrogated. "All my lecturers are up to hours."

"That's not what I asked," replied Junkin sharply. "What about your part-timers?"

"The Art ones are all specialists, so there's nothing there," Mort asserted, not wanting to concede anything to a coterie of elitists whose incorporeal staffroom conversations he'd found distastefully hypocritical.

"And English?" inquired Junkin, leaning back in his chair and looking down his nose at Mort.

"Well there's a couple of evening O level language classes…" murmured Mort.

"Don't do evenings, squire," Shaw sneered. "The part-timers do them. That's when we do our own thing."

"There must be something during the day," snapped Junkin, as he placed his hands behind his head.

He was still peering over his nose. Mort looked at Junkin, then at Shaw.

"Well, I have a couple of part-time classes aimed at adults…"

"How many hours are there in total?" asked Shaw.

Mort looked through the papers on his lap, but he knew the answer.

"Twelve – four three hour sessions," he said reluctantly.

"That's perfect," said Shaw, his flaccid face beaming with delight.

He looked at Junkin.

"He can have the servicing in return. We'll fix it up after this meeting."

"That's excellent," said Junkin, visibly relaxing too.

He eyed Mort narrowly.

"It'll do you good to teach the Engineers. They'll be more like the students you're used to. Now let's look at your plans for next week."

"But they're not English teachers," protested Mort.

"I've got a PhD and two others have master's degrees," said Shaw, dismissively. "I think we'll cope very well. All we need is the syllabus and a little support from Paul Honor."

"Has this happened before?" asked Mort, wanting to sound indignant but feeling that they'd already got the better of him, like two scheming dandies deceiving a lowly dogsbody.

"Every September," grinned Shaw spitefully.

Mort remembered what Junkin had told him about the 'controlled experiment' with marking schemes during the tirade after his interview and he began to suspect who was responsible.

"I thought you wanted me to put a stop to things like this," he said bravely, but he might as well have been wringing a cap in his hands.

"With the *English and Art* staff," said Junkin scornfully. "Jeff's group are no trouble. Let's move on."

Junkin listened to the enrolment plans in silence, nodding occasionally.

"Sounds good," he said when Mort, who spoke last, had finished. "Have another look at Mr Todd's plans for me, will you Jeff, when you're discussing those timetable amendments?"

Mort returned dejectedly to his desk.

"I bet fatso has a double desk all to himself," he muttered under his breath as he sat down. "I'm going to have to do those sodding timetables again over the weekend and I've promised Cassandra I'd take her to the coast on Sunday. What am I going to do?"

"Cheer up and stop chuntering," he heard someone say behind him. "It might never happen."

It was Ariadne who had followed him into the room and he hadn't seen her.

"What's up? You look dreadful."

"Have you seen the film *Planet of the Apes*?" he asked brusquely, as he turned round and looked up to see a smiling, concerned face.

"Once on TV," she replied, slightly taken aback at the harshness of this unexpected question.

"Do you remember the bit where Charlton Heston's locked up in a cage after a sham trial waiting to be castrated or something?"

"Vaguely. Why?"

"Well he screams in anger 'It's a mad house, a mad house'!"

She looked away wrinkling her brow as if she didn't understand.

"What is?" she said trying to sound less confused than she was.

"This place," he whined, "That, or I was killed in a car crash coming here last Monday – and I've gone straight to Hell."

CHAPTER 13

12 April 2005: 11.10am

When the female scene of the crime officers arrived dressed in their white overalls, looking like two ghostly, hooded figures who'd come to mourn their dead queen, Harrison returned to the cubby hole where Hugh was sitting, idly flicking through some of the old course files to while away the time.

"Get me the caretakers!" he ordered gruffly, safe in the knowledge that he could adopt this tone because at last he had a lead to follow.

"They're not called that anymore," said Hugh equally offhandedly.

He was unaccustomed to being spoken to in this way and he didn't like it.

"I presume you mean the estate manager and the site technicians."

"Hmm," said Harrison, continuing the acerbic skirmish. "As soon as possible please, then we might be able to get this place re-opened."

Hugh slowly rose to his feet to leave, but he'd only taken a few steps when he turned round.

"I'll have to make a couple of telephone calls, providing they're in their shed," he said. "Otherwise I'll have to use the walkie-talkie which is in reception. Am I free to walk about now?"

"Yes, yes, get on with it," snarled Harrison, waving him away.

He wanted to clear his nostrils of the foul fetidness of Hugh's breath as quickly as possible. Hugh went bright red. The last time someone had spoken to him like this was when he and his wife had sex.

"Look here, Detective Inspector," he said furiously. "Please remember that I'm the chief executive, albeit in an acting capacity and I won't be treated like this. I'll be contacting your superior officers when all this is over."

Harrison was unfazed by this forceful show of bravado.

"Please remember also, *temporary* Principal Jones that you remain a suspect until I say you're not. Now please find me the *caretakers*."

A few minutes later the Estate Manager and his two assistants arrived. Harrison flicked his fingers at the middle-aged man who was wearing a threadbare, grey suit which was mottled on the shoulders by the rain, and indicated that he was to go into the interview room.

"I'll start with you first Mr, er…"

"Wallace. Steven Wallace."

He then beckoned the Hulk, pointing as he did so at the remaining two men who were sensibly wearing oilskins.

"Constable, those two are to sit in the waiting area over there. They must not speak to each other. Is that clear?"

"Yes sir," the Hulk boomed in his customary way.

Harrison turned and went into storeroom to find Steven Wallace sitting on the desk. He'd pushed all the files that had been piled on top of it onto the floor.

"Health and safety hazard these files," he said wryly as if emphasising that he was there primarily in a professional capacity. "I'll get them cleared up when you've finished."

"Please sit in the chair Mr Wallace," said Harrison remaining standing, his back to the desk. "You are the head caretaker?"

Wallace had been called this many times before, mainly by people who wanted to wind him up and there were plenty of those in the College. He took himself very seriously and when senses of humour were being handed out, he'd been given a one that didn't work. He was a big man and could easily have been mistaken for the Hulk's more sinister, elder brother, had he had a crew cut instead of a fully shaven head. There was another significant difference, however; while the Hulk always smiled inanely, Wallace as a rule scowled ferociously. Needless to say everyone was frightened of him, and on the occasions anyone had the nerve to taunt him to his face, they did so from a long distance away.

"My title is Estate Manager," he replied. "I'm also in charge of security and I'm responsible for health and safety as well as stacking chairs and changing light bulbs."

"What time did you open the College this morning?" asked Harrison, ignoring Wallace's surliness.

He wanted to get on with his questions, which he liked to keep short and as simple as possible.

"Six o'clock as usual," Wallace replied mechanically, as if he knew what was going to come next.

"Was there anyone else with you?"

"Yes, Jim. He's the tall one sitting over there. There's four of us, see. Andy comes in at ten, and Brian comes in at two."

"Was there anyone else here?"

"No. The first person to arrive after we open up is the Principal. She's in at seven sharp."

"What time did she arrive this morning?"

"Seven o'clock as I just said."

"How do you know?"

"I usually wait for her to say 'good morning' and tell her all's in order – unless it isn't."

"Did you go with her to her office?"

"Oh no, I usually open the door to the executive wing – the one out there with the combination lock – and she goes in. I've no business in here anyway. Why should I go in with her?"

Wallace paused and rubbed his chin.

"I see what you're getting at, mister, er," he said smugly. "Sorry I didn't catch your name."

"Detective Inspector Harrison."

"Well me and Jim just got on with things. We had to set up a couple of rooms for an exam on the second floor here and then do a bit of routine maintenance in the engineering block – there's a leaking tap and we need a plumber. I expect it'll have to wait till tomorrow now, won't it?"

Harrison ignored him again. He wasn't going to be sidetracked into a discussion about plumbing.

"Were you and Jim together all the time?"

"Yes, except when I did my early rounds and when I went to ring for a plumber."

"What time was that?"

"Shortly after nine."

"What was the name of the plumber?"

Wallace looked as if he were going to explode. He stood up and found himself looking directly into the detective's eyes. Harrison tried to take a step back but all he did was to overbalance as the back of his legs hit the edge of the desk.

"Look, mate," Wallace yelled. "The first I knew about any of this was when the police cars arrived at about ten to ten. It was our tea break. Jim was brewing up for when Andy gets in and I was reading the paper."

"What about the cleaners?" said Harrison trying to conceal the lump that had developed in his throat.

He motioned to Wallace to sit down but he remained standing.

"What about the cleaners?" replied Wallace crustily.

"When do they come in?"

"Most of them come in at about four, although we have a couple on duty during the day."

"Have any cleaners been in this morning?"

"The two who come in at nine."

"So the Principal's room was cleaned last night?"

"Yes, after she'd gone home. There's no point in doing it in the mornings because, as I've just said, she's always in for seven. And before you ask she went home at about six thirty last night. Her room's usually among the last to be done."

"Are the doors to this part of the building locked every night?"

"Yes by whoever's on lates – last night it was Brian. The doors are locked after the cleaners have finished."

"Who lets the cleaners in?"

"Brian does. Reception calls him on the two-way radio. The cleaners let themselves out and the door locks automatically when they leave."

"Who else has a key to these rooms?"

"Apart from our keys, you mean?"

Harrison nodded. He knew that because he still had Jim's key to Ariadne's room, but he was making progress.

"All the managers have a key to the meetings room down at the end but only the Principal and her secretary have keys to their rooms. Only the estates team, the senior managers and Bernadette know the combination of the security lock, and it's changed every twenty four hours. It's circulated confidentially before teatime the previous day."

"Who has a key to this cupboard?"

Wallace paused and looked up at the ceiling.

"I'm not entirely sure," he continued and he sat down again and started counting on his fingers but he didn't get far. "Bernadette definitely has one and there might be one in the locker in the reception office, I'll have to check."

"Do that, will you, after we're finished," said Harrison.

He had two more questions.

"What time did Bernadette arrive this morning?"

"Can't say. I was trying to fix that tap."

"I can check all of what you've told me on the CCTV tapes…"

"No you can't," exclaimed Wallace, meeting Harrison's look of surprise with a wide grin. "We haven't got CCTV!"

"Last question," said Harrison, trying to regain his composure. "What time do most people start to arrive in the morning?"

Wallace wrestled with the question for a few seconds, stroking his chin again.

"Some come in at seven thirty but most come in between eight thirty and nine," he said finally. "There's no set pattern. It depends what they've got on that day."

Then he started laughing, which again took the detective by surprise.

"Oh and then there's Mr Todd – Head of Humanities. He always comes running in about quarter past nine."

CHAPTER 14

7-11 September 1984

Mort was fuming when he got home after his meeting with the two men he now regarded as 'underhand, slippery customers'. He was going to have to start all over again with the timetables, and he and one English teacher as a minimum were going to have to lose courses they'd been trained to teach. What made it worse was that the servicing lessons were spread out through the week, mostly at the end of the day or in the early evening, and they were in a subject that he knew little or nothing about. He'd been well and truly ambushed, just when he considered he'd handled himself really well and solved most of the problems he'd deemed were hopeless a few days before. Luckily he had another week before the students came in, but for some of that period he'd be involved in interviewing and enrolling applicants. What would Cassandra do?

"For a start we're going out on Sunday," she said defiantly, when he asked her that evening in the half empty pub near their home. "You can work on the changes tomorrow if you like because I'm going out for the afternoon with Suzie."

She'd taken it more calmly than he expected, perhaps because they were in a public place.

"I can do half of the servicing myself," he replied. "It's a matter of who does the other half."

"Do you know what I'd do?" she asked, grinning mischievously from behind her spritzer.

"What?"

"I'd teach them Basic English."

He looked up at the ceiling for a second or two. He wasn't going to let her believe she'd resolved it without more of an explanation.

"But I can't do that. There are syllabuses for a start."

She paused for thought and took another sip of her drink.

"You said that no one cares about the classes, particularly that orang-utan bloke. If you change it to English, you'll be building your empire. The situation won't arise again."

She sat back, the grin on her face becoming even wider.

"Yes, I see," he said, "But Shaw will want the English hours. He'll still have light timetables."

Then she played her ace, banging her glass down on the table a little too hard. The pub went silent as all eyes turned to look at the couple in the corner.

"You've several months to work on that, Mort," she said triumphantly, when the customary hubbub returned. "Go and see their Heads of Department and don't try to solve Shaw's problems for him."

"Well, there's only one really and that's the Head of Engineering," he conceded but he knew she was right. "Cookery comes under him as well, I think. I could go and see Maureen King too. She's the Youth Training Scheme Co-ordinator. Kettleman and a couple of others do some work for her in Basic English. They call it Communications or Social and Life Skills. They're fairly new subjects and I'm thinking of introducing Communication Studies at O and A levels."

He leaned over to her and kissed her. Where would he be without her?

The rest of the weekend passed quickly and, for the second time that week, Mort worked enthusiastically and excitedly. He rejigged the timetables on the Saturday and he and Cassandra enjoyed a delightful day at the seaside the following day. She liked this version of him much better; he put tapes on the car's cassette player as they drove and he sang along to some of the songs. They walked for miles and sometimes he ran along the beach, looking for pebbles to skim against the incoming tide. He looked like a little boy. She knew how much he'd relied on her recently to get him out of the black moods he got himself into, and she wondered which of the words she'd used in the pub had done the trick this time.

The first thing on Monday morning Mort arranged an appointment with Richard Head, the Head of Engineering (and Catering) who'd been there for about ten years by then and had risen to his lofty position extremely fortuitously at the age of forty. He'd arrived on promotion as a senior lecturer from a much larger college in the south of England, expecting a quiet life in the sticks, but to his dismay two days after he started he became the temporary replacement for the previous Head of Engineering who'd died suddenly playing squash. He ran things satisfactorily for the rest of the year as the department wasn't very large, consisting mostly of day-release students from nearby garages and small light engineering companies in and around Storbury, and he was simply handed the post permanently. Ever since he'd kept his head down, he wasn't very sociable and no one noticed him much. He ate all his meals in his office and was usually off the premises each day by half past four. No one even laughed at his name.

As Mort approached Richard's office in the Engineering building late on the Monday afternoon after enrolment had finished for the day, he thought he heard rock music coming from somewhere nearby. It sounded like Jimi Hendrix. When he knocked on the door the music stopped abruptly, followed by the sound of a drawer being opened quickly and then closed again with a bang.

"Come in," said a squeaky voice followed by coughing. "Come in." The voice sounded deeper now.

"Mr Head?" said Mort as he bent the top half his body into the room. "I'm Mort Todd, the new senior lecturer in English and Liberal Arts."

The room was smaller than he'd expected a senior member of staff to have, and it would have been empty if there hadn't been a desk, a chair and two grey filing cabinets. There was also a calendar on the wall, with crosses through the days that had passed so far that month. He couldn't decide whether Richard had recently moved in or whether he was getting ready to move out.

"Ah yes," said Richard, his voice even deeper. "You want to see me about General Studies."

"That's right," continued Mort. "I've been given the classes to cover and I wonder if I can talk to you about them."

"They were covered by Paul Honor last year, so why do you want to see me about them?" said Richard, looking as though he wasn't going to be very helpful.

It was twenty past four.

"Do you know the sorts of things the teachers did…I mean what topics they taught?" Mort persisted.

"Not really. Haven't you got a syllabus or something? Ask Paul or Jeff Shaw."

"No one seems to have anything, I'm afraid," said Mort not wishing to be thwarted so soon.

"I think Simon Junkin wrote a syllabus," countered Richard, intent on sounding positive that he had absolutely nothing to offer. "Paul might have one – I think Alice Riley had one too. Have you looked through her things?"

Mort paused. He remembered the four pages of *English for Craft Students* he'd found in the cardboard box she'd left on her desk. So that's what they were. No wonder he didn't recognise much in it.

"Did you say Mr Junkin wrote it?" he asked, narrowing his eyes and scowling.

Another black mark for Junkin.

"I think so. Not much good though," Richard continued, sounding more relaxed and warming to his theme. "The students didn't like it. It was about credit cards and health education – the dangers of smoking and drinking, that sort of stuff. They said it was inappropriate for them. I mean how many teenagers have a credit card these days? And the number of cigarette ends outside the workshops hasn't gone down, I can tell you. The caretakers are always complaining. In the end the teachers gave up and showed videos – educational ones, not films or anything like that. Some of them looked quite interesting. Anyway we don't bother much about the subject. It's not part of their exams. We have to give them an hour, sometimes two, to keep the boards happy. Why not try to liberalise the little fascists. There's a challenge for you."

He saw that Mort wasn't returning his smile. On the contrary, he looked horrified.

"I'm joking Mr Todd," said Richard, but he didn't look as if he was.

"That's what I wanted to hear, Mr Head," replied Mort, smiling belatedly. "May I make a suggestion? What's their standard of literacy?"

"That's not a suggestion, it's a question," said Richard, but he took it no further. "Well the best student I've ever come across is an erudite, articulate engineer. Lives in all worlds you see. I'm afraid most of the lower level ones can barely write and their attitudes to the female students are appalling. I get complaints about that too. In truth if there's ever any trouble in the refectory or the library they always get the blame, even if none of them is in there."

He sat back and looked appealingly at Mort.

"If you can do anything about that, Mr Todd, you'd be doing me a great service."

"I have several ideas which I'd like to discuss with you," said Mort.

He noticed that Richard was looking furtively at his watch.

"Jot them down and put them in a memo, please," said Richard hurriedly. "What I really mean is that you can do what you like as long as there are no rebellions like there were last year. And that includes the lecturers as well as the students. Please excuse me. I have to go to an urgent meeting off site."

As Mort was walking back to the main building and his staff room, he didn't know that Richard's important meeting was with Mick Jagger, Bill Wyman and Charlie Watts at the Albert Hall. Keith Richards had sprained his wrist again.

The next day Mort went to see Maureen King. It was warm and sunny again and he left his jacket on his desk.

"Hello Mort," she said, a wide smile spreading over her face as he entered the Business Studies staffroom on the ground floor of the main building.

He looked around and behind, as if expecting her to be greeting someone else. She knew he was playacting because there was no one else in the workroom.

"Come and sit down," she giggled. "Coffee?"

Mort accepted, mildly surprised at this unexpectedly pleasant welcome; only Ariadne had been this hospitable before. While Maureen was away making the drinks, he took the opportunity to have a look round. It was much the same as the Humanities staff room but slightly smaller. There were nine or ten desks arranged around the walls, all loaded with books and paper and box upon box crammed full of yet more books and paper. On the side facing the window the ledges were covered in multiple copies of text books which would disappear when classes started. In the middle was a low-lying coffee table on which there stood a tray of mugs, a crusty looking packet of sugar, two half empty bottles of milk and an opened box of chocolate biscuits. Very civilized, he thought. We've only got a kettle.

Maureen soon returned carrying two large cups.

"Bring our chairs," she said, indicating that she wanted to sit round the coffee table "It'll be easier to talk. Sugar and milk? Biscuit?"

He helped himself to all three.

"Can I smoke in here?" he inquired.

"Of course you can," she replied amiably. "I'll join you."

He offered her one of his but she politely declined, shaking her head.

"I smoke menthol ones. Now, how are you settling in?"

"Hmm," said Mort wondering whether to give the expected response or speak the truth – or should he tell her about how awful the traffic was each morning?

"I hear you've got eyes on the Prinny's job," she teased before he'd made up his mind. "Don't take it too badly. People have parked there before and they always will do until that damn hedge is cut. Iris shouldn't have bawled you out like that, not in front of all those people. I don't know who she thinks she is. She's only a jumped up secretary and a bloody lorry driver's wife."

He was slightly taken aback by the venom in her voice but he had no time to dwell on it. As they both took out their cigarettes, he couldn't help looking at her exquisite breasts as she bent over to accept his light. She was wearing a low cut white blouse, which wasn't leaving much to his imagination, and skin-tight jeans. He had to admit that she was the most beautiful woman he'd seen in a long time. Had she been a couple of inches taller she could easily have been a model, perhaps a film star. Even Cassandra was nowhere near as enchanting. He guessed she was about the same age as he was, early thirties probably. Yet somehow he knew she wouldn't be interested in him other than as a colleague. His instincts were correct. She was a one man woman and she'd married the man she loved when she was twenty.

"Tell me how you're settling in," she said, laughing again, as she blew smoke up into the air.

It swirled spectacularly as it caught the sunlight coming in through the windows.

"Well…" he said still hesitating.

"I bet you've had it rough with the English and Art set," she said, filling in the silence for him again. "I don't know how they've got away with things with for so long. Paul Honor told me you've sorted out the timetables without consulting him and he's not happy. You've taken his favourite group off him and he's furious."

"Yes," he droned, not sure whether he was happy either since she was setting the tone and direction of the conversation.

"And I bet you've had a few run-ins with Simon Junkin."

"Yes."

"And Jeff Shaw?"

"Yes."

"You're aware they're related, aren't you?"

She was smiling wickedly as he stared back at her in disbelief, his mouth slightly open.

"Oh yes," she continued. "Jeff's married to Simon's daughter. They all live together on his farm, Simon's that is. Not his wife though. She left him ages ago."

"That explains a lot," said Mort, screwing his face up as tried to come to terms with the pictures coming into his head.

He was imagining what Junkin's daughter looked like. If she were as thin as her father then what a strange pair she and Shaw would make.

"I can guess why you look bewildered," she said, still smiling roguishly. "Sarah, that's Jeff's wife, is nearly as tubby as him. "

"I wish I'd met you last week," he said, grinning and tapping the ash off his cigarette less manically than before. "I might have felt a bit better. What can you tell me about Roy Jolly?"

"Mr Arty Farty? He's mostly harmless. Damn good artist though. Simon worships him."

"What?" he cried, nearly spitting his coffee out all over the table. "Junkin told me he's never here – he works in his shop or whatever it is he has."

"He's been on a very long leash, Mort," she said, stubbing out her cigarette.

She'd only smoked about half of it.

"That's because Simon gets a lot of bargains – all originals. He's a collector and fancies himself an expert in rural watercolours."

"He told me that he wants me to sort him out before the inspectors do – adamant he was," he said angrily.

He became aware, as he spoke those words, what Junkin had meant by the word 'abrasive'.

"Be careful," she said, sensing he was riled and adopting a more serious tone. "It's not as easy as that. Around here, Mort, people don't just know each other – they're all related. Roy has powerful friends everywhere and most of them buy things off him. Besides you can't get rid of someone just like that – if that's what you're considering. You'll have to do everything through Simon and he won't want the union on his back for obvious reasons. Sounds like you're going to get into trouble. Of course you could frighten him a bit. The other art teachers are fed up of having to cover up for him and look after his students. Talk to them and use them to help you. He's not number one anymore now that you've replaced old, useless Alice the Alcie. From what I've been hearing, you've upset a few apple carts already and good for you. I'm glad someone's brave enough to do it."

She paused and looked him straight in the eye, then she burst out laughing.

"Incidentally, what did you want to see me about?"

Mort laughed too. He stubbed his cigarette out and picked his papers up he'd placed on the floor as there was no room for them on the coffee table. As he was about to speak, a middle-aged woman with a page boy haircut covering most of her face came into the room, pushed past them without looking at them and sat down at the desk furthest away from the door. She was smartly dressed in a grey jacket and well-pressed black trousers but the striking thing about her was that she was wearing a large pair of sunglasses. She turned her back on them, bent over her desk, put her head in her hands and started sobbing. He looked at Maureen, perplexed by this unconcealed show of grief.

"That's Anne Conroy," she whispered, tapping her lips twice with her right index finger. "Her husband's a

purser – Danish liners, I think – and he's home on leave."
"What's wrong with her?" he mouthed slowly and carefully
so that there would be no need to repeat himself.

"He comes home for a couple of nights and then he goes
back to port, and he stays on board his ship until he has to
leave again."

"Why?"

"You'll find out if you ever have the misfortune to be
introduced to her. I'll give you one clue. She talks so slowly
that someday we hope she'll finish a sentence in less than
four minutes. That'll be a new world record."

They both tried hard to suppress their laughter, succeeding
only by clasping their mouths with both hands. He coughed,
wagged a warning finger at her and started laughing again,
but the soft sobbing continued behind them.

"I've come to see you about the general studies classes I've
had dumped on me by Jeff Shaw" he said, resuming a normal
volume. "As the YTS Co-ordinator I hoped you might give
me some advice on what to teach, although I think I may
have solved that one yesterday for the engineering lads with
Richard Head."

"I don't like your use of the word 'dumped', Mort," she
said without any trace of humour in her voice.

"I'm sorry," he said hastily. "I wasn't expecting to be
teaching anything like this until last Friday."

"I understand and I sympathise," she replied, a little more
considerately. "It happens every year. Paul Honor was given
no choice when he took over, but he never got to grips with
it. He told the teachers to do what they wanted…"

He finished her sentence for her. "…and ended up
showing videos."

"Yes. I suppose Richard told you that, but he doesn't give
two tosses either. What do you intend to do?"

"I want to assess their language skills…"

"Be careful," she said interrupting his flow once again.
"They've got low thresholds of concentration and get bored

easily. Why not teach communication? I'll lend you a couple of programmes to look at. You could start with NVC – non-verbal communication, body language, that sort of thing. Bring in some video equipment, get them role playing. Make up an accident scenario and get them to write a report. They could write a script and make a film. They'd enjoy that and they'd be learning Basic English in a much more interesting way."

She was sounding more enthusiastic with every word. Then she stopped and looked at him. Once again he was staring at her, his mouth slightly open. He knew he'd found a new and unexpected confederate and he'd forgotten all about telling her how dreadful the traffic had been that morning. The sobbing had stopped too.

CHAPTER 15

12 April 2005: 11.25am

Steven Wallace was just leaving Harrison's make-shift headquarters when the two SOCO officers emerged one by one from Ariadne's office. They looked like twins in their identical white outfits. Both were very young and characteristically wore their dull, brown hair in pony tails making them look equally plain. The first one to appear smiled at Harrison but the second one shook her head at the Hulk as he closed the door behind her.

"You should be wearing gloves," she said fiercely. "You'll have smudged any prints on that handle."

"It's too late for that," he said apologetically. "People have been in and out all morning, even before we got here."

He wasn't telling the whole truth and he knew they knew, because they were looking at him even more disapprovingly.

"Give him some gloves," said Harrison gloomily.

The Hulk leered in his usual asinine way as they gave him purple ones when green would have been aesthetically much neater. The two SOCO officers turned away to report to Harrison.

"Not much to go on," the first one said, scarcely able to hide her disappointment. "We've dusted what we can for prints, including the desk, but it looks as if it's been cleaned recently. It's too early to say but we're pretty sure all of the prints belong to one person, possibly two max. You'd better fingerprint anyone else who's been in there during the last twenty four hours so that you can exclude them."

Harrison sighed. Things weren't getting much clearer and soon he'd have to re-open the College or even better close it down for the day, possibly longer.

"We've taken some pictures," said the second officer, taking over. "We've taken some of the prints on the desk and we've got the body from most angles. We're not sure what to do with the you know what, so we've left it. I think forensic will want to examine it for DNA, so I'll tell them to bag it up before they take the body away. There are some smudgy prints on it."

"Anything else?" asked Harrison, crossing his fingers behind his back.

"We think you should bag the book and the pen that are lying on the desk as well," said the first officer, not aware they were sounding like a double act. "We had a quick look in the book. It's a sort of diary and there are a couple of recent entries that might mean something. You'll also need to look at her computer obviously, particularly her emails."

"Good work!" said Harrison, uncrossing his fingers and placing his hands in his pockets but he saw that she was looking looked very uncomfortable.

"I haven't finished yet, sir," she went on, getting slightly more red-faced with every word. "We went through the drawers in her desk. Mostly educational stuff, nothing unexpected, except for this. In the bottom drawer, hidden under a load of files were a few sex toys. Vibrators and some, er, pleasure balls I think they're called."

"Another thing might have skipped your attention, sir," said the second officer, raising her eyebrows keenly. "We noticed that the deceased doesn't…didn't…have a handbag with her. At any rate we couldn't find one. It may have been stolen."

Harrison remembered that he knew he was missing something when he carried out his cursory sweep of the room earlier. Perhaps it *was* the handbag?

"Is there anything else?" he said, grateful for yet another lead. "I want to release the body to Charlie's mob as soon as possible and I want to close the College. When you get back to the station tell control I'll need a couple more plain clothes officers, and one of them had better be a woman."

"Well, sir…" It was the first officer again and she was trying to choose her words carefully. "You've been in there, haven't you? You corrupted the scene of the crime. You should have worn a suit…"

"I didn't have time to go all that way back to the car in the rain," he said halfheartedly, conceding that she was right. "Besides I didn't know what I was in for until I saw the body…"

"You always say rain's the policeman's friend, sir," she countered.

"There wasn't time," he argued, beginning to bristle.

"You could have closed the crime scene down immediately," she added, hoping he wouldn't lose his temper. "You should have waited. *Has* anyone else been in there?"

"As far as I'm aware only the woman who found her," he said sulkily. "Anyone else could have gone in there between then and when I got here."

The two SOCO officers nodded and made as if to leave, when the first turned back, smiling again.

"I don't think it'll matter that much," she said, trying to get back in his good books. "Bye sir – oh and get someone to put barrier tape on this door and the one at the end of the corridor."

When they'd gone, Harrison spoke briefly to the two site technicians, who corroborated everything that Wallace had said. After he dismissed them, he telephoned for back up but none was available immediately as the investigation into the bank robbery in the town centre was still in progress. Apparently there were two hostage situations to deal with. He'd have to cope on his own for a while longer, so he decided to take stock. He sat down in his little cupboard, surrounded by unkempt heaps of crumpled paper and files and started his initial analysis of what he'd got so far, greatly discomforted by his present predicament and the lingering stench of bad breath. The sight of the Hulk standing across the corridor humming to himself didn't help either.

What *had* he got so far? He'd got a dead body and a highly original and *very* suspicious set of circumstances. But there was no sign of a forced entry, no sign of a struggle and probably no fingerprints or DNA that would be of any use. Could it have been suicide? That would make matters simpler. Could she have been trying to top herself and messed it up? What *was* he thinking? Of course it wasn't suicide. Or could it have been an accident? Heart attack? No, Charlie would have spotted that. Her handbag was missing…he must order a thorough search of the buildings and the grounds. Could it have been a robbery? A robbery that had gone wrong and had resulted in murder to shut her up. Yet his mind kept returning to one thing. What was it that she was doing in her office? Why all the sex toys in her desk? Why? Why? Wait a minute…if it was a robbery gone wrong, had some sick bastard made it look like she was pleasuring herself to put us off the scent? This was worth pursuing. To think it through he drew up a timeline in his notebook, muttering softly to himself as he did so.

"She comes in at seven o'clock and starts working. The thief comes in a bit later, say ten past, before anyone else arrives, and she gives him – *or her* – *or them*…let's say there were two of them…her handbag, but she recognises them. Charlie said she was drugged so they chloroform her at quarter past. That would explain the marks on her nose and the smudged lipstick. But Charlie said she was asphyxiated – burked, he said – and that's why he assumed there might be more than one killer. A Burke and Hare duo and they leave the chloroform on too long and she can't breathe. Afterwards they set up this macabre scene…no that's not it. Hell's bell's, why would a couple of chancer tealeafs carry chloroform and sex toys…unless they weren't chancers and had planned the whole thing. Hold on, the outer door…it's locked electronically…the murderers must have known the combination! Well, whichever way you look at it, it looks like an inside job. It has to be one of that crowd down the corridor…or Wallace. Right, I'm going to sit this one out. I'm setting up camp here and I'm not leaving till I get a result. Sod the rule book and sod the Chief Inspector. He's left me on my own with Tim."

As he was making this decision, two men in light blue overalls from forensic pathology arrived wheeling a long trolley with a stretcher on it and told him that they were going to take the body away to the mortuary. One was carrying a black body bag. They looked like two surreal waiters bringing Ariadne an early lunch. He watched them go into her office and then he heard two gasps, which were soon followed by the rustling of a body being lifted and, shortly after that, the sound of a zip being fastened. Ariadne's reign at Storbury was over and so, much to Harrison's relief, was the ghastly scene of her last attempt at self-gratification.

"They say that death is the ultimate orgasm," he whispered to himself. "Well, it wasn't quite for Ariadne, was it?"

CHAPTER 16

Early October 1984

Once there are sufficient enrolments and timetables are agreed a college works like clockwork for most of the academic year. Students go to their appointed classes, they get taught, they learn, they get examined, they pass, and they move on. Well, most of them do. Mort had been correct in his prediction that he wouldn't see much of the other teachers once term had started and that included Maureen. He was able to get on with teaching his own classes and call all the meetings that mattered as Senior Lecturer in English and Liberal Arts and, although he didn't like to admit it, he soon settled into the term-time routine. His main gripe was that he considered nearly all of the people at the College to be shallow and pretentious – he dubbed them all 'the twee set' – and many times he felt alienated in what for him was an unbearably bourgeois backwater. They, in turn, found him distant, aloof and, what was worse, a trouble-maker and a 'smart arse'. The English teachers generally did as they were told and were nowhere near as bad as Junkin had painted them, except for Paul Honor. He went out of his way to be unhelpful, such was his overtly blazing bitterness at not getting what he thought was his job by divine right, and it came as no surprise that he was a constant thorn in Mort's side.

The same could not be said for the Art team, however, who were a law unto themselves. They refused to start until ten o'clock each morning, backed by Jeff Shaw and the union, who pointed out that Art teachers needed an hour's preparation time before classes to organise their studios and set up or lay out equipment – and another hour at the end of the day to put it all away. They lunched as a group in a nearby pub and were away by four o'clock even when they had an evening class. This was their saving grace in Mort's eyes because each one demanded two evening classes each week, and he guessed that it was because they could have a lie-in the next morning after extending their lunchtime and early doors drinking sessions with a few more rounds shortly before closing time.

He was, however, intrigued by Roy Jolly, whom the other Art teachers treated as something of a spiritual guide, despite their reservations about his behaviour. Roy was, as Maureen said, a successful and talented artist and owned the gallery in Mallory which Mort passed every day, the one in fact which was later to form part of his daily chant as he sat staring ahead at the barely moving traffic. He learned that Roy had bought an old Rolls Royce which he was restoring because it drove like a dream. Roy was an amiable, old rogue and they agreed that as long as he came to College more often and taught most of his classes, Mort would leave him alone. He could continue to set as many off-site projects as he liked as long as he filled in the appropriate paperwork and it was countersigned by Junkin. This mutually harmonious relationship actually turned into something more like a genuine, if fragile alliance when Roy let it slip, one afternoon when he and Mort were discussing the Art budget, that he detested Junkin. It happened that he'd been summoned to Junkin's office to be told that it would be a good idea to exhibit student work in a nearby public library, an exhibition which Roy had proposed the day before in a memorandum. Mort couldn't work out whether Roy was up in arms about having his own ideas pirated or whether it was because he'd put pen to paper for once and all his effort had been wasted – it wasn't the first time, he said, but it was equally as disgruntling all the same. Roy blew hot and cold, chiefly because Junkin pretended he was a connoisseur of all things art, especially water colours, when, as Roy put it, he couldn't tell the difference between a Girton and a Gilpin even if you told him. Occasionally he felt sorry for Junkin because of what his wife had done to him. She'd run off with his best friend, leaving him with a young daughter and an even younger son to bring up and a ramshackle cottage to rebuild in the middle of nowhere.

Then there was Ariadne, who always tried to see Mort at least once each day. She sat with him at his desk as he ate his lunch if she couldn't find any other opportunity. Occasionally she asked him if he had a minute or two for anything that had come into her head as soon as she saw him, such as who his favourite authors were – he just smiled and said he had a few. If she'd asked him about films it would have been a different matter. She worked as hard trying to think up original reasons to be near him as she did on most of the other aspects of her job, and it wasn't long before knowing glances and mocking sniggers accompanied her perambulations across the staff room. This made him uneasy – it was undermining the impression of solemn diligence he was trying desperately to create – but she ignored the sneers, more intent on finding out more about him. She once asked him what his hobbies and interests were and was astounded when he told her he hadn't really got any as he was too busy with College work and the refurbishment of his home. It was, she concluded, as if he didn't want to let her into his life at all. He made her laugh every so often, as when he told her that like most men from Yorkshire he liked sport and he couldn't believe that, as a woman from Yorkshire, she didn't have the faintest idea how to play cricket. Her enthusiasm didn't even cool when, in answer to her forthright question, he told her he was married – and very happily too. It never struck him that she might be coming on to him and he maintained a discreet distance from her in keeping with his role and status at the College. He thought she was keen yet inexperienced and she was simply talking to him about other things to disguise this. He did, however, notice that she took tremendous care with her appearance. She wore different clothes each day, sometimes wearing elegant, fashionable dresses or suits, at other times looking like a tomboy, but the lavish make-up and swaying earrings were nearly always present.

His favourable impressions of her were to change, however, about four weeks into the term. On his way to the refectory to have a snack before one of his twilight classes with engineering students, he saw her coming out of Junkin's office as he passed. She was arm in arm with Paul Honor and they were laughing and joking. He didn't think much of it until the next day when, returning from his late morning class, he saw her go into Junkin's office and heard the door being locked. That lunchtime he didn't see her and he felt a slight twinge of jealousy. What was she up to, he wondered? Nevertheless he didn't think too much about it again, except that it was a bit odd, and he was slightly disappointed to have no one talk to as he ate his sandwiches. He was soon to meet someone who would explain everything to him.

The following week he was sitting alone in the refectory drinking a cup of coffee. It was about quarter past six and the College was almost deserted except for the cleaners and those waiting to teach evening classes, and they were spread out all over the site in classrooms or staffrooms. It was early October and the nights were quickly drawing in. It was almost dark outside and most of the lights had been switched off, the women who worked there having long since gone home. Anyone who wanted something to eat or drink had to use the dispensing machines. He was reading *The Hitch-Hiker's Guide to the Galaxy* by Douglas Adams, who was soon to become one of his favourite authors he never told Ariadne about. He had just started it and he was becoming intrigued by the Vogons whose favourite pastime was shouting, and he was wondering if they were real and had recently colonised Storbury College. 'Resistance is useless' was their catchphrase.

The refectory wasn't very big considering the number of people who passed through it during the mornings and afternoons, but there were enough chairs and tables there to make even the bravest person feel uneasily insignificant when it was half lit and empty. It had been designed in the shape of a letter B lying on its side, which meant that there were two large bays at either end, both of which could be accessed from outside by two large glass doors. They were now in almost total darkness, which signified that they were out of bounds for the rest of the day. He was chuckling away to himself when out of the blackness came a ghostly voice.

"Hello Mr Todd", it said, as he sat there slowly turning to stone. "I bet you'll never guess who I am."

He looked in the direction from which this eerie sound had come but he couldn't see anyone. He was about to get up and make a run for it when the voice spoke again.

"Don't scuttle away, young man," it whispered. "I'm Alice Riley – Alice the Alcie they called me when I was here. Alcie – it's an anagram of my name, you see. They all thought it was hilarious, the cruel buggers."

"Oh!" said Mort, sounding like a small boy who'd just been told that Santa Claus didn't exist.

"Sit still and listen to me." Alice's voice murmured. "I've one or two things to tell you."

He stood up and walked towards the gloom anxious to see what she looked like, when she quickly raised her voice.

"Don't come near me," she hissed. "Stay there and listen. Then you can go."

Mort obeyed her for some reason he never grasped, and he couldn't hide his disappointment at not being able to see what she looked like.

"Why won't you let me sit with you?" he pleaded, returning to his seat.

"I'm not going to answer any questions either," she said as her voice rose even higher.

"Why not?" he asked, not realising it was pointless to persist.

"I said I'm not going to answer any questions. I'm going to tell you a story then I'll put you in the picture about a few things that will make you see things more clearly."

She was sounding calmer. He peered into the blackness and could barely make out her silhouette against the fading light outside.

"A woman died and went to Heaven," she began, her voice now at a more normal pitch. "As she approached the pearly gates, Saint Peter stopped her and asked her where she thought she might be going. 'To Heaven, sir,' she replied. He looked in his book where everyone's life history is kept, looked back at the woman, shook his head and said 'Oh no, you're not. You've been good but you've also been wicked and you haven't earned enough points to enter the Kingdom of God. You'll have to go to Hell.' 'Oh please let me have one more chance,' she beseeched him. Saint Peter looked again at his book and started counting. 'The number of ticks and crosses are about the same so it looks like you deserve one last opportunity to prove yourself worthy,' he said kindly. The woman thanked him profusely as he showed her a map of the world. 'Take this thimble,' he said pointing to the Atlantic Ocean. 'When you've emptied all that water out of the sea with it, you can come through these gates.' The woman fell to her knees and took hold of his ankles. 'But that'll take an eternity,' she wailed, 'Please choose another task for me to perform.' Saint Peter was moved by her show of humility and reconsidered. 'Oh all right,' he said, once again feeling compassionate. He showed her a map of Britain and this time he pointed to a small town. 'That's Storbury,' he continued. 'Go there and become the Senior Lecturer in English and Liberal Arts'. 'Give me that bloody thimble,' the woman shrieked as she snatched it from Saint Peter's hand."

She cackled and the sound echoed around the bay and out among the empty tables and chairs. He didn't laugh. He merely sat there trying to work out who this eccentric, possibly insane woman was.

"I've heard it before," he said a short time after the ghostly cacophony had subsided. "Last time it was about becoming a lecturer at my old technical college. One of my ex-colleagues told me it when I started there."

"I've told you the joke precisely to emphasise what I'm going to say," she said, her voice lowered to a whisper. "I suppose you've already found your Head of Department is a barrel of laughs. He and that son-in-law of his drove me to drink. Well, perhaps not altogether but they helped."

"Why did you take everything with you when you left," he asked, beginning to feel less frightened.

"I said I'm not going to answer any questions," she reminded him sternly. "But I was coming to that."

He heard her take a long swig of something from a bottle, then he heard her exhale noisily and smack her lips.

"They're both in it for themselves so watch them very carefully. They pretend they're passionate about education, even this place, but they're mainly interested in their social lives and holidays in Tuscany or wherever it is all the pseudo-tourists go these days. If anything goes wrong they'll stitch you up and hang you out to dry. The same goes for Paul Honor. He desperately wants to get in with them. That's why he became so obnoxious when you got the post he assumed incorrectly he was going to get. He saw Junkin's job as the next step, you see, to carry on the long line of pompous prats that have run this department for donkeys' years."

She paused and took another drink, while he continued to stare into the bay that was getting darker every minute.

"And before you ask," she continued, "Jeff Shaw doesn't want Junkin's job. That would be a betrayal of his socialist credentials."

She laughed again, although not as raucously as before.

"The rest, although extremely infuriating at times, are mostly harmless, including Roy Jolly," she added as if as an afterthought. "Unfortunately you're caught between a rock and a hard place. You've got the slime balls on one side and the skivers on the other. You can't win whatever you do. They'll drive you insane in the end."

He sighed and started to drum his fingers on the table. He'd heard something similar from Junkin and the teachers many times before.

"You think I'm crackers, don't you?" she asked, more gently than before. "I'm just old and tired. I wasn't always like this, you know. I was like you once when things were more civilised, before we got all these…"

He didn't let her finish. He was becoming bored with her and it was getting the near the time he had to leave to collect his things together for his lesson.

"I'm sorry I have to go soon," he said, careful not to ask any more questions. "Please get to the point of what this is all about."

"I'm here to warn you about someone," she whispered, sounding chillingly sinister again, and she sensed that she'd regained his full attention.

"I'm here to warn you about Ariadne Hopwood," she said, resuming her ominous tone. "She's very single-minded, she's very hypocritical and she's very clever. She wants promotion quickly and she works on anyone she thinks can help her particularly if they're male. She knows she's very attractive too and she plays miss goody-goody, miss keen-and-willing and miss sexually-available to any man that she thinks might be influential. She was all over Paul Honor till she heard about you and then it cooled slightly with him. She's after you both for two things – sex, if you're lucky, and her career. She believes the first leads to the second so if you're gettin' it, young man, you must have something else she wants. It's Junkin she's really courting because he has all the power in the department. But she'll keep making Honor think he's still number one when she's alone with him, and I bet she's been finding a hundred and one reasons to talk to you as often as she can. It all adds up. The job she's after is Honor's but she'll take anything going anywhere in the country, and she'll need a good word in the right ear from Junkin – even from you."

He heard her take another long drink.

"Haven't you noticed yet that she doesn't seem to have any female friends?" she added, becoming more acrimonious with every word. "Don't you think that's odd? But beware. She's a fervent feminist and if she ever gets to where she wants to be and has power over you, she'll eat you up and spit you out like a piece of half chewed meat. She treated me like something that had crawled out of the primaeval soup. I saw through her and she knew it."

He sat and listened to the old woman's diatribe, completely thunderstruck. He hadn't been expecting anything quite like this and, in all truth, he didn't suspect Ariadne of anything other than over-friendliness. Then he heard the top being screwed slowly back in place on a bottle and he knew Alice had taken her final mouthful of whatever it was she drinking.

"I've got one more thing to say," she said, and he detected a more melancholy tenor to her voice. "It's an answer to one of your questions. I've broken my own stipulation but I was going to tell you anyway. I took all my things with me when I retired because they're mine. I designed everything and I worked long, hard hours to produce everything myself. I worked here for over forty years. Why should the College get my soul as well as my life?"

As the silence returned he could hear the sound of voices somewhere in the distance, probably from outside as the early birds were arriving for their evening classes, or perhaps it was the cleaners? Then he heard the sound of a door being closed softly. He stood up and cautiously walked into the bay. There was no one there, although he could smell the lingering odour of whisky.

CHAPTER 17

12 April 2005: Mid-Morning

The first Helen knew about the mysterious death in the College was when she heard the sound of a police car's siren rushing up the drive, followed shortly afterwards by the equally piercing blare of an ambulance. She looked out of the office window and couldn't believe her eyes. Another police car was silently parking across the College drive near the entrance. A small, thin officer was stopping people and cars from leaving and, despite their angry gestures at the sky and soundless protests about the rain, he was making them return up the drive and back into the College's main building, leaving their cars stranded on the roadway. A burlier policeman was stopping anyone from coming in, ignoring the same silent pantomime about the rain. Detective Inspector Harrison had ordered a temporary lockdown of the whole campus and Bernadette had been dispatched to inform everyone to stay where they were.

Helen decided to leave the office to find out what was afoot. As she made for the staffroom down the corridor, she passed an empty classroom. She was surprised to see Gordon and Barry sitting at opposite ends, with their backs to each other true to form, amid a forest of unoccupied desks and chairs, both quite oblivious of each other and what was going on outside. She pushed the half open door silently and looked in. They made a fine pair, she thought, as she watched them idly staring at the wall in front of each of them. Barry, the tall, bony, fatuous dreamer who would trip over his own shadow, suddenly stood up and flicked his head to one side, the back of his white hair hiding his nondescript features. She smiled to herself as she considered them too tiny and out of place on a guy who was over six feet tall. Then there was Gordon, small, stocky, dark-bearded and bespectacled. His jet black hair was parted straight as a dye, as Simon Junkin's was but on the opposite side. The white line across his scalp reminded her of Thomas Hardy's description of the road traversing Egdon Heath in *The Return of the Native*, her favourite book which she re-read every year. She never told him about it because she knew he hadn't read it. She noticed he was picking his nose with his index finger and licking it occasionally as he read a magazine.

She went into the room quietly and sneaked stealthily up behind Barry, who was sitting nearer to her, grabbed his shoulders and shouted "Boooooooo", which made him jump out of his chair and stand up belligerently, fists clenched and teeth bared.

"What the frigging hell!" he shrieked, his unremarkably long face turning violet and his tiny eyes bulging. "What are you playing at? You nearly frightened me to death. I was in the middle of preparing a lesson…You could've given me a heart attack!"

"Barry, you were miles away," she retorted calmly but sheepishly. "Where were you? Away with the fairies?"

She couldn't have been more right. He'd just leapt like a salmon to head the winner in the Cup Final and once again someone from that bloody office had spoiled his moment of triumph. Gordon seemed equally shocked. He stood up too and gesticulated at Helen, his arms outspread, and he yelled at her "Take care, young…"

He stopped and swallowed the word 'lady'. He didn't want to be on a charge of sexual harassment, not at his age and with all his debts besides.

"Cool it, boys," said Helen, staying calm but beginning to feel a little foolish. "The police have closed the College. We have to find out why. Come on."

Neither of the men moved.

"Don't bother," said Barry negatively, sitting down again. "We'll find out soon enough"

"Yes," said Gordon smiling. "It's not as if there's been a murder, is it? I bet it's some lunatic students messing around in the refectory. You know how windy those women are down there. I remember one teatime being summoned by them to go and investigate two suspicious looking characters they believed were drug dealers. Turned out they were two black guys who'd enrolled on an evening course and they were having a coffee before their class began. Hysterical, all of them."

"That's sexist," said Helen ominously.

Gordon gulped. Had he just infringed the College's new code of conduct lately enacted by Ariadne and her 'Women's Group'?

"I'm not implying anything about gender here," he retorted before she could go on. "What's more I think you mean racist, don't you? I mean those women are clinically... or to put it more correctly for you, *over-reacting emotionally* to any possible threat because they want our..."

He was stopped in his tracks by a red-eyed Bernadette, who rushed in and ordered them all to leave the room.

"The Principal's dead," she panted, breathing heavily from all the running about she was having to do. "But don't tell anyone. It's not official yet."

Gordon looked at Helen and raised his eyebrows.

"The police are here," wheezed Bernadette "No one's to leave the building. Helen, please go round this floor and order everyone to stay where they are. No one's to leave, not even to use the toilet. You two gentlemen are to go back to your office and stay there. Helen, you too, after you've been round the rooms."

With that she hurried off, leaving the others stunned and frozen to the spot like cardboard cut-outs of themselves.

"You'd better do as she says, Helen," said Gordon pulling himself together after a few seconds. "Come on Barry, let's go back next door and wait and see what's really happened."

"But you *knew* someone had been murdered, Gordon," murmured Helen. "You said so. *How* did you know?"

"Oh don't be silly," said Gordon edgily. "I didn't say someone *had been* murdered. I think I said 'It's not as if there's been a murder'. It was a figure of speech."

"Not technically," interjected Barry contemptuously.

"Now's not the time to be pedantic, English teacher," Gordon snapped back.

He was beginning to feel like a prime suspect if Bernadette's message had been true, and he hoped that neither Barry nor Helen would mention it again. He was clearly rattled.

While Helen went off to spread Bernadette's message, Gordon and Barry returned to the Humanities office. Barry looked out of the window for a while but mostly they sat in silence, neither able to think of anything particular to say. As Gordon was becoming ever more nervous of the consequences that his stupid but wholly innocent *faux pas* might have, he decided to break the ice.

"Where's Mort got to?" he asked.

"He'll be with the others in the management meeting," replied Barry. "If we have to stay here, he'll have to stay where he is. I wonder if he's panicking."

"Why?"

"Well, Ariadne used to work here...with Mort."

As Barry was in the middle of his answer, Helen returned from her expedition and stood by her desk.

"What did you say, Barry?" she enquired more politely than usual which increased his apprehension. "Did Ariadne work here before she became the Principal?"

"Oh yes," he replied, nodding frantically. "Oh yes, yes. She was an English teacher before I came here, but yes, sometime in the eighties, I think."

He looked at Gordon for support but he only shrugged his shoulders.

"Before my time, mate," he said.

"Before my time too. I was working in London," continued Barry. "But I've heard a little bit about her. All I know is what Mort told me just after she started here eighteen months ago. He seemed very angry. He just blurted it out. Don't tell him I've said anything about her though. He'll kill me if you do. He's sworn me to secrecy."

"Well, I never," said Helen. "I didn't know that she'd worked here before."

"By all accounts she was very ambitious and would've sold her grandmother to get on," Barry added. "If she ever had one, that is."

They all grinned at this lack of sympathy for the recently departed, Gordon most of all since talking about Ariadne was taking the pressure off him. He stood up and sat on the edge of his desk eager to hear Barry's story. Helen sat down too. She leaned forward onto her desk, propping herself up with her elbows. Barry sat back, pushed his hands through his hair and continued, relishing the chance to share some forbidden gossip.

"She was here for about two...maybe three years. Mort was her boss. She was a good teacher by all accounts but she was pushy. She ingratiated herself with all the senior staff – they were all men then – and it's rumoured, and I said *rumoured*, that she slept with a couple of them. It seems she was what you'd call a sexual predator, Gordon."

"Hold on a second," said Helen indignantly feeling that she had to butt in. "Just because she chased after blokes doesn't make her a loose woman."

"I thought you'd say something like that," scoffed Barry. "Do you want me to carry on or not? I'd be grateful if you'd sit there and listen if you want to learn anything."

Gordon smirked at both of them. He felt that this had superseded *his* accusation of sexism.

"You sound like you're talking to your students," he grinned.

Barry sighed. "OK, OK, but that's what Mort said. Anyway there isn't any more except that he told me Ariadne didn't want anyone to know about her working here before. That means other people must know – like old Richard Head."

"I bet Mort was *mortified*, when she became Principal?" joked Helen.

"He doesn't…didn't like her and he's…was very suspicious of her for some reason but he didn't let on why," Barry went on, looking at Gordon for a possible interpretation.

Gordon shook his head, sticking out his bottom lip to illustrate his ignorance.

"He doesn't talk about himself much these days, does he?" he said quietly. "He's never said anything about it to me."

"Perhaps it's because she's made it to the top and he's jealous of someone who used to work for him," Helen chimed in. "It must be strange for him to be ordered about by her though, mustn't it? Imagine you two having to work for me someday."

She laughed again but the two men sat looking at each other and they both grimaced.

"We'd probably both do you in," said Barry. "Twice."

From the surprised look on Helen's face, Gordon knew he was off her murder suspect list. Or if he wasn't, it now contained another name or two.

* * *

As their Principal's body was being wheeled out of the College, the senior managers were getting very fractious. They'd had to sit around without a drink and they hadn't been able to take a 'comfort break'. This seemed to be affecting the three witches the most, each of whom had brought a bottle of water as they did to every one of Ariadne's meetings. Lucy was constantly crossing and uncrossing her legs and bouncing up and down on her chair like people with full bladders tend to do. Penny and Harriet were trying to take her mind off things by speculating what might have happened to Ariadne but no one else had any sympathy for her, least of all Iris who told her sternly several times to pull herself together. This inadvertent irony didn't pass unnoticed by Mort, provoking a customary, savage tongue-lashing from the old tigress. Hugh was the most agitated however and he was still seething after the way he felt he'd been treated by Harrison. He was sitting with his back to the table staring at the wall and muttering to himself that he needed a cigarette. Mike had been busy writing his press release and Richard was keeping himself entertained compiling lists of tracks he and his band would play that evening at a concert somewhere in the USA. Bernadette, now more disconsolate, was still in the chair in the corner and had started to cry again. There was also a detective in the room which was making things even more uncomfortable. He'd been speaking to them individually and he'd collected a sheet of paper from each of them.

An hour earlier Iris had tried to start the scheduled meeting ten minutes or so after the tall, uniformed police officer had told them to stay in the room but she was shouted down disapprovingly; it had taken only a few seconds for the others to grasp that she was *actually* serious. Their disbelief didn't last long however; she was soon called out of the room briefly to meet the detectives who'd just arrived to start the investigation. When she returned she was accompanied by a young man wearing a damp, grey car coat over his crumpled, green suit. He was looking round hesitantly as he entered. The first thing that struck them was that he looked very young. He was small but well-built with curly, tousled blonde hair. His face was boyish and flushed and his eyes and nose looked too small for the chubbiness that encased them. Were it not for his thick, protruding lips he could have been Iris's son – or Bernadette's for that matter.

"Good morning everyone," he ventured, immediately becoming conscious that this was not the appropriate way to start things off.

The weather was foul and there was the small matter of a dead body to deal with, but it had stopped the boisterous quarrelling he'd heard as he approached the room from outside in the corridor.

"I'm Detective Constable Hudson and I'm assisting Detective Inspector Harrison on this case," he continued as he took off his coat and placed it over the back of Ariadne's throne-like chair.

He hesitated again thinking he wasn't quite important enough or indeed daring enough to warrant such a brash gesture as to actually sit on it. He'd feel more comfortable in the seat usually occupied by Bernadette. He was conscious that everyone was looking just as antagonistically at him as they had been at the small, plump grey-haired woman as he came in, but he let it pass.

"I'm going to send round some sheets of paper," he said as authoritatively as he could manage. "I want you to write your name, your position at the College, your home address and telephone number – including your mobile number – and, finally your College and home email addresses, er…on one of them."

There was a collective gasp of exasperation.

"Do you need my vital statistics as well?" said Maureen gruffly and she didn't appear to be joking.

"Or my inside leg measurement?" added Mort equally mockingly.

Tim ignored these flippancies and passed a wad of paper to Penny who was sitting nearest on his right.

"Before you start," he said, looking at Penny. "Who's in charge?"

His instinct told him that for some reason the question had lightened the mood in the room, and it was Hugh who spoke next.

"I suppose I am," he said. "What do you want me to do?"

"I want you send someone round the buildings to tell everyone to stay where they are for the present." Tim declared more confidently. "Set up a relay system. You must be prepared for an eventuality such as this?"

Hugh nodded and looked at Bernadette.

"You go, will you?" he said as considerately as he could muster. "It'll take your mind off things."

Bernadette looked bewildered.

"You'll feel better doing something," he added as if he was talking to a child whose pet hamster had just died.

"Please don't tell anyone anything, madam, and don't mention what's happened" said Tim.

He turned to Hugh.

"Has anyone's seen the corpse?" he asked bluntly.

Bernadette was getting up to leave when she heard this question and she stopped dead in her tracks.

"I found the body," she said retaining her dignity, the expected flood of tears not materialising – perhaps it was because there was an outsider in the room.

"Anyone else?" said Tim, unsure why he'd bothered to ask.

It wasn't a very difficult question which required a lot of thought but no one spoke.

"I popped my head round the door," volunteered Iris after waiting to see if any of the others would inform on her. "I had to confirm what Bernadette had told us she'd seen. I locked the door afterwards and went off to call the police."

"Ah, it was you." he said, not yet fully aware of her ferocity. "The Detective Inspector wants to know why you didn't report a murder when you made the emergency telephone call."

"Because I didn't *know* it was a murder when I rang, Detective Constable", she replied, trying to keep a lid on her anger at what she regarded as brazen insolence. "Are you informing me *officially* that it was?"

"No, madam," he said, remembering what had Harrison said about keeping his mouth shut.

He was very pleased with himself; he'd obtained two of the answers he needed from one simple question. Since he was highly satisfied that he'd carried out all the Detective Inspector's preliminary orders, he rose to leave.

"I'll be back soon," he said as gravely as he could. "I have to acquire further instructions. The pathologist will be here soon. In the meanwhile I insist that no one leaves the room. Please excuse me."

When they were sure he was out of earshot, they all began to talk at the same time.

"We've got a right one 'ere!" said Maureen but no one wanted to indulge in comedy at that moment.

"How long does he think he can keep the College like this?" shouted Iris, trying to regain order. "There are hundreds of people on site currently and as soon as they see more police cars they'll be all over the place trying to find out what's going on."

"I bet most of them leg it over the fields," added Mort. "It's too large an area to guard."

"I expect the police will rely on stereotypical human behaviour," said Mike. "In a situation like this the teachers will act as surrogate prison warders…"

"Yes, for those in class," replied Mort. "Students are always hanging around the refectory at this time of the morning…"

"Why aren't they all in class, Mr Todd?" asked Iris.

She was a staunch believer in iron discipline and was frequently criticising the Heads of Department for not imposing tighter control.

"I think I need the toilet," said Lucy despondently. "How long do you think they'll keep us here?"

"You'll have to wee over there in the corner," said Maureen impassively.

"Or use your water bottle," added Mort equally poker-faced. "It would be more unobtrusive."

One or two saw the absurdity of Lucy's predicament and tried to force a laugh but Iris had had enough.

"Are you all aware that Ariadne Hopwood is lying dead a matter of a few feet away!" she bellowed. "You're all behaving like children. Control yourself, Lucy."

She stood up and looked around the now silent room.

"And you two over there," she went on, fixing Mort and Maureen with one of her deadliest glares. "Speak only when you've got something sensible to say. Do I make myself clear?"

They nodded obediently, bowled over by the savagery of her verbal assault. Her face reddened momentarily as her temper subsided and it was Hugh who came to her assistance.

"We're all a bit on edge, Iris," he said soothingly. "Sometimes humour helps, you know, even if it is of the gallows type. I suggest we try to work out a strategy for dealing with this. Clearly we can't do much at present but, as you said previously, the College is going to be closed and we have to put in place some contingency arrangements."

He turned to Mike.

"You'd better start to take notes," he said, enjoying his new role as acting Principal. "You handle the media."

"Yes, yes," replied Mike indignantly. "Iris told me before."

Hugh ignored this, such is the privilege of power, and addressed the meeting.

"The rest of you start working on your departmental plans. Iris, Maureen and I will work on a cross-college approach."

"Not more bloody action plans," said Maureen under her breath.

Hugh stood up and motioned her to follow him to the top of the table to sit with Iris. They hadn't even begun working when Tim came back into the room. He stood in the doorway and cut straight to the chase.

"The Detective Inspector wishes you to locate him a room that he can use for interview purposes," he said a great deal more officiously than he intended.

He was reacting to being in the presence of what he assumed were clever academics who understood grandiose language and therefore would expect him to use it.

"He requires it to be in close vicinity of this boardroom."

"Have we got a room he could use?" Hugh asked, looking at Iris.

Without looking up she licked her teeth noisily.

"There's an old office opposite Ariadne's room," she replied dryly. "It's now used as a store room but it's all I can suggest at such short notice. It's a bit small but it's bigger than the other one, which is a closet. That used to be a cloakroom in the old days for the principals and the secretarial staff before all the unnecessary alterations were made."

"What alterations were those?" asked Hugh, who didn't know much about the 'old days'.

"Before administrators and typists were replaced by computers," said Iris, even more sardonically than before. "The waiting area at the end used to be the room where they were based. It was sometimes used as an anteroom for interviews."

"That's why it's been converted into a proper waiting area," said Mort, ruefully remembering his interview all those years ago. "They use to push the desks against the walls and put a couple of extra chairs in, but it wasn't very comfortable when all the candidates were in together."

"If I may interpose," said Tim eager to regain command. "I'll apprise the Detective Inspector of the situation. When I return, Mr Jones, I'd be grateful if you'd go and see him."

With that he left the room again but Harrison was still in Ariadne's office. He asked the Hulk to follow him across the corridor and tried the door to the storeroom. It was unlocked.

"He won't like that," quipped the Hulk.

"No he won't," said Tim. "You'd better tell him."

"Go and see what the other policeman wants," Iris said to Hugh when Tim returned for the third time. "Otherwise we'll be here all morning. Now young man how can we help you?"

Tim sat down, again in Bernadette's chair, hoping she wouldn't want it if she came back earlier than he expected from her assignment.

"I'd like to speak to you all individually to ascertain a few facts about who you are and what you do here," he began. "I want to obtain a picture of what goes on in the College and so forth. We'll interview you more formally soon when we have a suspect or two."

He was trying to put them at their ease but it had the opposite effect.

"Oh no!" said Lucy panicking. "We *are* going to be here all morning."

CHAPTER 18

Mid-October 1984

Mort was uneasy for several days after his nightmarish encounter with Alice. He was baffled why she'd come to the College and particularly why she'd chosen to appear like some phantom from a horror story. The only thing missing was thunder and lightning. In the end he came to the compromise conclusion that she was genuinely trying to save him from the same miserable fate that had befallen her. It was an altruistic gesture from a bitter, old woman in an effort, as she might have put it, to save her self-respect. He didn't tell anyone about seeing her but he thought about asking around if Alice had been peculiar. Who to ask was the problem since he didn't talk to many people as it was. If he explained it was because she'd visited him when he was sitting alone in the refectory, and had remained out of sight while she warned him about Junkin and Ariadne and the rest, he'd have been considered crazier than she was.

There was worse to come. He learned a week afterwards that Alice had died alone in her town-centre, terraced cottage and that she'd drunk herself to death. It was then that he decided to visit Maureen again.

"What can you tell me about Alice?" he said getting directly to the point as he went into her workroom.

She was sitting and marking a heap of papers. As luck would have it she was the only person there.

"Hello, Mort," she replied playfully, smiling as usual, but a little bowled over by his sudden entry. "Nice afternoon isn't it? Yes I'm well. I'm a bit busy at the moment, thank you for enquiring."

He didn't return her smile; instead he stood and stared at her. He could hear pigeons cooing in the surrounding trees and they were a welcome distraction from the uneasy silence his offhand manner had generated.

"I'm sorry," he said eventually. "I'm in a bit of a hurry."

"She died last week," she said, her tone of voice fitting the solemnity of her rapidly changing mood. "You must have had the memo."

"Yes, OK," he said as intensely as before. "She drank herself to death, I know. But was she weird? Did she, like, do spooky things to people?"

"Not that I've heard," she said pushing the papers to one side and looking genuinely intrigued. "Why do you ask?"

"I'm not sure I want to say," he said.

The conversation wasn't going as he'd hoped it would.

"Hmm," she said, her curiosity well and truly aroused. "One of the greatest disadvantages of our line of work is that many teachers die very soon after they retire. Something to do with suddenly having nothing much to do after working all hours God sends year after year."

"When she worked here was she regarded as an oddball?" he persisted, aware that she was now deflecting his questions.

"Towards the end she was, I suppose," she answered, wondering where his line of questioning was leading. "She couldn't get on with Simon Junkin. She once thought she'd become head of department but he was appointed in her place. That was six or seven years ago. I wasn't here then but I've heard that they had some terrible rows. She started to let things go and she finally gave up when Paul Honor became section leader in English. She'd realised that she'd got as far as she was going and she started boozing."

He knew he wasn't going to discover anything by being enigmatic and he decided he had to tell her the truth – some of it at least.

"A few days ago she came to see me," he ventured, keeping to the bare bones of his story. "She told me all the usual stuff about Junkin and his cronies but she was most scathing about someone else."

"Who?"

"I can't tell you."

"Why not?"

"It may not be true. I'd be spreading malicious lies."

He paused; he was regretting his decision to talk to her and the conversation would go no further unless he gave her Ariadne's name. If he didn't she was bound to think that he was as unhinged as he was making Alice out to be – as he'd predicted.

"Why so mysterious all of a sudden, Mort?"

"Do you know if she disliked anyone else specifically?" he asked, waiting for a response he wasn't sure he wanted to hear.

"She bottled things up, if you'll pardon the pun," she replied, trying to lighten things. "She got on with most people as far as I know."

He couldn't think of anything else to say and it was Maureen who continued the guarded interchange.

"It's not me, is it?" she inquired hesitantly.

She stood up, breathing more heavily and clenched her fists as if preparing for a fight.

"No, no, certainly not!" he shouted, waving his arms in front of him. "It's…"

"Be careful, Mort," she cut in. "You never know who's listening. Maybe it's best if you don't tell me after all."

She smiled at him and he deemed it best to smile back, relieved that she'd calmed down. He'd never seen her so wound up in the short time he'd known her, but he made a mental note that she wasn't a woman to be trifled with.

"Look," he said cautiously. "I'll tell you what she said about the person and you see if it fits anyone you might recognise. Is that OK?"

She nodded and sat down again. He rested his arm against a filing cabinet and bent forwards slightly.

"Alice said the person in question was two-faced, highly ambitious and therefore exceedingly untrustworthy," he whispered, looking round to see if anyone had come into the room without his knowledge. "He or she uses underhand devices, for want of a better expression, to get in with influential people…no, she…or he… uses people as a stepping stone…or something…"

He paused again, tormented by the convoluted way he was reporting what Alice had said without disclosing a name. He saw that Maureen was looking at him extremely attentively. Even the pigeons had become silent outside. Perhaps the suspense was getting to them too.

"It must be a woman," she said when she realised he wasn't going to say much more. "And she's using her sexuality with men. It must be Ariadne Hopwood you're talking about because there's no one else who's young enough or good-looking enough – not at this College, for heaven's sake. I'm right, am I not?"

He wanted to say he knew of one other woman who fitted the bill but he knew it would be too forward. Instead he smiled faintly again and nodded.

"It's common knowledge, Mort," she continued, laughing occasionally as she spoke. "When you walked into the Principal's meeting with her on the first morning of term, everyone sussed what she was up to. A new senior lecturer and a young, handsome man to boot…or more accurately, *a new man*. Didn't you figure out why she took you to the front row, where no one ever sits unless they want to get noticed?"

He was lost for words. The one person who'd befriended him had turned out to be a two-faced fraud.

"But she hasn't got a reputation for sleeping around," added Maureen becoming aware that he was staring into the middle distance. "Exactly the opposite. I think she's a bit of a teaser. She won't give something away for nothing."

"Then why did Alice make the point of saying she was promiscuous?" he said, returning to the conversation with a jolt.

"Maybe she knew something the rest of us don't," she replied. "But more likely she was jealous of her. Ariadne's young and attractive and gets on with the very people Alice despised. It was just the ramblings of an old, confused and very jealous woman whose mind was addled with drink."

He laughed but he still didn't know how to continue or to end the discussion. It was Maureen as usual who did that for him.

"Why did you come to see me of all people about this?" she asked. "What's so important about Ariadne anyway?"

"Because you're the only mate I've got here," he heard himself say. "I thought she was a friend too but now I'm not sure."

She moved slightly closer to him and gently touched his arm.

"Do you fancy her, Mort?" she said, surprised by her own directness.

"Of course not," he retorted quickly. "I'm a married man. I wanted to find out if I'm being made a fool of."

"Have you considered that she might fancy you?" she said, ignoring his last remark.

He shook his head, and she wasn't certain whether he meant he hadn't considered it, or whether he was simply bewildered.

"Thanks, Maureen," he said as he turned to leave. "I'm sorry I interrupted you. I'd be grateful if this conversation goes no further than the two of us."

Unknown to both of them there was someone else in the room. Anne Conroy, the woman whose husband reduced her to tears because he spent most of their marriage on the seven seas, had been sitting reading quietly behind a huge mound of text books that had fully obscured her from view. She hadn't been listening to Mort's and Maureen's conversation but, as Mort left, she peeped over her makeshift barrier to see who had provoked such a lengthy and animated discussion. They'd make such a handsome couple, she sighed, as she watched them for a few seconds before tears welled up in her eyes, and she reached down into her handbag for her dark glasses.

CHAPTER 19

12 April 2005: 11.40am

News had reached Harrison that more police were to be assigned to the case as it now looked like a death in suspicious circumstances. The Chief Constable had phoned him to inform him that a Detective Chief Inspector was coming down from the city to take charge of the case and he had to have his notes ready for her when she arrived at about one o'clock. In the meantime he and Tim were to get all the preliminary formalities out of the way and provide her with a list of suspects, assuming that he'd already had some. Harrison had convinced the Chief Constable that, although it could have been any of a number of people, the murderer or murderers had to be working at the College, most likely as a senior manager. He'd suggest to the DCI that this should be their line of enquiry.

He walked slowly down the corridor and went into the meetings room. If he'd been a teacher he'd have thought he'd walked into a badly managed lesson. Tim was sitting and talking to Iris but the rest were muttering and moaning, a tall, boyish-looking woman with dyed blonde hair was wriggling about on her chair, and two of her colleagues were trying to calm her down. Hugh was sitting on his own, sulking.

"What's going on here?" shouted Harrison, directing his words at Lucy. "What's the matter with you, miss? Are you ill or something?"

"She needs the toilet desperately!" Penny shouted back. "And she needs it now!"

"Constable", he said sharply looking at Tim. "Get a female officer down here at once to escort this woman to the toilet."

"We all want to go," said Penny, thankful that at last relief was on its way. "The three of us."

Tim stood up and walked over to the door. As he passed Harrison he stopped.

"You said no one was to leave the room, sir," he muttered.

"Use your common sense, lad," said Harrison tapping the top of his head with his right hand.

As Tim was about to leave, Harrison motioned him to stay and called for attention. He wanted to get things moving, irrespective of the fact that a woman might soon wet herself.

"Can anyone give me a description of Ms Hopwood's handbag? It's gone missing?"

Bernadette put her hand up.

"She has several," she said, tears welling up in her eyes again. "As she was wearing black today, I think she'd have had her black leather one. It's Gucci, about a foot square."

"It's missing," he said. "DC Hudson will organise a search of the College and the grounds to look for it."

Tim left the room, searching his pockets desperately (again) for his notebook.

"I want to speak to Mr Jones and the person who deals with the press," Harrison continued resolutely, scanning the room for Hugh.

Hugh and Mike stood up and he indicated that they were to follow him in to the top corner of the room near the windows, where they stood with their backs to the others.

"I'm going to ask you to close the College," he said, his voice hushed. "Please do this as quickly as you can but I want the workforce – that's everybody, not just teachers – to stay on the site. I'll need a full staff list from your personnel manager so I can be sure…"

"The *Human Resources* Manager is off sick today," Hugh said, disrupting Harrison's flow.

"I'll need a full staff list," repeated Harrison. "The names of people absent must be clearly marked on it, and reasons for their absence. We'll need to check where they were this morning but we'll do that later."

He turned to Mike.

"Have you put a press release together yet?" he asked, too patronisingly for the Marketing Manager.

"Of course I have," Mike replied, more restrained than he thought he could be after all he'd been through that morning. "As Iris ordered."

"Good," said Harrison, as he turned away to speak again to Hugh. "Is there any immediate family to inform?"

"Her mother, I think. She lives in York," said Hugh, pleased that he was now being treated with the respect he deserved. "Ariadne wasn't married and, as far as I'm aware, she hadn't got a permanent partner. I don't think she was seeing anyone regularly, so I think we can rule out a crime of passion, Inspector."

Harrison looked away. Hugh considered he might have gone a little too far in his speculation but Harrison had just got a whiff of bad breath again. Hugh turned round and shouted across to Iris and Bernadette.

"Do you know if Ariadne is…was in a relationship with anyone?"

Both women shrugged and shook their heads.

"Anyone know?"

Everyone else shook their heads. It wasn't their place to tell him she was often seen in the company of a very powerful, public figure.

"Does that mean she wasn't or you don't know?" Harrison said, taking the lead again.

Again no one spoke so he turned back to Hugh.

"I want to use this room as our HQ," he said. "A DCI is coming this afternoon and I'll be handing over to her. I assume that's all right with you?"

"Of course," Hugh replied. "Does that mean that we can go now?"

"Yes," replied Harrison, keen to talk to Tim and even more eager to have this room bursting at the seams with police officers sifting the evidence. "One more thing. I'll need to be connected to the Internet. Can you arrange that for me?"

"There's a port and a phone there," said Hugh pointing to the wall behind where Mike was standing.

He turned round again and announced that they could all leave the room and return to their offices. As he finished, a female uniformed police officer arrived to act as toilet escort. She was almost knocked over by three women, also dressed in black, who'd decided to make a break for it no matter what the consequences.

When Tim returned Harrison was keen to hear what he'd found out from his questioning. Tim explained slowly that he'd obtained all the necessary personal details and held up ten sheets of paper. Harrison studied them carefully and contemplated whether it was worth bringing in a graphologist to see if any murderous tendencies could be gleaned from the different styles of handwriting on view. He put it immediately to the back of his mind, regarding it only as something he might reconsider if all else failed. He looked extremely pleased however when Tim told him that they might have a few suspects. He'd summarised everything in beautifully neat letters on one sheet and Harrison could read it as clearly as if it had just emerged from a laser printer.

Penny Castle – blonde, small – single, lives with…

Lucy Carlton – blonde, tall – black British – single. Left for work together c: 0800. Arrived c: 0815. Coffee till 0845 then both finalised staffing summary in PC's office for meeting at 0930. Several witnesses including their administrative assistants.

Harriet O'Reilly – blonde, glasses – married. Had to take children to nursery after dropping off husband at railway station at 0800. Caught in traffic at Mallory. Arrived 0855-0900. Says husband and nursery staff will confirm.

Hugh Jones – Acting Principal. Married. Left home at 0800, stopped off to buy newspaper at 0815. Arrived college c: 0840. Says wife, neighbours and newsagent will confirm.

Mike Smith* – tall, balding – married but stayed with friend last night. Arrived college c: 0845. Went straight to office.

Richard Head!!! – oldest manager, beard – single, lives alone. Left home 0835. Arrived 0855. Says neighbours might confirm.

Maureen King – oldish, greying hair – married. Left home 0800 to go shopping (Waitrose). Showed me timed receipt (0832). Arrived college 0845.

Mortimer Todd* – oldish, not wearing suit – single, lives alone in city. Left home c: 0800. Bad drive to work. Arrived at about 0920 – says office staff will verify.

Bernadette Arden – oldish, P's secretary – single. Took dog for walk 0730. Says neighbours and other dog walkers she met will confirm. Left home c: 0800. Arrived 0830. Straight to office. Says receptionist will confirm.

Iris Baxter? – old, married – the one who orders the others about – said her husband left home at 0600. She tidied house and left for work at 0800. Arrived c: 0830. Went to office to prepare for meeting.'

Harrison placed the sheets of paper on the table and sat down, relieved he had something to show the Detective Chief Inspector.

"Good work, Tim," he beamed. "A couple of questions. What do the asterisks mean?"

"They're my prime suspects from this group," he replied looking pleased that Harrison had complimented his efforts. "They don't seem to have anyone to corroborate their movements before they came here this morning."

"And the three exclamation marks after Richard Head's name?"

"It's the name, sir. I thought he was winding me up. Turns out it *is* his real name."

"Why is there no asterisk after his name? He looks a bit odd to me."

"He's quite old and he looks and sounds harmless. Put an asterisk after his name if you want, then."

"What's the question mark for after Iris Baxter's name?"

"Well, she's not very pleasant and she didn't mention anyone who could verify her whereabouts till gone nine when she arrived in this room for the meeting. Bernadette Arden confirmed that."

"She might blow and bluster but is she capable of doing anybody in?"

"I'm not sure, sir. I'd keep her in mind. 'Once you've ruled out the impossible, whatever remains, however improbable, must be the truth.' That's what Sherlock Holmes says."

Harrison smiled. He'd spoken to Doctor Watson already that morning and now he was talking to the great Mr Holmes himself.

"Let's see who our real suspects are," he said as he looked down the list again. "Mike Smith. He's the marketing man, isn't he? He doesn't look very dangerous to me. Too flabby. It says here he's married. Why didn't he go home last night?"

"He said he went out with some friends and stayed overnight with one," said Tim, more than a hint of scepticism in his voice. "He wouldn't say who. Maybe he's having an affair?"

"Yes," replied Harrison, noting that their roles seemed to have changed and anxious to regain command. "We'll interview him this afternoon."

He moved on down the list.

"This Todd chap," he continued. "I've heard his name before."

While he was thinking, Tim seized the initiative again.

"Seemed a nice enough bloke," he said. "Bit nervous. Doesn't look like a senior manager, does he?"

"I know where I've heard his name," said Harrison, ignoring Tim's question. "The caretaker said he always comes in late in the morning. He thought it was comical. We'll definitely have more words with Todd."

"He's got a long drive," said Tim. "He kept going on about it. He lives in the city and he said that every morning he's held up by slow drivers. He calls them the Countryside Vigilantes. He might be on CCTV somewhere."

"One more thing," said Harrison, again ignoring Tim. "Did you ask them if anyone saw Ms Hopwood before the meeting?"

"No one did," replied Tim. "Bernadette Arden and Iris Baxter have seen her body."

"Iris Baxter did too, did she?" said Harrison rubbing his chin. "That Jones chap said only Bernadette Arden had seen it. You'd better make sure that neither of them tells anyone what they saw, especially the media."

He picked up the list of names and quickly read through it again.

"I've another name for you," he added, glancing at Tim. "Steven Wallace, the Estate Manager. He told me he saw Ms Hopwood arrive this morning just after seven. He might have been the last person to see her alive, except for the murderer of course, but he'd all the time in the world to do her in, assuming the times of arrival on your list are correct."

Harrison was feeling happier with his morning's work. He had a list of suspects to show the DCI and sound reasons for questioning them, he had a lot of physical evidence to display and he had a computer to examine. He also had a good idea how the murder had been committed and he knew roughly when it had happened. He'd organised a search of the campus to try to find the missing handbag. There were some things he didn't like, however, and they were likely to be the DCI's first questions. Why had Ariadne been murdered and who had the know-how to do it so skillfully? As the problem gnawed away at his brain, a few doubts began to materialise. He might not have any real suspects at all. Anybody could have done it, so why was he concentrating on the people she was scheduled to meet at nine thirty? That might even be the DCI's first question. He hadn't even looked at the book that was on Ariadne's desk and he hadn't even switched on her computer. He considered for a moment what he might usefully do until the DCI arrived and then he turned to Tim, who was absently looking out across the fields.

"I know what our next move is," he said, his face lighting up. "We'll stop those two women talking to the media then we'll grab a bite to eat. After that we'll find out more about Ariadne Hopwood and get uniformed to check out the alibis of the rest of her crew of managers. Oh, I nearly forgot. We'll have to fingerprint the whole bloody lot of them – DNA swabs as well."

Part 3

CHAPTER 20

Late October 1984

Mort fretted more than usual for the next few days. He hadn't told anyone except Maureen about the strange episode with Alice, and that included Cassandra. He was weighing up whether Ariadne was, as he originally maintained, merely an enthusiastic and ambitious teacher or, as Alice had insisted, a ruthless, manipulative and devious seductress. Things were unpleasant enough at the College as it was, and he didn't want to be made to look a naïve fool who couldn't resist the charms of a good-looking, young woman. Since he didn't want an unjust reputation as a philanderer either, he came to the only conclusion feasible: he'd no choice but to carry on as normal without giving her a reason to suspect that he might have seen through her deceitfulness. He remained just as friendly (and just as distant) whenever she came to sit with him or when they met for a tête-à-tête over coffee. Two things he could be sure of however were that she rarely spoke to other women (although she was always superficially affable and courteous) and that she preferred the company of men – Junkin and Honor in particular. Yet there was nothing to indicate that she was sleeping with either of them. Perhaps Maureen had been correct and Alice was just being spiteful. If he wanted to find out more about her, he'd have to be exceptionally subtle and above all very clever so that he didn't give her the wrong idea about what he was doing. The last thing he wanted was for her to suspect that he was coming on to her, and he'd have to mark time until a suitable opportunity arose to continue his investigation.

It was on the Friday before the half term break in October, over two weeks since Alice had ranted at him, that he became determined to delve into Ariadne's background if she put in an appearance during the lunch break. If anything went wrong he'd have four days before he saw her again to come up with an excuse. As he sat rehearsing what he was going to say to her, he heard her voice in the corridor and, before he could turn round to say hello, she strode into the staffroom, told him to put on his jacket and accompany her to a nearby pub. When she said she'd drive it struck him how little he actually knew about her; he didn't even realise that she had a car. She looked appealingly at him, and then impulsively lunged forward as if to grab his arm to drag him out of his chair, but just as quickly, conscious that she might be going too far, she stepped back again.

"I'm dreadfully sorry," she said, "I don't know what came over me."

"It's alright," replied Mort, sensing he might be able to exploit her indiscretion. "Is that where everybody else is?"

"Yes," she nodded diffidently, looking down at her shoes. "The others weren't going to ask you to come, but I thought how unkind it would be if you were left here all by yourself."

Mort tried not to show his disappointment at being left out – not because he was the new boy but because he was unpopular. He supposed the 'the others' were the English teachers and they were showing their contempt by ostracising him.

"Where are they all going?" he asked hesitantly, uncertain whether he wanted to join them if he were unwelcome.

"They're going to the Bridge with Roy Jolly and the Art set," she answered, brightening up slightly.

"I don't think I'll come," he said. "Not if they don't want me there. I'd spoil it for them just by walking in."

"You'll be on your own if you don't come," she said, wide-eyed in anticipation.

"You must go," he replied moodily. "You should be with them. I'm used to my own company round here. I'm fine on my own and I have some work to do. It'll be good to have some peace and quiet for once."

She turned to leave and got as far as the door, where she stopped and turned round quickly, a faint smile on her face.

"Shall we go somewhere else?" she ventured; she wasn't going to let him play the martyr.

He looked at his watch as if he were deliberating her offer, but he knew that unwittingly she was providing him with the perfect chance to ask her about herself without suspecting what he was up to. After all, she'd proposed it.

"OK, I'll come," he smiled. "But I haven't a clue where we could go?"

"There's a bit of a dive on the way out of Storbury. It's called the Barred Gate near Mallory School."

"Oh yes," he grinned. "It's near Roy's gallery. I sit outside it every morning on my way in here!"

Mort's spirits rose perceptibly as they walked out of the almost deserted College and into the car park, where she led him to her car.

"Is this yours?" he exclaimed as he saw the gleaming, silver Ford Escort sports car.

"My father bought it for me when I got this job," she said, delighted that he was surprised.

"He must be worth a bob or two. What does he do?"

"He's a lawyer, the senior partner in Hopwood, Wells and Simpson. There are a lot of ancient farms and old houses where I come from, and he's an expert in flying freeholds or something. It's quite complicated but he makes a fortune."

As she drove, they discussed how pleasant it was to live in and around York and how Yorkshire was so misunderstood by most people south of Sheffield. It was a good starting point, he mused, for delving into the more private details of her life that he had to pull together to put his mind at rest.

The pub he'd studied many times from the outside was precisely as he'd imagined it would be on the inside; it was small, dark and gloomy. When he walked in, he saw a frosted glass door ahead of him, through which he could just make out three or four elderly men playing cards or dominoes – a tap room probably. He assumed he was standing in what passed for a lounge and he and Ariadne were the only people there. There were long, wooden tables with benches against the two side walls and four polished, square tables arranged in a horseshoe around the semicircular bar which was cluttered with ancient brass ornaments, toby jugs, two or three charity boxes and old newspapers. The ceilings were low, and the yellowing walls were covered in pictures of old Storbury, including one of a large, long since demolished toll gate which had given the place its name. The pub had been the gatekeeper's house, which explained both its cramped size and why it was the last building on the road, marking the eastern outskirts of the town.

She chose seats in the corner on the left hand side of room furthest away from the entrance while he went for the drinks, a half pint of beer for her and an orange juice for him, served by a grubby, old man in a moth-eaten cardigan – again exactly as he'd expected. They sat side by side in silence for a while on one of the benches, looking round the room and sipping occasionally until he decided it was time to throw caution to the wind.

"Where did you go to school?" he asked, sounding as if he were making polite conversation to get things going.

"I went to a private school in the south west," she replied, blushing slightly. "It was an all girls' school, very posh, but it was miles from anywhere. I hated it. It was like a prison, and dreadfully boring when I was in my teens. We were only allowed out at the weekends, and we had to be back by ten, so we couldn't go very far, not even to Exeter which was the only oasis round there. We were all cooped up together day after day, randy as hell."

"I see why you haven't got a trace of a northern accent," he said, taking another sip. "How long were you there?"

He wanted her to keep talking.

"Seven years – eleven to eighteen," she said, pleased that he looked more relaxed than usual.

"What did you do to pass the time?"

"I did a lot of homework, reading and such. I even played hockey and netball to keep me occupied. I wasn't much good though."

"Is that how you coped with all those awkward hormones?" he said, raising the stakes and hoping that this more explicit question wasn't going to shock her.

"We weren't lesbians or anything like that," she joked, not concerned by his bluntness. "Broom handles and wax candles were locked away at night, but I found lots of innovative ways to ease my sexual tensions!"

He considered changing the subject, but she seemed lost in cherished memories.

"I developed a whole load of masturbatory fantasies," she giggled, as she finished her beer. "Most were about pop stars or footballers and the boys I'd seen on my rare trips out. I can remember them all clearly and I still think about them sometimes…"

She stopped and looked directly into his eyes. He presumed she was hesitating because she thought she might have said too much.

"I'm having another drink," she continued surprisingly. "Same again for you, is it?"

While she was at the bar, he gathered his thoughts. He hadn't commented on anything she'd said and he'd tried to remain straight-faced as he listened. He'd given her complete freedom to talk as much as she wanted and she'd told him what he wanted to know: she did like sex, even if it was, as far as he knew at this stage, with herself. He had two more important questions and this was the perfect opportunity to ask the first one. When she returned, she sat down with a bump.

"I haven't shocked you, have I?" she said, slurring her words slightly. "I'm telling the truth. It was the danger of being discovered that excited me most. Is it the same in boys' schools? I bet you know all about that, don't you?"

"Not really," said Mort, guessing that the alcohol might be starting to affect her; perhaps she hadn't eaten anything before they came out. "I went to a grammar school in Leeds. It was a boys' school when I started but it went co-ed before I left. I lived at home so there weren't many restrictions on where I went or what I did when I was old enough to go out with my mates."

"Did you have a lot of girlfriends?" she asked, innocently taking over his role as questioner.

"No, not many," he replied tersely, wanting to shift the focus back to her. "I was too shy and nervous to ask. I preferred to wait till they asked me."

"I bet there were a lot more than you're prepared to let me in on, if that's the case," she grinned, tapping him gently on his arm.

"Did you have many boyfriends when you went to University?" he said, trying to regain his momentum. "At Hull wasn't it?"

"Yes to both questions," she replied still grinning. "I loved it there. No limitations. I lost my virginity in Freshers' week. The chastity belt was off forever. I went to bed with anything that had two arms, two legs and a dick."

She burst out laughing but he couldn't tell whether it because she was making fun of him or whether the beer had taken away her inhibitions.

"But I prefer masturbation," she went on, giggling again. "Because you know you're having sex with someone who truly loves you."

"You sound like Woody Allen in *Annie Hall*," he said, remaining pokerfaced.

"You're on about films again, Mort," she said mockingly. "I'm talking about real life. I enjoyed myself in more ways than one in Hull but I've settled down now, so don't start thinking I'm going to seduce you or anything."

He smiled uncomfortably. He was making progress and it hadn't taken long. He was convinced that Alice had been right, but possibly for the wrong reasons. Ariadne liked sex – that was perfectly true – and because of that she sought the company of men. It was time to change the subject again – his final question.

"Do you like teaching?" he asked.

"Yes," she replied, looking a little bemused by his sudden shift of focus. "Of course I do."

She was beginning to think she might have embarrassed him after all.

"Do you want to make a career out it?" he persisted, moving in for the kill.

"It's only a means to an end," she said coldly, turning away and staring at the bar. "I'm not going to *remain* a teacher forever. Not like old Alice. Look how she ended up."

"Have you already worked out your next move?"

"You mean in my career?"

"What else did you think I meant?"

She turned back and looked at him trying to discern if there was any trace of ambiguity in his eyes.

"Never mind," she replied, when her examination of his face had proved fruitless. "I want to go right to the top, if that's what you're asking, Mort. I'll be a Principal one day and then I'll come back here and force you to answer all *my* questions."

"To this pub?" he asked mischievously.

It was the first time he'd smiled since they arrived there. She looked bemused.

"Tell me what interesting things you're doing over the long weekend," he added, ending his interrogation on a neutral note.

They chatted for another few minutes about their respective plans – they both didn't have any other than resting before the hard slog up to Christmas – until he announced he had to leave as he had a class to teach. He'd found out what he wanted, and he was satisfied she hadn't guessed his real motives. He had a lot more to mull over but he had the weekend in which to do it, and he was going to ask Cassandra to advise him on what he should do next.

When they left the pub, he saw that she was walking unsteadily, swaying slightly from side to side. He tried to dissuade her from driving, but she insisted that she was perfectly capable since she'd only had two small drinks, excusing her rockiness as no more than tiredness. They hadn't gone very far when she lost control of the steering wheel. The car veered off to the left and mounted the kerb. Luckily there was no one on the pavement but unluckily for Ariadne a police car was parked a few yards behind them in a side street. She was still laughing at her carelessness when she heard a light tap on the window beside her, and she looked up to see a grim-faced, heavily built, uniformed policeman crouching down and looking into the car.

"Would you mind stepping out of the car, madam," he ordered politely but firmly as he'd been trained to do on such occasions.

"Yes, officer," she stammered as she unfastened her seat belt.

"Oh, it's you," he said, his attitude changing dramatically. "Had a couple of drinks, have we, Ms Hopwood?"

She nodded demurely.

"Well, drive more carefully," he continued, touching the peak of his cap deferentially. "Mr Crossley will want you in one piece tonight."

CHAPTER 21

12 April 2005: 11.50am

Mort obeyed Harrison's orders and returned to his office where he was surprised to see Helen, Gordon and Barry quietly working, and they stood up together when he came in, as they might have done had he been some very important person or other. They nodded sympathetically as he walked past them to his desk at the far end of the room.

"What's been happening?" Helen asked excitedly. "Tell us all about it, bud."

"I'm not certain," he sighed. "How much do you know already? I suppose the rumour mill's been at work."

"Bernadette said the Principal's dead," she replied. "Is it true?"

"Has she been murdered, Mort?" asked Gordon, eager to hear the gory details.

Before Mort could answer the door opened, and Maureen King and the three witches marched in one by one and sat down on the edge of each of the desks.

"You shouldn't be here," he said huffily. "The police will see it as collusion."

"Screw them," said Maureen who was sitting on his desk. "What's going on, Mort?"

"God knows," he replied, looking down at the floor. "We all know that Ariadne's dead, and, judging from the state of Bernadette, it must have been pretty horrible."

"What do you all make of those coppers?" asked Lucy, trying to think of something profound to say, but falling short as usual. "What about the one that looks like a bloodhound?"

"He can't help what he looks like," snapped Penny. "He's only doing his job."

"Do you think we'll get home today at all?" said Harriet, sounding panicky. "I've got to pick the kids up by six and my husband's not going to be able to do it. He's in Birmingham all day."

"Ring your mother," said Penny more soothingly. "She'll sort it out."

"Settle down everyone," said Maureen, standing up and moving forwards a little. "Let's look at it from the police's perspective. There's been a murder and it had to have happened this morning. It looks like they think one of us did it…"

"Well, I know I didn't do it," cried Lucy, panicking.

"That's why that young detective was asking us all where we were," continued Maureen, ignoring her. "I assume we can all vouch for our whereabouts? I'm sure I can."

The three witches nodded their heads in harmony as if someone had suddenly sent a mild electric current through their bodies, but Mort just stood there looking down at his feet.

"I can't, I'm afraid," he said gloomily. "I was at home on my own."

He'd no intention of telling them about his drive in the middle of the night.

"Yes, but your neighbours must have seen you this morning," said Barry, unsure if he would be allowed to contribute to the discussion.

"They're not the nosy types," replied Mort. "We keep ourselves to ourselves in Buchanan Road."

"It's not as if you leave every morning at the crack of dawn, is it Mort?" joked Helen, hoping her light-hearted interjection wouldn't be misconstrued as sarcasm. "Someone must have seen your car leave."

"I had to park in another street last night," he laughed dolefully. "There must have been a 'do' on near my house and there was nowhere to park till gone eleven. I couldn't be bothered to move it as I'd already had a couple of drinks."

"That's not like you," said Helen. "You must be getting more relaxed in your old age."

"Shut up, Helen," said Barry crossly. "You're not helping."

"It's OK, Helen," said Mort, yawning. "I know what you mean. What I'm trying to say is that I didn't see anyone last night or this morning. I sat in the back room working on my personnel report till gone one, which means the house was in darkness at the front. I'd switched the security lights off. No one can see much of the back because of the leylandii and the other trees in the garden. To make matters worse I couldn't sleep…"

"Why couldn't you sleep, Mort?" asked Helen mischievously. "Did you have something on your mind you don't want to tell us about?"

"Shut up, Helen!" shouted Barry and Maureen in unison.

"But we know you didn't do it," said Helen animatedly. "We know you never get here till after nine because of all the traffic. Surely someone must have seen you on your way to work?"

"The bloody Vigilantes did," he mumbled, too quietly for it to be heard.

"What was that?"

"Nothing. Nothing at all."

There was a long silence.

"How do they know that Barry, Helen or I didn't do it?" Gordon asked eventually, not worried that anyone would really think it was one of them since a genuine suspect was standing in the room.

"Do you know the combination to the executive suite door?" asked Penny none too warmly.

"Well do you?" echoed Maureen. "Do any of you? Barry? Helen?"

"They change it every day," said Helen quietly. "Bernadette told me."

"What else did she tell you?" asked Penny playing inquisitor.

"Well, I assume that the Principal had some changes in mind," confessed Helen. "That's why you were doing a staffing review, isn't it, Mort?"

He didn't reply. He was looking at the dust and other small pieces of detritus on the carpet.

"Does anyone think that might be a motive for killing her?" asked Lucy hesitantly, hoping that no one would assume it was a silly question.

"Hmm, we all saw that restructuring was on this morning's agenda," said Penny slowly rubbing her neck. "Good point, Lucy."

Lucy beamed with delight. Someone had agreed with her for once.

"My job's safe," she said, hoping not to cause offence. "What about everyone else?"

The others nodded, except for Mort.

"I'm vulnerable," he said, sounding even more depressed.

"I don't think you are, Mort," said Maureen, trying to cheer him up. "Ariadne might do something like that to anyone else, but not you. Remember the old days?"

"What old days are you referring to?" said Penny, now standing up also, her eyes bulging. "You've kept quiet about that! Why did Ariadne – or you for that matter – never mention that you knew each other? That could make you even more of a suspect, couldn't it?"

"I remember her too," said Maureen firmly, glaring at Penny. "You must know she was here for a couple of years back in the eighties?"

Penny shook her head and looked at Lucy and Harriet.

"I didn't," said Lucy followed by Harriet.

"Why haven't you said something before?" asked Penny crossly.

Mort shrugged. He didn't remember telling anyone much about Ariadne because no one had asked him. If they had, he still wouldn't have told them anything because Ariadne had forbidden him to gossip about her. Maureen knew anyway, and the other three were all too intent on getting well in with the new Principal and her unconscionable plans rather than delving into her past history.

"Mort was her line manager," continued Maureen diplomatically, turning round to face him and winking. "From what I recall, you were good friends. I remember you worried a lot about her being a bit devious and there were a few wicked insinuations about her."

"So it *is* true!" exclaimed Helen, again speaking out of turn. "Who was she screwing, Barry?"

"Don't bring me into this," he said, shifting about uneasily in his seat. "I told you I wasn't here. I was in London, remember?"

"Well, Mort?"

"What's it got to do with you, Helen?" said Maureen, mentally throttling her. "Yes, it was rumoured she had some kind of affair with Simon Junkin when she started looking for jobs to get away from Joe Crossley after she got engaged to him. She maintained that she was drunk when he asked her to marry him, and she couldn't remember anything about it."

"How do you know all this, Maureen?" said Mort, suddenly finding his voice again.

"You hear things in the ladies," she replied tartly. "Anyway, you told me you'd seen her leave Simon's bedroom at the summer ball."

"Ah yes," he said, staring sheepishly at the carpet again.

He was regretting telling her – and Barry – about one of the most poignant episodes in his life, but he was relieved that the attention was off him.

"I don't remember much about it. I had a lot on my mind. I don't ever want to imagine her sleeping with that twat, and I don't want to talk about her either. Let's change the subject."

"Language, Mort," said Helen, butting in again.

The others looked at her threateningly and she slapped her wrist in mock contrition.

"Wasn't he Head of Humanities?" asked Lucy. "I vaguely remember him when I started here. Tall guy with a snobby face and a funny moustache."

"He'd retired before you started," explained Mort, stifling another yawn. "He used to come into College occasionally to see how things were doing, so you might have seen him then. He couldn't keep away – meddling, old bastard."

"He didn't want to retire," added Maureen. "He couldn't cope when we went corporate…"

"He couldn't cope *before* either," Mort said bitterly. "Can we change the subject? Why do you all think Ariadne was murdered?"

The room became quiet again for a few seconds.

"That's an important question, Mort," said Harriet, forgetting her children temporarily. "I was at a community centre meeting in Beech Vale last week and one of the governors was there. He's from the bank and they needed some funding for a youth employment scheme they're trying to get off the ground. Well, one of the centre volunteers was asking why the College couldn't put some money in. I was about to answer but he beat me to it. He said there were some not inconsiderable financial worries – yes he used that phrase – and the auditors are definitely coming to check up on us next month. So it looks like Hugh Jones hasn't been able to resolve the issues he was talking about a few weeks ago…"

"Why didn't you mention this before?" exclaimed Penny, looking round the room for support. "That explains why Ariadne was planning to restructure, doesn't it? Does anyone know who was going to be made redundant?"

"Let's not speculate too much," said Maureen, trying not to let things escalate out of proportion. "We don't know what *all* her plans were."

"How could we?" added Harriet. "We knew she was a scheming so and so and we knew there were problems with finances, didn't we? Restructuring was on the agenda. Not downsizing."

Before anyone else spoke, the telephone on Helen's desk rang. They all listened attentively, but Helen merely nodded her head until finally she thanked the caller and replaced the receiver.

"That was reception," she said looking at Gordon and Barry. "Everyone can go home except the Heads. You have to go back to your offices and wait until you're called for interview."

"I told you they'd try to stop us talking to each other", said Mort sanctimoniously. "You'd better go."

"How did they know we were all here?" asked Penny, beginning to feel paranoid. "Did you rat on us, Helen?"

"Certainly not," replied Helen forcefully. "I expect reception's ringing your office at this very moment."

As the interlopers began to file out, Helen looked up at Mort.

"I'm going to stay if that's alright with you. I'll go and sit somewhere else if it bothers you."

"I'm staying as well," said Barry.

"Me too," said Gordon. "If you don't mind."

"Oh and one other thing before you all leave," said Helen to the four women. "No one knows where Richard the Dickhead is."

CHAPTER 22

End October 1984: Half Term Break

"What a fuss over nothing!" screamed Cassandra when Mort had told her briefly about his lunchtime escapade with Ariadne. They were lying in bed on the Saturday morning after his trip to the Barred Gate.

"I made sure they were the sort of questions anyone might have asked," said Mort calmly, getting up onto his elbow and taking a cigarette from the packet on the bedside table to his right. "The sort you ask when you don't know someone very well. I didn't ask her about her sex life. She told me about it and brought it up in every bloody thing she talked about from then on. She's obsessed."

"No Mort, it's you that's obsessed and you can't see it," she yelled, pulling the duvet over her face. "And don't smoke!"

"I don't like it when people use you to get on," he said, remaining calm even without the essential palliative. "In particular when it's so underhand. That's what bugs me about her – she's *untrustworthy* and you never know where you stand with people like that."

"I don't follow you," she said, her head still covered. "She's just keen. It's not really much different from being seen to work hard or going in when you're poorly, or volunteering to cover other people's classes when they're ill."

"It was Alice who started it," he retaliated. "If she hadn't told me everything that evening…"

"Who's Alice?" she shouted.

She pushed the duvet back and sat up.

"Oh I remember – the old woman you replaced. You said she'd died. How did *she* start it?"

Mort wasn't very good at arguing with Cassandra, even when he tried to work out in advance what he was going to say. By the time they reached her first riposte whatever he'd planned crumbled to dust. He was surprised that it had gone so well with Ariadne the day before, but now he was in full retreat already. He'd no choice but to give an account of the disquieting incident with Alice that had aroused his suspicions about Ariadne, and he threw in his thoughts about her relationship with Junkin and Honor for good measure. Cassandra sat with her head in her hands, laughing occasionally, more heartily when he told her about Alice's mysterious departure from the refectory. This made him all the more frustrated because he knew she wasn't going to give him much attention after that. He wished he'd spoken to her about Ariadne earlier, as soon as his suspicions had been aroused, simply because she might think he was trying obliquely to boast that he had an admirer. Instead he'd gone to see Maureen and if he told Cassandra about that too, she'd feel he'd betrayed her. She was his wife and confidante and he should have unburdened himself to her first.

"Have you asked anyone else at the College about this Ariadne woman?" she asked, using the tone of voice reserved for those she held in contempt.

"Such as who? I don't know anyone there I can talk to about such matters."

"Well that's your next move," she said, brightening up. "There must be someone there who can help you. Ask a woman. A woman will let you know without hesitation, especially if she's the jealous type or, like you, a prude."

She sprang out of bed and put on her dressing gown that was draped over the end of bed.

"There, I've solved it out for you yet again," she trilled as she sashayed out of the room. "What would you do without me?"

He lay back down in the bed and lit the cigarette he'd discarded before. He'd been right after all, he mused. Cassandra had advised him to do what he'd already done, so clearly he'd made the right decision. He didn't need to put her in the picture yet but when he did, he vowed he'd tell her everything that Maureen had said. Then Cassandra would laugh at him again and let him know in no uncertain terms that she'd told him all along that Ariadne was harmless. She'd put it down to female intuition and that would be the end of it. She'd been very patient with him over the last few weeks, and she'd provided a solution for all of the crises he'd had to face. He wanted to do the same for her but she didn't seem to experience any difficulties of her own. She breezed through life avoiding any complications and it was she who always seemed to be helping him, never the reverse. She'd been like that at university. No matter what emotional calamities she found herself in, and she'd had quite a few with men before they met, she solved them quickly herself and ended up cheerful and completely unscathed. She was very similar to Ariadne in some respects, he concluded; they'd both let their hair down when they'd had their first taste of unfettered freedom but had settled down when they acquired adult responsibilities. He left it at that, promising himself that he wouldn't make a fool of himself again with Ariadne, although he'd continue to be on his guard and maintain a strict, professional distance.

He stubbed his cigarette out and got out of bed. He was still brooding about the College as he was getting dressed, and he began to reflect on how he'd suffered every day that he'd spent at that appalling place, including all the time he'd had to waste getting there and back. He was becoming more neurotic than ever, fussing over the slightest problem that came his way. He was even driving more carefully and scrupulously observing all speed limits which made every journey longer and harder to endure. If Cassandra hadn't been there to cheer him up, he'd have turned into a sullen, bad-tempered, old man long before his time. He needed a new job and he needed one as quickly as possible. He had to devise a strategy – an escape plan – immediately. For once he'd perked himself up and he was going to work hard at making sure he wasted no opportunity to gain more experience in the management aspects of education. He'd start digging tunnels out of Stalag Luft Storbury as soon as the half term break was over…

Suddenly, out of nowhere, an odd thought entered his head. Why had Cassandra started to wear pyjamas? He couldn't grasp the connection between a prisoner of war camp and female nightwear. Perhaps it was because he'd imagined her laughing at the analogy he'd invented a moment ago? She'd never worn pyjamas before; usually nothing at all, sometimes her underwear, occasionally a short nightdress. He assumed it was because winter was coming and the nights were getting colder. She'd been going to bed earlier recently so she needed the extra clothing to keep warm while she was waiting for him to join her. That was it. His new job had given him a lot more to do at home than when he was at the technical college and he'd regularly had to burn the midnight oil. It had resulted in a change in their sex life and he had to admit that he'd been neglecting that side of his marital obligations for too long. He began to feel very selfish. She was right. He was the one that had become preoccupied with his petty worries at the expense of her. She'd never complained once. She was so very considerate. Or had she gone off sex…or him…and the pyjamas were a symbol that their marriage had metamorphosed into a new phase called middle age?

As he struggled to understand what was happening to this part of his life, Cassandra was happily humming to herself in the kitchen whilst she made her breakfast. She'd stopped him moaning and groaning for the next few days, and that afternoon she was going shopping. She needed a new dress.

CHAPTER 23

12 April 2005: 1.10pm

Harrison was speaking to Iris on the newly installed, internal phone when Tim returned to the meetings room, appropriately renamed the incident room. The young detective had been talking to Bernadette, and he'd managed to get the personnel lists and a copy of the morning's agenda as well as Ariadne's curriculum vitae from her. He waved the bundle of papers he was carrying and pointed to their titles. Harrison made an exaggerated thumbs up gesture to acknowledge that he'd spotted them. They'd changed the room around to accommodate the physical evidence that had been brought in by a uniformed officer. The large, oak table had been pushed back against the top wall of the room nearest the computer port and most of the chairs had been stacked neatly along the wall opposite the window. On the table were Ariadne's hardback exercise book, her pen and her computer which the uniformed man was currently examining. The contents of her desk drawers had been spread out in small piles and the sex toys had been neatly placed in a row towards the back of the table, each wrapped in clear plastic bag and numbered. It looked as though they were setting up for a jumble sale or a short auction. A small desk had been brought in from one of the classrooms and three chairs had been arranged around it. They would have to suffice for interviewing.

"There doesn't seem to be anything irregular in her files or inbox, sir," said the uniformed officer, sitting with his back to the two detectives and staring at the computer screen. "The usual business and educational stuff, and nothing personal in her sent items and deleted folders either."

"Right," said Harrison impatiently to Tim. "Go round to her address and see if you can get in without the keys. But don't smash any doors down or break any windows. Post a guard if all else fails."

Tim picked up his car coat and was about to leave when he turned round.

"You'll be on your own again, sir," he said quietly. "It's not on, is it?"

"I should have sent someone straightaway," replied Harrison. "But there's been too much to do. This place should be swarming with coppers, Tim, and they put a sodding bank job ahead of a murder! Hostages or no hostages."

"We *are* understrength," said Tim sympathetically. "The lads can't be in two places at once, and you've only got one pair of hands."

"Thanks," said Harrison. "I hope the DCI takes the same view when she gets here. She should've arrived by now."

Before Tim could say anything else to appease Harrison, the door opened and a short, rain-soaked, young woman walked hurriedly in.

"Sorry I'm late," she said without introducing herself. "I got held up outside Storbury. Bloody tractor had shed its load all over the road, and there weren't any wooden tops there to keep the traffic moving."

She took off her sodden, full-length, black raincoat and threw it, together with her shoulder bag, onto the nearest chair. She ran her fingers through her long, brown hair in an attempt to tidy it up, revealing fleetingly her large ears from which hung a pair of blue and green, parrot-shaped earrings. Her face was flushed from rushing in from the car park, but it added to the boyish plainness of her features. She was wearing a black trouser suit, the jacket short enough to reveal her backside, and a low cut, white blouse which some of her more conservative colleagues might have considered too revealing for a senior police officer. She looked about forty but this was without make-up, so she might well have been a few years younger. She scanned the room and looked surprised to see that there was such a small squad dealing with the case. Harrison pulled one of the chairs from under the desk and invited her to sit down.

"DI John Harrison, ma'am," he said respectfully.

If he'd had a hat, he'd have doffed it.

"Detective Chief Inspector Carol Miller," she replied with the easy calmness of someone who wanted to be in command. "Please call me Carol. I've been tasked with getting to the bottom of this suspicious death as efficiently and speedily as possible."

He was pleased that she was keeping things on an informal level but he'd imagined she'd be older, taller and more conventionally dressed. He dragged another chair towards him, placing it at right angles to her, and they both sat down together. She brushed her thighs briskly twice, crossed her legs and leaned over towards him.

"Bring me up to speed," she said, pointing to the table behind her. "I've been told you've started a murder investigation and you've decided, unilaterally it appears, to close the College and carry out your enquiries here. Let's start from there."

"I'll explain as we go along," said Harrison guardedly.

He related to her the events of the morning, although not quite in the order or the way that they'd taken place. He reasoned that it would save time and probably his reputation for thoroughness too. She stopped him regularly, mainly for clarification, and she showed no flicker of emotion, not even mild surprise, when he told her what position the body was in when Bernadette had found it.

"The key to solving the case is the combination lock on the door," he said to indicate that he'd nearly finished his report. "The murderer could only gain entry that way. That puts the caretakers and the people who were in this room in the frame."

"So why not take them all down the station and interview them there? We'll have all the technological advantages of a modern police force at our disposal."

"This place is fairly secure. It saves all the fuss. Besides we don't have the manpower at the moment. They'll have to be isolated and guarded."

"I'm not a man, John," she cut in icily. "You mean human resources. The police force now contains women."

"We can probably discount all bar four or five..." he continued disregarding her remark.

"But you haven't isolated them," she interrupted.

"It's too late for that."

"All the more reason to take them to the station. It's a more intimidating place. Someone might make a run for it if we stay here. Then we'll have a lot of explaining to do!"

He stood up and threw his arms in the air so vehemently that she had to sit back in her chair.

"OK, let's take them down there," he said, raising his voice. "That'll look dramatic. Then there'll be solicitors and the media crawling out of the ceiling. We'll probably be able to start the interviews later in the week. Right now we can tell them they're all helping us with our enquiries. Keep it low key. Let's give it two or three hours. After that it's up to you what we do."

"Right, I agree. You're still the SIO for the time being. On your head be it."

"Can I take the credit if I'm right?"

He sat down again, breathing less heavily. He smiled at her unconvincingly and she didn't return his attempt at warmth.

"Let's discuss what we're waiting for, shall we," she said phlegmatically. "We need the post mortem report. That will tell us how it was done. If, as the pathologist says, she was asphyxiated without a struggle, then we want to ascertain what kind of drug was used to keep her immobile. It might be pufferfish poison but it's more likely to be curare. The right dose relaxes the muscles to the extent it paralyses the body but leaves the victim still sentient. I suppose pufferfish poison would do the trick, although it works much more slowly. Curare can produce almost instant paralysis – just ask the Amazon Forest hunters. If it is curare, we need to find out three more things. First, how it got into her body, secondly, who had the skill to administer it, and last, where did the murderer get it from? That should narrow things down a bit."

She looked up at him and smiled.

"Have you found out if any of your suspects has been to South America recently?"

He shook his head. How could he have done?

"The next thing we need is for that handbag to turn up," she continued. "If there was a robbery it's likely that the thief emptied it out, took what he wanted and then threw it away in the bushes or dumped it in a bin. If we find it, we might be able to work out what's missing. He was probably after her purse, her car keys and her house keys, if he knows her. Or, as you say, he might have made it look like a robbery."

He wanted to remind her that the 'thief' might have been a woman but he thought it better not to.

"Aren't you concerned about what the deceased was doing before she was murdered?" he asked instead. "I've never seen anything as bizarre in my twenty odd years on the force." "Yes, it is interesting," she said, uncrossing her legs and sweeping imaginary dust off her thighs again. "Why would she want to touch herself intimately in this room when she could have done it totally privately at home? You said she only lives about half a mile away."

He nodded but he knew she couldn't think of a reason why. She hadn't seen the body so she couldn't imagine the ludicrousness of the spectacle.

"Let me look at your preliminary list of suspects," she said, holding out her hand. "If your golden hour hunch is right and she was murdered between seven and nine this morning,

I agree it has to be one of these because they all know the combination to the security lock. They're given it the day before, you said, so they can come and go freely each day rather than waiting to be given entry. This has to be our first line of enquiry. It's too late for any other MO and we won't be able to make use of anything else…which is a bloody nuisance."

She glanced down the list, pausing once or twice to think.

"Yes, that's his real name," he said after the second pause. "Thank goodness he doesn't call himself Dick."

She looked up, puzzled by what he'd said. "I don't follow you," she replied eventually.

"Richard Head. He's sixth on the list. That's his real name," he repeated.

"Oh I see. I hadn't noticed that. Do you think it's important?"

"It might be. It must be hard going through life with a name like that, especially at a college."

"I assume the asterisks are the main suspects because they haven't established an alibi. We need to find out if any of them have got a record and take their fingerprints and DNA samples." she said, quickly changing the subject.

She still couldn't see why he attached such importance to someone's name. He nodded again.

"So you've narrowed it down to four," she continued. "I note they're all men. Are you implying that women don't kill?"

"Not at all. Why, what do you think?"

"I can't possibly imagine why *anyone* would kill her in such a way. We'd better speak to all your suspects as soon as possible and take positional statements. We can't keep everyone here all day." "I was coming to that," he said impatiently, again interrupting her flow. "DC Hudson has already taken preliminary statements. That's how we ended up with a list of main suspects. Fingerprints and DNA won't tell us anything as they've all probably been in the Principal's office. I suggest we detain the eight managers involved plus the estates chap, let most of the other staff go and ask them to come back in the morning. We can check their names on the personnel lists, do a T-I-E and if anyone's not come in, it could be because they've done a runner. Then we'd have other suspects."

"Sounds a bit speculative," she said, ignoring him again. "It's a pity there's no CCTV. That would've helped."

She stood up and went slowly over to the table. She brushed her thighs again as she walked, as though she'd just eaten a sandwich and spilt crumbs on her trousers.

"We should take a look at her papers and that exercise book," she added. "It's more than likely she'd have written more personal, intimate things there than on a computer."

She put on her cotton gloves and started to flick through the pages.

"There are a lot of observations, the sort you make before and after meetings. It looks like she took notes during meetings also. Everything's titled and dated. She had beautiful handwriting – italics. All so neat and clear."

He went over and stood next to her as she read, craning his neck over her shoulder.

"Is there anything in there for today?" he asked. "It might tell us something."

She flicked around looking for the last entry, then she stopped and turned the pages back.

"Got it!" she shouted excitedly. "It's a list of the main points for the meeting, entitled 'Restructuring'. It looks like she was going to re-organise the College…yes, departments into faculties."

"Let's see if it was on this morning's agenda," he said. "There's a copy over there on the table."

He walked over and picked up the agenda.

"It *was* on," he said, mildly surprised. "Item three."

"There are a lot of fancy names with initials after them," she continued without looking up from the book. "The first is Faculty of Arts – MT…blah blah blah…Finally there's a heading – 'Downsizing SMT' and a list of initials: RH, MS, and two other sets of initials in brackets – MT again and HJ."

She paused and looked at Harrison who'd strolled back over from the table.

"Let me see your list again…"

"No need!" he exclaimed. "RH is Richard Head and MS is Mike Smith. They're two of our main suspects. HJ is Hugh Jones, the acting Principal and MT is Mortimer Todd."

"Perhaps she knew she was going to be murdered," she joked, referring to Ariadne. "She's left us a list of suspects *before the fact.*"

"That leaves one more," he said, ignoring her unexpected frivolity. "Steven Wallace – we know he was the last person to see her alive."

"That puts Smith and Head top of our list then. Now each has a motive. I wonder why Todd's and Jones's initials were in brackets."

He frowned and then he remembered that Wallace had seen Mort arrive that morning.

"Todd has a sort of an alibi," he sighed. "He was seen coming into this building sometime after nine. That puts him out of the picture because the murder must have taken place before half past eight. That's when Bernadette Arden said she got here this morning. I didn't put two and two together on that. We now have a fairly accurate time of death: between seven and eight thirty."

She was still looking at the book and she grunted an acknowledgement of his deductions.

"I'm not so sure you're right about Todd, John," she said, showing him the very last thing Ariadne had written.

"My God," he gasped as he read it. "She's written 'Mortimer – then prep meeting'."

CHAPTER 24

Early November 1984

"Smoking?" screamed Junkin, his voice reverberating round the building. "Which one of them was smoking?"

He was sitting in his office with Mort and Roy Jolly who'd just told him that he'd caught two students 'having it off' in the gents' toilet in the art block, and one of them happened to be smoking a cigarette at the time.

"It was the young man," said Roy.

"Was the girl smoking as well?"

"Not as they were doing it, Simon, but she might have been if I'd let them finish. They were going at it hammer and tongs! She might have ended up in flames."

"What are you going to do about it, Mr Todd?" asked Junkin more quietly, but the veins were standing out on his temples and his face had turned a dark shade of puce.

He evidently hadn't understood Roy's joke.

"He's done all he has to," said Roy before Mort could answer. "He's referred it to you."

"I don't believe I asked you, Mr Jolly," said Junkin haughtily, his gaze fixed on Mort.

"Your role is to decide the nature of the disciplinary action," said Roy, ignoring him again. "We don't have the necessary authority."

"I have enough to do running this department," said Junkin fixing his gaze on Roy.

His head was tilted backwards slightly and his top front teeth were jutting out over his bottom lip. Mort smiled to himself. Not only had he heard that several times before, but Junkin's facial expression was making him look every inch the feckless fop both men took him to be. In contrast Roy looked calm and relaxed; he knew how to handle Junkin. He was small but sturdily built wearing the regulation Ben Sherman shirt, Levi jeans and Doc Martin boots that made him stand out as a trendy artist in any company. He was about the same age as Junkin, and, although his clothes, his round, rimless glasses and long, brown hair made him look younger, he was balding at the front and his face was haggard as a result of too much drinking.

"Why were they smoking in a non-smoking area?" Junkin reiterated, trying to avoid having to make any sort of decision.

"That's hardly the issue at stake," said Roy firmly. "They both had their trousers round their ankles and he was giving her a knee trembler against the wall in one of the cubicles."

"How old were they?" asked Junkin impatiently, hoping that he wouldn't have to call their parents in.

"Both final year Diploma students," replied Roy, now grinning genially. "And luckily for you they're both over eighteen."

"You'd better arrange for them to see me," said Junkin, relieved that he might be able to get away with a stern talking-to or a short suspension. "I want you both here when they come."

He paused, sat down in his chair, and flicked through his diary. "Are you both free on Friday at ten?"

"Yes," said Mort and Roy in unison. "We'll make sure we are!"

"I wouldn't miss this for the world," whispered Roy as Junkin filled in the appointment.

"I'll have to speak to the Principal first", said Junkin phlegmatically. "I'll have to check on procedure."

"He's going to ask him what to do," Roy whispered again out of the side of his mouth.

He was loving the cut and thrust.

"That reminds me," said Junkin, standing up and walking round his desk towards them. "It's Ani Hopwood's twenty fourth birthday on Friday. Paul Honor and I are arranging a surprise lunchtime get-together for her in the Bridge. I expect you'll be there anyway, Mr Jolly, but I think you should attend in your capacity as her senior lecturer, Mr Todd."

This wasn't the only instance that term of Junkin's involvement in a lavatory related incident. Three weeks before he'd put a sign up in the gents' staff toilet complaining about 'the incorrect use of urinals' which had made him the laughing stock of the College for days. Mort's dealings with Junkin had already made him recognise that he'd developed two new glorious weaknesses, failings that would make him even more miserable: he didn't suffer fools gladly and he hated those in authority – and he regarded every one of them as fools. Now he was being ordered to go for a drink and pretend to be enjoying himself with a bunch of people he didn't much care for, knowing that the feeling was mutual. Luckily Friday was the day when he had a class immediately after lunch so he wouldn't have to stay long. He was still feeling ashamed about the episode in the Barred Gate, and he was apprehensive about speaking to Ariadne for the first time since half term, albeit more formally and in the presence of others. He hoped she'd have too many distractions to care about him, especially if Junkin and Honor were there too.

* * *

When Mort arrived at the pub the following Friday, the party was in full swing. The Bridge was close enough for him to walk to, and a total contrast to the Barred Gate. It was large, spacious and modern: there were several booths arranged on opposite sides, and twenty or so tables, all full, encircled the bar which was situated centrally. On entering anyone would have thought that this was the only room but off to the right and left, hidden from view by the large numbers of customers who had to stand, were a snug and a large games room, which were also full to bursting. It was the same in the evening and at weekends since it was the largest and most stylish watering hole in Storbury, conveniently adjacent to a large and rapidly expanding housing estate.

He spotted Junkin first standing out head and shoulders above the rest. He was holding court but as far as Mort could make out from his position in the doorway, it looked as though his audience was laughing at him rather than with him. As he pushed his way through the crowded lounge he heard Junkin boasting about how that very morning he'd dealt with the two Art students who'd been caught *in flagrante*.

"Of course I could have expelled them," he proclaimed to what he supposed were his admirers. "I considered a two week suspension but I let them off with a slap on the wrist. They told me they were very much in love and were getting engaged as soon as they finish their studies here. They were smoking, you see, when they were doing it, so I confiscated their cigarettes…"

He stopped momentarily to gauge the reaction to his leniency, but no one uttered a word. They were glowering at Mort who was standing behind him.

"Ah, Mr Todd," said Junkin forcing a smile. "Glad you could join us. I expect you've met everyone here."

"Yes, yes," replied Mort eying the stony faces of the Social Anthropology set. Only Jeff Shaw was missing. "Where's my lot?"

"Your lot, as you put it, are over there in the corner with the birthday girl," replied Junkin and this time his audience did express their amusement.

"Spoken like a true parvenu," Mort heard someone say as he made off quickly.

He'd just seen Paul Honor with his back to him talking to Ariadne.

When Ariadne saw him slowly threading his way towards her, she touched Honor lightly on the arm and excused herself.

"Happy Birthday!" he said as they came together near one of the booths.

"Have you brought me a present?" she asked, clapping her hands like a small schoolgirl.

"Yes, and I've got you a card."

"Let me see them. Let me see them."

He passed her a small parcel containing the card and a copy of *The Unbearable Lightness of Being* by Milan Kundera. He'd chosen it because it was a multifaceted love story which he hoped might serve as a homily for her. He hadn't read it, but it had received excellent reviews and one critic had explained that one of the male characters, caught up in a love triangle, had many 'dignified qualities'.

"This look *intereshting*," she slurred when she'd torn off the paper. "I'll open the card later."

He realised that she must have had a few drinks already, because she was swaying from side to side as though she were trying to keep upright in a rapidly moving train.

"I want another *preshent*," she giggled. "I want you…to give me a *kish*."

He stooped down, put his arms on her shoulders and gently pecked the side of her face so that it looked as though he was saying hello – or in this case goodbye.

"I have to go," he said, uncomfortable at the intimate contact.

It wasn't a thing he usually did; his working class background made him uneasy among touchy-feely types.

"Enjoy the rest of your birthday," he said, turning away.

"That might not be as easy as you think," she garbled, scarcely able to disguise her disappointment that he was leaving so soon. "I'm *sheeing* Joe again tonight and we're going for my birthday meal with his 'comrades' from the *counshil*. That'll be a barrel of laughs."

"Are you seeing him regularly?"

"Yeah, I think he wants to marry me but there's absolutely no *chansh* of that!"

"Try to have fun all the same. I won't see you again until Monday so have a nice weekend."

He left her standing alone and looking disappointed. The brief tableau had been witnessed by the dragon Iris Baxter and several of the teachers who were wholly unaware that they'd completely misread what had gone on between Mort and Ariadne, but their tongues were already beginning to wag. They were silenced permanently the following week when they found out about Ariadne's engagement to Joe Crossley.

CHAPTER 25

12 April 2005: 1.45pm

The Hulk was half-heartedly pushing a heavy, rectangular, mobile whiteboard into the incident room. He'd been sent to find it in one of the classrooms at the other side of the building and he felt it was a demeaning task for a police officer to have to do. Where were the caretakers? Hugh Jones had readily agreed to Harrison's request to provide the board if it meant that the investigation was progressing. He wanted desperately to go home and clear the gruesome events of that day out of his mind. He needed time to work out how he was going to run the College which would be difficult enough without all the turmoil of having to deal with the repercussions of his predecessor's unsavoury death. He knew more or less what to do to keep the place ticking over as Ariadne had kept few secrets from him, and he'd often had to stand in for her in the past when she was away at conferences and such like. That hadn't been too challenging as he'd never had much to do, except once when he had to give out some diplomas at a celebration dinner for beauty therapists and he'd enjoyed that enormously. But he had his own job to do also and he knew he couldn't trust any of his assistants with the masses of data he had to collect and process. That would present too many dangers to the way he liked to operate.

While Hugh brooded away behind the screens which served as his office in the open plan information services room, Harrison was writing the names of the main suspects on the whiteboard. He'd have liked their photographs to stick on with the blu-tack he'd managed to purloin, to go with the grisly ones of Ariadne's last few moments that had been delivered not long before. He hadn't considered it his duty to prepare Miller for what she was about to see, but she'd pulled rank and opened the envelope before he could warn her. She was currently sitting on a chair with her back to him, trying to catch her breath and sweeping imaginary crumbs from her thighs again. He stuck the photographs to the centre of the board and then drew four boxes at each corner for the names of each of the potential 'villains', as he now called them. He added the information about where they were between seven and eight thirty, which consisted mostly of a number of question marks. The staff lists had told him that only the Human Resources Manager and a kitchen assistant were absent that day, so Miller had agreed to narrow the suspects down to Richard Head, Mike Smith, Steven Wallace and Mort Todd. She'd discounted the others although they all had a possible motive – the restructuring of the College. Yet none of the senior managers had seemed worried about it. Although it was on their agenda, it was deemed reasonable to assume that Ariadne hadn't shared her plans with them and was going to make a sensational announcement at the meeting. If that turned out to be an incorrect inference, each manager would still be on site and available for grilling.

It was nearly two o'clock and they'd got as far as they could without a provisional post mortem report from Charles Edwards and further news about the handbag. However, they'd drawn up a revised modus operandi: Miller and Harrison were to conduct the preliminary interviews and Tim was to be set to work on compiling the case file when he returned from Ariadne's flat, so that he could act as collator and intelligence centre to be consulted if necessary. However there were two major tasks to complete before they could begin. The first was to hold a short press conference and afterwards they could send everyone home except the senior managers and a skeleton staff to deal with enquiries from the public, which the Acting Principal would take care of. The second was to see if Ariadne's curriculum vitae would throw anything up.

As they were discussing whether or not to bring in a psychological profiler, the Hulk put his head round the door again and told them that reporters from the Storbury Tribune and regional radio and television were waiting impatiently in the rain outside the entrance for a statement about what had happened that morning. They'd been tipped off about the strange happenings at the College by a number of students, but they'd known about them long before then because of the emergency services activity in the area. The local police station had confirmed that two serious incidents had indeed taken place in Storbury that morning, and they'd been unable to get anything further either from the police or from the College despite frequent telephone calls.

"As senior officer I'll handle this," said Miller without waiting for Harrison to nominate himself. "Have you done a statement yet?"

"Mike Smith, the Marketing Manager, has prepared one," he replied. "We can use that if it's OK."

"Have you read it?" she asked frostily.

She was getting over her nausea caused by the photographs.

"I haven't had time," he said defensively. "I told Tim to tell him what to write but I think that Baxter woman had seen to it already."

"We'd better have a look at it in that case," she added, staring at the Hulk. "Constable, please ask Mr Smith to come here with his press release."

"Hold on, Naylor," ordered Harrison. "I strongly advise against that. Smith's a suspect. I'll go and get it, have a look at it and then bring Jones in here so you two can go and meet the media together. Do you agree?"

Miller nodded and Harrison quickly went off with the Hulk, leaving her temporarily at a loss what to do next. She went over to the table and rummaged through Ariadne's papers but found nothing of immediate interest. She remembered her unfinished conversation with Harrison about whether they might need a profiler to help them identify the murderer. He'd only muttered something about it being a waste of police time and she concluded that he was against it. Then her eye caught the words 'Curriculum Vitae', protruding from under the sheet of paper containing the morning's agenda that Tim had been given by Bernadette. She supposed neither he nor Harrison had read it yet and, as she'd a few minutes to kill, she decided to have a look through it before he came back. She smiled to herself again; she'd have something to tell him at last, even it was merely that she'd changed her mind about sending for 'Cracker'.

The first page of the curriculum vitae was the title page and the second contained basic information – address, telephone number and so on. The next few contained the standard summary of her career history and her personal skills and achievements. Nothing much of note, she thought, just the usual long-winded, boastful stuff about how talented a teacher, manager and leader she'd been. Miller noted that Ariadne had had five posts up and down the country before she'd arrived back at Storbury eighteen months previously, but what was most interesting was that she'd been there before as a lecturer in English from 1983 to 1985. This could be important: someone might be holding a grudge over what happened all those years ago and she'd have to ask Tim to check who'd been at the College during that short period. Towards the end was a section entitled hobbies and interests which didn't throw up anything that looked significant: reading, writing educational papers, theatre, art and personal fitness. Finally her references included two senior education authority directors and Joseph Crossley, the Member of Parliament for Storbury. Nothing unusual there but she'd ask Harrison if he knew anything shady about them.

Meanwhile Harrison was reading Mike Smith's press release. He'd have to make alterations and rewrite the section concerning the progress of the investigation, but it would do for now. He gave Mike no forewarning of what was in store for him, stating insensitively that DCI Miller had decreed that she and Hugh Jones would present the statement to the waiting journalists, and he was to wait in his office for further instructions. He gave the same message to Hugh and told him to meet Miller in five minutes in the foyer. On his return he quickly amended the statement and gave it to her for approval. Without mentioning what she'd gleaned from Ariadne's curriculum vitae, she agreed to the changes and went off to make the early evening news.

Hugh was already waiting for her, looking anxiously out at the four reporters and two TV cameramen who were huddling together under the small canopy over the entrance door which was providing shelter from the rain. They didn't look too pleased at having to hang around outside, wet and bedraggled, for what was probably not going to make much of a story, but they knew they had to stay to get whatever they could. Further away in the car park their technicians were at least dry in their vans. When at last the doors were unlocked and two people emerged, there was a brief commotion and some jostling for position as everyone moved out into the forecourt and prepared for action.

It was Miller who was to do the talking. Hugh was holding a large, black umbrella over both their heads.

"Good afternoon," she said gravely. "I am Detective Chief Inspector Carol Miller and this is Hugh Jones from the College. I will read a brief statement after which I will take questions, but at this moment in time I cannot promise, as you will see, to be very forthcoming with my answers."

She paused, cleared her throat and started to read slowly and clearly, pausing after each sentence to look up at the cameras.

"At approximately nine thirty this morning the body of a woman believed to be in her forties was found in the main building of Storbury College. The body has yet to be formally identified. Evidence has emerged which showed that she died in suspicious circumstances. It is not yet clear how she died, but details should become clearer after the post mortem. Storbury Police are taking this matter very seriously and are dedicating a number of investigative resources to this. We are treating it at this time as a murder enquiry. We have a number of leads at this very early stage, and we are confident these are directly related to the enquiry. Finally, we do not believe there is any risk to the residents of this town."

"Can you tell us who the woman is…was?" shouted a female reporter from one of the regional television stations.

"I'm afraid I can't reveal her name until the body has been formally identified."

"How do you believe she died?" another woman shouted, presumably from BBC radio as there was no cameraman with her.

"I can't tell you that until after the post mortem," replied Miller keeping to the script.

She'd obviously done this before.

"I'm Ben Briscoe from the Storbury Tribune," said a bearded man in a dark blue duffel coat. "Can I ask why Ms Hopwood isn't here representing the College?"

"She can't be with us just now."

"Why has she closed the College?" he persisted.

He knew Ariadne and because of this he was certain she wouldn't willingly miss such a spectacular opportunity for publicity.

"It is now a murder scene. We cannot carry out our investigation efficiently and the College cannot function normally in such circumstances."

"Do you have any suspects yet?" It was BBC radio again.

"A number of people are helping us with our enquiries, but it is too early to say what the outcomes will be."

"I'm Zulfiqar Ali from BBC local TV," said a young man in a well-soaked jacket. "Do you think the murderer is from the College?"

"That is our first line of enquiry."

"Why is Mr Jones with you?" asked Briscoe sharply, more than ever convinced that he was on to something. "In what capacity is he representing the College?"

"Mr Jones is the Deputy Principal and as such he is currently acting as Principal. That is normal procedure in such circumstances."

She turned to look at Jones who was looking directly at Briscoe and nodding frantically.

"That's her car over there in the car park, isn't it, Hugh?" grinned Briscoe.

They'd met on a number of occasions before at College promotional events and he wasn't impressed with Hugh's ability to give a straight answer to any question.

"Yes it is, Ben," Hugh replied, glancing nervously at the silver Porsche which was parked nearby, confounding the newshound.

"When will you be able to tell us anything more?" asked the female reporter from one of the regional television stations, which she'd identified as ITV.

"There will be a further bulletin at noon tomorrow," said Miller. "Thank you for the present. I hope to be able to update you then."

"One last question," said Briscoe menacingly. "It's for Mr Jones."

"Yes?" said Hugh looking attentively back.

"Will Ariadne be here then?"

"I can't say," he said confidently. "She may be away for some time."

"Why is her car still here?"

"I think that will be all," said Miller cutting in.

She didn't want Hugh to cave in and say out loud that Ariadne would be away forever and was, at that very instant perhaps, lifeless, laid out on a slab having her chest and stomach stitched up.

CHAPTER 26

Mid-December 1984

It was getting towards the end of Mort's first term at Storbury and the Christmas break was fast approaching. The weather had turned much colder and there were frequent flurries of snow, which made his journey to and from the College not only wearisome but extremely hazardous, especially on the country lanes. There was one small consolation, however. The cars driven by the people he'd christened the Vigilantes were nowhere to be seen. Perhaps they thought they weren't needed as the poor driving conditions were doing their jobs for them, or perhaps they themselves considered it too dangerous to venture out on the freezing, winter mornings.

Things were winding down everywhere in the last timetabled fortnight, and classes were being regularly cancelled in the afternoons as students failed to return from extended drinking sessions in nearby bars and pubs. For the teachers that meant some much needed extra time to produce lists of marks and grades and complete reports on academic progress. Then they could look forward to their annual party at the Alpaca Club in the town centre. Mort hadn't put his name down for this. He didn't want to spend an evening among people he disliked when he couldn't have a drink to compensate, and he didn't relish a long, difficult journey home in the snow late at night even though he would be sober. He had other plans in any case which he didn't reveal to anyone.

A week before the end of term, after he'd submitted his

reports for his English groups, he received a note from Paul Honor asking him to explain the low coursework marks he'd awarded to his O level English Language students. When he checked what they were, he found that he'd given what he considered to be accurate grades, mainly Bs, Cs, and Ds, which was what most students usually achieved at this stage of the course. He was summoned to a meeting that afternoon to 'go through the paperwork' and Ariadne would be there to act as an observer. He was staggered, uncertain whether this was an attempt to make him look incompetent or whether it was nothing more than 'Diss' Honor's vainglorious attempt to show that standards were indeed higher at Storbury than anywhere else. He was more than curious to find out which it was.

When he arrived in the classroom at the appointed time, they were both already there, with two large desks covered in cardboard folders. He placed his own set on another desk, and without speaking, he pulled up a chair and sat down opposite them at the front of the room.

"Thank you for coming," said Honor condescendingly, but Ariadne barely smiled. "We want you to have a look at the way we've marked our scripts, and then we'll have a look at yours to see why your grades are much lower. It could simply be that we have better students, or, and I hope you'll take this in the spirit intended, we might be, shall we say, better, more experienced teachers."

"There could be another reason," said Mort curtly." We'll wait and see, shall we?"

He stood up and went over to the student files.

"Which are yours?" he asked.

"Those are mine and those on the next table are Ani's."

He read the mark sheet that had been placed on top of Honor's papers. Every piece of work had been given an A or a B. He looked at Honor and raised his eyebrows in disbelief, hoping that it would be perceived as a look of admiration. He picked up a pile of what looked like essays and read the first one slowly and carefully. He did the same to the second and then quickly flicked through the rest.

"On what basis did you give this piece on capital punishment an A?" he asked, holding the first one up.

"That means it's of a very high standard, Mort."

"It should be more or less perfect, shouldn't it?"

"Of course."

"What does that mean?"

"It means that it's well written and the case for and against the death penalty is well argued."

"What about spelling and knowledge of sentence structure? Should they be perfect too?"

"Of course."

"Then why does this one contain several spelling mistakes that haven't been highlighted, and sentences which are separated by commas, not full stops. There's also a complete absence of definite articles. It looks like the person who wrote this essay doesn't have English as a first language. It's gibberish. I thought so, a foreign name."

He held up the second one.

"As far as I can make out after a brief first reading, this one sets out an argument *against* the death penalty. There are no contrasting views at all. I could give it a D at best, and the first one no more than an E, both of which count as fail grades academically."

He paused for a response but neither Honor nor Ariadne had one; they merely smiled at one another.

"My final comments are that none of the essays appears to me to have been read. Basic errors haven't been pointed out. No corrections have been made, there are no suggestions for improvement or critical comments and there isn't a verdict on the standard of each composition."

Honor turned to Ariadne and grinned.

"This is the nineteen eighties, Mort," he said still smiling. "That's the old Victorian way. This is the new way. Our marking scheme's been approved by the moderator. The

Social Anthropology teachers invented it…I mean *devised* it last year."

"Ah, I see" said Mort recognising what was happening. "So it wasn't a couple of drunken English teachers after all. What if we get another moderator, one who's got a brain?"

"I don't follow you."

"It's a highly irregular way to present work to an exam board."

"It's been approved. He said he was going to write a monograph on it. He sees us as revolutionaries. We're not demotivating the students by pointing out their errors. No more red ink."

"Have you seen this *monograph*?"

"Well, no…"

"I think we should be providing the means for the students to motivate themselves first."

"We are. We're giving them As and Bs."

"You're also saying the person who wrote the first essay can demonstrate he or she understands and can apply the mechanics of English?"

"That's irrelevant. Her arguments are cogent."

"If you can comprehend them without all the grammatical errors intruding. What if she gets a job based on this grade and her employer finds she can't write a sentence properly?"

"There's an equal opportunities issue here, Mort."

"Irrelevant, Paul. She's not yet able to express herself correctly. This is English Language we're discussing, isn't it?"

Honor frowned and turned appealingly to Ariadne for support.

"We've a very good reputation here," he stammered. "Do you realise you're ruining it?"

"I thought we were coming to that," said Mort sternly. "It's your status you're worried about. That's why you're inflating the grades isn't it? So you'll look good. What about the students? They haven't been able to learn anything."

He turned to Ariadne.

"Are you in on this as well?"

She stared down at the desk in front of her, moving uneasily around on her chair.

"I warned you at the beginning of term. From now on I'm going to look at a sample of your coursework," continued Mort. "You'll have to re-mark this lot tonight so that the correct grades can be placed on the reports."

"I'm taking this to Simon," said Honor angrily.

The next thing that Mort saw was a blur of movement as Honor stormed out of the room, slamming the door behind him.

"I'm surprised you went along with this, Ariadne," said Mort breathing heavily.

The strain of the argument had taken a lot of out of him.

"I was doing what I was told to do", she replied, forcing back the tears. "I'll start the re-marking immediately."

"Thank you. It shouldn't take too long."

"We got away with it last year," she sniffed, "What's it going to be like for me now that my grades are going down? It will cramp my style no end."

"I haven't seen much of you recently," he said, changing the subject, hoping she wouldn't start crying.

"I've been very busy with all my reports," she said, brightening up a little.

"Congratulations on your engagement, by the way. I'm very happy for you."

She looked up at him and shook her head disconsolately. She'd started to cry after all.

"I'd better go and see what Honor's up to," said Mort, gathering up his folders hurriedly. "Please don't do anything until I find out what Junkin has to say."

Junkin didn't react as Mort assumed he would – by siding with his ally and erstwhile protégé. He refused to discuss the matter until both parties were present, and when Mort knocked and entered he seemed pleased that he'd be able to resolve the matter speedily. He acted with scrupulous propriety throughout the debate, taking the view from the outset that he'd asked Mort to look into the idiosyncratic way that certain English teachers had been awarding marks, and he was satisfied that the appropriate action had been taken. He proposed however that a compromise might be reached: Mort should allow Honor and Ariadne to reduce each grade by one or two points so that they didn't have to spend an inordinate amount of time on adjustments and the interim student reports would still go out as planned. Mort agreed reluctantly on the condition that Junkin wrote a memorandum to the effect that, as Head of Department, he'd made this decision. He also insisted that Junkin add a paragraph expecting the English team to re-mark all their students' papers and demanding that a more reliable assessment would take place in future. Junkin agreed willingly, Honor less so and, as the routed section head couldn't think of any demands of his own, he had to confess, if solely to himself, that Mort had got the better of him.

Mort was ecstatic. He drove home happily that evening for the first time he could remember. He couldn't wait to tell Cassandra that Junkin had at last shown his mettle. He expected her to say that she'd told him to be patient and that soon he'd start to enjoy working at his new College. He'd mutter something about swallows and summers, and they'd laugh and hug and dance around the room. When he arrived, however, he found the house in darkness and the breakfast dishes were stacked unwashed in the kitchen sink. She'd gone out and she'd forgotten to set the timer for the hall light. The back door was unlocked. He'd have to speak to her yet again about her featherbrained attitude to home security.

CHAPTER 27

12 April 2005: 2.45pm

It was approaching three o'clock and Mort stared at his computer as if willing it to offer him some advice on what to do or provide him with something comforting. He was worried that he'd been spotted in Storbury during the night and, if anyone had seen him, they'd recognised him and informed the police. He was angry also with Barry for betraying a confidence that everyone now seemed to be aware of. Furthermore, he wasn't sure whether he was pleased or not that the three of them were hanging around. Gordon had brought him some sandwiches, but he wasn't convinced that they were there simply to give him support. Perhaps they were waiting to see him arrested and taken away with his coat over his head. Then they'd be able to tell everyone that they were there when it happened. He looked up to see that they were all busily working on some task or other, or at least it appeared that way. He had to find something to take his mind off the events of the day so far, and he clicked his mouse on the email icon in the hope of finding one or two that were out of the ordinary, maybe even droll.

The latest email he'd received was from 'Rick-Rock-n-roll' about ten minutes previously which turned out to be Richard Head's home email address – so that's where he's buggered off to, he thought. He knew that Richard lived in Storbury but not where exactly. Richard must have walked – or run – home because he couldn't have driven out unless he'd smashed through the police car at the end of the drive and the whole College would have heard about that by now. He opened the email. It read:

'I'm sending this to you Mort because you and I (plus Iris Baxter and maybe Maureen King) are the only people who were here when Ariadne Hopwood was a young lecturer. I don't know how well you knew her but I seem to remember you taught the same subject so you must have come across her quite a lot. I'm writing to ask you if you can remember anything devious she was involved in back then. I heard that there was some fanciful marking going on involving English teachers but it might have been before you came here. You see, I think there's more to her than meets the eye. Apart from her appalling behaviour towards me, she spends too much time with Dog Breath Jones and Fatty Smith for my liking and we know they were both up to something which could be a reason why someone wanted her dead – and maybe them into the bargain. My suspicions about her were aroused by accident when I looked at the pictures on her wall when she summoned me to her palace after she was made Principal. She liked to show off who she associated with – there's one with Dodgy Joe, our MP, taken in 1997 at the Houses of Parliament, and another of her with Kurt Cobain – he of the rock band Nirvana – dated 1999. They're getting out of a Bentley with an S registration plate. It must be a forgery of some kind because S reg cars dated from 1998 and Kurt Cobain topped himself (or so it's believed) in April 1994. Interesting eh? Nevertheless, I think you should do some digging about her.

I'm also writing this to ask you if she confided in you about her plans for restructuring (as she put it). At my last appraisal with her, she asked me if I was thinking of retirement, so when I saw today's agenda I assumed I was going to be made redundant to make way for a younger person. I've been here for over thirty years and I've kept the wheels rolling but I don't think she reckoned that was good enough. It looks like my goose is cooked. She hinted that she was planning to dismantle my department and transfer the constituents to Business Studies and a new department she was setting up with a fancy title. I protested of course but she laughed at me and I didn't like that.

I've come home because I believe I'm a key suspect. I haven't got an alibi for last night or this morning. I live on my own but I don't get on with my neighbours because they say I make too much noise. I like to listen to loud music but I've bought some earphones for late night sessions so the threat of an Asbo has been lifted. The police will also think I have a motive, won't they? I ran away in the hope that it'll soon be over and the real murderer will have been arrested. It wasn't me, Mort. I hope you believe me. I can't snoop around from here, but you can do some research for me. Start in the store room opposite her office. Before my review she was in there wading through some old paper folders. When she saw me, she stopped what she was doing and locked the door quickly.

I'm going to sit here and play some bluesy music while it all blows over. Please try to do what you can.

Rock on

Richard Head'

Mort blinked, shook his head and read the email again. What's Richard doing, he thought? The sad, stupid fool. They'll go and arrest the poor sod and before he can say 'not guilty' they'll pin it all on him. He sighed and Helen looked up.

"What's up, boss," she said kindly. "You sound as if you've got the weight of the world on your shoulders."

"What a day!" replied Mort.

He observed that Gordon and Barry had also stopped what they were doing and were listening intently for an explanation. He wanted to tell them to go and have a coffee because he needed time to work out what to do.

"I was deep in thought," he said, trying to avoid another tedious discussion. "On the way here this morning I thought

I'd never be able to do that journey ever again. Two hours a day minimum in my car each day. That's ten hours a week. I do more than one day's work every week sitting in my car. No wonder I'm always tired and tetchy, especially when I've not had much sleep. And what do I do when I get here? I can't remember when I get back home. I seem to spend each day going to meetings about meetings, dealing with all these bloody emails…"

"You can come and live with me," said Helen, eager to hear Mort's reply but he didn't react.

"Do you want to hear a joke?" asked Barry, expecting that his request would be shot down in flames.

"Go on then," Mort nodded.

"There's this very rich man," he began. "He has three young sons. One day he decides that because he loves them so much he's going to buy them a big present each. He calls his eldest son into his study and says 'Son, I love you so much I want to give you a very special gift, anything your heart desires.' The son's a big football fan and asks for an electronic football game, so his father buys him Aston Villa. He asks his second son, who's a bit younger, what he wants and he asks for a model aeroplane, so he buys him Gatwick Airport. His third son is much younger, seven say, and comes to see his father dressed as an Native American with two feathers stuck in his hair. 'Oh father,' he's says, 'I'd love a cowboy outfit…'"

"So he buys him Storbury College," shouted the other three in unison.

"We've heard it before," laughed Helen.

"Never mind," chuckled Barry. "The old ones are always the best ones."

"I've got one," said Gordon, wanting to keep up the tempo. "What's green and got wheels?"

"I don't know," mocked Helen, "What is green with wheels?"

"Grass."

"Grass?"

"I lied about the wheels. It's from the Beano."

They all groaned and the high spirits seemed to have cheered Mort up.

"Thank you," he said, "You're all very kind. But I want one of you to do me a favour. If no one wants to do it for me, I think you should all take the rest of the day off."

"Well, what is it?" asked Helen.

"I need to get into the executive suite and I need someone to distract the policeman guarding the door."

"What do you want to do?"

"I need to look at some files. Just look at them, that's all."

"I could go for you…"

"Why?"

"I can say that I need them for a job I'm doing. The copper can escort me and I can grab a few for you."

"Hmm, that sounds interesting, except for two reasons. He's bound to ask you why you haven't gone home, and two, if I murdered Ariadne you'll be an accessory after the fact."

"Whatever, sunshine, it's better than sitting here listening to Morbid Mort and the Two Ronnies."

CHAPTER 28

19 December 1984

Mort didn't say goodbye to anyone on the last day of term. He waited until the building had more or less emptied at lunchtime and everyone had gone drinking or to do some late shopping. He had to hang around in any case for the start of his scheduled half past one class, despite having told the students the week before that it was cancelled. He was confident that there would be one spotty youth who would turn up because he'd nowhere better to go and he knew he'd be early. Sure enough at one fifteen he saw the young man standing outside the classroom, wiping the condensation off his glasses. He was holding a small envelope in his mouth which he took out and gave to Mort, who thanked him and wished him a Merry Christmas before gently ushering him down the corridor to the top of the stairs. Breathing a long sigh of relief, he waited for the sound of the exit door closing on the ground floor. He then went back to the staffroom, collected his things and dashed out to his car. He was running away to meet his old pals from the technical college. He'd arranged to meet them that evening in the city centre tavern where they usually began their pub crawls, and he'd plenty of time to get ready before the six o'clock start. When he arrived home, the house was empty but securely locked for once and he was pleased that Cassandra was out buying presents – that was what she'd said she was doing that afternoon. He could be on his own for a while, and there'd be no distractions to stop him formulating the most humorous way of telling the gang all about his misfortunes at Storbury. He was particularly looking forward to seeing Old Stan again hoping that his best friend would be at his most scathing and make it sound like there was always something worse – liking being a lowly lecturer at forty five or was it forty six?

He ran a bath and lay back in the warm, soapy water and contemplated how he'd portray his most dreadful tormentors. That would include almost everyone he'd met since September but he'd concentrate on Junkin, Honor, Kettleman and Alice the Alcie. He decided to include Ariadne in this band of rogues but he'd leave out his visit to the Barred Gate and the subsequent fraught investigations into her nature. They all seemed so far away now, in another world that had ceased to exist. It was if they'd been put into storage somewhere for the next two weeks and would only reappear when the new term began in January. He lay there and relaxed, hoping that soon he'd be more like his old self, the one that didn't have a care in the world. He chuckled at this self-deception; he'd never been like that before and he knew he never could be. Yet he was content with things as they were at that moment, and he wanted this newfound sense of calm and lightness to remain with him as long as he could make it last.

He remembered that he'd told Cassandra that he'd probably sleep on someone's floor that night if he became too drunk to make it back home and he let his mind wander over her body for a while. They hadn't had sex for several weeks and he couldn't remember the last time he'd seen her naked after that first Storbury morning when she made him breakfast. He'd make it up to her over the holidays. She was pretty, she was clever and she never worried about anything. He was a lucky man, and he was glad that he wasn't married to someone like Ariadne who was so untrustworthy that she might want to sleep with any man she met. He shivered when he thought of the poor soul that had just asked her to be his wife. Then he became conscious that his bath water had gone cold and his abstraction would have to be put on hold unless he wanted to freeze to death.

When he arrived at the bar that evening, he knew at once that something wasn't as it should be. Old Stan, the man he'd been longing to see for weeks, wasn't there. He was told, rather cagily he thought, that Stan had been 'having it off with some woman' regularly ever since he returned from Majorca, and that this was very much out of character for a man whose catchphrase in matters of the fairer sex was 'never buy the book when you can join the library'. Perhaps he'd finally settled down now that he was well into middle age, and, like most men in the first flush of a passionate relationship, he'd relegated his mates into second place. The consensus was that he'd be dutifully carrying bags of shopping back to her flat precisely when he should have been downing his first three pints. Mort said Stan should meet someone he knew at Storbury College but he didn't go into detail.

The evening went well despite the absence of his long-lost adversary, and he kept everyone well entertained with his tales of the Hellhole, as he'd chosen to call Storbury, because it summed up his feelings in the presence of men he liked and a college he wished he'd never left. There were gasps of horror when he told them of his first day there and he was frequently accused of exaggerating. There was much derisory laughter also; it was his own fault, they taunted. If he hadn't been so determined to seek promotion, he'd still be happily grinding his way through life with them instead of suffering among his tormentors. He knew they were right, but he missed Stan's take on things and for that reason he didn't feel as cheerful as he hoped. He hadn't drunk as much as he intended either, and shortly after closing time he found himself standing alone at a taxi rank waiting for a cab home.

The house was in darkness, except for the hall light and a table lamp in the front window, when the taxi pulled up outside. He shut the front door quietly and tottered into the kitchen, resolving to get timer switches installed so that he didn't have to remind Cassandra again to switch them off before she went to bed. He needed a drink, and he was debating whether it would be coffee or another beer when he noticed things weren't as he expected them to be. There were two unwashed glasses in the sink and Cassandra's handbag was lying on the floor under the kitchen table instead of being upstairs in the bedroom. He glanced at his watch. It was five to midnight. She must have had an early night after all, he guessed, tired out after a hard day spending money. He wanted more than ever to reawaken his mood of the early afternoon and sitting and chatting to her would have compensated for his disappointing evening. Instead all he could think of doing was to light a cigarette and have that drink. He chose a beer from the fridge and went through to the sitting room, taking up his customary recumbent position on the settee.

He spent the next few minutes blowing smoke rings up in the air and when he'd stubbed out his cigarette, he closed his eyes. Visions of the past few weeks kept flitting in and out of his semi-consciousness and he was about to fall asleep when he heard a loud thud from somewhere above him. He thought he must be dreaming and decided to go to bed. He got up and staggered out of the room, returning falteringly to switch off the light, and made for the darkened staircase. It was then that he heard surreptitious whispering noises coming from his bedroom and a naked Cassandra emerged on the landing above him. When she saw him, she screamed and ran back into the bedroom, leaving the door open. She must have assumed he was a burglar – he'd said he wouldn't be home that night. He had to get to her and hold her and tell her everything was fine. Then she could fall asleep in his arms. In his drunkenness he found the climb tricky and stopped half way up to catch his breath. It was a man's voice he heard next, a voice he recognised, a voice that he'd wanted to hear a few hours earlier. As he sat there, the voice materialised into the absurd form of someone he hoped more than anything it wouldn't be. There stood a suntanned middle-aged man with a tattoo on his left arm, his chiseled features and crew cut identifying him immediately. It was Stan, naked also, and he was brandishing a woman's stiletto-heeled shoe high above his head.

Part 4

CHAPTER 29

12 April 2005: 2.45pm

Harrison used the time while Miller was away to turn the whiteboard round so that the suspects wouldn't see their name, or anyone else's, when they were being questioned. He pushed it up against the wall nearest the door and wondered whether he should write something on the blank side to make it obvious why he was using it. He decided on a simple timeline of the events of the day so far. That wouldn't give anything away other than that he was being thorough. He wrote:

0700	*AH arrives at work – seen by estates manager (SW)*
0935	*Body found –by AH's secretary (BA)*
0940	*Police called (IB)*
0950	*Patrol car arrives – ascertains not false alarm*
1000	*SIO called*
1015	*SIO arrives – calls for uniform back up*
1025	*Preliminary examination of AH's office (SIO)*
1035	*TH interviews managers (to 1135)*
1040	*SIO speaks to HJ (acting Principal)*
1050	*Pathologist*
1105	*SOCO*
1110	*SIO speaks to SW (Estate Manager)*
1130	*Body removed*
1140	*ID of next of kin established (mother in York), SIO speaks to managers in meetings room*

He was standing back admiring his handiwork when Tim walked in.

"I wondered where you'd got to, lad," said Harrison with his usual gruffness. "Doesn't your phone make outward calls?"

"Sorry sir," said Tim, taking off his coat and throwing it on the interview desk.

He was soaked to the skin.

"Not there, lad – you'll get everything wet!"

"Sorry sir," repeated Tim, putting the damp coat on one of the stacked chairs behind the whiteboard and catching sight of the photographs on the reverse side. "I see you you've been busy while I've been away."

"Anything to report?" asked Harrison, motioning him to come and stand next to him.

"Not really. Uniform haven't found the handbag yet and there's nothing at Ariadne Hopwood's address. It turned out to be one of those new, posh flats behind the Bridge Inn. There's an intercom system there and I managed to find someone to let me in. The flat's on the first floor. I don't know where we're gonna get a key as they're all owner-occupied. I spoke to two people there but neither had noticed anything unusual."

"That's disappointing," grumbled Harrison, annoyed that he couldn't add anything new to his summary of the case. "Why didn't you break in?"

"You told me not to. Anyway what was I looking for?"

"Did you post a guard?"

"Yes, you said I had to do that. I thought we were waiting for someone to show up there."

There was a pause as they both became conscious that the investigation might be grinding to a halt.

"Have you got any further?" asked Tim, keen to discover if Harrison had had any better luck.

"One thing's emerged since you left. The DCI and I had a look through that exercise book over there, the one that was on Ariadne's desk. The last thing she wrote might be important. She'd written 'Mortimer – then prep meeting'. What do you make of that?"

"That puts Todd in the frame," said Tim excitedly. "She must have been meeting him well before 9.30!"

"But why? He was seen arriving after nine o'clock."

"He'd could have come in early, knocked her off…er… killed her I mean, then dashed off home and driven back again after nine to give him the perfect alibi."

"Where did you say he lived?"

"In the city. That's an hour's drive in the rush hour but at six or seven in the morning it'd take about forty minutes – less if you put your foot down. I think I know where I'm off to next…"

"No! That's a waste of time. I'll get Carol to call the City mob and they can send someone to have a look round."

"I told you he didn't fit the bill. He doesn't look right somehow. Are you going to have him in first up?"

"I'll see what Carol has to say. Personally I don't like the look of that Mike Smith. There's something fishy about him too."

"Such as?"

"When I went to see him about the press release he was very jumpy. He's hiding something."

"We've all something to hide, sir."

"Speak for yourself, lad. If you've any skeletons in your cupboard, let's hope you're never a suspect in anything serious!"

They both laughed and Harrison's mood improved. He liked to talk things through with Tim because he possessed a positive clarity of thought, the ability to see in black and white. He could also rely on his detective constable's dogged single-mindedness to give their cases a clearer focus. Or was it just talking things through with him? He was musing on this when Miller walked back in.

"I'm glad that's over," she said sitting down on the interview desk and sweeping her thighs again. "That Jones chap nearly gave the game away. I've promised the media another conference tomorrow and I don't want him with me."

"I think we've made a bit of progress while you've been away," said Harrison, more and more fascinated by her peculiar habit.

"So have I!" she said elatedly, becoming aware of the writing on the whiteboard. "What's that?"

"It's what's happened so far," he replied, unable to hide his satisfaction at what he considered was a job well done.

"Hmm," she said. "Any news on the handbag?"

"Not yet. We've also drawn a blank at Ms Hopwood's address. We'll need a key to get in – otherwise it's the battering ram boys. Tim here thinks Todd's done it."

"Because of her last entry in the book?"

"And the fact that he could have done it..."

"Hmm, I think we may have another suspect, John."

Harrison grimaced. This was all he needed. She'd only been here an hour or so and she was already coming up with new names – but how could she have dug one up so soon? She'd also ignored the best lead yet without even listening to it.

"I've been reading her CV. What do you know about Joseph Crossley?"

"He's our local MP," said Tim, keen to impress a City detective. "He's a Conservative. He was elected in 1997 when there was a Labour landslide and again in 2001. He's up for re-election next month, but he's bound to get in. The Tories could put a sheep up round here and no matter what the other parties do, it'd get voted in."

"There's a picture of him on the wall in Ms Hopwood's office," said Harrison, anxious to show her that he'd been systematic in his search. "I'm sure I've seen her in town with him."

"He was a long-standing Labour councillor before that," said Tim, eagerly. "He changed sides about two years before he stood as an MP."

"He was involved peripherally in a murder a couple of years ago," said Harrison, considering Tim's history lesson unnecessary when he'd more relevant information to impart. "You remember, Tim. A young man was found dead in an alley behind the Alpaca nightclub. He'd been strangled."

"What's the correlation?" asked Miller, unable to see any connection.

"Crossley owns the Alpaca. It's named after some kind of camel. Apparently he's farming them somewhere up in the hills. He brought them in after he'd been to Peru."

"Why did he go to Peru?"

"On a business exchange trip organised by the town council. He's well in with everyone around here. Storbury's twinned with Piura."

"Where's that?"

"Tim?"

"Up in the north, ma'am," he said with absolute confidence.

"How was he implicated in the murder?" asked Miller still unsure where this was leading.

"I said only *peripherally*," replied Harrison. "We suspected that drugs might be involved in the murder and the club might be a distribution point, but we never proved anything."

"You said 'we'. Were you involved?"

"*Only peripherally*," repeated Harrison wearily. "I was a sergeant then and I interviewed Crossley. Smooth as silk. He co-operated fully and we found no trace of any drugs in the club, not even in the toilets."

"Is that all?" she asked, unsure whether Harrison had any more to add.

"Well, I was thinking. You supposed that curare might have been used to knock Ms Hopwood out, didn't you?"

"No I didn't. I said the curare – and we don't know whether it was yet – could have been used to keep her awake but immobile."

"Yes, OK. That's the connection. Curare comes from South America!"

"But does it come from Peru?"

"Check it out on the Internet, Tim. This could be important."

Tim went over to the police laptop on the table by the window. It was a few minutes before he found anything interesting and by that time both Harrison and Miller were impatiently looking over his shoulders.

"Curare comes from the rainforests," he said at last. "Mainly from the Amazon region. No, hold it…crude curare is found in the Peruvian rainforests as well."

"I think we should have a few words with Mr Crossley," said Miller when Tim had read out the last pages he'd found.

"I'm not so sure," said Harrison cautiously. "It's a long shot. Why should he want to kill her? He was obviously her friend. Our murderer's more likely to be one of the four we've identified already. Probably Todd."

"Crossley could have supplied the drug," suggested Tim. "Even inadvertently. I agree with DCI Miller. He must be involved in some way – like he probably was in that other murder in Storbury."

"We got someone for that," sighed Harrison. "He's doing life in Strangeways. It was an open and shut case. The lad even confessed. There was no connection with Crossley whatsoever. It happened outside his nightclub, that's all. Both the victim and the murderer were from Leicester. The murdered boy was knocking off the other one's girlfriend.

Simple as that. It wasn't even drugs related, although the murderer had form for dealing back in Leicester."

"How do we know if he's in Storbury?" asked Tim, "Shouldn't he be in London?"

"We can check," said Miller. "If he is, then he's in the clear, but I've got a funny feeling about him nonetheless. The South American link is too much of a coincidence."

"I think we should start with our four from here?" said Harrison. "I want to start with Jones, then Head, then Wallace, and finally Todd."

"Why Todd last?" said Tim. "He's our main suspect."

"I want to make him sweat."

"Add Crossley to the list," ordered Miller tartly. "Tim, check him out please. He must be connected to the curare somehow. If he's in London, I want to speak to him anyway. Better still, ask him to phone me. I'll inform him of Ms Hopwood's death and then ask him to come up here. He might remember if he's ever had any curare and, if so, who he might have sold some to."

"Before you do that," said Harrison. "Ask one of the uniform boys to bring Smith in here."

Tim hesitated. He looked at Harrison and Miller and then he said courageously:

"I've changed my mind. I think you're wrong about Crossley, ma'am. You're building a case against him on pure supposition, starting with the curare. As you said, we don't even know if it was used. If he's in London the whole thing falls apart."

Miller sat down again and looked angrily at Tim.

"Go and ring London and leave the thinking to me," she barked, brushing away specks of dust from her trousers again.

CHAPTER 30

Christmas and New Year Break 1984/5

It's often said that there's nothing worse than being alone at Christmas with only gloom and despondency for company. It's a time when everyone else seems to be enjoying themselves and the spirit of the season is goodwill to all men and women. There's no escape from the collective joy and merriment unless you shut yourself away and pretend it's not happening, but in the middle of a large city the chances of doing that are negligible unless you're deaf and blind. You have to eat so you have to procure food supplies and in 1984 that meant going out shopping and seeing all the ornamented trees, the lavishly overindulgent decorations and the permanently smiling faces. The first thing you notice is that it's harder to buy for one than for two and not much cheaper unless you get it all separately from different shops and stores and that necessitates having to maintain the façade of bonhomie over and over again; it's quicker and easier at a supermarket. Then there's the lack of companionship to cope with and no one to talk to when you come home, no one to share your booty or the account of your escapades in acquiring it. Worst of all, when your wife has just run off with your best friend, no one calls you up to chat, even to sympathise in case they're accused of taking sides. There's no longer anyone to give special presents to, even the ones you bought months ago and hid in a secret place, and you're sure that you're not going to receive many, if any at all. It's a desolate time and you can't wait for it all to end, and then it's cold, miserable and dark midwinter again.

When Cassandra and Stan finally recognised that it was Mort and not a burglar that was sitting in the dark in the middle of the staircase, they hurriedly got dressed and left the house. Mort only knew that they'd gone when he heard the front door click shut. It wasn't even a dramatic exit and he never heard Stan's car start and move away. When it finally dawned on him, sitting alone in the dark of the kitchen, that his wife had been having it off with his best friend in his own house and in his own bed, he couldn't work out what he was expected to do. He'd joked with her in the past that if he ever caught her with another man, he'd simply say sorry and excuse himself. Yet reality was different and a lot more difficult. He hadn't anticipated she'd leave him immediately. At first he hoped he might have dreamt it all, but he'd heard the noise coming from upstairs and he knew that what he'd seen had to be real. The next thing that forced its way into his semi-consciousness was that he might no longer have a wife, and that any say in the matter had been entirely taken away from him. It was now her decision and presumably Stan's also. He even considered what he'd have done if they'd decided to stay. Could *he* remain in a house where another man was sleeping with his wife? Would they want *him* to leave? He hadn't reached the stage where either pleading with her not to go or instigating a violent confrontation came into the equation, when he realised that they'd moved out. Swallowed up by the cold night air. Gone. Vanished.

After he became fully aware that he was now alone, a practical matter entered his head. Where was he going to sleep? Certainly not in *that* bed. He was slowly sobering up but he was dog tired and he didn't want to spend the night on the settee. It was too cold. It would have to be the spare room. He shambled wearily upstairs and got into the ornate, brass bed fully clothed and closed his eyes. No matter how hard he tried he couldn't drift off into unconsciousness since his brain wouldn't stop repeating the same picture over and over again. Eventually he must have fallen asleep because the next thing he remembered was the sound of the telephone ringing. He stumbled downstairs, still groggy, to hear Cassandra's friend Suzie's voice. He heard it telling him in a matter of fact way that she was coming round at lunchtime to collect Cassandra's clothes and other things of intimate value, and she hoped that he'd co-operate and not try to stop her or do anything silly. He grunted back that she could take what she liked and hung up. It was nine thirty and he had over two hours to get himself together. He'd have a wash then he'd make a list of his demands.

He surprised himself with this strange, new sensation; he wanted some kind of immediate retribution, even though he wasn't sure in what form this would manifest itself. The first message he wanted to send via Suzie was that he wanted his *ex*-wife's house keys. That would suffice as a preliminary salvo. What had been troubling him most was that she'd be able to come in whenever she pleased when he went back to work, and he didn't fancy her poking around in *his* house and leaving doors unlocked and appliances switched on. It made him angrier just thinking about it. She had to be punished and he knew what it was that would hurt her most. He would refuse to speak to her ever again. He'd always told her everything that was happening in his head and that's how she'd controlled him. When she'd been listening to all his many recent dilemmas, she'd been planning her next assignation with Stan. Or was it his own self-obsession that had made him blind to what was going on around him ever since he'd applied for that job at Storbury? That's why Stan was so keen for him to go for it in the first place, that's why Stan had read out the advert for it, and that's why Stan had convinced him it was worth taking financially by subtly trying to put him off. Stan had wanted him out of the way.

When Suzie arrived with two empty suitcases, she looked very uneasy. She said nothing other than that she needed half an hour and went straight upstairs. Mort went into the kitchen, ostensibly to make something to eat but really he was trying to look unconcerned. He filled the kettle and decided to make a sandwich. He was still pottering about when Suzie reappeared in the doorway, and he offered her a coffee which she declined. He was about to ask her to tell Cassandra to return her keys, when Suzie held up her hand and jangled them at him. As usual Cassandra had read his mind.

"She's not coming back, Mort," said Suzie as she turned to leave. "She's going away with Stan. She told me to tell you that she'll sort everything out financially in a few months."

"Merry Christmas," said Mort cheerfully as he bit into his sandwich.

She smiled and thanked him but didn't return his insincerity; she knew he was putting on a show for her sake. She simply said goodbye and left, shutting the door behind her as quietly as the two fugitives had done the night before.

"I wouldn't have her back after what she's done to me," he shouted but she didn't hear him.

The following Tuesday was Christmas Day and Mort decided to ring his parents to break the news to them. He wasn't going to do the same for Cassandra's parents – that was her responsibility. He'd spent each of the previous four days moping, shopping, lying around and moping again, reading, watching television and drinking, roughly in that order, and he decided to make the call in the morning while he was sober.

"Eeh, our Cassandra, and at Christmas," he heard his mother's say in her thick Yorkshire accent when he told her the news. "You'll 'ave to go get 'er back…"

There was a muffled rustling on the other end of line after which he heard his father's voice.

"Are you all right, lad?"

"Yes, dad."

"Pay no attention to your mother. As long as *you're* all right, that's all that matters. Do you want to come and stay with us?"

"No, dad, I'm not spoiling your Christmas as well."

"That doesn't matter. I've 'ad plenty of good ones. Shall we come down and stay with you?"

"It's best you stay where you are. I'm OK. I'm managing on my own."

"Well, don't go running after 'er and make sure you change the locks. I'm saying nowt else…for the time being."

"Thanks, dad. Merry Christmas to you both."

"Merry Christmas from both of us too and your mother says you 'ave to ring if there's owt you need."

The rest of the day passed quietly. He had a modest dinner but it looked like the real thing except that most of the trimmings that Cassandra would have made were missing. He opened the bottle of Bollinger champagne he'd bought in a rash moment when they were out shopping together and when she complained about the price, he'd told her that she was worth every penny of it. It was a special gift for her because she'd helped him survive in the mad house that was Storbury College. Instead he proposed a toast to himself and the hope that he'd soon be in another job – any job away from that place. He no longer felt any affection for her; it had been replaced by a malevolence towards her and Stan that he couldn't shake off. The psychological scars of being discarded by a woman he'd been in love with for so long would take a long time to heal. He'd learned the hard way that however close you think you are to someone, you never really know them.

Gradually he became more resilient as the days crawled by but his new mental toughness came at a price. He began to live in an imaginary world where inanimate objects became real and he imagined that even these were out to get him. Perhaps this is what had always lain behind his neuroses that his beloved counsellor had somehow patched up for him. He'd always dreaded something terrible happening and now that 'something' *was* happening, he didn't know how to fight it without her. He began to shout at the furniture because it was old and ugly and he constantly ranted at the TV for being "so bloody annoying". He hadn't seen a real human being since Suzie had been round to collect Cassandra's things, and he ignored the telephone even though it might be his parents who were calling. The world had started to revolve around him and he didn't want to stop it. He was in a place where he was being forced to choose between truth and delusion, a place of his own making where reality and fantasy blended together because it was better than a life of despair, and it wasn't a difficult decision to make as he was never sober enough to make it. What troubled him most was that he had no friends. He'd invested his friendships in Cassandra and the boys from the technical college and both had betrayed him in equal measure. He was alone in a hostile world – only his parents were left to care about him. Life had to some extent come full circle. Someone – no, many people – would have to pay sooner or later. For the present Cassandra and Stan would do.

On New Year's Eve everything changed. He received a letter from Cassandra's mother.

'Dear Mortimer

Cassandra has telephoned to inform us that she has left you. We are both very sorry indeed to hear this news but, to be honest, we knew it was coming from the day she told us you were to marry, so it has not come as too much of a shock. She did not give many reasons but she did say that she was tired of your moods and that you could be depressed at nothing at all for weeks. We have never doubted that your working class background has not prepared you to live in a middle class world, and so it is with some relief to us that she is free of you.

We hope that there will be no acrimony between the two of you and luckily for you both in the circumstances there are no children, so it will be a clean break. Since Cassandra did not say where she is living at present, it will be no use you contacting us to find out,

if the thought ever crosses your mind. She says that she has found
another partner and they wish to start a new life abroad.

Yours sincerely

Dorothy Hamilton'

Mort didn't know whether to laugh or weep but the letter transformed him. It was as if he'd woken from an insane nightmare and the dizziness of sleep was preventing him from seeing clearly or realising where he was. He looked around and found he was in the sitting room surrounded by brimming ashtrays, empty bottles and crushed beer cans. The curtains were drawn shut and the TV was on but he couldn't remember why. He saw a wild face he didn't recognise staring back at him from the mirror above the fireplace, with a half-grown beard and disheveled hair. Then it all came rushing back to him and he knew he was through the worst. Whatever had been going on had stopped as suddenly as it had started. Cassandra, through her mother, had done him one last favour. She had, as she'd have put it, "solved it for him again".

Whatever he felt for her now wasn't love. That woman had gone forever and had been replaced by another who was a stranger, an impostor, a barefaced liar, and, most of all, a shameless adulteress. He would remember her as she was while they were together but that person had died. She would exist as nothing more than a fond, distant memory. He'd survived and, despite the madness of the last few missing days, he knew he was stronger for it. He'd become his own man.

CHAPTER 31

12 April 2005: 3pm

"I didn't do it, if that's what you're trying to imply," squawked Mike Smith more in anguish than self defence.

He'd been quickly disconcerted by the situation he found himself in when Miller and Harrison had started asking questions, even though Miller had told him that it wasn't a formal interview and he wasn't under caution. He was simply helping them with their enquiries in order to eliminate him. Nevertheless he wasn't used to high pressure situations like this, except when he was behind with his deadline to publish the annual college prospectus.

"I'll tell you where I was last night," he continued, loosening his tie and searching his pockets for something with which to mop the sweat from his forehead. "I was with Penny Castle round at her house. She shares it with Lucy Carlton."

"Why didn't you say so before?" asked Miller who was playing bad cop.

"I'm married with two children."

"You're a stupid boy. What's more, you're a liar as well."

"I'm telling the truth! Ask Penny. She'll back me up."

"I might ask Lucy first. She must have seen you there."

"No, she didn't. I slipped in quietly while she was having a shower. Later she went out somewhere with some man or other. When she came back, Penny and I were asleep in bed."

"What about this morning? Didn't she see you then?"

"No, they both left before me."

"What about your car? Where did you leave it?"

"They live on a new estate in a semi. I parked it a few houses away. It's a red Volkswagen. It doesn't stand out around there. I let myself out of the house when they'd gone and came straight here. I got changed in the gents."

"You're very well organised, Mr Smith. How do we know you didn't come *straight here* and kill Ariadne Hopwood?"

Harrison could feel that Mike was beginning to crumple.

"I see you shaved," he said, stroking his chin as if to point out the absence of bristles.

"I keep an electric razor in my office," replied Mike. "It's useful for late appointments with clients."

He was visibly calming down at what sounded like someone believing him.

"What time did you arrive here this morning?"

"About a quarter to nine, as I told the other detective."

Harrison searched through the notes that Tim had made and found Penny's address.

"She lives fifteen or so minutes away. She says she left home at eight and got here at eight fifteen. Why did it take you half an hour to drive here?"

"I didn't leave right away. I didn't want her neighbours to see me leave immediately after she and Lucy had gone."

"Why ever not?" Miller cut in. "What's it do with them who you're having illicit sex with?"

"You never know," replied Mike trying his hand at humour. "Someone might be acquainted my wife. Storbury's a very small world!"

"Have you any idea who might have wanted Ms Hopwood dead?" asked Harrison, quite sure that Jones wasn't their man.

He put his notebook on the desk and leaned back in his chair.

"No, I've no idea," replied Mike beginning to relax. "All I know is what the rest of the managers know. Ariadne was planning a reshuffle and some of the older ones might have felt threatened."

"Who, for instance?"

"Well, the men for a start. Penny told me in confidence that Ariadne didn't want any old men working here."

Miller couldn't stop herself laughing at the thought of what sounded to her like middle-aged, male paranoia, but Harrison carried on.

"That puts you at risk too, doesn't it?" he said shrewdly, remembering that Mike's initials had been on Ariadne's proscribed list.

"Yes, I suppose it does. I assumed she meant academic managers – the Heads."

Harrison looked at his watch, then at Miller. He was satisfied that he'd obtained what he wanted from the interview, and he wanted her to give her approval to finish.

"Any more questions, ma'am," he said formally.

She shook her head.

"OK, you can go. You can make a statement later. Please stay in your office until you're contacted again."

When Mike had gone, Miller glared at Harrison.

"You were soft with him considering he's your main suspect."

"We can't be too hard on anyone at this stage. As soon as we put too much pressure on, they'll be shouting for a solicitor and we'll have to continue down at the station. Besides, he's more scared of his wife."

"Why didn't you ask him if he had a reason to kill Ms Hopwood?"

"I'd written him off after his tale of sex in the semis. It's obviously true. He'll be crapping himself thinking his wife's going to find out he's been playing away. Shall I go tell him that we're bringing her in for questioning?"

"You rotten bastard! I don't want a suicide on my hands on top of everything else!"

Harrison stood up and, chuckling to himself, made his way to the door.

"Naylor," he shouted and beckoned to the constable who was standing outside the locked door to the executive suite. "Where's Tim?"

The Hulk turned round and pointed to his right. "Down the corridor," he mouthed slowly. "In the cubby hole."

Harrison shouted at the door of the store room that had once been his makeshift office. It was slightly open and Tim's head appeared as if by magic in the narrow gap."

"Yes, guv?" he shouted back.

"What are you doing in there?"

"I've got to sit somewhere, sir. I'm getting the case file up to date."

"Did you ring Crossley?"

"I got through to his office. He's sitting on a committee this afternoon. They said they'd get him to ring back as soon as he's finished."

"He *is* in London after all! Was he there yesterday?"

Tim came out of the store room and began to saunter towards Harrison, talking as he walked.

"According to his movements he was. They looked in his diary…"

"Who are *they*?"

"His secretary. Very nice lady. She said he'd a breakfast meeting this morning."

Harrison scowled as Tim approached him.

"Another one bites the dust," he said sourly. "Two down, three to go."

"Have you finished with Smith?"

"Yes, he said he was having it off with Penny Castle all last night."

"The lucky bugger. I'd like to get my hands on those knockers."

Harrison scowled again.

"Go and get Richard Head. He's next on the list."

As Tim went off, Harrison followed him through the door, and tapped on the Hulk's shoulder.

"Go down to the canteen and get us two cups of coffee, please," he said as the Hulk turned round.

"The door will be unguarded, sir," replied the Hulk.

"I'll leave the ops room door open. It shouldn't take you long and the outer door will be locked."

"How do you want your coffees, sir?"

"Bring some of those cartons of milk and some sachets of sugar and sweetener. We'll sort out who takes what when you get back."

When Harrison returned to Miller he found her looking at Ariadne's exercise book.

"We didn't ask him if he knew what 'Mortimer – then prep meeting' was," she said looking annoyed.

"He wouldn't have a clue," replied Harrison, sure of his ground. "It's obviously something between her and Todd. We'll find out soon what it means."

"It's all a bit too slapdash, John. I'll take the lead with the next chap. Richard Head isn't it?"

Harrison nodded. "Whatever you say, Carol."

As they stood there, they heard the door to the executive suite click shut.

"That'll be Naylor with our coffees," said Harrison rubbing his hands, but no one entered the incident room.

They waited for about half a minute before he went out into the corridor. There was no one there.

"Did you hear that door shut?" he said when he came back in.

"I heard a noise," she said, shrugging her shoulders. "What of it?"

"I thought it was Naylor."

"It must have been a ghost!"

They both laughed although he didn't find the mystery as funny as she did. Then they heard the door click shut again.

"That'll be him now," said Harrison expectantly but again no one appeared in the doorway.

They both laughed again and stood there waiting as if uncertain what was going to happen next. About a minute later they heard what sounded like the door closing for a third time and in walked the Hulk, followed by Tim.

"Did you pass anybody on your way in?" asked Harrison.

"There were a couple of young women chatting at the reception desk outside," said Tim, as the Hulk passed each of them a hot, disposable plastic cup.

"I asked him to get me one as well," said Tim. "I met him on his way to the canteen."

"I took the liberty of ordering one for myself, sir," grinned the Hulk slyly. "I'll drink it outside at my station."

As the Hulk left, Tim turned to Miller.

"Bad news, ma'am. Richard Head's not in his office and a couple of stragglers from the Engineering department said they hadn't seen him since this morning. He must have run off."

"Damnation!" she screamed. "Bloody Hell. What's going on here?"

"Go round to his house sharpish, Tim," said Harrison, ignoring her angry outburst. "I bet he's gone there. Take a couple of men with you."

"I hope for your sake he has," snapped Miller. "If he hasn't, he could be anywhere by now".

CHAPTER 32

January-March 1985

Mort arrived at Storbury on the first day of the spring term as a man reborn. He set off early enough to negotiate the hazards and holdups of his long drive and he sang all the way there. Strangely, the Vigilantes seemed to have disappeared altogether. He was wearing a suit for the first time since his interview, and he'd bought a briefcase in the January sales for good measure. He strolled from the car park into the main building and wished everyone a cheery good morning as he made his way to the staff room, where he found Junkin talking to Jeff Shaw in the doorway.

"Good morning to you, gentlemen," he beamed. "Happy New Year! Did you have a good Christmas?"

"I see you've changed sides," said Junkin ignoring the question and raising his eyebrows. "Whatever's come over you?"

"You sound like Ebenezer Scrooge after his conversion!" joked Shaw.

Mort laughed out loud as if he'd never heard anything so funny.

"You've bought a briefcase!" shouted Junkin, loud enough for the others in the room to stop what they were doing and look up to see what was going on.

They hadn't heard such frivolity so early in the day for a long time, not from Junkin at any rate.

"Join me for coffee at ten if you're free, *Mortimer.*"

"Thank you, *Simon*. I'd love to." Mort replied brashly. "I want to discuss Communication Studies courses. I'm thinking of introducing them from next September, and we'll need to start the validation process as soon as possible, if you agree."

The rest of the day passed just as serenely. Junkin readily approved all Mort's ideas and invited him to lunch. Mort asked graciously to be excused – he'd a previous engagement, he said mendaciously; he wasn't yet wholly prepared to socialise with a man he still found arrogant and foolish. His afternoon English Literature class went surprisingly well, and his students remarked to him that they'd never seen him so buoyant. When he drove home in the evening, singing and whistling as he went, he remembered that he'd intended to seek out Ariadne and ask if she'd had a good holiday, but he hadn't seen her. He'd forgotten even to look for her, too carried away with his newfound happiness to be concerned. There's always tomorrow, he mused, as he put his foot down and impetuously overtook a slowly moving truck that once he'd have hesitated to pass in case he met something coming the other way and hit it head on.

His life since the first day of 1985 had involved a series of important decisions as he came to terms with the idea that if he wanted a less stressful existence at Storbury, he had to accept it for what it was for a while longer. Similarly, when he arrived home that evening, he didn't miss Cassandra. He found living alone gave him more time for everything, and he could please himself what he did and when he did it. There were no compromises to make, and he no longer had to keep anyone entertained other than himself. He cleared out every trace of his former wife that Suzie hadn't taken but he didn't throw anything away; he put it all out of sight under the spare bed. That included most of her books, records and photographs and all of the clothes, perfumes, make-up, trinkets and bathroom products that she'd left. Cassandra had made no claims on anything. She hadn't even contacted him, and he no longer cared where she was or what she might be doing. He felt the same about Stan and the rest of his old associates from the technical college. They could all go to blazes. He also changed the lock on the front door.

His contentment lasted for weeks. He didn't worry about the delays on his early morning journey since he gave himself enough time to arrive comfortably before the nine o'clock start. This made him more relaxed for the rest of the day and he found no problem too insurmountable that he couldn't solve with a smile on his face. Most things went as he planned them and naturally this made him more popular with everyone, even Kettleman, for whom he occasionally made a cup of tea. The only person who seemed to avoid him was Ariadne, but he hardly noticed that she no longer came to sit with him or ask him anything about teaching. Whenever she did, she seemed very preoccupied, as though she was struggling with some unfathomable quandary that she couldn't discuss. He concluded that she was worrying about her hasty decision to get married, and he felt he was in no position to involve himself in such matters after all he'd endured recently.

He was now able to separate work from his personal life. He hadn't told anyone at the College that Cassandra had left him because it wasn't affecting his conduct and therefore it was of no concern to them. He'd learned to be superficially even tempered enough to take everything in his stride during the day and he found plenty to do when he was by himself in the evenings. All was going well again and by the end of March he'd accomplished most of what he'd set out to do. His team meetings were well attended, and an atmosphere of willing and co-operative diligence had replaced the indolent cynicism that had pervaded previously – so much so that collective ambition was outstripping the financial resources available to provide it. This was also of considerable benefit to the students to the extent that in the short period that Mort had been in charge, English and especially Art were gaining a deservedly first-rate reputation that they hadn't enjoyed for many years. Occasionally he remembered that Alice had started to tell him about her dogged conscientiousness when she became a senior lecturer, but he didn't dwell on it. He knew how her story had ended and he was determined that the same thing wouldn't happen to him.

* * *

One Saturday towards the end of March Mort ran into Suzie in the city centre. He'd gone there supposedly for a change to his regular weekly expedition to his local supermarket but actually he felt he needed to spread his wings further afield. For the last three months he'd spent most of his time existing in two bubbles – home and college – connected by a tube that was his drive to and from work and punctuated only on Friday evenings when he did his shopping. It was Suzie who approached him after she'd attracted his attention by waving at him from across a busy street. Although he knew she was one of Cassandra's best friends, he'd never seen much of her, and he'd have walked past her if the street had been empty.

She didn't look like the sort of woman that Cassandra would associate with. Whereas Cassandra was flamboyant and extroverted, Suzie was dowdy and unassuming. She seemed to be dressed in the same clothes whenever he met her, and this time she was carrying the same scuffed brown leather shoulder bag and wearing the same pinky-white anorak and faded blue jeans she'd worn when she'd collected Cassandra's things. Her long, blonde hair was as usual tied in a pony tail at the back and she wore no make-up which made her look drearier than she was; on closer inspection anyone would've observed that she was quite pretty and, if they'd have taken the trouble, they'd have advised her gently to try to make more of herself.

"Hello, Mort," she said as soon as she was close enough for him to hear her. "How are you?"

"I'm fine," he replied, uncertain whether he wanted to prolong the conversation.

"You look great!" she smiled in return.

He wanted to think of some cliché to repay the compliment, but he noticed that she was blushing and he didn't want to walk away without asking how she was too.

"I'm fine," she laughed and went an even deeper shade of red. "Do you fancy a coffee or something? I've one or two things to tell you."

"If they're about Cassandra, I don't want to know!" he growled back sharply.

"Oh," she sighed, crossing her legs and looking awkwardly down at the pavement. "I thought you'd be interested to learn where she's got to."

"I'm sorry," he said contritely. "I didn't mean to be rude. If you must know, I don't give a tinker's where she might be."

"What have you been doing with yourself?" she asked delicately, hoping that the question wouldn't make him even more irritated.

"Let's go for that coffee," he said and he laughed. "Perhaps we do have something to talk about after all!"

As they looked for a café, he saw that she was smaller than he remembered, although she was well above average height. Possibly it was because he'd only seen her sporadically before and he'd never stood next to her. Or was it the role she'd played in Cassandra's leaving that had made him assume she was an evil accomplice and consequently much taller? Yet he knew that Cassandra had chosen Suzie to collect her things because he'd hardly ever met her.

They soon found a small coffee shop with lots of empty tables, and he startled the elderly waitress as he ordered two cappuccinos before they sat down. Suzie undid her anorak to reveal a tight, grey woolen sweater and instantly he was reminded of feelings he'd not had for a long time. He hoped she hadn't noticed his surprise and what he'd been looking at. To his relief she wasn't paying him any attention but fumbling with her handbag.

"I'll have to buy a new one," she said as she tugged at the zip. "This thing keeps on locking itself shut."

He offered to help and opened the bag straightaway.

"Thank you," she said as he passed it back to her. "You seem to have the knack!"

He wanted to say something like he'd had lots of practice with Cassandra's handbags but that would bring them back to the delicate subject he'd absolutely no wish to discuss.

The only other people in the café, a young couple who'd been holding hands as they whispered secretively to each other, left their table and walked out leaving Mort and Suzie with the place to themselves except for the waitress who was about to bring them their coffees.

"We get a lot of love birds in here," said the waitress as she placed their drinks on the table.

Mort and Suzie smiled back at her in the way that people do when they don't want to start a conversation with a stranger. They both took a sip of their drink and it was Suzie who broke the ice, although rather more inelegantly than she intended.

"How've you been keeping?"

"I'm coping. In fact, I'm doing much more than that. I'm thriving!"

"Cassandra was certain that you'd have a nervous breakdown!"

"That shows how little she knew about me!"

She put her hand across the table and gently squeezed his arm.

"Don't get angry, Mort," she said soothingly. "It was a rotten thing she did. Just before Christmas. I felt terrible having to come and pick up her clothes."

"Then why did you do it?" he asked morosely but he didn't move her hand.

"Would you rather she'd have come – or Stan?"

"Yes, you're right, I suppose," he frowned.

"I've had a postcard from her," she said, deciding to risk depressing him even more.

She watched his face for further signs of annoyance, but he kept on staring at his coffee. She took this as a sign she could continue.

"She's in Majorca with Stan."

"You might as well give me the gory details," he said, resigned to letting her finish what she was obviously set on telling him.

"Stan quit his job," she said, taking her hand from his arm. "He simply walked away. I think he sent a letter or something. They've gone to join a hippy nudist colony there!"

Mort screeched with surprise – so loud that the waitress turned round from the counter to see if anything untoward was going on.

"I see it all now," he shouted as he recalled how a naked Cassandra had made him breakfast before his first day at Storbury. "I remember her telling me about Stan's wonderful summer holiday in Majorca."

"She joined a naturist club at the end of August to see if she liked being in the nude all day," added Suzie when he'd calmed down. "She used to go with Stan."

"Did you go too?" he asked. "She used to leave me notes saying she was out with you."

"No, I didn't go," she replied. "I don't think I've got the sort of body to be an exhibitionist. To tell you the truth I didn't see much of her…"

Her face flushed as she realised what she'd just said.

"You know what I mean – after you started at Storbury. We did meet briefly once or twice but she told me you were having a lot of problems and needed a lot of comfort and support, so I assumed she was busy – with you."

"She played us off one against the other, Suzie," he said bitterly. "She used us both and all the time she was frolicking in her birthday suit with my old mate Stan the Man."

He was pleased that she'd been determined enough to tell him about Cassandra and Stan, but he was puzzled why she felt she had to. Perhaps she thought he needed to be told because secretly he was missing his wife, and she wanted to make him see the pointlessness of it all. Or perhaps she needed to find out what state he was in so that she could report back to Cassandra. He sensed he might be falling into some kind of trap whichever way he looked at it, and he knew that up till then their exchanges had been focused on him. He wasn't satisfied that he'd persuaded her that he no longer cared about Cassandra, and he still had to convince her that he'd sorted himself out after the break-up. He had to prove that he was no longer the self-absorbed man she'd have heard so much about by shifting the attention to her.

"As you can see," he said, looking directly into her eyes. "I'm OK. I'm through it and I'm a stronger, better, happier man for it. She did me the biggest favour she could've done by leaving me and your little story has rounded everything off nicely. Thank you. But that's enough about me."

Her eyes widened as she felt the effect of his piercing stare.

"I don't know much about you at all," he continued, now smiling and looking past her at the waitress who was sitting quietly on a stool at the counter and reading a paperback book. "I've only met you…let me see… twice…three times before, is it? And you never spoke much to me – usually to Cassandra."

"Once I came to your house with John and we all went off to that party in…oh, where was it?"

"I remember," he interrupted. "Nice bloke, John – how is he?"

"We split up a year or so ago," she said, almost apologetically. "He wasn't that nice, though. He was having an affair with…"

"Cassandra?"

She blushed yet again. "What do you want me to say?"

"Anything you like!"

"Yes, it was her."

"And you still remained friends?"

"Who? John and me or Cassandra and me?"

"Either…both."

"Yes with both of them."

"You're an impressive woman."

He wanted to say "stupid" but it would have ended their dialogue.

"Not really. I was seeing Stan at the time."

He exploded with laughter once again, but the waitress didn't look up. She was enjoying eavesdropping on Suzie's disclosures.

"How long did that last?" he asked, knowing what the answer would be.

She sniffed and looked past him at her reflection in the window.

"A few months."

He laughed out loud again, this time for much longer, but Suzie wasn't smiling; she was staring intently at him and gripping his arm.

"You know what we should do, don't you?"

He understood instantly. Oh perfidy, thy name is Suzie, he thought. And Cassandra. Even Ariadne. You're all the bloody same.

"What's that?" was all he could think of to say.

"Your place or mine?" she said, still not smiling.

"Does it matter?"

"I suppose not. Do you fancy me?"

"Does it matter?" he joked.

"I suppose not," she echoed. "But it would help if you did."

He didn't reply and they sat in silence for a few seconds until he got up to pay.

"That's one pound twenty," grinned the waitress. "I hope you both enjoy the rest of the day."

CHAPTER 33

12 April 2005: 3.30pm

The two clicking sounds that Harrison and Miller imagined they heard were real. The security door *had* opened and closed twice. What they didn't see as they waited optimistically for their drinks was a young woman in spectacles creep stealthily up to the store room door, remove as many cardboard folders as she could carry without dropping any, and tiptoe back down the corridor and out again. What Tim and the Hulk didn't see as they each concentrated on carrying two hot coffees across the foyer back to the incident room was the same young woman place the folders on the counter of the reception desk and strike up a conversation with another young woman they knew only as the receptionist. As they passed they nodded at the second women as they neared the locked security door.

"Could you let us in, please?" asked Tim, turning round slightly self-consciously.

"I don't know the combination," the young, bespectacled woman answered without turning round.

"I'll let them in, Helen," said the receptionist as she lifted the hinged section in the counter and walked over to the door.

"I'll be off then," said Helen when she was certain that both the policemen had their backs to her.

"Thank you," said Tim as she tapped in the numbers. "You'll have to change the combination now, I suppose."

"You're asking how I know it, aren't you?"

"Well?"

"Hugh Jones gave it to me this lunchtime. He said that there were bound to be comings and goings all day and there might be no one to open and close this damn thing."

"Do you ever open this door to strangers?"

The receptionist shook her head.

"No, I have to call the site technicians as a rule."

* * *

Mort had finally agreed that Helen would be the best person to purloin the mysterious files from the store room opposite Ariadne's office. He warned her that she was on her own if it ended in tears and he called Gordon and Barry as witnesses.

"It's a hanging offence in Storbury," quipped Gordon. "It's the same as driving without due care and attention."

"The combination is 1-6-2-6," said Mort. "Don't tell the cops I gave you it."

"Give them name, rank and serial number," grinned Gordon. "Even if they torture you."

"I'll say *you* forced me to do it, Gordon," replied Helen, as she opened the door to leave.

The three men sat in silence whilst Helen was away on her quest, looking down at the floor for most of the time, occasionally looking up and smiling at each other. Once Mort got up and looked out of the window. It was still raining. Then all of a sudden Helen rushed in breathless, with about a dozen of the files he was hoping for.

"Mission accomplished!" she yelled triumphantly.

"Well done, you beautiful creature!" shouted Gordon clapping his hands in genuine applause.

"Flattery will get you nowhere, pal," she panted, and she dropped the folders in a heap on Mort's desk.

"How many did you get?" asked Mort.

"A generous armful," grinned Helen. "Precisely what you asked for."

Mort picked one from the top of the pile and saw immediately what it was.

"This is a student folder from 1984/5," he whispered. "That's strange. What would the Principal want with these?"

He sat down at his desk and began to read the contents of each file. After a few minutes during which his three accomplices eagerly waited for an answer, he looked up and shook his head.

"I still can't quite grasp why she'd want to retrieve them from the archive. Each one of these files contains the student's history from the day he or she applied to study here. There are copies of all their reports, their marks and their references et cetera. All on paper in those days. Everything seems to be in order."

"How do you know she had anything to do with them?" asked Barry. "Someone might be clearing out the archive."

"A little bird told me…"

"Had she got anything to hide?"

"One or two things," continued Mort. "There were the marking irregularities, but they happened the year before I came here."

"What sort of irregularities?"

"There was a problem about how the English Language mode three grades had been awarded and these files look like they date from that period."

"What's it got to do with Ariadne?" asked Helen.

"She was in on it."

"How do you know?" asked Barry.

"I sorted it out. She and the section head were trying to inflate the grades to make it look like they were super-teachers."

"Isn't it all water under the bridge?"

"Of course it is – to us. For some reason she must have wanted to get rid of these files, or something in them, something that's in her past which could've embarrassed her in her present position."

"Surely it's far too long ago?"

"They all have feet of clay, Barry."

"Yes, but…"

Helen suddenly perked up again.

"Do you think we'll be in the Sunday papers?"

"Maybe someone's blackmailing her, Mort?" said Barry.

"*Was*," Gordon reminded him. "Whoever it was won't get anything now!"

"Is that why you did her in, Mort?" teased Helen, but he didn't smile. "You're the only one who knows anything about it – whatever *it* is!"

"Let's just say *it* is interesting," said Mort quietly.

"Mort," she said quizzically, her head on one side. "How did you know the files were there?"

"Ah," he replied, sucking in air between his teeth. "I wondered when you were going to ask me that."

He tapped his nose.

"Let's say for the moment that it's none of your business."

"Oh go on," she begged, like a schoolgirl asking her father to let her go to a party, but he shook his head.

He picked up the folders and placed them carefully under his desk, making sure that they wouldn't topple over onto his feet. As he sat up, he saw that he had another email from Richard Head, sent ten minutes earlier at three o'clock. He was about to click it open when Helen shouted across to him.

"Don't start reading emails," she insisted. "Not at a time like this!"

"Shush," he said, waiting for the email to open itself.

"I think I *will* go home," said Barry, hoping that Mort wouldn't think he was sulking. "I'm tired and I don't think I can be of any use just sitting here."

"Me too," said Gordon as he got up to leave.

"Thanks for staying," said Mort, looking away from his computer screen. "I really appreciate your support. When this is all over we'll all go out and celebrate – and I'll pay."

"Looks like the Greasy Spoon again," joked Gordon for one last time as they left.

Mort began to read the email, sent a few minutes earlier.

'Hello Mort

It's me again. I hope this is going to be coherent as I've had a few whiskies and I'm feeling great, man. I want to tell you, as my oldest acquaintance at the college, that I'm going to go out like a true rock star. Just like Jim and Jimi, just like Keith and Kurt. OD-ing just like them, the lucky sods. All my life I've dreamed of being up there on stage winding up my axe (guitar) with the Wild (name of my band) and rocking it to you all for an hour or two. Well I failed, didn't I? I never got the chance and if I had I'd have been too scared anyway. God, what a truly boring life I've led. No wife, no kids, not even a lady friend for God knows how long. I've earned loads of money though and I've spent it all on records, tapes, CDs – oh and music videos, books and concerts. I've never done anyone any harm and now I'm going to be arrested for a murder I didn't do. Well, they're not going to get me. I've got a bottle of secanol capsules and I'm going to take the frigging lot right now. Jimi took these. I don't want to be part of the first army of geriatrics to snuff it listening to the Rolling Stones on their ipods.

Bye bye.

Ricky Headbanger

PS I didn't do it. I didn't do it.'

"You look like you could use a drink," said Helen sounding genuinely concerned for once.

She was sitting forwards, her head resting on her cupped hands as she watched his facial expression change from mild amusement to total dismay, then to outright panic as he read on.

"That's the last thing I need after reading this email," was all he could say as he turned towards her. "It's getting worse and worse, Helen. I think we might have another body on our hands. Richard Head's just told me he's committing suicide."

"Aren't you going to do something about it?" she yelled, jumping up and running over to look at the email.

"Why?" he asked, chillingly calm for once. "That's the way he wants to go. Read it for yourself."

She read the email quickly and looked more horrified as she scanned each line.

"He's barmy," she said when she'd finished. "You're right, but you should call the fuzz. You could even go downstairs and tell them. They'll send someone round…"

"And do what exactly? You're going to say 'save his life', but it's too late…"

"He might be bluffing!"

He wasn't listening to her. He was in another world. His eyes were glazed as if he was looking inwards into his mind.

"I've caused enough deaths as it is to worry about one more," he drawled. "Death will come to all us all one day."

"*I'll* go and tell the police," she said and turned away to leave but she stopped herself. "I've just realised something and I don't understand why it came into my head out of the blue. It must be what you've just said. Your name, it means 'death' in French."

"It's called nominative determinism," he smiled, but he wasn't looking at her. "And I'll tell you something else. Todd means 'death' in German as well although in German it's spelled with one D. Richard's parents weren't the only ones to have made a daft mistake when they gave him his Christian name, although I expect mine never recognised what they'd given me."

"What will the police do to us if he dies, and they find out we knew all along and could have prevented it?"

He looked up at her and reached forward for the mouse to his right. He closed Richard's email and, with a flourish, he deleted it. He then clicked the mouse three more times and removed all trace of Richard's last words from his computer screen.

"It's too late, Helen," he said quietly. "He's better off dead. If he's gone through with it, the best case scenario is that he'll be a vegetable for the rest of his days. If he hasn't, have you considered what he'll feel like when he recovers? Let's leave it and see what happens."

CHAPTER 34

23 March 1985

They decided to go to Suzie's house as it was nearer. They drove there in his car as she'd left hers at home that afternoon – very conveniently, he thought. It was a small, terraced house, built for factory workers in the late nineteenth century, but now it was part of a fashionably bohemian enclave populated mainly by single women, the recently divorced and well-off, young couples on the first rung of the property ladder. He hadn't even put his car keys in the pocket of his leather jacket when she flew at him frenziedly, forcing him down onto an armchair under the large window directly overlooking the street. He tried to return her passion but he felt it was all going far too quickly. He wanted to take it more slowly, one step at a time, and feel more in control. He was out of practice at the impromptu gratification of lust and he was scared. He couldn't work out whether he was frightened of her, or whether it was a fear of failing at something he hadn't done with a stranger since before he met Cassandra. He pushed her away gently with his arms and tried to think of something appropriate to say, but all he heard was his distant voice asking her something about having a drink first. She laughed and released her grip on his arms.

"Would you rather go upstairs?" she asked invitingly. "If you do, you'll have to wait a bit."

She jumped up and strode quickly out of the room, turning right and disappearing, which must have meant she was running up a staircase because he heard the sound of thumping feet gradually receding above him as she climbed. He stood up and ran his hands through his hair. The low-ceilinged room was tiny compared with the spacious dimensions of his own house. It was just big enough for the armchair under the window and a settee placed centrally facing the fireplace. A television stared blankly back at him to the left of the settee, and apart from a few ornaments here and there and pictures on the white painted walls, that was that. Diagonally opposite at each end of the room were two doors, one leading out onto the street and the other to a back room just after the opening to the staircase. He opened the back door soundlessly and saw opposite him a well-appointed and very tidy kitchen at the rear of the house, through which he could make out a small yard with a long, narrow outhouse to the right – probably the outside toilet and dustbin shed in days gone by, he assumed. He knew the layout well; he'd been brought up in a similar two up two down and his parents still lived there. He was grateful for the familiarity of his new surroundings, and he was beginning to feel more settled.

He found an ashtray and returned to the armchair where he lit a cigarette and waited. How long's a 'bit', he fretted as he sat and smoked. Then he heard the sound of footsteps again, coming downwards this time, and she emerged looking much different from the woman who'd left him a few minutes earlier. She'd untied and brushed her hair so that it now hung down below her shoulders and she'd put on eye shadow and lipstick. She'd also taken her trousers off and was wearing only a pair of scanty, flesh-coloured knickers below her sweater. He was overwhelmed by the transformation, and he knew without a shadow of a doubt that he wasn't going to disappoint anyone – least of all himself – that afternoon.

He stood up and she dragged him towards her by his arm. She led him slowly up the stairs, smiling at him every step of the way. They entered her bedroom where she told him quietly to sit down. She took off her sweater and threw it onto the dressing table at the foot of the bed. He was entranced – but not quite enough for him to ask himself why women always take off their clothes and leave them inside out. Then she removed her bra and he couldn't wait any longer. He quickly took off his pullover and made an attempt to fold it neatly, but she grabbed it out of his hands and flung it onto the floor. She jumped up and pulled him towards her, more tenderly and unhurriedly than she'd done when they first got there. She undid his shirt and slipped her hands inside it while he undid the cuffs. He removed his trousers, shoes and socks and they were on the bed, kissing and caressing each other wildly. That's the difference between married sex and passionate sex with a new partner, he thought, as they threw back the duvet and got into bed. In the first case it's more of a well-rehearsed ritual with both partners aware of each other's likes and dislikes and it takes place at pre-arranged, mutually convenient times of the week. This was more turbulent and more spontaneous and he wasn't sure whether he'd be able to keep up with her, let alone satisfy her. So he let her take the lead because she'd undoubtedly done this many times before and knew what to do.

"Who's that hiding behind all the make-up?" he asked when it was over and they were lying in each other's arms, her head resting on his chest.

"Who's that hiding behind the beard?" she replied, running her finger around his shoulder.

They both giggled but he was laughing at his reluctance to ask the hackneyed post-coital question of whether it'd been pleasurable or not. Nevertheless he decided to throw caution to the wind; it had sounded as if she'd enjoyed it.

"Was that OK?" he heard himself asking.

"What do you think?" she teased. "Cassandra was a lucky woman!"

"And Stan was a lucky man!"

"Stan was an animal!" she said angrily. "Don't talk about him, please."

"I'm sorry", he said soothingly.

He squeezed her arm as a postscript to his apology to show her that he was being sincere. He'd let her explain at her own pace.

"Do you realise something?" she asked, lifting her head and looking slyly at him.

"What?"

"We've just killed two birds with one stone!"

"I don't follow."

"I've got Stan out of my system and you've got revenge on Cassandra!"

"I'm merely a rebound, am I?"

"No, I'm serious. You know what I mean."

She lay back down and he stroked her arms for a while. He hadn't considered that sleeping with Suzie was any kind of vengeance, but he had to admit that it was very clever of her to have connected it all together like that. Or perhaps this is what she'd planned. He needed another cigarette but he wanted to ask her more about Stan no matter how much she might protest.

"How long is it since you and Stan broke up?"

"If you must know, it was about eight or nine months ago, before he went off to Spain last summer. Why do you keep asking me about him?"

"Are you still getting over him?"

"In a way, I suppose. It was worse when he started seeing Cassandra, because I introduced them to each other. I didn't see much of her after that but I knew what was happening."

"She left me notes when she went out if she knew she wouldn't be back before I got home from work. She usually mentioned she was out with you or the girls, as she put it."

"That's awful. If I'd found out I *definitely* wouldn't have come round for her things at Christmas."

"Why are you so reluctant to talk about Stan?

"I don't give myself easily to a man, Mort. I haven't been with anyone since he dumped me, if that's what you mean?"

"No, no! I don't understand why you're so upset when it was merely a casual affair for him. That's Stan. No complications. Find 'em, feel 'em…"

"He was frighteningly evil, Mort. The things he did to me and he wanted me to do to him! I was glad when it was all over."

"Why didn't you finish with him then?"

"At first he was OK. He's good company – you know that. He's charming, witty and very generous. I think he believed he hadn't completely conquered me, so he pestered and pestered me, hoping I'd give in to his monstrous…desires. But I never did. That's why he broke it off in the end."

"How long did it last?"

"I told you before. A few weeks. Let's change the subject. I don't want to talk about him."

He was now desperate for a smoke and he'd have to go downstairs to get one. He raised himself on one elbow and gradually untangled himself from her.

"I'll be back in a tick," he said, pulling on his trousers.

He wasn't going into her goldfish bowl of a sitting room naked.

"You're not going to run away and leave me all alone, are you?" she said, and she put her hands across her face theatrically.

"Not without my shoes," he smirked, winking wolfishly at her. "Besides, we haven't done it at my place yet. Then our revenge will be complete."

CHAPTER 35

12 April 2005: 3.30pm

Miller took her mobile phone from her handbag. It had started to ring as Tim was leaving to go to Richard Head's house and Harrison had gone with him out into the corridor to give him further instructions.

"Miller," she said, sitting down to listen to the Chief Constable's request for a report on how the investigation was going. "At the moment, sir, we've got three suspects and we've ruled another one out. Harrison and I will interview at least two more of them this afternoon."

She listened again.

"Yes sir, 'they're helping us with our enquiries at this stage' would have been a better way of putting it…No, sir, I don't want any more CID but I think I might need a few more uniformed. I expect to have something more concrete this evening but it would be help if you could get the coroner's office to give me the results of the p-m…oh, that's good, it's on its way, is it?"

She paused again.

"Thank you, sir. I'll ring at six o'clock. Bye."

She looked up as she pressed the end-call button to see Harrison standing over her.

"That was the Chief Constable," she said. "He's actually pleased with progress and the preliminary results of the post mortem are on their way. It must have been a clear-cut autopsy." He looked relieved. He might not be 'on the carpet' after all.

"Thank goodness for a bit of good news," he replied but he screwed up his face peevishly. "Did I hear you say we don't need any more CID?"

"Yes – why?"

"There's only two of us. We could be here for hours."

"So?"

"We've got two more to interview here. Then there's that Head chap to find…"

"That's why I asked for more uniformed."

"Then there's the MP. Who's going to deal with him?"

"I will."

"On the phone? We want him up here."

"I'll ask him to be here by tomorrow morning. He can catch an evening train or a plane."

"Are you planning to stay here overnight?"

"Yes. We'll need to take formal statements tomorrow – if that's all that's left to do. I'll stay in town or at a pub or something. It doesn't matter, John."

"Have you, er, got a change of clothes?"

"I keep a packed suitcase in the boot of my car."

Harrison couldn't have known that Miller was determined to crack this case on her own. Like him, she'd been recently promoted – fast-tracked they'd called it – and she needed to prove that she'd deserved it ahead of longer-serving, more experienced detectives, most of whom had been men. She was already unpopular at headquarters, and she'd volunteered for this case to get away from the hostile atmosphere for a while.

"Right," she said as decisively as she could. "Let's get the next one in. While you're fetching him, I'll ring my HQ and get a car round to Todd's place. Let's keep things moving."

Five minutes later, he returned with Steven Wallace. She was on her phone, talking to someone about a squad car. He heard her give Mort's address after which she ended the call.

"Ah, Mr Wallace," she said, pointing to the chair in front of the interview desk and indicating that he should sit down.

"I understand that Detective Inspector Harrison has already spoken to you about your movements this morning, but I'd like you to tell me again what you did and who you saw."

Harrison took out his notebook and listened impatiently to what Wallace had to say, checking every now and again that it concurred with his previous, informal statement. When he'd finished, she tilted her head on one side and looked at him suspiciously.

"You didn't see anyone else go into the executive suite, did you?"

"No I didn't, and I told him the same thing before. I had a few early chores to do."

"Why couldn't you have followed her into her office and killed her?"

Wallace sighed and sat back in his chair.

"Am I a suspect?" he said. "Shouldn't I have a solicitor?"

Miller stroked the side of her head and smiled.

"I have to ask you in order to eliminate you…"

"OK, I'll tell you," he conceded. "I couldn't have killed her because I'm her minder."

"What?" she shouted, leaving her mouth open wide.

She looked at Harrison who was sitting next to her and then back at Wallace.

"I…look…after…her," he said slowly as if clarifying a complex technical term for her.

"How do you mean?" she asked, still looking incredulous.

"You've obviously not checked me out yet for previous, have you?" he scowled. "I'm an ex-copper. I was on the local force twenty years ago but I gave it up. I was offered a contract I couldn't refuse."

"What sort of contract?" asked Harrison, butting in.

He knew he had to take over while she recovered from the shock.

"I got into a bit of bother. Let's leave it at that. I owed someone who fixed it all up for me."

"Get to the point," barked Harrison, trying to recall any

incidents in which Wallace might have been involved but it was too long ago.

"I was paid to keep my eye on her wherever she went. I didn't follow her or anything like that. I had to see that she came to no harm and report back every so often what she'd been doing."

"Who's paying you?" It was Miller again, getting back to her normal self.

"I can't say," he replied, pursing his lips. "I'm in deep enough shit already seeing as someone's topped her."

"So let me see," she continued, leaning forward and meeting his gaze. "You're asking us to believe that for the last twenty years you've been 'minding', as you call it, Ariadne Hopwood?"

"Yep," he replied, wanting to spit in her face. "Have you bothered to check where she's been for the last twenty years yet?"

"As a matter of fact I have!" she replied and she stood up and walked over to the large table, where she picked up Ariadne's curriculum vitae. "Now you tell me where she went when she left here."

"Chester," he replied without a pause. "For two years. Then London. Two colleges there, for eleven years. Five at one, six at the other."

"You could have got this information anywhere," she interrupted, but she was beginning to believe him.

"Five years in Newcastle before she came back here in 2003."

"How come she didn't know about you?" asked Harrison, also impressed by his plausibility.

"She might have done," he said, scratching his head. "She didn't at first...well, perhaps not till she got to Newcastle. She wouldn't have had a clue at Chester – and London colleges are massive."

"What happened in Newcastle?"

"What do mean 'what happened'?"

"How did she recognise you there?"

"She knew me when I was in the police here in Storbury. I let her off a couple of driving offences. Once I saw her in her car with Mr Todd. Nearly wrote it off, she did…"

Harrison and Miller looked at each other and their eyes widened.

"Did you say Todd?" she asked. "That's a name that keeps cropping up."

"Does it?" he answered, looking casually out of the window.

"You were saying."

"Well, it was easier to get jobs in colleges in those days. I worked as a caretaker in Chester, then again in London although at the second college they called me a site technician. But at Newcastle I got a job as a security officer. That was easy being an ex-cop."

"You were lucky with all these…convenient vacancies, weren't you?"

It was Miller, interrupting again, her head tilted, and she was staring wide-eyed at him.

"I think the wheels were sometimes greased for me."

"By the same person who you won't name."

"Possibly. But I got the job here on my own. I'm a hundred percent positive about that."

He smiled, but perspiration was starting to form on his shaven head.

"I'd got a lot of experience in estates and security by then, hadn't I? And a good record. I walked it."

"I want to know the name of the person you're working for," she barked dictatorially.

"I'm saying nothing more until I see a solicitor," he replied sharply. "I know my rights."

"I could charge you with withholding evidence…"

"Go on then," he said, challenging her. "I've told you more than enough. I haven't *withheld* anything. I've cleared a lot of things up for you. Either arrest me or let me go. I've got a lot to do sorting this place out now you've closed it down."

He sat back and folded his arms, waiting to see what they'd do. Harrison scowled. He'd remembered where he'd seen Wallace before.

"Steven," he said. "I do recognise you. You were a constable, weren't you? You drove a Panda…I was a raw bobby on the beat…do you remember me?"

"I've a good memory for faces. Yes, I remember you. You're PC Plod – aren't you?"

Harrison ignored the remark. He didn't want to have to explain it to Miller in front of a man he was starting to dislike intensely.

"You remind me of someone, you know," he continued, half in jest but hoping to redress the balance. "You look like Albert Naylor, the constable standing out there."

Wallace laughed.

"You mean the Hulk?"

He leaned forward and leered.

"I should do, Mr Harrison, sir. I'm his father."

CHAPTER 36

Late June 1985

Mort had to admit that he'd fallen on his feet for once. He started to see Suzie regularly although they continued to live separately, meeting occasionally during the week and spending each weekend together. They both preferred it that way. They had time to themselves and they had time for each other; neither suspected that one was taking advantage of anything, and there was little or no need for compromise. They tentatively discussed living together, as the money they'd receive from the sale of one of their houses combined with their two salaries would make them extremely well off, far richer in fact than either of them had ever been before, but they couldn't agree on which one to sell. They both gave countless reasons why they preferred their own home, and they let it drop. In addition, he wasn't sure whether he wanted to commit himself to a permanent relationship so soon after his marriage had ended, and she was worried about his continuing stability having heard so much about the lack of it from Cassandra. Besides, they had different ideas about how houses should be furnished and decorated.

He was a new Victorian renovator and liked large, cluttered rooms; she was a minimalist moderniser and preferred simple neatness and order. They even disagreed about bathrooms, revealing more starkly their contradictory natures. She had cupboards packed with lotions and creams of all shapes, textures and sizes, bath products, hair shampoo, depilatory creams and razors, pumice stones, scissors, nail files, towels for this, towels for that, flannels, loofahs, sponges, soaps, deodorants, aromatic candles, mouth washes and toothbrushes galore – which would remind him too much of Cassandra if they lived together. Nevertheless they were content with themselves and each other as long as they had somewhere to escape to whenever they needed to. She admired his practicality and he adored her cooking – she cooked like his mother and he wasted no opportunity to tell her.

She enjoyed her job working for the local council in Environmental Services but she rarely spoke about it. He on the other hand would entertain her with tales of the Storbury crackpots but he never told her about Ariadne. He embroidered the account of his meeting with Alice the Alcie as a mysterious ghost story, so well that occasionally he believed the revised version more than the disturbingly true one. Yet the thing that cemented them together was their joy of being with each other and this included their ever blossoming sex life. She told him she never understood why Cassandra could leave a man as tender and loving as he was for a man who was, in her words, vile and perverted. He never contradicted her but he believed he knew why. It was something in Cassandra's blood, he would say whenever she brought it up. Suzie never told him why she was in town on the day they met by chance but he often wanted to ask her. If he had, she'd have told him simply that she found him attractive and had promised herself that if she ever got the chance of sleeping with him, she'd take it, no matter what the consequences.

Things were still good at the College apart from the occasional spat with 'Diss' Honor, and he felt particularly drawn to Maureen. They shared the same cruel sense of humour, and they spent many a free half hour lampooning the people they mutually disliked. They were harshest of all with each other and a casual bystander might have believed they were squabbling like husband and wife had they not cottoned on that it was no more than playful badinage. He flew to work each morning, or it seemed so to him that he did. He overtook everything that blocked his path, sometimes too daringly, narrowly avoiding colliding with the oncoming traffic. The indignant drivers blew their horns and flashed their headlights, they shouted obscenities and shook their fists, but he sailed on serenely regardless. Nothing seemed to trouble him or make him anxious, and there was now no need for lengthy self-examinations of what had taken place on any day – he could spare Suzie that.

He found, as summer approached, that his workload at the College diminished and everyone began to relax and look forward to their holidays. One lunchtime towards the end of June, just before the college broke up for the summer, a glum-looking Ariadne asked if she could sit with him so that she could seek his advice. He hadn't spoken to her about anything personal since her birthday over six months earlier, and he was hoping that it would be a work matter rather than some emotional crisis she was going through. He was planning on going away with Suzie and he was busy reading through a brochure as she approached.

"Mort, I've got something to tell you," she said as she sat down and tore the cellophane wrapper from her sandwiches. "I've got another job."

"Congratulations," he replied, relieved that he wouldn't have to do much thinking. "What is it and where at?"

"I'm going to be a section leader in Chester. I went for the interview yesterday. Simon says he's going to release me early so that I can start in September."

"No one informed me," he said, feeling a little slighted that he hadn't been told beforehand.

"Paul covered my classes, as a favour. Well, actually he owed me one."

"Why didn't you ask me for a reference?"

She could see that he was becoming annoyed, and she put her hand on his thigh and gently stroked it.

"Simon said he would," she said as she took her hand away.

"I see," he said huffily. "I suppose he pulled rank, did he? Is he aware we're one down for next year now?"

She smiled good-naturedly and he understood that she was trying to explain to him the difficult position she'd found herself in. She needn't have told him anything at all, he realised. He moved his chair and turned to face her.

"What does your fiancé think about it all?"

"He's not very pleased. It means we can't get married this summer."

"You don't sound too upset yourself."

"I'm not. That's what I want to ask you about."

She paused and moved slightly closer to him.

"How do I tell him I don't want to marry him?" she whispered.

He looked round to see if anyone was within earshot. He had the perfect answer.

"Just tell him," he said, speaking normally and remembering Cassandra had walked out of his life without even so much as a goodbye, never mind an explanation. "He'll soon get over it."

She looked bewildered by the harshness of his answer.

"I'm sorry," he went on soothingly. "I didn't mean it like that. I know a bloke whose wife left him recently and it didn't take him long to get back to normal. You'll both soon find someone else, I expect. Yes, that's what I wanted to say."

She leaned forward again, more closely than before so that their faces nearly touched, and she lowered her voice.

"There's only one man I want," she whispered again.

"Ariadne, you can have any man you want," he said unthinkingly.

"There's only one man I want."

She paused, uncertain if she should continue. He hoped she wouldn't say that it was Simon Junkin or Paul Honor, but he fully expected that it would be. Why else would she be telling him? He sat back and looked behind him but he could see no one else in the room. She'd chosen her moment well, he thought.

"It's you," she said fervently. "You. I've loved you ever since I saw you sitting miserably alone in your car on your first day here. You looked so helpless. Why else did you think I came and spoke to you so often?"

Tears came into her eyes and he was unsure what to do or say. Life had become intricate again and he didn't want that. Not at all.

"But you're happily married," she sobbed. "You've always told me so. That's why I'm leaving, Mort. That's why I never told you anything about Chester. Do you understand?"

He didn't but he nodded anyway. He knew that, no matter how much he wanted to, he'd never be able to tell her that his 'happy' marriage had been over for six months. She'd made all her decisions based on a false supposition and it would be too cruel to tell her the truth. Not now anyway, now that he was with Suzie.

"You're a very attractive woman, Ariadne," he said, and it occurred to him as he said it that he wasn't trying to flatter her.

Something had stirred inside him, something dormant that he too had felt that sombre morning of his first day at the College. Something that had got lost amid misguided suspicions and doubts fueled by his neuroses and insecurity and intensified by a jealous old witch's drunken rant. He wanted to put his arms around her and comfort her but he held back.

"I'll have you with me, when I'm in Chester," she said, regaining her dignity. "Wherever I go, you'll be there. Whenever I'm alone and in need of comfort I'll think about you. I know you know what I'll be doing so I'll call it after you. Please don't laugh at me. I'll call it 'Mort'…no, I'll call it *Mortimer*. That sounds much better."

She stood up and started to walk slowly out of the room. She paused and turned round as she reached the door.

"Goodbye," she whispered. "I love you and I wish we could have got to know each other a lot, lot more."

CHAPTER 37

12 April 2005: 4pm

Miller was confident that they'd narrowed it down to one, maybe two suspects that had come to light so far, but Harrison still wasn't satisfied. He wanted every alibi checked, and he reminded her that it would be the perfect task for the extra officers she'd drafted in. He also wanted to find out what was delaying the criminal record checks. They'd already received a report from the City force that no one had seen a Mortimer Todd during the last twenty four hours, and the attending officers had only been able to confirm from speaking to his neighbours that his address was correct, that he lived alone, and that he drove a large, black Mercedes. No one had said anything untoward about him; the general consensus was that he kept himself to himself and he was polite, sociable and helpful. They hadn't heard from Joseph Crossley MP yet, but a message had been received from the York police that Ariadne's mother was on her way to identify her daughter's body.

Steven Wallace hadn't yet been dismissed as a suspect, and he was warned as he was roughly manhandled out of the interview room by Harrison, that he had a lot more explaining to do about his involvement with Ariadne and her mysterious guardian. "We're checking out every bit of your story," had been his parting shot. Miller had gone to speak to Constable Naylor about his 'father' and hadn't witnessed this unwarranted act of violence. The Hulk laughed as he told her that he was indeed Wallace's son but that he was illegitimate.

Neither he nor his mother had seen anything of his father since he'd left Storbury. He knew that he'd returned recently and was working at the College, but they hadn't got in touch.

Miller and Harrison were preparing to interview their last suspect when Harrison's phone rang. It was Tim and he was speaking from Richard Head's house in Mallory. Harrison looked at his watch. It was two minutes to four.

"We've found him, sir, but he's in a bad way," Tim reported. "When we arrived there was raucous music blaring out, and the neighbours had already called the police to complain. They mistook my team for the response unit they were waiting for."

"Get to the point, Tim!" snarled Harrison, beckoning Miller to come closer. "Go on."

"I looked through the front window and saw an IC1 male lying on the floor, so we broke in. The place reeked of alcohol and there was an empty bottle of pills beside him. I called the paramedics and they're on the way."

As Tim was speaking Harrison had mouthed the words to her that they'd located Richard Head and she was looking on expectantly.

"When will we get a diagnosis?" he asked.

"Dunno," replied Tim. "I'll see what they have to say when they get here. The neighbours said the music started over half an hour ago. I'll get back to you as soon as I can."

Before they were able to discuss Tim's account of what had happened, the door opened and the Hulk walked briskly in. Joseph Crossley had called the College and was waiting to talk to someone in authority, hoping that it wasn't something trivial as he was extremely busy. Miller rushed out and the Hulk shrugged his shoulders and followed her. Harrison took out his notebook – things were moving swiftly again and he needed time to write it all out. He was still scribbling when she returned and promptly sat down.

"He's not a very nice man," she complained, rubbing her thighs. "Not a nice man at all."

"Why?" he mumbled, looking at his watch.

He was trying to recall what time he'd bundled Wallace out of the room.

"He told me how *very* important and busy he is, that's for sure!" she replied.

He looked across at her and he couldn't work out whether she was shocked or angry – or both.

"Are you OK?" he asked, but he sounded too patronising.

She stared back at him and he knew that it was anger.

"Of course I am!"

"What else did he say?"

"He was very put out when I ordered him to come up here tonight."

He knew that Crossley was what he'd have called 'an arrogant bastard', and he wasn't surprised at all at the reaction her overbearing attitude would have elicited.

"Did you notify him that Ms Hopwood's dead?"

"Of course I did. That shut him up for a second or two, I can tell you."

"Is he coming?"

"Yes."

"Did he sound upset?"

She nodded and a sadistic grin came over her face. He sat back, perplexed by her sudden change of mood. Why couldn't she have kept it simple, he thought? The man must be devastated, although it was obvious he hadn't given anything away. A professional liar at all times.

"What else did you say to him?" he asked.

"I didn't mention the circumstances of her death, if that's what you mean. I asked him where he was this morning and he hit the roof."

"Was that wise?" he said, trusting that she wouldn't misinterpret his genuine misgivings as impertinence.

"I bet he's running up the M1 right now!" she laughed.

He wanted to tell her that they'd lost all element of surprise. She should have simply gauged Crossley's reaction to the bad news rather than intimidating him like that.

"Did he say anything when you told him she was dead?" he said, ignoring her attempt at humour.

"He went silent and then he said how sorry he was. He asked if that was why I'd contacted him. I told him that I knew he was a friend of hers because of our investigations and that I assumed he'd want to know."

He was beginning to lose the thread of the chronology of her account of the phone call. If she'd been a witness he'd have asked her to go back to the beginning and tell him the story in the order it happened.

"So give me a minute to take all this in," he said. "At what point did he lose his rag?"

"After I asked him his whereabouts. He asked if he was a suspect."

"That's natural."

"Maybe to you, but why should he not simply say that he was in London…"

"As we deduced."

"Then I asked him to come here and he refused."

"I bet that's when he said he was busy – so did his secretary."

She stood up and turned to look out of the window.

"You're saying I handled it badly, aren't you?" she said with her back to him.

"I think he would have come voluntarily," he said quietly. "It doesn't matter anyway – he's one hundred per cent kosher."

He didn't want her to lose her temper again since she outranked him, and that would be too undignified for both of them. He thought for moment, attempting to conjure up something that might repair the damage to her self-esteem.

"Actually I don't think you did badly at all. He'll be able to tell us a lot more about Ariadne Hopwood than anyone we've seen so far, even Wallace."

"You're a kind man, John," she said, her back still turned. "I wonder if Wallace kept a diary. That would be useful if he did. We'll see him again after we've interviewed Todd."

They were interrupted by a knock at the door, and a constable they hadn't seen before came in with a large brown envelope. It was the preliminary post-mortem report from Charles Harrison at the coroner's office. She opened the envelope carefully and perused its contents, occasionally going back and rereading a section to check on something.

"It's much as you suspected, John," she said as soon as she finished and she started to summarise it for him, reading occasionally. "Death by asphyxiation caused by prevention of air entering the lungs through both mouth and nasal cavity simultaneously. Preliminary surgery reveals that internal organ trauma supports cause of death. Lack of marks on body or bruising establishes that there are no signs of a struggle, although there are marks on her chin and nose consistent with the cause of death. There was also a small puncture in her neck to right of oesophagus and another on her right arm."

She looked up at him to see if there was any sign of a reaction.

"What do think made those?"

"I don't know," he said vaguely. "Some kind of dart?"

"Ultraviolet tests show little external residue on clothing or skin," she continued. "All clothing unsoiled and body recently cleansed by bathing or showering."

She paused again and turned over to the next page.

"Traces of curare were found in her blood. He adds that the amount of curare found would have rendered her completely immobile in a matter of seconds and unable to resist her assailant…"

She gave him a glance which said 'I told you so'.

"Any sign of sexual activity?" he asked impatiently, feeling uncomfortable that she still wanted to engage in some sort of competition.

"He says that, from the position the body was in, it's likely that she was masturbating when the curare was administered. In addition, there was no semen in the vagina, only traces of lubricant. Nothing in her pubic hair."

"Does he say how the curare was administered?"

"No. We'll have to work that out."

"I expect he has an idea," he said, sounding disappointed. "Any traces of DNA?"

"There's nothing in the report. There won't be any results yet, although he's sent some swabs to the lab in case we find anything else they can analyse."

She looked over to the other things on the table.

"We'd better send that lot off when we're finished here for the day."

"What time does he say she died?" he asked, curious to find out if his earlier guess had been correct.

"Lividity was present in the lower parts of her legs and rigor mortis had partially commenced in the face and neck on first examination of the body at 1100 hours and, as the room temperature was twenty one degrees centigrade, it can reasonably be determined that death occurred between 0700 hours and 0935 hours when the body was found."

"He's hedged his bets, the old..." he snapped. "We knew that already."

"I haven't finished," she scowled. "Rigor mortis had started when the post-mortem began at 1330 hours. He goes on to say that, allowing for the normal two to six hours before it sets in at the room temperature indicated and the fall in body temperature by approximately five degrees, he *estimates* time of death to be between 0730 and 0800."

"Good old Charlie!" he exclaimed. "Seven thirty – only the caretakers are in at that time," he said, excitedly. "That means the murderer knew that she'd be all alone until the rest of the staff start coming in after eight."

"Does that mean you've ruled out Wallace and the site technicians?"

"Oh yes, Wallace didn't do it," he said convincingly. "He was trying to protect her. Smith was still at Penny Castle's..."

"What about Richard Head? He ran away."

"Shit, I forgot to ask Tim if there was a suicide note. I'll get onto him now."

Harrison quickly reached for his phone and Tim answered straightaway.

"Anything to report, Tim?" he asked, picking up his notebook and opening it at a new page. "Hmm...yes. Oh dear, yes, I'll let her know."

He listened for another few seconds.

"Tim," he said impatiently. "You can bring us up to speed when you get back. Did you find a suicide note?"

He ended the call soon afterwards, and she couldn't make out what had been said from his blank facial expression.

"Head's tried to do himself in and he's not expected to live, forty-sixty at best," he said, and she couldn't infer from his tone whether it was sadness or disappointment in his voice. "He's pretty far gone, the paramedics said, but they've rushed him to hospital to see what they can do there."

"Did he leave a letter or something?"

"Yes, but the handwriting was a bit shaky, probably due to the amount he'd drunk – they found a half empty whisky bottle there. The letter was addressed to Mort Todd. He said he was sorry for all the trouble he'd caused by running away but that he didn't kill anyone. He said he was going to be with his buddies in rock heaven."

"What did he mean by that?"

"Tim said there was a room upstairs in Head's house that resembled a stage with a microphone on a stand and an electric guitar lying on it, but there weren't any amplifiers..."

"Perhaps Mr Todd can enlighten us, John," she said confidently. "He's mixed up in all of this, and I'm glad we've left him till last."

CHAPTER 38

5 July 1985

Mort's colleagues were still under the impression that he was a contentedly married man and, since this was half true, it left him with a difficult decision to make. Each year, on the last day of term before the summer holidays, the College held its annual summer ball, a formal occasion at a residential country club about six miles outside Storbury in the opposite direction from which he lived. Everyone was expected to be there, with their spouse or sweetheart, providing that they had one or the other, and single people were especially encouraged to join in so that they might find a partner. Richard Head was too shy to attend and surprisingly neither Kettleman nor Maureen went along, the former because he was too mean to buy two tickets and the latter because she hated dancing. Simon Junkin had gone unaccompanied ever since his wife had left him, and this year Paul Honor came alone, his wife being eight and a half months pregnant. It was usually organised by the Principal's secretary, and for once she had a willing and able assistant in senior administrative officer Iris Baxter, who had designs on her job and saw this as an opportunity to impress. Furthermore both the Principal and his secretary had announced their retirements which would make the occasion extra special, another reason why Kettleman didn't attend; he was too stingy to contribute to their leaving presents, fueling the lighthearted rumour that he was saving up to be a miser.

He had however the most perfect of excuses: he visited his invalid son every weekend in Oxford.

Mort didn't want to go by himself but he didn't want to go with Suzie either. This would leave him with too much explaining to do, and he didn't want to tarnish his growing reputation as an up and coming replacement for Junkin when his chance came. She accepted this argument willingly and she was more than happy to oblige him. She hadn't told him that she'd also been invited out on the same Friday evening by 'old friends' and she was looking for a plausible reason why she wasn't going to be able to spend it with him. His relief at having escaped this uncomfortable predicament was predictably immeasurable and she was content to let him believe that he was in her debt, safe in the knowledge that he'd make it up to her in the way she liked best when he returned. He'd also decided to tell anyone who asked whether Cassandra was away for the weekend which, being correct, meant that he wouldn't have to tell a lie.

When he got to the country club, the party was in full swing and he had difficulty finding somewhere to park. He'd left it as late as possible to set off as it was, but he didn't expect to have to leave his car in an overflow area which more closely resembled a ploughed field. If it rained, he'd have to be towed out. There was no formal supper, but Iris had arranged a magnificent buffet with sufficient food to allow the guests to eat as much as they wanted, whenever they wanted. He hadn't had an evening meal at home and he was ravenous by the time he made his entrance at a quarter to nine. He headed straight for the well-stocked tables and the drinks bar at the back of the brightly lit ballroom, and he stood and watched the dancing as he ate. The first people he saw as he looked around were Ariadne and Junkin jiving together in the middle of the dance floor, and he smiled as he watched them gyrate crazily to a rendition of Bill Haley's 'Rock around the Clock' by the veteran four piece band that had been hired for the night. They made an incongruous couple with Junkin in a dinner jacket standing a good foot and half above her. She was wearing a long, flowing, low-cut, black ball gown and her pendulous earrings were whirling dangerously close enough to her neck to garrote her whenever she spun around. He soon spotted Honor, also in a tuxedo, talking animatedly to Jeff Shaw who was predictably dressed in a brown, tweed suit with a clip-on turquoise bow tie that didn't match.

Although he had no companion there was plenty to maintain his interest. The hotel was a rambling, old manor house, extended to connect with a nearby barn which was used for large functions. He admired the elegant décor and presumed no expense had been spared to attract such events as this, along with business conferences and weddings. He didn't have long to wait before the Principal and his secretary were presented with their farewell gifts, and both made short speeches of thanks; surprisingly the former told no amusing anecdotes, merely expressing his relief that he could spend his retirement playing golf.

Mort found lots of people to chat with and he managed an enjoyable dance or two with some of the younger teachers. He avoided Ariadne and she made no attempt to approach him, content to spend the whole of her evening alternating between Junkin and Honor as her dance partners. He lost sight of her for a good half hour towards eleven o'clock but he spotted her again later looking tousled and flushed as she helped herself to a few small sandwiches with Honor at her side. As midnight approached the revellers increasingly began to say their goodbyes and went home or made their way upstairs to bed. He decided to follow the residents and slipped off unnoticed to his single room on the first floor across from Junkin and Shaw, who each had double rooms. To his annoyance he couldn't sleep despite having consumed several glasses of wine. He tossed around for a while before abandoning any idea of rest and he spent a good two hours reading the book he'd brought for such an eventuality. At three o'clock he heard the spattering of rain on the window and he looked out to see a heavy shower illuminated brightly in the floodlights outside. He dressed quickly and went downstairs, telling the night porter that he intended to move his car to a tarmacked area. He was hoping that someone had driven home rather than staying the night. Luckily there were a few vacant spaces and, much relieved, he was able to drive off the soggy, rutted swamp to firmer ground.

When he returned to his room he managed at last to doze off until he was woken abruptly by footsteps coming from the corridor, followed by a hushed voice and the sound of a door opening and closing. He assumed that it was Junkin who had been disturbed by someone as the whispering had taken place immediately outside his room, and Junkin's room was directly opposite. He attempted to sleep for a third time, but he couldn't settle, now and then speculating who had disturbed Junkin – as well as himself – in the middle of the night. He switched on his bedside light and supporting himself up on his left elbow, he reached for a cigarette. He lay back and despaired, occasionally blowing long plumes of smoke up at the ceiling to calm himself. He looked at his watch – four thirty; it would soon be dawn. Intense frustration was getting the better of him and he sat up and beat the mattress beneath him with his fists. The pantomime would have continued had he not been distracted by the same door opening again and this time he got out of bed and opened his door a fraction. There stood Ariadne on her tiptoes reaching up to kiss Junkin who was naked. She held her ball gown and shoes across her left arm in front of her and her right arm was stretched upwards around his neck. The corridor was dimly lit but Mort could easily make out that she was wearing nothing more than a skimpy, dark G-string and a black, strapless bra. Junkin kissed his hand and pressed it tenderly against hers, after which he mouthed something which might have been 'good night, my dearest Ani' and disappeared back into his room. She turned round and looked at Mort's door, which she must have noticed was slightly ajar because she slowly walked towards it.

"I'm repaying a couple of favours," she murmured softly before turning and running off.

It was the last he saw of her for eighteen years, but he cherished the memory of that moment and the sight of her almost naked buttocks that had preceded it.

He left at around a quarter to six as soon as he judged it was light enough to drive on the unfamiliar, narrow country lanes, not caring if anyone missed him at breakfast. They'd doubtless have forgotten that he'd even been there come September, he thought. The road was still wet after the downpour that had disturbed him earlier and he drove slowly, the wondrous vision of Ariadne vying alternately with the absurd spectacle of Junkin's unclothed beanpole of a body. He was thankful that she'd been standing in front of it. When he reached familiar territory, he put his foot down and was home more quickly than he anticipated. He'd forgotten it was Saturday and there were very few vehicles on the roads that morning to slow him down. He picked up his milk from the doorstep, kicked his morning newspaper out of the way in the hall and went to bed. It took him a while to fall asleep as he kept thinking about Ariadne. Why, he pondered, had she confessed she loved him and then openly and unashamedly slept with Junkin? Why was she so intent on letting him see that she had? Which was the real Ariadne? He'd left it too late to uncover the truth, and it in turn puzzled and saddened him deeply.

He woke around lunchtime to the sound of someone banging on his front door. It was Suzie. When she saw that he was in his dressing gown, she looked even more worried than she did when he saw her standing outside from his bedroom window. She ushered him hastily into the kitchen and made them both a mug of coffee. He was reading his paper and scratching his head lazily when she came to sit with him at the kitchen table.

"Mort," she said, getting straight to the point. "I've got some bad news."

"What is it?" he yawned. "I've had a crap night and I want to get some kip."

"Cassandra's dead."

She'd wrestled for a similarly sleepless night with how she would tell him what she'd learned the evening before with some of her – and Cassandra's – oldest friends. It had ruined their evening completely and they'd all gone their separate ways early, tearful and depressed.

He froze. She didn't know whether it was the shock of hearing the news or whether he hadn't heard her.

"How did it happen?" he asked, putting his newspaper down and sitting back in his chair.

"She'd gone snorkeling with some people from the commune," she replied, taking a deep breath. "On their way back their boat hit a submerged rock – or a reef or something – and sank. They were quite a way out to sea maybe, I wasn't told, but she drowned. You know she wasn't a strong swimmer and she didn't make it back to the shore."

"What about Stan?" he said, clenching his fists. "Why didn't he save her?"

"He tried, Mort," she said.

She put her hands over her face and burst into tears.

"He's dead too."

"Were they wearing any clothes, bathing costumes or anything?" he asked truculently, trying to visualise the tragedy.

"I don't know," she sobbed. "Does it matter?"

"To me it does," he replied coldly. "I have to see the whole thing. How many others died?"

"I don't know. Angie didn't mention the body count!"

"Who told Angie?"

"Cassandra's mother. Angie keeps in touch. Cassandra went to school with her."

He stood up and went over to the sink. He splashed cold water on his face and, without drying himself, he looked abstractedly out of the window.

"I killed her," he said dryly. "I did it."

"What do you mean?" she said, blowing her nose.

"If I hadn't been so bloody worried about my job, she might be alive…"

"It's not *your* fault," she said softly.

She moved her chair backwards and got up to go to him, but he turned round quickly.

"She must have been sick and tired of all my moaning," he said, not looking at her. "You said so yourself."

"I only said she told me she was."

"I neglected her. I put my career before her. No wonder she went out and had affairs."

"Mort, she had other men long before you went to Storbury."

He looked thunderously at her, a foolishly deranged look she'd never seen before.

"I killed her, but I'm glad I did. I've got you now."

He moved quickly towards her and kissed her, but as he did so she felt he was somehow different. Had he revealed something inside him, some facet of his personality that she hadn't seen before? Or was it the shock of hearing about the death of someone he'd loved? Perhaps he was still in love with Cassandra.

"Come to bed with me, please?" he asked, now smiling sweetly as though their last conversation had never taken place. "I wanted you last night and I need you to show me what I was missing."

CHAPTER 39

12 April 2005: 4.15pm

As the detectives were studying the post-mortem report, Helen was contemplating what would happen to her if the police discovered that she'd aided and abetted a suicide. Was it the same as murder or was it more like manslaughter? She sat at her desk, head in hands as usual, and studied Mort. He was the major player in ignoring Richard Head's doleful email but she hadn't done anything about it either. She imagined he had his reasons, but he hadn't spoken since he told her to wait and see what happened. He'd been standing for at least half an hour at the other end of the room looking out at the rain and to her he appeared every inch the tragic, romantic hero she'd always desired. He was Clym Yeobright and she was Eustacia Vye from *The Return of the Native*. He was after all a teacher and that's what Clym had planned to be when he returned from Paris. She was the proud, bohemian, beguilingly beautiful, young woman with long, curly black hair whom the local peasants believed erroneously to be a witch, and she, like Eustacia, loathed the rustic isolation of where she lived. She yearned for him to sweep her up in his arms and carry her off to some outlandish place but his house in the city would definitely suffice.

"Mort," she said dreamily, "Tell me something. When was the last time you had it off with a woman?"

"Shut up Helen," he grumbled, long accustomed to her provocative teasing. "I'm your boss. You shouldn't say such stupid things."

"I've been thinking about you, that's all. Do you know who you remind me of?"

He shook his head but he didn't turn round.

"You've read *The Return of the Native* by Thomas Hardy, haven't you? You remind me of Clym Yeobright."

"And who are you?" he replied, and this time he did turn round to observe a warm, amorous face he'd never have expected to see. "His doting mother?"

"I'm Eustacia, of course!" she laughed. "Take me away from all of this."

"You are aware what happened to them, Helen?" he said, adopting the tone of the English lecturer he'd once been. "He couldn't, he wouldn't, he didn't, and she ran away from him and died. He ended up lonely and miserable."

She sat up, ready for the challenge of a debate.

"It's ambiguous! There was a storm. She might have slipped and drowned *on purpose*."

"You think she felt guilty about leaving him for someone else?"

"Yes but she didn't want to really. She wanted him to stop being a bumpkin and be the man he once was."

"So actually you think she killed herself because he wouldn't do what she wanted?"

"Yes! At last you're seeing it from my perspective. She loved him."

"I've done that already, Helen. I killed my wife. By neglecting her."

She wasn't going to be beaten, especially as it was her favourite book by far, as she would have put it.

"Let's rewrite it!"

"You mean write a sequel."

She didn't answer. Her brain has just received the message that he'd killed his wife.

"Did you say you killed your wife? I didn't know that. I thought you were divorced."

"It never got that far. She ran off with another man, like Eustacia nearly did, and died in a boating accident."

"Oh Mort, how romantic! She drowned. You are Clym Yeobright and I'm sharing an office with him!"

"Who are *you* then? I've already met my Eustacia."

"I'm Helen Armstrong and I want what she never had!"

She'd stopped caring about Richard Head or whether she was an accessory to any crime she might or might not have committed. She'd fantasised for most of her unhappy and rebellious existence about finding her Clym, no matter how contrived it all seemed. What had depressed her most of all in her short life so far was that she hadn't met any man she wanted a meaningful relationship with, having had to make do with a series of disappointing one night stands. Her paramours all ran away – as quickly as they could after it was all over and sometimes before it had even started – and like all the other unpleasant incidents that happened to her, she didn't understand why. Every now and then she considered she might be a witch since that's what most people she knew ended up calling her but, try as she could, she never managed to turn anyone into a frog or make them disappear in a cloud of smoke. Mort was the first person she'd told about her much loved heroine, and he'd refused to accept the analogy, but she no longer needed an alter ego now that she'd finally stumbled on the man she'd been searching for.

Mort had been thinking again about whether anyone had seen him in Storbury during the night but he was thinking about Richard Head too and how curiously superficial people are. Richard had appeared to be no more than a quiet, self-effacing, old man who did his job efficiently and then went home. Yet inside he was profoundly emotional, driven by a secret craving he could never satisfy. Why hadn't he dropped a hint or two? He must have ached to share his love of music with someone and now no one would discover why he hadn't. In truth no one would ever know more about him than he'd confessed in his final emails. Then there was the oddest thing of all to consider. What dark inner forces had led him to run away and commit suicide? Helen had interrupted his train of thought by rambling on about Eustacia Vye, and he didn't feel much like crossing swords with an immature twenty-something, particularly when she was talking nonsense. He'd often thought that about some of his prettier, young female students: they looked alluring enough until they opened their mouths. Then whatever fleeting notion of desirability there might have been vanished, never to return. Helen wasn't good-looking and he was tired of her endless belligerence.

"You look dog-tired. Come and stay at my house tonight," she said genially. "You've still got to be interviewed and you won't feel like driving all that way home afterwards, will you?"

"They won't keep me very long," he said, searching for an excuse to turn her down gently.

"I could ease your tension for you," she went on, not listening. "Anything. Hand job…"

"Helen, please," he shouted in exasperation. "Not now, not here of all places. The Principal's been murdered, remember, Richard Head's topped himself and all you can think of is sex. Do me a favour!"

"I didn't mean do here it right here and now, you daft brush," she corrected him. "I meant tonight…"

Someone banged heavily on the door and they both stood stock still. It was the Hulk.

"Mortimer Todd?" he enquired as politely as he could manage. "Will you come with me, please? Chief Inspector Miller and Inspector Harrison would like a word."

"Good luck, Mort," said Helen as he walked past her towards the policeman. "I'll be waiting for you when you get back."

"Don't forget to switch your computer off and close the windows before you leave if I'm not back shortly," replied Mort fretfully. "And make sure this door's locked."

As he followed the Hulk downstairs, he felt like he was going to the gallows and he began to speculate how he'd got himself into this mess. He'd chosen the wrong career, there was no doubt about that, and for some reason he was reminded that as a young man he, like Richard, had wanted to be a musician. At that stage in his life he'd been captivated by the many complex, awe-inspiring compositions he heard and he couldn't fathom how they wrote them. He wasn't thinking of the sort of music that had electrified Richard, more the classical sort. He felt the same about artists, writers and scientists. They all had the same thing in common. Somewhere in their heads were countless shadowy ideas that no one else possessed, like the stones that Michelangelo said already contained his sculptures and all he had to do was give them form. He swore he'd find out how they did it before he died, but he'd never got round to it. There hadn't been enough time. He knew all about writing of course but it was passive knowledge learned from reading and lectures. If he got through this, he'd write something because he'd make himself do it.

It occurred to him suddenly that if he hadn't been so narrow-minded about Ariadne all those years ago she would still be alive. She might even have been his wife. If only he could turn back the clock and start again...then he thought of Helen and he despaired. What could she have been thinking about to reveal her infatuation so starkly? She was no doubt regretting it at that very moment and there'd be hell to pay when...if he came back. He was starting to feel apprehensive. He'd never had anything to do with the law before – he hadn't even committed a motoring offence – so the experience would be entirely new. He'd have to be careful, because he was so sleepy. What did they know that he didn't? They'd try to trip him up and they'd purposely misinterpret his words and twist everything. He hadn't got any kind of alibi, and he'd worked with Ariadne before she returned to Storbury as Principal. Did they know that they were no longer friends? They were bound to suspect him. As he trudged along behind the Hulk, he realised why Richard had run away. It was the dread of the interrogation. He gripped his left hand with his right as his mother had frequently told him to do when he was a child. It felt like someone was with him and it used to soothe him whenever he was frightened – like whenever he went to the dentist for a filling.

They passed through the foyer and, as he walked, he tapped his hand three times on a wooden table that was used for exhibiting pamphlets and leaflets.

"Touch wood," he murmured and the Hulk turned round.

"Who would?" he asked, looking puzzled but Mort didn't answer.

When they reached the door to the executive suite, he asked Mort to wait whilst he pressed in the security code.

"You're the last for today, sir," he said casually, as if he were escorting a candidate to a job interview.

He waved with equal indifference at a chair and told him to sit down. Mort remembered that twice before he'd waited here in similar circumstances, once in 1984 when he'd got his post as a senior lecturer and again in 2003 when he'd made Head of Department. He'd taken the first purely to further his career and the second one to save it. He could have walked away from either, but he hadn't and he was going to regret both decisions. If he'd turned the first one down he'd never have met Ariadne Hopwood. But he couldn't refuse either job, could he? He'd had interviews at other colleges during those nineteen bleak and barren years and he hadn't even come close in any of them. When he'd asked for feedback, they consistently gave the same reasons for not employing him. 'Poor interview technique, Mr Todd' was the standard response and now his mediocre skills were going to be put to the test like never before; he was going to be grilled as the prime suspect in a murder investigation. He closed his eyes and tried to come up with something convincing to prove his innocence, but he couldn't think of anything they'd ask him other than where he was this morning. He was driving slowly behind streams of heavy traffic, wasn't he? He'd been by himself inside a black, metal box all the way. There were no witnesses to corroborate that. It was then that he remembered again he'd been out all night too, driving around. Why had Helen asked him this morning if he'd been 'up to something'? Had he been seen? As he sat there racking his brains, it gradually dawned on him that they couldn't force him to admit he'd murdered her if he didn't know *how* she'd been killed. That was it! Stay cool, Mort, you've got them!

The door of the meetings room-cum-incident room opened and Harrison's head appeared. He snapped his fingers, pointed at Mort and beckoned with his head that he wanted him to come in. Mort felt the dull ache inside him intensify as it usually did when it was his turn to be questioned, and he put his left hand into his right again, holding them both across his chest, looking as if he were about to pray.

"Ah, Mr Todd," said Miller smiling vindictively, as he came in. "Take a seat, please. We've been wanting to meet you all day."

Part 5

CHAPTER 40

1985-1998: The Wasted Years

Dark clouds were gathering in 1985 and the good old days were over. The Audit Commission published a report showing that further education was wasteful financially, poorly managed and in need of considerable reorganisation. This resulted in two significant Acts of Parliament which from 1992 made colleges independent, profit-making corporations, but still dependent on central government for the bulk of their income. Their governors and principals, the new captains of industry, were free to act more like private sector company directors, and this necessitated the creation of many previously unnecessary and expensive managerial posts as they set off on their journey to make lots of cash. Simon Junkin had been right all along. Education became big business, money a paramount concern – and the current generation of pedagogues didn't like it. Not one bit.

The early euphoria didn't last long and the first casualties were older principals accustomed to being protected by local authorities and the relatively generous, 'historic' budgets they received each year. They soon took early retirement to be replaced by younger, more dynamic *chief executives* with masters' degrees in business administration. The lecturer career ladder shrank. The easiest way for teachers to gain promotion was to take on more non-educational roles to ensure the complete satisfaction of 'customers' with the rapidly expanding number of new 'products' that were being developed as the government expanded the vocational curriculum it now largely dictated. The main sources of revenue were still provided by the state which had set up a central funding council to deal directly with each college. This entailed the development of complex, computer-programmed formulae based on the level of the course a student was following and whether or not he or she completed it and gained the appropriate qualification. The more students that could be enrolled and the more successful they were, the more the funding increased. In addition colleges were at last allowed to create extra 'services' and as many exclusively designed, high cost training courses as they could sell to anyone that could afford them – and retain the profits. As *losses* seemed to be more common, many establishments used this 'opportunity' to try to make up any deficit. Naturally shortfalls led to cuts in internal budgets and redundancies followed, mainly of teachers, with those that survived having to work longer hours. Soon colleges lost their national collective bargaining power, and the extensive, inter-term holidays became a thing of the past; salaries, which had hitherto been well above those schoolteachers earned, diminished substantially. Lastly, to ensure that standards were rigorously maintained, regular inspections were to be carried out by the adult learning arm of the much-dreaded Ofsted.

It was against this background that Storbury College evolved, or more accurately struggled for the next seven or eight years, burying its head like the proverbial ostrich and hoping it would all go away. To their collective horror, all who served there were soon facing bankruptcy and, tragically, closure. Worse was to come. The college was deemed to have serious educational weaknesses by the inspectorate in 1994. The Principal, a carbon copy of his predecessor who had retired in 1985, soon suffered a nervous breakdown and retired in 1995 on health grounds. He couldn't take the pressure of dealing on a daily basis with officious, quango mandarins, but most of all he was worn down by Jeff

Shaw and his Union cronies who opposed everything that the government proposed. Simon Junkin soon followed in a similar fashion and Shaw was persuaded to apply for his job; to universal amazement, he was selected as one of two internal contenders. It was felt by the next Principal, one of the new breed of slashers and burners, that since the only way forward was to 'rationalise, re-organise, downsize and rebuild', it would be wisest to avoid the disruption of constant industrial action this would involve by promoting him out of harm's way.

Mort was the other candidate chosen. On the day of the interview Shaw turned up in a pinstriped suit, clean-shaven with a smart, short haircut. He'd removed his Doctor Zaius costume to reveal the actor inside and he looked like a stockbroker. Mort wore his usual work suit but he'd trimmed his beard for the occasion. Shaw got the job and was immediately christened the Poacher turned Gamekeeper, later, more pejoratively, the Traitor. When Mort asked why he hadn't been offered the post, the Principal said that the panel hadn't taken to a man with designer stubble. He shaved his fuzz off that same evening.

Mort had been reasonably content for the most part of the decade of halcyon days before devastating reality hit Storbury, increasing in competence and confidence and he was on good terms with both of his teams. He'd warmed to Junkin's glaring ineffectiveness, often using it to his advantage, but he steered clear of Shaw, whom he still regarded as duplicitous, rightly so as things turned out. He'd already been applying intermittently for other posts, but the escape tunnels he was trying to dig all collapsed on top of him whenever he was called for interview, and it wasn't long before he grasped the horrifying truth that if he hadn't obtained another post by the Whit holiday each year he'd be staying until Christmas. It was during this time that he finally plucked up enough courage to announce that he'd become a widower in tragic circumstances. He became a sympathetic figure for a few weeks before everyone forgot about it, although Maureen King wasn't too happy that he'd kept it from her for so long.

Many of the old brigade that had been at the College for as long as anyone could remember took voluntary redundancy or retired but some went reluctantly, struck down by the bullet of renovation. The older members of the Art team were culled, including Roy Jolly, who devoted his twilight years to his painting and his gallery, making a stack of money in the process. Paul Honor resigned in a fit of pique at not being considered for a more senior role, took his family to the Inner Hebrides to devote himself to painting, writing and homeopathy and never returned. He was replaced as section leader for English by Barry Roberts, a Mancunian, who'd previously worked in London. Kettleman was also disposed of summarily, there being no compassion for an old man who needed most of Fridays and Mondays off, and by the end of the butchery of the mid-1990s only Maureen remained for Mort to talk to about anything other than work.

Richard Head also survived; some said that it was because the Principal had slaked his thirst for blood by the time he got round to Engineering and was satisfied to leave things as they were. The old-timers and those looked upon as unmanageable sceptics were nearly all replaced by younger, cheaper, more pliable optimists, many of whom were employed part-time. Despite the carnage an ambitious, grant-funded construction programme was instigated to accommodate new subjects introduced by the governing body. A third large complex of training salons, workshops and classrooms was built, and the old Art studios were converted into leading-edge computer suites and joined onto the Engineering block. A modern training kitchen was created on one side of the ground floor of the main building and only the library remained untouched by the march of progress. Even the car park was doubled in size. Storbury College was going to be 'world class' and set its sights on 'meeting the needs of the rapidly expanding regional service sector'. Mort asked Maureen wryly which 'world' this claptrap referred to, but all she could say in reply was that regrettably the bullshitters were now completely in charge.

He'd become much better off financially after the death of Cassandra since he no longer had to support her. He sold his ageing Astra and bought a brand new Volvo. He continued to see Suzie and their relationship thrived although they still lived separately. They went everywhere together including several expensive holidays abroad, and they were very happy until things started to go wrong for the College. They were forced to meet less frequently during term time, when he had too much to do each week to give her his undivided attention. She became bored with sitting and reading or watching TV until she fell asleep while he worked in the dining room, which he'd converted into a study complete with an Amstrad computer and printer. Increasingly they only got together on Saturdays and gradually they drifted apart. The end came in 1993 when she rang him to tell him that she had to go away for a fortnight's training in Scotland, promising to contact him when she returned. He never saw her again (although he was to hear from her once more briefly) but he didn't care. By then Suzie didn't have the patience to listen to his moans and groans, and therefore she'd become more or less surplus to requirements.

He withdrew inside himself again, depressed by his long-held fear of being in a repetitively meaningless job for the rest of his life and existing for long, monotonous hours among people he still felt very little kinship with – fuelled the more so by the gruelling professional demands of maintaining the high standards he'd set for them. Moreover, his constant failures to break out of his 'prison' and a growing sense of hopelessness that he'd never find another job had bred within him a cynicism that soon would be frowned on by the draconian senior managers, and this compounded his loneliness and isolation. He began to dislike the younger students as the age gap between him and them widened, and his individual relief at the end of each year at not having to teach them again far outweighed their collective indifference towards him. He stopped wearing suits and relished this new-found non-conformity. Paradoxically he espoused some of the elements of the new, more regimented culture as they fitted in with his raison d'être of disciplined efficiency and academic rigour.

Despite his animosity to most things human then, his conscientiousness was unwavering, and he saw to it that the English and Art students' accomplishments continued to rise until they reached their zenith in time for the next inspection in 1998. Whilst he'd managed successfully to separate his professional responsibilities and what was left of his personal life, he remained a fish out of water, and he needed a woman far more easy-going and understanding than Suzie could ever be. When in the depths of despair he went to see Maureen, and it was she who kept him out of trouble during these confusing times, especially when he became frustrated and was about to shout his mouth off. She ensured that he focused on work rather than his petty grievances against anything or anyone that riled him. Yet she was out of reach, and he needed much more than the common sense and admonishments she was able to offer. He needed a soul mate.

He had a few casual affairs as the years rolled on, including, in September 1997, a very brief, passionless fortnight with a recently appointed, young teacher of beauty therapy called Lucy Carlton, the first person of colour to be hired by the College. He ditched her, he said, because he found her immature, scatterbrained and silly, even though she had an advanced diploma with a distinction in nails. He admired her, nonetheless. She flirted with all the right people, and he included himself in that category – until she fell for a younger, taller, more athletic Senior Lecturer in Computing. He thought once in a while of contacting Ariadne but he'd had no news of her since she left for Chester. The last vision of her and the warm memories of her chatting to him in the staff room and touching his knee when he made her laugh often cheered him up, but these were always replaced by a hollow aching that she was a hypocritical opportunist who'd tried to make use of him. He rarely attended the annual summer ball and on the last occasion he did go in 1997, he went by himself, only to be pestered all evening by a small, plump administrator, Bernadette Arden, who was, to put it kindly, very well-oiled. Likewise inebriated he told her very coarsely to stop pestering him and went upstairs to bed, where, oddly enough, he slept like a log, not worrying at all about where he'd parked his car. He also met Iris Baxter's husband Vic, but he was too drunk to remember anything much about their conversation other than it was about the amount of slow traffic – and one particular articulated lorry – on the roads every morning on his way to Storbury. The next July the summer balls were cancelled.

When he reached his late forties and the new millennium approached, the face he saw in the mirror each morning had taken on the aspect of a grotesque caricature of the man he'd hoped to be. He drank heavily, smoked no less than two packets of cigarettes every day and he'd put on weight. His hair was turning grey at the temples and puffy bags were developing under his eyes. He was losing his will to make things happen for himself and his life had become dreary and uneventful. He needed to find a new purpose but, other than taking up a hobby, he had absolutely no idea what to do other than to continue breathing in and out until the day he died. It was then that it struck him that, since university, his social life had revolved around Cassandra, and almost immediately afterwards around Suzie. The only friends he'd made himself had been the gang at the technical college, and he couldn't bring himself to get in touch with them again after they'd betrayed him that harrowing night when Cassandra left with Stan. Unsurprisingly they didn't contact him either. He'd come to the point in life where the older you become, the fewer friends you make unless you force yourself to go out and make them for yourself. He didn't – and that left only his parents and work colleagues as people he communed with regularly.

He whiled away what free time he had watching television or going to the cinema, occasionally accepting an invitation to dinner with his neighbours but he never reciprocated. He justified his self-imposed isolation by convincing himself that he preferred his own company – but this came at a price. He seldom thought of Cassandra or Suzie and although Ariadne remained his one constant source of hope and longing, it was still tinged with bitter animosity and regret. After all he'd been through he didn't think he was at all misogynistic, but he needed a woman for the one thing he missed most – sex. He now understood why Ariadne had found comfort in masturbation as a teenager, but he was reluctant to touch himself whenever he tried. Unlike her, he couldn't conjure up erotic images, and even when he bought soft porn magazines to stimulate his efforts, he still failed. As a child he was told at Sunday school that 'playing with yourself' was 'self-abuse' and that had conditioned him to feel uncomfortable whenever 'unhealthy ideas' excited him in an inappropriate context. He didn't want hair on the palms of his hands, and he didn't want to go blind.

He was at a loss what to do with himself until one bright, autumn evening in 1998, he bumped into Penny Castle, lately hired as a Business Studies lecturer with an extra responsibility for selling specially designed, tailor-made courses to local business and industrial companies. It was the Friday of the first week of term and they were in the car park, both carrying large crates to their cars; his were filled with books and hers with computer equipment. They didn't see each other until it was too late, and the contents of their respective boxes were scattered all around.

"Who the hell's that?" shrieked Penny as her backside collided with something that shouldn't have been there.

"Look where you're going!" hissed Mort, unsighted by his pile of copies of *Richard II*.

They both apologised simultaneously and laughed as no damage had been done.

"I'm Penny Castle," she smiled, introducing herself. "Business Liaison Officer. Who are you?"

"I'm Mort Todd," he joked "I'm an old lag serving a life sentence for crimes against education."

"You're the first person I've met this week who has the merest semblance of a sense of humour," she said, laughing again.

"No one's ever said anything like that to me before," he returned, trying to keep up the developing affability.

"What do you do here?" she asked regally but jovially enough for him not to give a sarcastic reply.

"I'm in charge of Art, English and Communication Studies."

"You're the very person I've been wanting to meet. I've got some ideas about selling interpersonal skills courses to the small businesses in Storbury. Can we meet tomorrow for coffee, say ten o'clock?"

As he drove home he was happier than he'd been for some time. He'd met a woman who was interesting to talk to, she seemed keen on him, and she had the most fascinating pair of breasts he'd ever seen. It was when he was unpacking the same box of books that evening outside his house, it flashed through his mind that tomorrow was Saturday and he'd have to wait until Monday to see her again. Later that evening in bed, when he thought of her once more, he managed to do something he'd never done before. He'd discovered he could become aroused by the power of his imagination. He slept well. He'd invented his own 'Mortimer' and he called it 'Penny'.

CHAPTER 41

12 April 2005: 4.40pm

While the Hulk was bringing Mort to the interview room, Miller was standing by the whiteboard, studying it to see what Harrison had recently written. He'd added the timings of the two interviews so far and the details of Richard Head's disappearance and his subsequent attempted suicide. She noted that he'd included the time of her telephone conversation with Joe Crossley but not commented on it. She noticed also that he hadn't included the post-mortem report. The checks on the alibis and criminal records hadn't appeared yet from uniformed although they only been at it for about half an hour. She wondered if he might be getting tired; he'd been there for six and a half hours, and she hadn't seen him take a break except for the coffee they'd had well over an hour ago. Then she observed what she took be a timing error around eleven o'clock that morning.

"John, why did the pathologist arrive before scene of crime?" she said, pointing to '1105 SOCO',

"He's keen," yawned Harrison. "He hasn't had a body for ages."

"They should've been here first. Why were they late?"

"There was a big bank job in town this morning. That got priority. The living take precedence over the dead, the Chief Constable said."

"This is murder!"

"We didn't know that. We believed it was another nuisance call. Besides, this is Storbury and money comes before everything including murder!"

"I'd change the times if I were you."

Before he could reply the Hulk's smiling face appeared in the doorway.

"Wait outside, Naylor," she commanded, folding her arms. "I need a word with the Detective Inspector."

"I'm not changing anything," he replied when they were alone.

"You haven't exactly followed standard procedure, have you, John? I'll have to mention it in my report," she said quietly as she sat down next to him.

"You might as well mention that Charlie didn't wear any overalls, gloves or covers over his shoes and neither did I," he said casually. "We've got all the forensics we're going to get from the post-mortem."

"Let's leave it for now," she said, giving him a knowing look. "We'd better get Todd in."

"No, wait a minute," he went on waspishly. "If you're going to be that damned picky why have you made Joe Crossley come all the way up here when he could have made a statement in London? He'll be furious and he's going to have you for breakfast..."

"Calm down, John," she said, trying to pacify him. "Let's get Todd in here and I don't want us to be arguing at a critical time like this."

"I want to clear the air," he replied, raising his voice as she started to sweep her thighs with the backs of her hands. "I've let you take the lead for obvious reasons, but has it occurred to you that Todd might *not* be the murderer? What if he isn't? This isn't a repertory murder play where we unmask someone in the library at the end. He's our last suspect except for the chap who tried to do himself in – and *he* might yet die on us. If Todd's clean and Head snuffs it, where do we go from there? The *real* murderer could be anywhere by now. I believe we should have asked everyone who was in early this morning if they saw anything."

"It was you who insisted it had to be an inside job," she retaliated. "That's been our methodology ever since."

"You didn't disagree!" he snapped. "And you didn't recommend anything else!"

"Let's leave it," she said again. "I believe Todd's our man. If not, we'll sort it out afterwards – or tomorrow."

Mort was brought in and directed to the chair that had been carefully placed about two feet away from the interview desk. The two detectives sat directly opposite with Miller on the left. She was convinced at once that Mort looked guilty. His head was bowed, his posture hunched, and he was holding his left hand in his right, pressed close to his stomach, as though he'd hurt his wrist. He was trying to imagine them as children but, although it was fairly easy with Miller, he couldn't imagine Harrison as anything other than some sort of dog with a sagging face.

"Interview commenced at 1645 hours," began Miller, strangely because there was no tape recorder.

Presumably she intended Harrison to log it or perhaps she wanted to intimidate Mort.

"Now, Mr Todd, where were you at seven o'clock this morning?"

He wanted to reply that he was in bed trying to sleep but instead he told her that he was getting ready for work.

"Can anybody corroborate that?" she asked, her head on one side again and her eyes wide open staring aggressively.

He shook his head.

"Where were you at seven thirty?"

"Still getting ready for work."

"What time did you leave home?" interjected Harrison, wanting to end this pointless line of questioning.

"Hold your collar, never swallow till you see a four-legged animal," chanted Mort under his breath.

"What did you just say?" said Miller turning to look at Harrison and raising her eyebrows.

"About eight o'clock," he muttered.

"No you didn't!" she shouted, and she sat back and folded her arms again, glaring fiercely.

"That's what I meant to say. I was talking to myself before."

Harrison sat back and also folded his arms, thrusting his legs out beneath the table.

"Mr Todd," he said in his most comforting voice. "We're simply trying to establish your whereabouts so we can eliminate you from our enquiries."

"Right," replied Mort. "I left home shortly after eight and I arrived here shortly after nine."

"What did you do in between?" It was Miller again.

"I drove."

"Yes?"

"And I stopped a lot. It's those Vigilantes..."

"What are you talking about? What Vigilantes?"

"The people who slow me down each day. They're an army of secret agents who patrol the roads every morning..."

"Mr Todd, Mr Todd," said Harrison patiently. "Please take this seriously. I assume you're saying that between seven and nine you got up, got ready and drove to work, and that you got held up on several occasions on the way."

Mort nodded again, but he wasn't really concentrating. He wanted to extricate himself from this menacing ordeal as speedily as he could, but he'd no idea how to do so other than to get up and leave. He was brought back to reality by Miller.

"How well did you know Ariadne Hopwood?" she asked but he didn't answer immediately.

"In what sense?" he said a few seconds later.

She looked meaningfully at Harrison again but this time her wide-eyed expression and a slight nod of her head suggested she knew that Mort was hedging, and he was playing games to break the fluency of their questions. She'd seen it done before on a training video.

"How long have you known her?" she said slowly, as if speaking patiently to a shy, hesitant child.

"I met her in 1984 when she was working here as a lecturer in English," he replied.

He knew how to answer this question because he didn't suppose that it was loaded, and he was reassured in a way. They were asking about the distant, not the recent past.

"I knew her for about a year before she left and went to Chester, I think."

He paused, looked around the room and pointed vaguely to his left.

"It was somewhere up that way. Then she came back here, of course."

"What was your relationship with her?" said Harrison, relishing the ambiguity of the question.

"I was her senior lecturer," replied Mort, shifting his gaze away from Miller.

"So you were *senior* to her, were you?"

He wanted to explain to the detective who sounded like one of his more loutish students, that the meaning of the word in this sense could be interpreted as something like 'higher in rank' but he bit his tongue. Miller knew precisely where this was leading, and she wasn't going to let Harrison beat her to the next obvious question.

"How did it feel when she came back here and was *senior* to you, Mr Todd?" she shouted, a little too loudly.

She was getting excited.

"How did that feel? Were you jealous?"

Mort understood why Richard had tried to kill himself. The old man's life had chugged along nicely because he'd controlled it cautiously and wisely so that things didn't go wrong, but when something he perceived as utterly devastating had shattered this routine, he couldn't take the pressure. He had no defence mechanism and he ran away. Mort hadn't run away because he was waiting for some calamity to catch up with him as it invariably did, and he was half expecting it. For him life had been a dreary slog interspersed with periods of baleful misfortune, but this was not merely another ill-fated, petty incident; this time it was much more than that. This man and this woman were openly attempting to prove he was a murderer, and they were serious in their intent. His glass would no longer be half empty; it would be lying shattered in pieces on the floor. He had to think carefully.

"There are two questions there," he said, sitting upright.

He unclasped his hands and crossed his legs.

"Which one do you want me to answer first?"

"How did you feel when she came back here as your superior?" she repeated.

"Nothing much. I felt a bit uncomfortable because she was different before."

"In what way?"

"She was sort of mixed up, I suppose."

"How?"

"Well, I remember she was very ambitious. I supposed that she was using me to get ahead like she used the others."

"What others?"

"The members of staff she believed could help her. Her Head of Department mainly."

The potent image of Ariadne standing in her underwear and tenderly kissing Junkin floated into his head, and he smiled. Miller took this as a sign that he was relaxing and that he was preparing to be more co-operative. She leaned forward, eager to maintain the initiative.

"So you resented her ambition?"

"It was the way she went about things. Everybody knew. Ask Maureen…Maureen King."

"Let's say *you* resented the way she went about things in that case, shall we? What kind of thing annoyed you?"

From this he concluded that she was attempting to make him say that he'd held a deep-seated grudge which had spurred him on to kill Ariadne. She'd decided that was his motive and he had to discountenance that right away.

"She used to make excuses to come and talk me so that I'd think she was a good, conscientious teacher and keen to learn," he said employing a matter of fact tone of voice. "She wanted to create a halo effect to give her an advantage if an opportunity for promotion cropped up. That's all."

"Did she use you 'to get ahead', as you put it, Mr Todd?" asked Miller.

She's patronising me, he thought. Who does she think she is?

"No, she didn't need me," he said, hoping this would make her realise she found the wrong tree and was barking up at nothing. "She had other more influential associates."

"You must have resented that also," she said, confident that this tree did conceal something although she wasn't sure yet what it was.

"I didn't resent her at all," he retorted calmly. "In fact I quite liked her."

He considered that he'd done enough to thwart her. It was Harrison who continued the questioning. He'd sat in silence enjoying the rough and tumble of the recent exchange and Miller's failure to get Mort to admit any ill will towards Ms Hopwood.

"Do you know what 'Mortimer' means, Mr Todd, other than that it's your Christian name?" he said when Miller paused for breath.

"That's a strange question," said Mort playing for time.

He was trying to make sense of how they could possibly have stumbled on this secret bond of intimacy between him and Ariadne and if they knew what it really meant.

"The last entry in Ms Hopwood's personal notebook stated, and I quote verbatim, 'Mortimer, dash, then prep meeting'," added Miller earnestly.

They could see that Mort hadn't expected this. He'd opened his eyes wide and shook his head several times very quickly as if someone had slapped him violently across his face.

"What's the matter, Mr Todd?" inquired Harrison sardonically. "Something rattled your cage?"

Mort was actually shocked for two reasons. First, he was delighted and flattered that Ariadne had kept her promise and was thinking of him every time she aroused herself, and, secondly, he was trying to fathom why on earth she'd written it down like that. It was the sort of stupid and childish thing a lovesick, immature teenager would do but no one could have cracked her code. Were the detectives keeping something from him? Nonetheless, did she genuinely love him? Had he driven her away, first to Joe Crossley and then to Chester and elsewhere? Was this the bad thing he'd been dreading: to find this out too late in his life – and now hers – to do anything about it? Or was there yet worse to come? He tried to steady himself, but his mind was wandering between intense regret and fear of what might happen in the next few minutes, and he was filled with anguish and terror in equal proportions. She'd written his name on a piece of paper that to them signified the last thing she'd done before she'd died, and they'd understandably interpreted it as an appointment with him, an appointment with death. His name was Mort and if they'd been French, they'd have arrested him already.

CHAPTER 42

Spring 2003

In January 2003 Mort had a stroke of luck. Jeff Shaw died suddenly of a heart attack and although this was a period of sadness and mourning for everyone, it was very inconvenient for Storbury College. The inspectors were coming again and there was no Head of Humanities to help see them off. Mort was offered the post temporarily as he was the more experienced of the two senior lecturers. Barry Roberts, who had replaced Paul Honor in the Great Cull of 1996, was drafted in to cover for Mort on the same basis.

* * *

Shaw, an Oxford graduate, had been an excellent modern manager. Known always as the Traitor, this gave him the licence to become inflexibly dispassionate and authoritarian enough to control things without fear of rumour or reprisal. He got results and that's what counted. He never uttered one more word of socialist rhetoric and in the 1997 general election he voted for Tory Joseph Crossley, who himself had changed sides shortly before. He was the antithesis of Simon Junkin, and although Mort hated him unwaveringly, they worked well enough together to gain the respect of all in the Department.

Gordon Moss, a mild-mannered Cumbrian from Barrow College, had taken over from Shaw and proved himself to be a capable Senior Lecturer; he imbued the previously bolshie Social Sciences lecturers with such an exceptional esprit de corps that they achieved remarkable examination results each year, and they even taught the Engineering and other lower level students without complaint. The three of them made a formidable team and impressed the 1998 Ofsted inspectors so greatly that the Humanities Department achieved the only top grades awarded to the College in what was a more than a highly acceptable result and measure of its progress. Things were on the up and Mort had been shaken out of his melancholic, mid-life crisis by this hard-earned academic success. He cut down on his drinking and smoking and lost weight. Moreover he'd found a new woman – or at least he thought he had.

He met regularly with Penny Castle in her office for the first few weeks of the autumn term in 1998 ostensibly to discuss his ideas for profit-making courses, a hard way to earn our pennies, she said, cleverly sending up her own name and job at the same time. He should really have delegated the task to Barry but he wanted some hands-on experience. That's what he told Barry, who hadn't yet seen her – and when he did, he knew what Mort's wink had meant. Yet while he made steady progress on the syllabus design front, he made little headway on the other. Whenever he tried to steer the conversation round to her, she skillfully manoeuvred them back to the topic in hand, and he knew what that signified. He was using almost the same tactics that Ariadne had employed when he suspected she was trying to charm her way into his affections. This sudden recognition tempered his well-meaning if sly inquisitiveness as he recalled how much Ariadne's transparent prying had annoyed him. All he was able to discover about Penny was that she was recently divorced and was looking for somewhere to live in Storbury; that was all that Ariadne had more or less accomplished with him especially after he encountered Alice the Alcie.

With all this firmly in the forefront of his mind, he abandoned all attempts to seduce Penny and he asked Barry to take over and finalise the discussions. He berated himself for his own lack of courage and courtship skill, not because he was too timid or unsubtle but because he'd never had much practice. Most of the women he'd met had introduced themselves to him and he didn't know how to enchant a woman unless she made all the running. His self-chastisement was short-lived, however. He overheard Shaw mention to Gordon that she was a lesbian and, as she was perfectly open about it, it would look good on their staff equal opportunities breakdown. Shaw was wrong and she was obviously lying to him as they'd all find out some months later when Mike Smith became Head of Marketing. Penny and Mike worked very closely together at first, so closely that they started a covert affair which flourished when she moved in with Lucy Carlton and they had somewhere nearby to go at lunchtimes or in the early evenings. Mort tried to forget her, but he'd become too fixated on her breasts to put her out of his head entirely, principally late at night when he had difficulty sleeping.

The millennium came and he celebrated it alone on that Friday night reminiscing about his past. It was a significant watershed. As a child the year 2000 had seemed a long way ahead and he wasn't able to comprehend what life would be like for him as a forty seven year old. He hadn't become an engine driver or an astronaut but that didn't trouble him. It was something else and it rumbled around inside him and wouldn't go away; he hadn't made a real success of anything. He'd been doing the same job for fifteen years and, although he'd worked hard and had gained a good reputation, it was all somehow meaningless. He often asked himself what he might have become had he devoted half that time and effort to himself. Even people who commit murder get time off for good behaviour after such a long stretch, but he was there for the rest of his miserable existence, no matter what. He despaired when he heard that many of his previous colleagues at the technical college had gained more senior posts than his, albeit in places he wouldn't have wanted to live, but he was trapped in some far-flung outpost as it was.

He convinced himself as the champagne took effect that he should have been a writer, even if it had meant living in a cramped attic somewhere foul and squalid. How much worse off would he have been? When he opened the second bottle as he watched the extravagant celebrations of the massed crowds of revellers on TV, he felt a sudden loneliness envelop him. He started to think about Cassandra who should have been here with him, but she'd betrayed him and walked out on him for Stan. He missed them both because they entertained him and no one else, not even Suzie, had done that since they'd disappeared into that crisp Christmas night. He wondered where Suzie might be, what she was doing and who she was with, but he felt so little for her that she soon faded away to be replaced by Ariadne, the woman who said she loved him so unreservedly. Had he really misjudged her or was it the cheap champagne that was making him sad and gloomy? It was bad timing, he decided finally. Had they met five months later things might have been entirely different.

He was romanticising the past but what else was there to do when he foresaw nothing changing in the future? His desperation intensified the more he drank – he was on his third whisky – and he realised it was time for bed when he lamented the demise of some the old 'characters' at Storbury like Roy Jolly, Kettleman and even Simon Junkin. At least he knew where he was with them, even if it had been somewhere rather uncomfortable. These days the new generation of managers and most of the teachers all looked alike to him and spouted the same mixture of business jargon and pseudo-psychotherapeutic gibberish. This was the age of conformity, and their lineage was perpetuated by carefully predetermined selection procedures based on fashionably spurious management training theories, so that their own bland image was scrupulously perpetuated.

Yet in the end he accepted it all. He woke the next morning and settled for what he was. He'd been in limbo for too long and, providing things remained much as they were, he'd be OK. He wanted no more troubles, no more complications and no more worries. It was his destiny to be ordinary and no one would remember him when he was dead. He resolved to make the best of what life he had left and to stop making rods for his own back, although it might be amusing to satirise some of his more narcissistically bumptious colleagues once in a while, especially the senior managers. If you can't beat them, join them, and if you can't, for whatever reason, join them, keep your head down and your nose clean. This would be his philosophy. Before the spring term started in the new century he gave away all but one of his suits to charity and traded in his Volvo for an old, black Mercedes limousine. His soul-searching was over – at any rate it was on hold. He was at ease with himself and he'd have to make do with his own company.

* * *

He made a good acting Head of Department. He'd learned what to do from working with Shaw and what not to do by paying heed to all the appalling mistakes that he'd observed Junkin make. Gordon and Barry were also very capable and a more relaxed but never casual atmosphere permeated Humanities. The inspectors were enormously impressed, so much so that they devoted a whole paragraph to him in their 2003 report. They praised his '*inspiring leadership in providing a stimulating climate in which learners achieve at the very highest level*'. They went on to say that this '*emanated from the impressive informality created by the Head of Department by his not wearing a suit on any occasion*'. No one was more staggered than the Principal who commented in his review of the inspection that in all his years in further education, he'd never read anything so crassly misguided and doubtless never would again. Mort was overjoyed with both accounts of his triumphant accomplishments and retaliated by turning up in jeans and a t-shirt at the next senior staff meeting. His post was made permanent, and no longer would he refer to himself as Mr H H Acting, frequently causing raucous merriment in the office when someone telephoned and asked for him by that name.

As 2003 progressed and Easter approached, the Principal decided he couldn't take things any further at what was becoming an institution of excellence and he announced he was looking for another challenge elsewhere. He'd become acclaimed as a man who could turn round ailing colleges and it was not long before he was tempted to Scotland to restore the fortunes of some higher education institute or other. He resigned at Whit and a replacement was immediately sought; the advertisement attracted over forty applicants, eager to run a prosperous and thriving establishment in a delightful country environment. Mort was invited to meet the short-listed candidates and among them, to his astonishment mixed with more than a touch of pleasure, was Ariadne Hopwood.

She looked older and her face had gained a few more lines and wrinkles, but to him she looked radiantly sublime, although he'd have preferred to see her in her black ball gown rather than the mushroom-coloured trouser suit that she'd chosen as her first day interview outfit. When their eyes met across the crowded meetings room, temporarily converted for a buffet lunch, they both smiled, and she cocked her head which he took to signify that she wanted to speak to him. He moved too late for, as he worked his way through the chattering clusters of assembled glitterati, she was already chatting to two dark-suited, white-haired governors. He quickly changed course and weaved his way carefully towards the refreshment table where Iris Baxter's famously lavish banquet awaited. He took plate, napkin and cutlery across its full length before choosing what to eat, looking here, there and back again until his eyes had had their fill. His stomach would be next. Food in hand he moved to a corner near the windows to view the room, at present a place of comfortable bonhomie that would soon become a horrifying torture chamber for some when the formal interviews began the following day.

"You didn't get away then?" he heard a familiar voice say before he had chance to finish his first forkful. "Still teaching spelling and punctuation?"

He ignored this teasing opening salvo, wishing to savour the moment he met Ariadne again. His earlier, first impression had been fairly accurate except that, close up, her features had hardened, and her eyes no longer sparkled when she laughed. He shook his head, miming to her that he couldn't talk because his mouth was full.

"You're quite a legend I hear," she added, taking over as he continued to chew.

He shrugged his shoulders and tried to swallow but he'd overloaded his mouth. This was hardly the reunion he'd anticipated.

"What have you been doing with yourself since you left here?" he inquired politely after a few uncomfortable seconds, licking his lips to dispose of any stray crumbs.

"I've been around," she said, taking a sip of her orange juice. "I'm currently Vice Principal at a college near Newcastle… upon Tyne."

"You've done very well, but you promised yourself that you would."

She pouted and looked away, not sure what to say next.

"How's the family?" was all she could think of, but she was sincerely interested in what his reply might be.

"There is no family," he said. "Cassandra's dead. She died in a boating accident."

He wasn't going to give her any details or that she'd left him beforehand.

"I'm sorry," she said looking concerned. "You must have been devastated."

"For a while…"

"Have you remarried or anything like that?"

He shook his head.

"How about you?" he asked, and he too was hoping for an answer in the negative, but, as usual, he was disappointed.

"I'm with Joe Crossley from time to time. When he's not at Westminster and I'm not too busy, that is."

She pointed vaguely in the direction of the door.

"He's somewhere over there. He's agreed to be one of my referees."

"Do you think you'll get the post, Ariadne?" he said changing the subject now that his curiosity about her marital status had passed.

"Oh yes," she said confidently. "I've made sure of that."

Before he could determine what she meant by her enigmatic reply, she was called away by two women he'd never seen before, guessing that they must be two of the other interviewees.

"I see you've reacquainted yourself with Ms Hopwood" said Iris as she passed by, carrying a plate full of vol-au-vents.

"I hope she doesn't get the job," she added fiercely as she walked on. "I don't want to work for a woman and there are three of them on the short list."

He continued his meal, looking around to find Maureen who, as Head of Student Services, had also been summoned to attend but she was nowhere to be seen. He didn't have long to wait for someone to talk to, however. He was approached by two gaunt, early middle-aged men, both grinning from ear to ear and each carrying a drink. They wore the same thick-framed glasses and identical black suits, black shoes and white shirts, only the colour of their ties making it easy to tell them apart at first glance. They were obviously there for interview.

"What do you do here?" the first clone asked him.

"I'm Mort Todd," he replied, hoping it would be a brief conversation. "Head of Humanities."

"Are you on leave today?" asked the second clone.

Mort wanted them to go away, but he laughed politely.

"Why do you ask?"

"We've been watching you," sneered the first clone brashly. "We noticed you come in and wondered at first if you were here to mend something."

"Don't you have a dress code here?" said the second clone, furrowing his brow. "What sort of example is this for a senior manager to set to staff and students?"

Mort had heard this before in the distant past from someone similar to these two buffoons and he had a ready answer.

"Are you two related in any way to Simon Junkin?" he murmured and, placing his as yet uneaten lunch on the table, he excused himself and left them standing there, dismayed at how rudely he'd behaved towards them.

As he was about to leave he bumped into Maureen – literally. She laughed and made a clichéd joke about sweeping a lady off her feet as she usually did, but she'd something more serious she wanted to ask him.

"Have you seen who's here?" she said, taking him to one side out of the way of the door.

"If you mean Ariadne," he said coldly, "Yes I have."

"How do you feel?"

"Why? I haven't seen her for yonks."

"How *will* you feel if she's made our new leader?"

"I don't know. She'll be in charge. We'll have to wait and see what she's like."

She knew that he was deliberately playing his cards close to his chest, and she was becoming annoyed by his prevarication.

"You know what I mean, Mort. Will it open any old wounds?"

He looked at her incredulously.

"She's a part of my past I'm not happy to think about, never mind talk about. Anyway, she hasn't got the job yet, although she seems pretty convinced she will."

"Same old Ariadne. She'll come a cropper one day, you mark my words."

"That's not a very nice thing to say, Maureen. What do mean by that?"

"Pride comes before a fall. Wait and see."

He was becoming more and more troubled by what she was implying. It was the second time in a matter of minutes that he'd heard a woman say that Ariadne would be an unpopular choice.

"I don't know what you mean," he said, turning round and leaning against the wall. "Are you jealous?"

"I am a bit," confessed Maureen, folding her arms tightly over her breasts. "I don't like her style. Perhaps you were right about her all those years ago when you came to see me…"

"I was wrong," he said crossly. "What makes you think anything different from what you did then? It was you who put me right, as I remember."

"It's probably tittle-tattle, but I heard that she's done some strange things to get where she is today…"

"From whom?" he interrupted for the second time.

"From my cousin in Newcastle. She works at the same college as Ariadne, although she never mentioned her by name, which is why I've never told you before. Your old friend's got something of a reputation as a hard-hearted slavedriver. Apparently she hates men and, if she gets the Prinny's job, it's her unconcealed ambition to have this college staffed completely by women before she moves on."

"What a load of rubbish," he laughed. "Come on, let's grab something to eat and have a bit of sport with some *pushy* buggers. There must be a few we can bate. Captain Bollocks and his twin brother over there will do for starters."

CHAPTER 43

12 April 2005: 5pm

Tim sat in his car listening to a news broadcast by Zulfiqar Ali of the BBC on the radio. He heard the reporter describe a suspected murder incident at Storbury College and speculate that the victim might be a 'very senior manager' according to unconfirmed rumours. Ben bloody Briscoe, Tim thought, up to his old tricks again. He'd have to notify Miller and Harrison. He unfastened his seat belt and opened the door just as two uniformed police officers walked briskly past with Briscoe held fast in between them.

"We found him prowling round the grounds between those two buildings," said one of the officers, a sergeant, indicating the Art, Hair and Beauty studios and the main building with a backward nod of his head. "We're escorting him off the premises."

Tim smiled. So it was Briscoe after all.

"Thank goodness it's Tuesday and the local rag doesn't come out until Friday," he shouted as they disappeared down the driveway arm in arm with the scowling, protesting journalist.

He strode over to the main building and saw a group of four people staring fixedly at him through the large, rain-soaked foyer windows; from the looks on their faces they appeared to be waiting for him.

"How much longer are you going to keep me her?" Iris boomed in her customary manner as soon as he entered. "I'm going away on holiday tonight and my husband is coming to pick me up later this afternoon."

Since he'd no answer for her he turned to the next person, the young receptionist he'd been chatting to an hour or so earlier.

"I've had dozens of calls from furious evening students," she said, looking agitated. "They're demanding their money back for this evening's cancelled classes. What do I say to them? Is the college going to be re-opened?"

He'd no answer for her either so he waited to hear the next complaint from two white haired men in dark suits, one of whom stepped forward and glared.

"I'm Henry Flower, Chairman of the Governors," he said. "I want to know why I've not been informed about the murder. Why has no one contacted me? The first I heard about it was on the radio half an hour ago."

Tim took a step back. He didn't like the look of this self-important old man. He'd met his sort before, and they didn't ask for anything nicely if they thought they could bully people into submission. This chap had the same well-groomed look and high and mighty expression they all had. Clean, well-manicured fingernails, neatly brushed hair, expensive clothes and the emblematic tie denoting some exclusive club or other.

"I'm afraid you'll have to take that up with Hugh Jones," he said gesturing vaguely in Iris's direction.

He didn't want to have to tackle her as well and he could slip away quickly while they sorted it out among themselves. Flower turned to her and held his arms out in frustration.

"Will no one enlighten me as to what's going on?" he bellowed. "Where's Ariadne?"

Tim decided it was time to go and, as he quietly crept away, he heard Iris ask Flower to come to Hugh's office where everything would be explained to him.

The Hulk was grinning as usual when Tim approached the security door. He'd overheard the shenanigans in the foyer and added that bad-tempered confrontation to his lengthening list of anecdotes for the pub later that day. Tim's face was still red and his hair was wet but he was calming down. He wanted to hide in his cubby-hole.

"Wait a minute, Tim," said the Hulk as they passed. "I've got some reports for you from PNC and the boys checking the alibis. It's good news and bad news."

"What's the good news?" asked Tim impatiently as he was handed the files.

"Well," said the Hulk, enjoying the opportunity to put a fellow policeman in the picture for once. "Only my dad's got form – Mr Wallace, I mean. All the others are clean except for a couple of motoring offences…"

"What's Wallace done?"

"GBH – twenty years ago in Storbury."

"What's the bad news?"

"There's more good news. No, it's middling…"

"Get on with it, Albert!"

"Most of the alibis check out apart from Richard Head's – but he won't need one now. They're still checking on one."

"Who?"

"Iris Baxter."

"What about Todd?"

"He hasn't got one either. He's in there being grilled."

"What's the bad news then?"

"There's only one CCTV camera between here and the city and it's bust."

"What about the petrol stations?"

"It'll take a while to check them out, seeing as he probably didn't stop for any."

Tim frowned.

"You shouldn't read these…"

"It's boring standing out here all day. It gave me something to do. You don't have a newspaper, do you? I've read all these college brochures twice."

* * *

"We have a witness who saw you alone with Ms Hopwood back in 1984 or 1985," rasped Miller, unaware of all that was going on outside. "You were in her car, so I assume you knew her a little more informally than you said before."

Mort was still reeling from the last question about his name being in his Ariadne's exercise book and it wasn't evident to him why they'd moved on. Harrison settled back in his chair to see what Miller was up to.

"I vaguely remember going for a drink with her one lunchtime," he said, being less than honest.

His memory was crystal clear, but he didn't recall anyone seeing them in the pub together.

"Were you having an affair with her?" asked Miller, smiling evilly again.

"Certainly not, but I know a few others who were," he replied testily, hoping to throw them a red herring.

Miller persisted.

"Were you jealous of that? Did she turn you down?"

"I wasn't envious of her then and I'm not envious of her now. I'm pleased she had affairs. It's natural for an attractive woman to have many admirers."

"And you weren't one of them?"

"No, I was a happily married man."

"You live alone, don't you?"

"My wife died twenty years ago, in 1985."

"That's a coincidence…"

Harrison couldn't wait any longer. She was missing something obvious.

"Did you kill *your wife*, Mr Todd?" he said, admiring his own lack of subtlety.

Only a policeman could have asked a question like that.

"In a manner of speaking, yes," said Mort unaware of the foolishness that had just passed his lips.

"So, let me summarise," Miller resumed, looking at Harrison as she spoke. "His wife dies in 1985 and Ms Hopwood was working here as a young lecturer. I think there's a connection, don't you, John?"

"My wife left me and died in an accident in Spain," protested Mort. "I had nothing to do with it."

"You just said you killed her?"

"If I hadn't neglected her, she might be alive today."

He recalled the same exchange with Helen less than an hour ago, and he realised what he'd said to her would have made far more sense to her than it did to the detectives.

"After your wife left you, were you seeing anyone else?"

"Not for a while…"

He decided it would be best not to tell them about Suzie. He didn't want her involved in this.

"You missed female company and you tried it on with Ms Hopwood…"

"No I went out with her once. To a pub near here. It was *before* my wife left me."

"I find it interesting Mr Todd that the only two people who can verify your last statement are both dead."

"You said you had a witness who saw us out together. He or she will tell you it was towards the end of 1984 before Christmas – not 1985. My wife left me at Christmas 1984."

"Did you see Ms Hopwood socially again?"

"A couple of times but I wasn't *with* her. She was with other people."

Miller knew she had to keep going because her intuition was screaming at her that what happened in 1984 had to be directly related to what had taken place that morning. Yet he wasn't breaking. He was deflecting everything with the assurance of man who, despite his nervousness, was speaking the truth.

"Do you mean she was with other *men?*" she asked with conviction.

"Yes, she was with a local councillor once, I think, and she was with some colleagues of mine at a summer ball," said Mort quietly, looking down at his hands.

If he kept on answering quickly, they'd have to assume he wasn't lying but he was too late.

Miller looked at Harrison again, who was writing something down; she leaned over and saw that he'd written 'Crossley' and drawn a circle around it. Perhaps he'd changed his mind again?

"Mr Todd," she continued. "I believe you were infatuated with Ms Hopwood. I believe you made advances to her because you wanted an affair with her and, because you were higher-ranking than she was, you expected her to comply. I believe she turned you down. Your wife found out and she left you. You said you neglected her and that resulted in her death. You also said you as good as killed her. You then saw Ms Hopwood with other men and it was too late. You couldn't have her, and you became jealous. You harboured that resentment and when she reappears many years afterwards, now senior to you, that jealousy was reawakened and intensified. I believe you waited until an opportunity arose for you to take revenge on both accounts, and this morning that is precisely what you did."

She sat back and watched for his reaction but there was none. He merely sat and gazed blankly at the floor grinding his teeth. He must have been seen this morning, he thought. They've put two and two together and made four. Miller, however, was ready for the next part of her speech, which she was feeling very pleased with. She couldn't have made a better one if she'd planned it.

"I also believe that this morning you came here very early, before a meeting with her later. The entry in her personal notebook confirms that you had an appointment with her. You went into her office and then you killed her in the most bizarre fashion possible to throw us off the scent. When you'd done the deed, you got back into your car and drove away. You may even have gone home. You didn't get back here until after nine, which explains why you were late. This also gave you an alibi, even if it was a flimsy one."

She paused and pushed her luck.

"Tell us what you were really doing first thing this morning. We don't have anything on CCTV that places you anywhere between where you live and this College at the times you've indicated."

"That doesn't surprise me," he said, wearily. "Otherwise you'd do something about the traffic. The Vigilantes must love you…"

"Stop going on about those bloody Vigilantes," she howled. "They're a figment of your bloody imagination."

He went on grinding his teeth, but now he was looking at her. She'd got up suddenly and rushed over to the whiteboard. She turned it round with a wave of her hand and there were the last gruesome photographs of Ariadne, one with her feet on her silver desk taken side on, and two more of her face and neck, taken in opposite profiles. He craned his neck around to look and immediately averted his eyes. This wasn't how he wanted to remember her, and these grotesque images had made all his other, fonder memories vanish in an instant.

"What do you make of that?" she said, fighting for breath.

Her frantic performance had taken more out of her than she imagined it would.

"Did you sexually assault her before you murdered her, Mr Todd? You did, didn't you?"

"No," he mumbled. "But I know what she was doing before she died."

Harrison steadied himself, waiting for Mort's confession, but Miller kept holding onto the whiteboard, gasping for air.

"That's what 'Mortimer' means," Mort whispered. "It means 'masturbation'. She was masturbating. She was thinking about me. It was me…"

He looked up at Harrison, a baleful look on his face.

"It was me," he said, raising his voice. "It was *me*…"

"He knows she was masturbating, John!" screamed Miller. "He said she was masturbating *before she died*. No one else has seen the body apart from us, Iris Baxter and poor Bernadette

Thingy, the woman who found her body, and I'm not sure they fully appreciated what'd been going on."

"He said '*It was me*'," roared Harrison. "He said it three times. He's confessed. He killed her."

He wanted to clap his hands and run over and hug her. She'd done it. She'd cracked him. She *was* good, after all.

"Yes!" he exclaimed, and he turned and looked down at Mort, who was drooping forward in his chair, arms between his knees.

"Mortimer Todd, I'm arresting you for the murder of Ariadne Hopwood. You do not have to say anything, but it may harm your defence if you do not mention when questioned something which you later rely on in court. Anything you do say may be given in evidence."

Tim poked his head out of the storeroom further down the corridor. He'd heard Harrison's roar of triumph and he detected from the Hulk's face that he'd heard it too.

"Looks like they've got a result," he said. "We might get down the pub tonight after all, Albert."

CHAPTER 44

1 September 2003: Morning

"I have some interesting announcements to make," said Ariadne regally, looking round the meetings room at her assembled senior managers. "They concern changes I propose to make in the next few months that will take this College into unchartered waters and onto new continents as yet undiscovered."

"What's Lady Ariadne up to?" whispered Maureen out of the corner of her mouth. "We'll be off to the moon next."

Mort didn't look up. He'd been busy doodling throughout the meeting, and he was drawing a complex, surrealistic aeroplane having already completed a similarly creative sailing ship. This was Ariadne's first meeting as the new Principal at the start of the new academic year in 2003 and she wanted to make a favourable impression. She'd already made some alterations to the room before the meeting began which had been carried out unofficially during the summer break. All the pictures had been taken down from the walls which had been repainted beige, the computer had been removed and the telephone had been placed on the floor. The biggest difference, however, was that each of the comfortably upholstered wooden chairs had been replaced by hard plastic seats, except for one. At the head of the antique oak table (which she had allowed to remain) was a magnificent, opulently crafted, high-backed, throne-like symbol of her power. This would be her personal statement, not only that this was a place intended for undistracted work and hard-nosed business, but also that she was in absolute command.

She'd started the meeting at precisely nine thirty by introducing herself after which she asked each of the managers in turn to introduce themselves. She then outlined her procedural rules for conducting each session, including the abandonment of coffee and biscuits both before and during the meeting. The agenda would be rigorously followed, and all discussions and questioning were to be through her as the chair. A grudging consideration for flexibility was the date of each meeting, which would be set at the beginning of each month, varied occasionally according to her diary commitments, and she expected everyone to comply with this arrangement.

"I intend to expand our portfolio of courses," she continued, eager to explain her latest but most surprising pronouncement towards the end of an otherwise routine event. "I want to introduce sciences, not in the purest sense, but in the applied sense. This will include such things as pharmacology and forensics and will involve the construction of a purpose-built suite of laboratories. I have already secured funding with the help of Joseph Crossley, our local Member of Parliament, who has agreed to open the building when it is completed, and it will be named after him. Provisionally these courses will be placed with Richard Head, although in due course I intend to modify the College's management structure to accommodate them. Are there any questions?"

There was an uncomfortable silence. Everyone was too dumbfounded by the impassive assuredness of a woman who'd barely been in post for a couple of hours, and by the insensitive conviction she was displaying in her own judgement without the merest hint of prior consultation or warning; the agenda item had simply said 'Announcements'. Mort and Maureen were affected most of all as they were the only people in the room who would have recognised Ariadne in her previous incarnation as a friendly, unassuming, young lecturer with a penchant for chatting up older men. Mort knew many other things besides, including the intimate details of her personal sex life.

"Who *is* this woman?" he said under his breath and Maureen nodded.

"Exactly what I was thinking," she whispered, again out of the side of her mouth

"I assume the plan meets with your approval," said Ariadne as she glared at Mort and Maureen. "I'll move on in that case. I also propose to look for opportunities further afield. To begin with I am looking at another college with a view to taking it over. I'm sure you'll have an idea which one I mean as it's in trouble, both financially and academically, and, if you'll forgive the expression, 'ripe for plucking'. Hugh Jones and I will oversee this. I'm also looking into expanding overseas and Mike Smith and I will work together to find some suitable locations. I have located one already in Greece. I have the draft action plans."

She turned to her right and nodded to Iris, who was sitting next to her taking the minutes.

"Finally, I wish to announce that I have appointed Iris Baxter to the new post Head of Finance and Educational Support with immediate effect after the meeting. This will relieve both Hugh, myself, and the Human Resources Manager – who I note is not here today – of many onerous duties. Iris will be replaced by Bernadette Arden, one of the administrative officers, as my PA. Now, is there any other business?"

She looked round the room to see a series of shaking heads. It was five past eleven and everyone needed a break.

"Thank you, that's all. You may go. Mort, I'd like a word with you in my office at twelve thirty sharp. Tell Bernadette that I've sent for you."

Mort walked Maureen back to her office on the ground floor. They were both in shock after what they'd witnessed, and they agreed not to tell anyone what they really knew about

Ariadne – for fear of scorn and ridicule. They speculated for a while why she might want to see him, and decided that all she probably wanted to do was to talk over some changes she had in mind for his department, although he didn't let on to Maureen that he hoped it might be more of a pleasurable reunion with an old friend. At twelve twenty five he duly arrived outside Ariadne's office and knocked on her secretary's door as ordered. To his surprise it was Bernadette who answered; he'd forgotten that Iris had been promoted an hour ago and she'd left already.

"Can I help you?" she said curtly, as though she'd never clapped eyes on him before. "What do you want?"

"I've come to see Ariadne," he replied, entirely aware why she was so frosty, adding tactlessly, "It's not you I want."

"I know that all too well!" she hissed. "Wait there and I'll see if she's free, although there's nothing in her diary until two o'clock."

She tapped quietly on Ariadne's door and went in, returning almost immediately. She indicated that he could go in, went back into her office and slammed the door.

He was staggered when he saw what had Ariadne had done to her room. Gone were the cheap, austere wooden furniture and the dated pc that her predecessor had used. Instead everything was 'cutting edge', expensive and, he found most surprising, apparently made of highly polished, stainless steel. The walls had been painted beige and the pictures of past dignitaries had been replaced by photographs of herself with people he couldn't quite make out.

"Do you like it, Mort?" she asked when he started to blink again.

"It's absolutely remarkable," he said trying to sound impressed.

He wanted to say "palatial" but he suspected it wouldn't go down too well, and he already detested her refurbishment as garish and tasteless. She sat back in her silver-grey leather, reclining chair and looked at him, waiting for him to go on but he was looking inquisitively around. She looked relaxed, he thought, like a judge who'd adjourned for the morning and had taken off her wig and robes, or, more aptly, a queen who'd removed her crown and ermine.

"Why do you want to see me?" he inquired when he deemed it appropriate for him to have finished admiring the room.

"I want to bring you up to date on who I am and where I've been," she replied, leaning forwards and clasping her hands together on top of the desk. "We never kept in touch, did we?"

"No, we didn't," he smiled. "You left here for Chester and came back here from Newcastle. I haven't heard anything else."

"I was in London in between, at two colleges. A steady ascent to the stars. Joe's very useful, of course. I let him screw me occasionally and he fixes everything. It's been like that ever since I met him."

She sat back again and laughed. He wasn't sure why she was being so charmingly explicit, and it was making him ill at ease, as it had done many years ago in the Barred Gate.

"I wanted to explain to you as soon as I could that things have changed, Mort," she continued, looking him directly in the eye. "I've moved on. I'm a Principal now and therefore your superior. I haven't made a formal announcement that I worked here before and I'm not going to do so because it's irrelevant. It may as well have never happened. Only you and one or two others might remember me and you're the only person I was even slightly close to. I forbid you to gossip about me. I know what it's like here. I don't want any rumours or innuendo on the bush telegraph."

She sat forward again still fixing his gaze, although now more malevolently.

"Whatever I may have said or done before has gone. It went when I left. I don't want you to think that I feel the same as I did once, and that things will be as they might have been between us."

He remained expressionless, intentionally making no attempt to show that anything she'd said had touched him. She'd changed from affable to cruel too quickly, but he understood completely why she'd chosen to tell him at the earliest opportunity. Impeccable timing Ariadne, but she'd obviously never had an inkling about her notoriety. She also couldn't know that he'd thought about her many times from the day she left, even when he was with Suzie and all the others, and that she'd wounded him far more than she could imagine.

"But that's enough about me," she grinned. "What have you been up to since Cassandra died."

"I've had one or two relationships," he said hesitantly.

He didn't wish to give many details after what she'd just said. "They were meaningless."

"Do you miss her?"

"Not at all…"

He stopped. She'd turned the tables on him and was undoubtedly enjoying this as some kind of perverse retribution. How much should he tell her? What the hell, why should he care now?

"She ran off with my best mate…"

"Oh Mort," she giggled in the way she once had done long ago. "You're such a loser!"

"They both died, and I've never held it to be a laughing matter."

"How about a quote? Come to think of it I've never heard you quote anything, not even from Shakespeare and you're an English teacher."

"I'm not Horace Rumpole either, lacing every conversation with grandiose crap."

"You used to make references to films, I remember. Planet of the Apes, wasn't it? Some nonsense like that. Haven't you been to the cinema lately?"

"I'll give you one right now if you want…a quote I mean. '*I wasted time, and now doth time waste me; for now hath time made me his numbering clock*'. Richard the Second, act five scene five."

"I hoped it might be about me, but it's still all about you, isn't it? Here's one for me...for a change. '*All the world's a stage all the men and women merely players. They have their exits and their entrances; and one man in his time plays many parts*'. As You Like It, act two scene six. That last bit's sexist and I'd rather have said 'one *woman* plays many parts'!"

He knew then why she'd asked him to see him. She wanted him to recognise without reservation that she'd fulfilled her ambitions but also she wanted to humiliate him to wipe away the past. It had been a game and he'd never meant anything to her. Old Alice had been speaking the truth when she warned him back in 1984. There's no fool like an old fool. He'd always been a fool.

"I think I'd better leave," he said quietly.

He didn't go back to his office. Instead he went out into the car park and sat in his car. He needed a smoke. It struck him that he'd done something similar on his first morning here and it was then that she'd rapped on his window and brought him to his senses. Nearly twenty years later, it had come full circle but this time she'd snuffed out everything fully and finally. For a brief moment he felt angry, picturing himself reaching over her desk and throttling her, but it soon passed to be replaced by a hollow sadness as much for her as for himself. Only a selfish, spiteful, little girl could have done what she'd just done to him and he pitied her. Her character had been formed at her boarding school where her adolescence had consisted of long, lonely hours dominated by strict discipline, hard work and sexual frustration. These elements had more than likely combined to fuel her innate cunning and the aspirations instilled in her by her middle-class upbringing to produce the heartless monster that had finally revealed itself in the meeting that morning, and a matter of minutes ago to him specifically. Perhaps he was going too far but he'd found out finally who she was and all his doubts, suspicions and, above all, the ebb and flow of his soul-searching were over. His gut instinct had been spot on for once and this offered him an unfamiliarly large measure of gratifying compensation. His sadness evaporated and he felt stronger. He stubbed out his cigarette and slapped his thigh. He was looking forward to thinking about Penny's chest in bed that night, but he knew in his heart of hearts that Ariadne wouldn't be far from his thoughts either. When he returned to his office and saw Barry sitting there alone, he remembered all at once that he'd already told him one or two stories about 'the old days' and he ordered him sternly then and there not to repeat them to anyone else – on pain of a slow death and eternal suffering.

Ariadne began to prepare for her next appointment. It was with Penny, Lucy, Maureen and Iris and she'd something interesting to run past them. She opened her hard-backed exercise book to make a few notes when she remembered that she would enjoy herself later that day thinking about 'Mortimer' and how beautifully and ruthlessly she'd crushed him. Afterwards she would cry, because it would reawaken the memory of that glorious year and her final, tearful conversation with him when she'd told him she was leaving Storbury.

"You were the only man I couldn't get, you handsome, intelligent, miserable, weak man," she sighed. "I hate you. I hate you because the only thing you'll feel about me is revulsion."

CHAPTER 45

12 April 2005: 6pm

Miller and Harrison were very pleased with themselves. They'd solved a category one murder in less than a day without any need for extra help. Now it was purely a matter of tying up the loose ends at the station, getting Mort's confession down on paper and establishing how it had been carried out. That process would take considerably longer, another few hours at least, and they both wanted to enjoy the next few minutes to empty their brains of the surplus information they'd been carrying around all day. Soon they'd come to a decision about who else to take statements from – probably only Wallace, Iris and Bernadette and they'd do that in the morning. They'd already made arrangements to meet those still on site in the foyer to inform them that they'd arrested Mort, and Tim was working with the receptionist to gather them all together at six o'clock. Their high spirits were somewhat dampened, however, when Miller phoned the Chief Constable to give him the good news but she wasn't very pleased with his brusque reaction. Instead of offering his warmest congratulations, he told her crustily that they'd 'got lucky' and thrown standard police procedure completely out of the window. He added that there would be a full internal inquiry about 'police protocol' and why Harrison had set up an investigation *in situ* so quickly, without authorization and with so few officers. He also advised her to inform the local press and broadcasters immediately so that they might be allocated a slot on the late evening television news. He wanted more good publicity after the bank robbers had been apprehended late that afternoon along with the stolen money, particularly as no one had been harmed, and the two hostages that the raiders had taken during the night had been safely rescued.

Mort had been taken to the store cupboard as Tim had no further need of it and he was being guarded by the Hulk, who was noticeably flagging. He was sitting on a comfortable looking armchair, which he'd brought over from the waiting area, and he was keeping himself occupied reading a magazine he'd found on the coffee table there. Mort was sitting with his head in his hands, pondering how he'd got himself arrested so quickly without a shred of physical or witness evidence. It was all circumstantial and they'd not even asked him how he'd done it – which he'd have found highly interesting because he'd no idea at all.

"How could I have done it?" he said, suddenly standing up and shaking his head.

"Feeling a bit remorseful, are we, sir?" smirked the Hulk, turning over a page. "It'll go down well in court if you tell the detectives that when you make your statement."

"No, no, I don't mean it like that," replied Mort in frustration. "You misinterpreted my intonation. I was asking myself how I could have killed Ariadne if I don't know how she died. Do you know, constable?"

"I'm afraid I can't discuss a case with a suspect."

"Did she die a horrible death?"

"You should know, Mr Todd, shouldn't you? Now please remain quiet and be patient till they come to take you away."

Mort was about to sit down when a high-pitched woman's voice could be heard out in the foyer, followed immediately afterwards by Helen who came running into the executive suite, pursued equally quickly by Tim.

"He didn't do it!" she screamed. "He can't have done it! He's too nice a guy."

Tim took hold of her by her shoulders and gently pushed into her into the incident room, where a startled Harrison and Miller were waiting to see what was going on.

"Who left that bloody door open?" shouted Harrison, looking sternly at Tim. "What's she doing here?"

"He didn't do it, you stupid buggers," said Helen calming down and returning to her normal self. "He can't have done. He was with me all last night from six o'clock until nine o'clock this morning."

The three detectives gaped at each other in astonishment, until Miller burst out laughing.

"Who are you?" she asked, sitting back in her chair and studying the interloper's naturally confrontational expression.

"I'm Helen Armstrong, Mr Todd's personal assistant," she replied. "He was with me all last night."

"Take a seat, miss," said Harrison, also smiling. "Tell me all about it."

"Don't patronise me, sunshine," she said fiercely, curling her lip. "You can't arrest him. He was with me."

"How did you know we'd arrested Mortimer Todd?" said Miller, putting her head on one side.

She wasn't going to let this fractious slip of a girl dictate to her.

"When I was told I could go home and Mort hadn't come back," snarled Helen.

"Young woman," continued Miller coolly. "I shouldn't say this to you, but he was given every opportunity to establish an alibi and he failed to do so. He's also confessed. I know what you're trying to do and it won't work. Now get out of this room before I have you charged with trying to pervert the course of justice."

"Helen…Helen," came a distant voice which sounded like Mort's. "Do as they say before you get yourself into serious trouble."

"There you are," said Miller, cocking her head in the direction of the makeshift cell. "What more do I have to say?"

"What about Richard Head?" asked Helen, by now so wound up that she'd lost any sense of concern for what kind of trouble this question might cause.

"What about him?"

"He's topped himself, hasn't he? He did it, it's obvious."

"You seem to know a lot about our investigation. How could you possibly know that?"

"Shut up Helen and go home," yelled Mort's voice again.

It sounded more like a cry of anguish than an order.

"She's making it up. She doesn't know anything. Go home Helen."

"Oh Mort," she groaned. "I'm trying to save you…"

"That will be all, miss," said Harrison as sweetly as he could without offending her again. "Do as he says and we'll forget about the whole thing."

"Hold on a second, John," said Miller, still puzzled by Helen's inference. "I want to know how she knows about Richard Head…"

"Shush!" he said, interrupting and putting his finger to his lips. "She's only trying to help her supervisor."

"I beg your pardon!" Miller snapped.

She'd had the initiative taken away from her and she'd lost face into the bargain.

"He sent Mort an email this afternoon saying he was going to do himself in," exclaimed Helen. "We disregarded it because he was drunk when he wrote it."

"Why didn't you inform us immediately?" said Harrison, starting to feel confused by this unanticipated complication. "You might have saved his life."

"Because he's a dickhead," she replied scornfully. Richard Head – dick head! Geddit?"

"Helen, what are you doing?" wailed Mort's voice again.

"Someone shut him up," roared Miller.

She turned to Tim.

"Take this woman's name and address."

She turned back to Helen and smiled cruelly.

"I haven't finished with you yet. Now get out of my sight and that's a bleeding order."

Mort was devastated. Helen had clearly made matters much worse for them both. The police would see her outburst as more damning proof of his guilt, and she'd invented a false alibi as well as admitting they did nothing about Richard Head's email.

"What was all that about?" the Hulk inquired without looking up from his magazine.

"They'll think I did it and she was trying to save me," sighed Mort.

"Yes, sir, they've got you bang to rights and that woman's hysterics aren't going to help. Not looking good is it?"

"Yes, you're right," said Mort grimly. "I've worked here for twenty years, and I've been desperate to leave since day one. I never guessed that the only way out of this place would be in handcuffs."

When Miller had calmed down, Harrison suggested she should prepare a statement for the press, and he'd deal with discharging the managers and the other staff who'd stayed on to help. He made his way to the foyer where he was met by a silent crowd standing around in overcoats or jackets, eager to learn about what had happened but equally intent on going home as soon as possible. Standing with his back to the exit, he outlined the bare bones of Mort's confession and Richard's attempted suicide which were greeted with continued silence. It looked as if they were expecting something like this and he found it very odd.

Everything changed, however, when he told them that they were required to report back tomorrow so that a written account of each of their whereabouts early that morning could be made. Hugh Jones was the first to protest since it would mean keeping the College closed for yet another day, and the logistics of contacting a vast array of students and teachers would be enormous, he said angrily. The three witches, turn by turn, voiced their concerns about interrupting the educational process so close to the examinations, and Steven Wallace asked, more politely than usual, when the College could be re-opened. No one seemed at all concerned about Mort and Richard. Then Iris pointed at the large windows which looked out onto the car park.

"I can't come tomorrow," she said smugly. "I'm going on holiday in the morning and I have to be at the airport for five thirty. My husband's already here to pick me up."

Everyone laughed as they saw Vic's face pressed up against the glass as he squinted in to see what was going on. He was a large man, well over sixty years old, and he was dressed in dirty overalls and a flat cap which made the spectacle even funnier.

"Let him in please, Mr Wallace," she added, beckoning to the scowling estates manager. "He looks stupid standing out there."

"What's going on?" said Vic as he came in, taking off his damp cap as he did so, to reveal a full head of white hair, slightly receding at the temples.

"There was a murder first thing this morning," said Iris importantly. "They've arrested Mort Todd…"

"That's enough," shouted Harrison. "You can tell him the rest later. You'll have to come to the station now I suppose. Or you'll have to postpone your holiday."

"This is preposterous," said Iris, winding herself up for a force ten screaming match. "Vic, say something."

Vic wasn't listening. He was thinking about his trip to the city that morning, in particular about his journey back.

"When is Mr Todd supposed have done the murder?" he asked Harrison, as he scratched his head.

"I'm afraid I can't discuss the matter," replied Harrison impatiently. "Certainly not with you in any event."

"You see," continued Vic slowly, ignoring the detective. "I saw him *first thing* this morning. About eight o'clock. I had to wait a bit longer than usual for him."

"You what?" croaked Harrison, nearly choking. "How do you know it was him?"

"He drives a big, old, ugly, black Mercedes. I have a lot of fun with him."

He smiled and looked round the foyer at the startled, frozen faces.

"What have I said?" he asked incredulously.

"What the hell are you going on about?" said Harrison.

He could feel drops of perspiration starting to form on his forehead and his stomach began to feel queasy.

"I saw Mort Todd this morning at about eight o'clock. I was on my run back here from the city. I'm a lorry driver, see?"

"You saw Mort Todd this morning at eight o'clock?"

"That's what I just said."

"*In the city?*"

"Yes, at about that time."

"At eight o'clock?"

"Yes, just after. It's the same nearly every weekday morning. He lives on my route back to Storbury from my early run to the city in the artic. I hang around so I can see him coming out of Buchanan Road. Always in a hurry, he is. I try to beat him to the traffic lights and, if I do, that's where the fun begins."

Harrison didn't hear Vic's last few words. His mouth was dry and his heart was beating faster than normal. He could feel it thumping into his rib cage as he swore silently to himself over and over again.

"No one's going anywhere tonight," he shouted, taking out his notebook and reading hastily through his list of names. "I want to speak to Bernadette Arden, Iris Baxter and Steven Wallace. You'd better come as well, Mr Baxter. I'll have to start again right from the very beginning."

CHAPTER 46

1 September 2003: Afternoon

The four women trooped slowly into Ariadne's office at two o'clock. Penny and Lucy had come together but Maureen had come separately, and Iris was the last to arrive. She'd been introducing herself to her new underlings and instructing them on how things were going to change now that she was in charge. She'd gone on so long that she had to take a late lunch and she just made the meeting in time. They were dazzled by what they saw as they entered, just as Mort had been an hour and half earlier. Maureen let out a whistle of admiration and Ariadne sparkled with delight. They couldn't decide which feature they liked the best as they clucked around admiring everything. When Penny asked innocently how much the 'revamp', as she put it, had cost, Ariadne merely shook her head and deflected the question by asking the others which of the photographs and the paintings that hung on every wall they liked best. Lucy asked who the people were in each of the photographs and Ariadne, slightly miffed by this, explained they'd been taken with celebrities she'd met on her travels, identifying Joe Crossley on one, Kurt Cobain on another, and a group of minor television personalities at a charity dinner on the third. She told them that they'd been arranged for her by a close friend of hers, and they were among a large collection she'd amassed intentionally to create the impression that she moved in glamorous circles.

The mood changed however when she told them they had to get down to business and they saw what they had to sit on. Four grey plastic chairs had been stacked in one corner of the room, and she asked each one of the women to take one and gather round her lustrous desk.

"I've called you here to sketch out my special plan," she began earnestly. "I want you to treat what I have to say as strictly confidential between us and these four walls. I want to move towards making this college staffed, as near as the law will permit, by women. This will enable us to rule out many problems associated with the male gender, such as aggression, coarseness, immature lewdness and all forms of sexual harassment. I could go on and I will if you want me to. I've battled my entire career against those four despicable qualities, and I want to eradicate them at Storbury. This will naturally be of benefit to all male students as they will be allowed to blossom in a caring environment replete with sensitivity, empathy, tolerance and self-awareness. I will introduce a strict code of conduct to ensure that this is robustly and rigidly implemented. Two of the major tenets of this code will be that it will be misogynistic for a man to criticise a woman and to talk about any kind of male-dominated sport. Do I have your support?"

She looked up from her notes to see four women who were, as a traitorous Maureen told Mort later about the tenor of the meeting (but not the details), completely staggered. Iris's mouth was wide-open. Her normally ashen face had changed to a dark shade of plum and she looked as though she were about to have a heart attack. The others, however, including Maureen herself, simply looked confused. Ariadne took this as a sign of approval but observing Iris's starkly changed demeanor, she asked her directly for an opinion. Iris mumbled something incoherent and looked away out of the window.

"What are you doing about the current male managers?" asked Lucy.

She assumed this would be a sensible question in the circumstances and was heartened to hear Ariadne praise her for her astuteness.

"I've thought that one through already," she said, leaning forwards across her desk and clasping her hands together. "Hugh, Mike and Mort are, in the short term, indispensable, but we'll have to put up with that until I can encourage them to leave or find a reason to dispense with their services. Richard Head and the others, however, are not, and that brings me to the second part of my plan."

The women looked on, restlessly crossing and uncrossing their legs as she spoke.

"I want to phase out all traditional male subjects such as Engineering and I want to ban…"

"Isn't that counterproductive," said Maureen interrupting. "What about the female students? And what about our gender policy of encouraging young women to…"

"Let me finish," said Ariadne in such a tone that Maureen expected Ariadne's eyes to turn a shimmering red and emit a death ray and blast her to smithereens. "I want to replace them with sciences, as I said at this morning's meeting. It's a must-have in a location like this and I've learned from our local MP Joseph Crossley that a new pharmaceuticals company is planning to move near here, so we have to be ahead of the game to ensure we meet their employment and training needs. In addition I want the laboratories to be able to synthesize certain products Mr Crossley imports from countries in South America. It will diversify our portfolio of services, Penny, and I'm sure you agree that's a good thing. It will bring in extra revenue. As for Richard, he's too old to deal with this. He contributes very little to the College as it is, and it will be way out of his comfort zone to take on something innovative and exciting. I want an intelligent and ambitious young woman. Besides, to be frank with you, I don't like him. He turned his nose up at my photographs although he wouldn't say why. Above all, it's his name. I can't stand it. How can we be taken seriously when the first interface our customers will have with him is that stupid name? Good God!"

"Have you told him?" asked Maureen.

She was concerned that Ariadne was going too far and although she didn't have too much 'interface' with Richard herself, she liked him. He ran a tight ship, although perhaps Ariadne was right in everything else she'd said. Yet it was too harsh, and she had to know if he was aware he was a marked man.

"Of course, not," laughed Ariadne. "I wasn't going to mention to him casually that I'm phasing him and his department out when I saw him last week."

"You've already seen him?" said Maureen. "In the holidays?"

"It was last Friday afternoon actually. He was in here prowling about so I asked him to come and look at my glossy new den."

She turned to the others.

"What do you think about my plan?"

"Sounds wonderful," said Penny. "However I agree with Maureen about developing female roles in the workplace."

"Me too," added Lucy nodding sycophantically.

Maureen's expression remained unchanged; only Iris demurred.

"Not with us, Iris?" said Ariadne more in disappointment than animosity. "I thought you'd be the first to agree after working for all those men for so long. No more wandering hands, no more demeaning duties, no more running their errands…"

"I quite liked it," said Iris. "They treated me well. I've nothing against them. Not like that anyway. There were never any attempts to touch *me* up."

"Out with the patriarchy, in with the new matriarchy, Iris," said Ariadne, almost pleading.

"Put it that way, I see what you mean. There are some men I don't like here, and I'll be glad to see the back of them. Take that Mort Todd, for instance. He doesn't look like a senior manager, he doesn't talk like a senior manager, and he doesn't act like one either – no matter what those lefty inspectors said. How desperate were we that we had to give *him* a job?"

"That's more like it," cheered Ariadne in triumph. "Mort's too valuable to us to lose straightaway. I'm working on it though, don't worry."

She paused and looked down at her notes again.

"Right. You're all with me. The core working party to get things moving will be me, Lucy and Penny and I hope we'll be joined by the new Adult Education Manager when *she's* been appointed. I'm not excluding you, Maureen and Iris, because I have other tasks for you, but more of that later. That's all for today."

She motioned them to go, but Maureen hung back. She wanted to see for herself how much Ariadne had changed and how sincere she was about her controversial plans in the light of her past reputation, but she was most concerned about Richard and Mort. She closed the door and sat down.

"It's good to see you again," she began tactfully. "I didn't know you very well when you were here before, but I heard a lot about you. I'm very pleased that you've achieved so much in such a short time. Your career's been glittering, but I've stayed here all my working life and I've got as far as I want to go. I like Storbury and I'm married to a good man. Do you mind if I ask you the secret of your success?"

Ariadne laughed nervously. She hadn't been used to such casual openness lately and she had to consider how to reply without appearing either too friendly or too offhand.

"The first thing I'd say is 'be your own person', plan exactly where you want to go and what it is you want from other people, if that answers your question?"

Maureen smiled and looked at Ariadne's left hand.

"I see you're not married. How've you managed to stay single this long?"

Ariadne twitched and she wanted to end the conversation.

"Frankly Maureen it's none of your business," she replied, raising her voice.

"I meant you're a very attractive woman," said Maureen calmly. "I'm surprised, that's all."

She wasn't afraid of Ariadne, and she could see that she was flustered.

"And you're not very hard to read, Maureen," said Ariadne, regaining her serenity. "What's your real reason for asking me all these things?"

"I'm worried about Richard. Don't play games with him. Like me he's been here for ages. Don't simply throw him away because he's a man."

"What do you mean? I'm not throwing him away. You heard what I said previously."

"Are you going to get rid of Mort too? You let Iris say all those awful things about him."

"Don't worry about him. He's going nowhere until I've finished with him entirely. I know Iris dislikes him and I allowed her to speak out to get her on board."

Maureen had found out the one thing she wanted to know, but she was assured enough to leave Ariadne with something to brood over before went.

"You're very cunning, aren't you?" she said with complete disregard for any consequences of what she was saying. "You use people, don't you – men in particular."

"I beg your pardon!" said Ariadne, seething with irritation. "Are you accusing me of using my gender?"

"Ariadne, where did your views on men come from? I'm not sure I agree with them. There's nothing more fascinating than the certainty of women in their own company when the topic is the opposite sex. You talk as if all men are violent, uncouth sex maniacs. It may sound obvious but they're not all like that."

"They see us as imperfect versions of themselves when the opposite is true."

"Why then do you regard women as superior and continue to see us as some sort of abused victims at the same time?"

"You're starting to annoy me, Maureen…"

"There's one man who's levelheaded, reliable, patient and fair. He's also gentle, kind and funny."

"You mean Mort," laughed Ariadne. "You won't save him…"

"I mean my husband," said Maureen sharply. "I understand clearly that Mort will have to save himself."

"Do I take it that you've decided not to help me with my vision?"

"Of course not," chuckled Maureen. "I'm a woman. I recognise that you take everything seriously, you're committed to your plans and you'll work hard to see them implemented. I'm delighted to be invited to join you."

She stood up quickly, regretting that she'd been unable to include the word 'solutions' somewhere in the last sentence but she'd had as much as she could take.

"I have to go," she said as she turned to leave, "I love my job and I won't jeopardise it over a philosophical matter. Thank you for an interesting chinwag!"

"Before you go, Maureen, there's one other thing," said Ariadne, pointing her finger. "You're not to tell anyone that I worked here previously nor are you to discuss me with those who remember me. Is that understood?"

Maureen smiled one last time as she quietly closed the door.

Ariadne sat back and stroked her ear. The unveiling of her special plan hadn't gone as well as she'd hoped, and she was perturbed by their initial, impromptu reactions to it. Perhaps she should issue them all with pleasure balls which they'd have to wear whenever they were in her presence. She'd have a remote control, and she'd press it to make them squirm with delight whenever she wanted them to agree with her. She'd easily won over the two younger women, but not Iris or Maureen. She could dominate Iris easily, but she hadn't met anyone as shrewd and brazenly candid as Maureen for many a year. She'd grown accustomed to obsequious toadies, and she was puzzled by this wildly inflated, rebellious mockery from a woman without fear of anything – or anybody for that matter. Maureen had foolishly shown her true colours, and she would have to keep a close eye on her. As she began to calm down, it struck her that Maureen would be the anticipated corollary of the ambitious social engineering programme for which she was striving; a self-fulfilled, assertive, secure woman. She was, in short, the perfect image of herself but she wasn't sure if she wanted that, and she would reflect on it later. She had another secret meeting to chair, this time with Hugh Jones and Mike Smith.

* * *

Maureen went directly to Mort's office, where fortuitously he was alone. She was bursting to tell him everything that Ariadne had put to her and the other women, but she dare not. She liked to laugh with him about the idiosyncrasies of the people they worked with but she would never reveal anything which had been imparted to her in confidence. All she told him was that their Principal was "utterly bonkers" and how her "daft ideas" had affected Iris specifically. When he protested that she shouldn't give him half a story, she reminded him that there'd been another occasion, many years ago, when he'd done exactly the same after his strange encounter with Alice the Alcie. He did concede however that there was a common denominator in Ariadne and, now that she was back, she was already causing a lot of trouble.

"You should have seen Iris's face, Mort," said Maureen trying to brighten his mood and move the emphasis back to Iris. "She looked like a beetroot! It looked at one point as if she wanted to do away with the Lady Ariadne she was so angry!"

"I guess the new Principal's hatching a plan to get rid of the old timers," he replied, ignoring her and switching the subject back to Ariadne. "We've too much history here and she'll want to rid herself of the excess baggage."

"If that's true, why were Iris and I invited to be in on the conspiracy?"

"Iris is bossy and cantankerous. That's why Ariadne wants to keep her. She doesn't take prisoners and she doesn't care what other people think about her. As for you, you never had much to do with Ariadne, and she never saw you as a threat…"

"She might do now after what I've been saying…"

"There you go, playing the mystery woman again. What *did* you tell her?"

"I won't say. I can't say."

"Did she mention me?"

"Yes. You're *very* safe for the foreseeable future, if that's what you're worried about, but Iris definitely doesn't like you."

"She's made that perfectly clear ever since my first day here! She seems to have had a star role at your witches' coven."

"For all the wrong reasons, old lad. Ariadne should never have promoted her. Hell's bells, Mort, she's so stupid and so out of touch with the modern world. Anyway, what did Ariadne want to see you about?"

Mort raised his eyebrows.

"I won't say. I can't say," he said with an unforgiving look in his eye.

CHAPTER 47

12 April 2005: 6.30pm – 7.30pm

Confusion reigned as the three detectives argued about what they should do next, and their voices echoed out into the corridor. No one had told Mort or the Hulk what had taken place in the foyer a few minutes earlier and, as they'd both turned to look in the direction of the commotion, they were surprised to see Wallace, Bernadette, Iris and Vic marched briskly past them by two uniformed officers who ordered them curtly to sit down in the waiting area. Mort, still hunched with his arms between his legs, asked who the elderly, boiler-suited man was but the Hulk shrugged uninterestedly and went on reading his magazine. He stared out at the glowering quartet and assumed it had to be someone Iris knew well because she was talking sharply to the man about losing his car keys.

Suddenly, like a train rushing out of a tunnel, Harrison darted out of the incident room and shouted for 'Mr Baxter' to accompany him. It was Iris's husband! Mort vaguely remembered Maureen describing him as 'only a bloody lorry driver' when he first went to see her in his second week at Storbury. It had stayed in his mind because Maureen's tone had been cruelly disparaging, but Iris's airs and graces frequently indicated that she would have considered it more fitting if she were married to a professional man. As Vic Baxter stood up he looked over at Mort, who was peering out of the store room door, and waved cheerily. Mort considered it a strange thing to do, as he'd have sworn they'd never met before, although there was something about him that he hazily recognised. Iris, still scowling, pushed Vic indecorously away and told him to hurry up as she was anxious to leave. He glanced back at her ruefully and walked off, smiling again at Mort as he passed by.

When he entered the incident room, he was greeted with the same facial expressions that he'd just left behind, and he scratched his head again in bemusement.

"Mr Baxter," began Harrison determinedly. "Please take a seat. I am going to ask you a few questions and I must warn you that you will be under caution throughout the whole of this interview. Do you understand me?"

Vic nodded and did as he was ordered, unclear why he wasn't speeding home to pack for his holiday. Harrison gestured towards Miller.

"Will you please tell Detective Chief Inspector Miller what you said about seeing Mr Todd this morning," he added with equal fervour.

Vic obliged with his account of seeing Mort that very morning and he saw her gulp hard.

"What have I done?" he asked nervously when he observed both Harrison and Tim do much the same, but his question was met with what could only be described as a stony silence.

It was broken by Miller who was trying to form words, but nothing came out other than short, disjointed sounds. Eventually Harrison found his voice.

"Are you prepared to make statement to that effect?" he said, clearing his throat.

Vic nodded and Tim quickly thrust the appropriate form onto the desk in front of him.

"Can me and the wife go then?" he inquired hopefully. "We're off to New York for a few days."

Harrison remained unmoved.

"Please write down what you've just told us," he said coldly. "Then you can go. Please leave details of your movements, where you're staying and what airports you'll be using with Detective Constable Hudson before you leave. We'll no doubt want to speak to you and your wife again on your return."

When, ten minutes later, they had Vic's evidence on paper, Tim showed him out and they heard Iris's loud, scolding voice reverberating harshly around the corridor. The stridency subsided gradually as the delayed holiday makers swiftly made their way out of the executive suite and off into the twilight. Harrison bit his lip agitatedly and Miller began slowly to brush her trousers, neither looking at the other. Tim was hovering near the whiteboard.

"Shall I release Todd?" he said cagily.

"Bring him in here first," replied Harrison while Miller was sweeping her thighs. "I'm still not sure he didn't do it."

This perked Miller up.

"I'll speak to him," she said wearily. "I don't want a series of false arrest charges on top of all this mess."

Mort sat impassively contemplating his knees as Miller told him that a witness had by chance come forward to support his alibi.

"Was it Iris's husband?" he asked, hardly believing that he wasn't dreaming, and he was in some dark, damp cell in the centre of Storbury.

"Yes, it was," she said girlishly, as though her previous incarnation as grand inquisitor had never existed. "He's a lorry driver and he's signed a statement to the effect that you were twenty miles away from here at eight o'clock this morning. This means that unless you own a helicopter, you couldn't have murdered Ms Hopwood and got back there at that time. It looks like your story checks out." "I've never seen him before," said Mort without realising that he might be further incriminating himself. "How does he know me?"

"He has a regular, early run to the city in a lorry most mornings. On his way back he drives ahead of you for the first part of your journey and deliberately slows you down.

He said he has a few accomplices who do likewise all around Storbury. It's some kind of childish, old man's game they've been playing for years…"

"The Vigilantes! You didn't believe me, did you?"

"It's lucky for you he came here to pick up Mrs Baxter," said a familiar voice behind him.

It was the Hulk. He'd become fond of Mort as he guarded him, and he wanted to see the look on his face when they told him he was free to go. He'd appreciated being spoken to you like an equal, the more so because Mort had asked him questions and listened to his answers.

"Come on, Mort," he added, grinning as usual. "You can buy me a cup of coffee to celebrate, if the canteen's still open."

It was after seven o'clock and Harrison and Miller were now hungry as well as tired. They asked Tim to buy some sandwiches and strong, black coffee even if it meant going into town and back again. They could interview Bernadette while he was away and grill Steven Wallace again when he got back.

* * *

"Tell me what happened when you went to fetch the Principal at nine thirty this morning, Ms Arden," said Miller now recovered enough to lead again.

"I opened the door," said Bernadette, cotton handkerchief in hand. "Then I saw her. It was ghastly."

"Then what?"

"I went back and told the others."

"What did the others do?"

"They all looked shocked. It was Iris, I mean Mrs Baxter who took charge. She told the other managers what to do and then she left the room to call the police."

"I appreciate it's difficult for you, but can you remember anything about what you saw when you opened the door?"

"I saw a woman who looked dead with a gruesome face. She was lying back in her chair…I'm sorry I can't go on..."

She burst out sobbing and streams of tears were rolling down her cheeks. She put her handkerchief in her mouth.

"Take your time, Ms Arden," said Miller softly.

"There's nothing else I can tell you," blubbed Bernadette. "Nothing. I hope I never see anything like that ever again. It was horrible. Horrible!"

"One more question," said Harrison gently. "What did you do after seeing Ms Hopwood like that?"

"I ran away. What else could I have done?"

"Did you lock the door?"

"I can't remember. I don't think so – but I had to unlock the door when I went to fetch her, which was odd. It's never kept locked except when she's out. Oh…and Iris borrowed my key to lock the door after she went to check that I hadn't imagined it all."

"Thank you, Ms Arden," he said with finality. "You can go home after you've given us a statement. Do you want me to arrange for someone to drive you?"

"I'll be alright," she replied softly.

As she left, Tim and the Hulk returned with food and drink. The refectory was open, and Tim said that most of the detainees were in there having something to eat.

"Why did you assume you could let her go without consulting me?" growled Miller as she opened her sandwiches.

"The door was locked when I arrived here this morning," said Harrison excitedly. "I had to borrow a key from one of the caretakers – the one called Paul. That Iris woman had locked it before she made the 999 call. But, and this is the important thing, the door was locked when Ms Arden went to find out why the Principal was late for her meeting. That means that the murderer must have had a key. There's no other way in or out of her office."

"That means" said Miller hesitantly, catching on. "Someone locked the door after…!"

"Bingo!" said Harrison jubilantly. "Bloody hell, are we lucky or not? It must be Wallace. He's the only one with a key who we can place at the scene of the crime. The other caretaker was busy somewhere else. That's what Wallace said this afternoon."

He turned to the Hulk who was sitting on the wooden table munching something.

"Naylor, get Wallace in here right now!"

"Begging your pardon, sir," he replied, sounding like a character from a Dickens novel. "I'd rather not. Can someone else go? He's blood and he has nasty contacts. I don't want to upset him."

All at once Miller looked interested but her ponderings were disrupted by Tim.

"If I was playing with myself, I'd lock the door," he said irreverently. "That's why Bernadette found it locked."

Harrison smiled but Miller didn't find it amusing.

"OK, I'll go get Wallace," Tim added, his aside dismissed by her dirty look. "Let's hear what he has to say. Come on Albert, stand guard outside again or something."

* * *

Wallace slumped into his seat and grimaced sulkily. Harrison was standing behind Miller and Tim. He'd handed over to the young detective because he wanted to watch Wallace carefully, and he had every confidence in Tim to help her break him down.

"We haven't spoken before, have we?" Tim began after he cautioned the Estate Manager. "Tell me what you did when you got here this morning?"

Wallace wearily recounted the story once again that he'd already given Miller and Harrison that afternoon, missing out no details as far as Harrison could remember. Then Miller took over. She was still thinking about the Hulk's last words.

"Mr Wallace," she said fussily, pausing for effect. "You said you were Ms Hopwood's minder. You were very protective of her, weren't you? Who were you protecting her from?"

Wallace stroked his chin and then rubbed his nose frantically.

"I want to see a solicitor," he said, and for the first time his overconfident swagger evaporated.

He looked scared.

"Who are you afraid of?" she asked sharply. "If you won't tell us, your son will."

For a moment his mouth moved and it looked like her ruse had worked.

"I haven't got...a son," he stuttered.

"You told us before that Constable Naylor is your son – and he's confirmed it. He also admitted that you had a relationship with his mother before you left Storbury. Is that why you left? Did you run away from her and your responsibilities?"

"I want to see a solicitor," he repeated. "I'm saying nothing else."

"Are you trying to protect him? He's frightened of you. He says you have powerful friends..."

Miller stopped. She wanted to let him 'simmer' for a while before she 'turned up the heat'. She liked the allusion. She was playing rough, tough TV cop and she was loving every second of it. It was invigorating and she wriggled in her seat with the thrill. She could see he was sweating.

"Shall I have him come in?" she said, choosing the phrase carefully so that it sounded vaguely American. "I'm sure he'd tell me if I ordered him to."

"No, no, don't do that. I don't want him dragged into this. He won't squeal and I don't want him in bother either."

"You weren't minding her, were you? You were being paid to *keep an eye* on her. I believe they were your very words. Is that what you were doing this morning? Were you watching what she was doing?"

"I want to see a solicitor," repeated Wallace.

Then all at once he jumped up and ran and opened the door, only to find his escape route blocked by the Hulk. For the second time that day he was roughly treated by a policeman but in this instance he was bundled back into the interview room.

"I want to see a solicitor," he shouted frenziedly.

"Sit down, Mr Wallace," commanded Miller. "Thank you Constable Naylor. Please stay if you will. I have a question or two for you."

"I told you to leave him alone, you smartarse bitch," he screeched, struggling to free himself from the Hulk's grip. "It's Joe Crossley who's paying me."

He relaxed his body and looked compassionately at the Hulk.

"Get out Albert."

It was the Hulk's turn to look stunned.

"Shut up, dad," he yelled as he let go of his father.

"It's OK, *son*," said Wallace shaking himself and straightening his jacket. "They'd have found out sooner or later."

The Hulk hung his head and sloped out of the room. Wallace sat down and looked up at Harrison.

"She's a good one, eh, Plod?" he said sarcastically. "Right, who's taking notes? I'll start from the beginning."

He took a deep breath.

"Joe Crossley was in love with Ariadne but she wouldn't marry him. So when I got done for beating up a prisoner, he used his influence with the Chief Constable to get me off. In return I had to watch her and report anything unusual."

"Unusual?" asked Miller.

Her head was tilted to one side again.

"If I ever saw her with another bloke. The first time I did was with Mr Todd, but I've told you about that already. Joe was very pleased, so I made up a few more sightings – all innocent ones, like – and this seemed to please him even more. Then when I got into a fight – off duty, by the way Plod – and got chucked out of the police, he hired me to follow her wherever she went…"

"Isn't that a bit farfetched?"

"Have you met Joe Crossley? He's completely smitten with her, and I don't know what's he's going to do now."

"Go on."

"I followed her around as I said. It was easy at a college but outside it was impossible – even when I found out where she lived, and I could tail her from there."

"How did you manage to keep going for nearly twenty years?"

"Joe really seemed happiest when I wasn't reporting anything. Occasionally I sent him something to keep him sweet, but I did see her with other men and I told him about them once in a while."

"How much was he paying you?"

"What do you mean?"

"How much was he paying you?"

Wallace looked bemused.

"I don't see what you're getting at. Well, not that it matters but it varied. Thirty quid a week at first. It was index-linked. It went up as the cost of living went up."

"What's he paying you these days?"

"He hasn't paid me for ages. He recommended me for this job and that's more than enough."

"I still don't understand why a man like Crossley would go to such lengths. He's an MP. He could take his pick of dozens of women."

"He probably can, but he's obsessed with Ariadne. Did you know they've been engaged since nineteen eighty something and she accompanies him on all the big occasions? I bet that helped her rise up the ranks. They need each other, you see."

"Ah, so Mr Crossley isn't a shadowy figure in the background to this murder. He's a very jealous man. Why did they never get married?"

"He wanted to, but she didn't. She must have been in love with her career…"

"Or someone else?"

"Like who, for instance?"

"Like Mortimer Todd."

"Naaah, not him. Never in a million years. He's a tosser."

"The last thing she may have written was 'Mortimer – then prep meeting'. What do think that meant?"

"Dunno. Funny thing to write."

Miller looked at her watch. It was nearly eight o'clock.

"Did you kill Ariadne Hopwood this morning?" she snapped. "Before anyone else except you and she were in this building?"

She saw that he was looking frightened.

"I let her in to this part of the building but I didn't go back to my office. I knew what she was going to do. I'd seen her all excited a few times before and I knew she was going to… masturbate…"

"What did you say?" exclaimed Miller. "How could you possibly recognise when a woman is going to masturbate?"

"I could see it on her face like she was excited. There was this weird glint in her eyes. She walked a bit quicker, you know, that sort of thing. It's not like that every day. Most mornings she's gruff with me."

He paused as if reliving the experience.

"She loved the danger, I expect. She never locked the door and she never fully closed the curtains."

Harrison nodded at the other detectives with a 'told you so' look on his face but Wallace thought he was laughing at him.

"I'd seen her do it before – by accident" he continued more earnestly. "I was outside the building checking the state of the windows one morning a few months ago and when I walked past her office I saw her going at it like the clappers. She was well out of it. The ceiling could have caved in and she wouldn't have noticed. That's why I got into the habit of letting her in each morning. It wasn't a courtesy. I was waiting for that special look on her face."

"You were there this morning weren't you?"

"Yes, but she'd just got started when Paul called me on the two-way radio asking me where I was, so I left her to it."

"She heard the radio, didn't she? Then she saw you. You came in and had to stop her telling anyone – like the police. You'd have been sacked and you panicked like you did five minutes ago."

"No I came back into this building to help Paul upstairs. She didn't see me. I said she was somewhere else – on another planet."

"What was she using to, er, pleasure herself with?"

"You don't really want me to tell you, do you?"

"No, but I get the picture – or rather I wish I didn't!"

Harrison had been watching the dialogue with great interest. It was a lesson for him in how to make a man tell the truth quickly and they had another suspect. Yet he wasn't going to get carried away and make another hasty decision. He didn't want two complaints against him in one day.

"What time was that?" he asked.

"About quarter past or twenty past seven."

"Think carefully Steven. Did you see anyone else around?"

"Not until after half seven, maybe a bit later, when I happened to look out of the window. I saw Helen Armstrong walking up the drive. Oh and I saw a car drive past her in the opposite direction. Frigging hell, I see what you're getting at. Why didn't I remember that before?"

"Can you describe the car?"

"It was black, I think, or certainly a dark shade. That's all I recollect. I'm sorry."

"Do you keep a list of staff cars?"

"Yes, but we only register make and number plate in case we want one shifted if it's blocking another one in the car park – and things like that."

Harrison paused and stroked his chin.

"One final thing," he said slowly and deliberately, fixing Wallace with a thunderous look.

"Did you check those keys I asked you about this morning? Are there any missing?"

Wallace looked away and then suddenly smiled.

"Yes I bloody well did. I forgot to tell you because you never asked. There's one full set missing. They're the keys to all the doors in this suite."

Harrison looked at Miller and smiled. She knew what that signified.

"Thank you, Steven," he said cordially. "Wait here will you please."

Without pausing he looked at Miller who was beaming. She motioned to Tim.

"Go and bring that vile, young woman in here without delay," she shouted clapping her hands.

CHAPTER 48

November 2004

Storbury College had become a much changed institution. Ariadne had been Principal (or Chief Executive as she preferred to call herself) for nearly four terms and she'd made her presence felt. Anyone who'd known her as a young lecturer wouldn't have recognised the woman that now ruled the roost. The lovely face, sharp features and the shoulder-length, black hair were all more or less the same as were her shapely, diminutive figure, but they disguised a loathsome beast lurking within. Where once she'd been judged as devious and ambitious by those who suspected her motives, now she was openly egotistical, obsessive, tyrannical, confrontational and vengeful. She brooked no opposition to her many pioneering projects, most of which were aimed at increasing the amount of money flowing into the College's coffers. Her closest allies were Hugh Jones who managed the government funding contracts and the complex data streams to regulate income, and Mike Smith who constantly sought new students from private business abroad and prosperous local companies. They met in secret in far off hotels so that no one knew what they were planning. The other managers were entrusted to run the curriculum, and they too were charged with increasing enrolments on courses by dint of the draconian targets she set them. They were also responsible for raising educational standards although the former often led to problems with the latter, many of the so called learners who were registered were simply not good enough and either dropped out or failed their examinations. This inevitably led to their teachers being severely reprimanded and, in some extreme cases, dismissed for incompetence. The fearless Ariadne took on any legal opposition and employment tribunals with importunate relish, commonly settling out of court before proceedings began, to her and the College's substantial advantage.

Work had begun a year earlier on building the science block, and the foundation stone was laid with abundant fanfares and publicity by none other than Joe Crossley himself in his role as local MP but also as a generous benefactor. He and Ariadne often attended important local and regional functions together as 'partners' (in every sense of the word), particularly when some pecuniary gain could be acquired either for themselves or for the institution. It had been a long era of suffering since she took over the reins but, to all intents and purposes, it had been a good one financially. Moreover, she spared no expense on herself and, as well as redecorating her office with the silver desk and the equally costly matching accessories, she bought a silver sports car and moved into an exclusive, luxury flat in the most stylish part of town, conveniently situated very close to her workplace. In contrast, within the College she was immensely unpopular with the lecturing staff and to say that the majority abhorred her is a colossal understatement. She made them work the longest hours allowable in the classroom, she cut their salaries and holidays, and she replaced any teacher who'd worked full-time with half-time equivalents on the premise that she could squeeze more out of two part-time teachers on more flexible timetables and hourly pay. Yet people still applied for the many vacancies there, and she was resolute on her policy of positive discrimination towards women. She paid no heed to her reputation within the college, secure in her unprincipled belief of *oderint dum metuant*[1] and she was feted outside of

1   Let them hate so long as they fear.

it by the people she cared most about. By the end of her first academic year she was coming to the notice of those in high places who saw her manifest merits as a model of modern managerial pragmatism in what had become difficult days for further education. And so it proved for Storbury when in early November 2004 the financial auditors made their annual visit and found, to everyone's horror, 'substantial irregularities', and announced starkly that they would return in six months if the 'issues' hadn't been resolved.

Hugh Jones chaired the first senior managers meeting after notice was given by Ofsted as well as the auditors that the college was to be inspected the following year, although assurances were given that this would be on an 'informal interim basis only', such was the high esteem in which Ariadne was held. She was, however, absent without explanation at this meeting, and this gave the assembled managers not only a cause for unanticipated conjecture, but, more significantly, a licence to talk more openly and freely as a group. Hugh's bulging face was redder than usual and the bags under his eyes looked blacker than ever, probably through lack of sleep. Mike Smith looked worried and fidgety, taking off his glasses and cleaning them unnecessarily from time to time as though he was hoping that he'd be able to see more clearly for some reason. Hugh called the meeting to order at nine forty; had Ariadne been there he'd have explained this lateness as uncertainty about how to begin and he needed to compose himself. He rapped on the table and explained that this was to be an unminuted, extraordinary gathering and what was to follow was not to be spoken about. This was why Bernadette Arden was not present.

He made his announcement quickly and waited for the predictable response. Mort, basking in the limelight of his status as leading academic Head, opened the inevitable process of seeking clarification.

"Can you give us some details?" he asked without looking up from his blank notepad. "I can't imagine how this can affect my department."

"There are some challenges with data returns to the funding agency, including the courses in Greece," replied Hugh, shuffling his papers. "In addition there are, er, shall we say, glitches in the software they sent us. They apply across the board."

"Can you summarise the implications of these challenges?"

"We've been claiming too much money."

"Is that all?" said Lucy, not at all alarmed as she hadn't fully got to grips with the apparent severity of the situation. "We must have banked all the money and if we have to pay back anything, surely it can be paid off from the interest we've earned."

"It doesn't quite work like that," said Penny in frustrated disbelief at Lucy's ingenuousness before fixing her gaze on Hugh. "All my department's enrolment forms and registers are in order. The Quality Manager has checked them and therefore I can assume it's your section that's responsible for these 'challenges', whatever that means."

The other Heads murmured their agreement and Lucy, trying not to appear the complete fool Penny had made her feel, sought again to make a salient point.

"They'll believe us, won't they?" she said cheerfully. "We're a successfully expanding college thanks to the Principal…"

"That's a good point," Mike broke in. "But the big picture's somewhat more delicate than Hugh has indicated. I've obtained some databases from the larger firms in the area…"

He paused and wiped his glasses again.

"I've obtained them without their knowledge via a few contacts and I've been using their employees' details…"

"In plain language please enlighten us how deep the shit is," said Mort more by way of cussedness than curiosity before Mike could finish.

Hugh shuddered.

"It can all be rectified by a few adjustments here and there," he explained. "Most of the data's at the raw stage and we can blame the software for being overoptimistic. Similarly any creative accounting can be wiped away at the flick of a few switches and the accidental destruction of a couple of laptops…"

"This is utterly despicable," fulminated an incandescent Iris, looking near to a full eruption. "You two should be sacked on the spot. This is corruption at its most flagrant."

"We're not entirely responsible," admitted Mike to Hugh's fulsome consternation. "We were only obeying orders."

"Hold on, Mike," Hugh tried to intercede, but he was too late.

"Sounds familiar," sniggered Mort, placing his index finger between his nose and his top lip.

"Mr Todd!" exploded Iris. "This is no laughing matter. This place is going to rack and ruin."

She raised herself up and pointed at Mike as though she were about to leap over the table.

"I assume we're attributing this entire muddle to the Principal. Have the governors been informed?"

"Yes and no," answered Hugh as Mike was too busy cowering back in his seat.

"What does that mean?" asked Iris, sitting back down and fanning herself with her notepaper pad. "Have the governors been informed?"

"No, not yet. They don't need to be advised of the current situation at all. I can smooth it over before they even find out."

"Who apart from us knows about this?" said Maureen calmly.

She'd been weighing up the argument from a discreet distance and she was impressed by Hugh's coolness and level-headedness.

"No one, as I said in my initial remarks."

"Then why are you letting us in on this sordid, pathetic matter?"

"It's a collective responsibility…"

"No it's not, it's yours and Ariadne's. How can we be to blame?

"You're responsible for the electronic registers for your teachers' activities, aren't you?"

"You've been doctoring them, haven't you? What have you been doing? It's some kind of fiddle, isn't it?"

"I wouldn't quite put it like that – but you're getting the picture."

To everyone's amazement it was Richard Head who voiced the inevitable finale to their dispute.

"I've not heard of this one since the age before computers when *cardboard* registers were the norm and you could do what you liked as long as you weren't found out," he said jadedly.

"I've told you I'll fix everything," said Hugh confidently. "It may take a short while but I can do it, I promise you."

"Why have you let us in on this?" asked Maureen looking sceptical.

"You may need to work on your stories for the auditors-slash-inspectors if I don't manage to sort everything out before May. You could look out for two or three scapegoats from the lower ranks…"

"What's the worst that can happen?"

"You'll probably get a reprimand, I might be sacked and the Principal could go to prison."

"This is intolerable," shrieked Iris, now at force nine on the Baxter Scale and steadily climbing.

Hugh ignored her, thanked the assembled managers for their attendance and walked out, hastily followed by a repentant looking Mike.

"Ariadne has to go," whispered Mort to Maureen as they rose to leave but he'd been overheard.

"Can I have a word with you, Mr Todd?" said Iris, more as a command than a request. "In my office, please. In five minutes."

Mort went directly to see her as instructed, eschewing his customary analysis of the proceedings with Maureen. He supposed he was in for a ticking-off for his childish levity when the ship appeared to be sinking with all hands, or more decorously, all officers. He arrived early and met her in the empty corridor outside her room.

"Thank you for coming, Mort," she said uncharacteristically capriciously.

He'd never seen her like this before and he took an involuntary step backwards.

"What did you mean when you said that Ariadne should be got rid of?" she continued. "I thought you were fond of her, or, more to the point, you were her friend, were you not?"

"That might have been your perception of our earlier relationship but I assure you things are different now. She's changed radically. It's not the same woman. She's the personification of evil and amorality, if you ask me."

He concluded that he might have exaggerated the final image but he wanted to let her suppose that he was on her side.

"Thank you Mort for your candour," she answered. "Are there any other reasons?"

He thought for a second searching for the most inappropriate thing to leave her with. "She's a wanker too," he wanted to say with an inscrutable deadpan expression. Then he'd be able to amaze her with the painfully gory account of Ariadne's secret which he alone was privy to. Of course he didn't because that would have been contemptible, and it would have invalidated the total number of brownie points he'd earned. If he *had* said it, however, it would have been his jaw that dropped first because she'd have replied "I know, I've heard her do it." Instead he ended with "I think I've given you enough to reflect on but if I come up with anything else I'll let you know."

"Two other matters," she said, resuming her normal haughty manner. "Your behaviour at our weekly senior management get-togethers is appalling. You should smarten yourself up too."

CHAPTER 49

12 April 2005: 8pm

Mort was having a cigarette in his office, in a no smoking area, which, as Gordon might have joked, incurred the death penalty in Storbury. It didn't bother him as he gazed vacantly out of the window into the darkness. He'd smoked four or five already. He was going over the events of the day, and he winced whenever he recollected how he'd allowed Harrison and Miller to run rings round him. They'd accused him of killing a woman that he still cared for despite her coldness toward him. They'd arrested him and he'd put up no defence whatsoever, merely gibbering and mumbling inanities as they toyed brutally with him and twisted his words mercilessly. Then his brain slowly sent out a message to his consciousness that Ariadne must have wanted to masturbate earlier that morning and that, while she was doing whatever she did to herself, she'd have been fantasising about him. Was that how she'd intended him to interpret her quotation from *As You Like It*? Why had she been deliberately ambiguous? Was she a consummate actress and trifling with him also? How many times had he misunderstood her before? She loved him, she loved him not. Which was it? It didn't matter to him that she was dead.

He stubbed his cigarette out on the carpet, leaving one more charred stain and lit another. Why had he crumpled so easily in the face of the detectives' hostile intimidation? Was he a coward, too accustomed to living in a comfortable, middle class world of maudlin self-indulgence and flaccidity, concerned obsessively with not making mistakes or letting his house burn down? Then it hit him. His major problem – the one he'd never even considered – was that he'd vastly overestimated himself. This was what had disadvantaged him throughout his life, and he finally realised that it had contributed to his utter failure to leave Storbury. He thought he could handle himself without Cassandra but as the years passed without her, he couldn't. Suzie had been no use to him and Maureen, well, Maureen was a workmate and couldn't be anything else. Inertia had led to paralysis and finally to utter stagnation. His recent success, if that was what it was, had been no compensation when Ariadne had returned and reduced him to ashes. He had no tactics to deal with her cruelty and likewise he had no idea how to deal with the police. He was a pathetic failure and it was his own fault.

If things were to change, he had to face up to this novel sense of his personal reality and finally do something about it. He'd always wanted to be brave, strong and noble like his father had been when, in the Second World War, he'd repaired the broken-down engines of a tinder-box of a rocket ship in the middle of an enemy mine field. His father was recommended for a medal but one of his team went drunkenly berserk out of fear and tried to wreck the engine room. This valiant man did a deal with his captain and lost that medal, so that the poor bastard wasn't court-martialed. There it was! He was his father's son. He'd inherited the bad luck gene and there was nothing he could do about it.

"Well, dad, we'll see about that!" he said aloud to his reflection in the window. "I've been pushed around all my life and I've let them all do it. I worried about doing the right thing in the hope I'd be seen to be honest and fair. So much anxiety and look where it got me. My God, I could have gone to prison for a very long time! I've been the biggest wimp ever but that's going to stop. I might as well be hanged for a sheep as a lamb…a whole bleeding flock in fact. There's nothing left for me to fear but myself. What have I got to lose except my life? Bollocks to Ariadne, Bollocks to Cassandra, Bollocks to the police, Bollocks to Storbury bloody College – Bollocks to the whole bloody lot of them!"

He was woken from his dark contemplation when Helen ran excitedly into the office. She'd be called down by Miller to answer a few more questions and she was bursting to give him her news.

"They've found out who did it, Mort," she cried. "You can relax. They've gone off to make an arrest. We can all go home."

"I don't want to go home," he answered sourly, looking at his watch.

It was ten past eight and he was tired and hungry, but most of all he needed a drink of something that would take away his pain, his sorrow and his despair.

"They asked me what time I came to work this morning," she went on regardless. "Then they asked me if I'd spotted a car coming along the drive as I walked in."

"Had you?"

"Yes. They asked me if it was yours, but I don't know what sort you've got. Anyway, it was a dark red Alfa Romeo. Its front number plate's offset to the left. Very stylish and distinctive. That's why I remembered it."

"I think I know who it belongs to," he said, suddenly interested.

"Who?"

"You'll find out soon enough."

He saw that she was exasperated by the ominous look on her face, and he waited for the expletive-filled tirade that was bound to be bubbling up inside her.

"You must be knackered after all you've been through today, what with losing a woman you knew well and then being blamed for her death," she said quietly. "Come back to my place and I'll make you a bite to eat."

"As long as I can buy a bottle of something strong on the way," he said, putting on his jacket and taking out his mobile phone. "Get your things."

"What about making sure everything's turned off properly," she replied impishly.

"Bugger that," he loured, as he gently took her arm and led her out into the night.

It was dark but the rain had cleared so they walked to her house, passing no one on the way. They only stopped to buy the seventy percent proof Scotch he'd promised her. She was ecstatic at finally having lured him back to her home and she insisted on going into the off-licence to buy it for him. When they arrived at her house, he presumed that there was someone already there as the curtains were drawn and the downstairs lights were on. He thought it odd as he lingered out of sight in the shadows that she had to ask her neighbours for a key to let them in and, once inside, she hastily ran upstairs to make her bed – just in case.

He went into the kitchen searching for glasses, and nearly burnt his arm on the iron she'd forgotten to switch off that morning. She soon joined him, and he offered her a well-filled tumbler of whisky but she declined it, complaining that she'd be too drunk to cook if she started on an empty stomach. He watched her as she effortlessly prepared their supper of Spanish omelette and a green salad and he was reminded of Cassandra and Suzie, who'd both been excellent cooks – almost as good as his mother. What was it about women, he pondered, that makes them such experts when men as a rule are so useless? He hated cooking although he prided himself on being a good short-order chef – that is as long as it took less than twenty minutes from packet to plate.

He leaned against the wall and sipped his drink and, as he admired her dexterity, he realised he was seeing a different version of the glib, bombastic façade she presented to the office.

"Helen," he said when she was turning the thick, browning pancake. "Why did you call me lady boy this morning?"

"I said *lazy boy*," she replied without taking her eyes off the frying pan. "It was a joke, that's all. It's my mouth, you see. It's rarely in tune with my brain. Things come spewing out. I don't know what I'm saying half the time until I've said it."

"I hope things will change after today…"

"And after tonight…"

She dropped the skillet and ran over to embrace him. He let her do it but it felt somehow wrong, and he carefully unwrapped himself from her arms and pointed to the oven with the glass he was holding in his outstretched right hand.

"You'll spoil the dinner," he muttered, and she released him from her clasp.

They ate in the kitchen and afterwards moved into the cosy, half-lit sitting room where they sat together on the sofa. It was then that it registered that her house was identical to Suzie's, even down to the positioning of the furniture and lack of pot plants, pictures, ornaments and knick-knacks. Perhaps some women don't bother with much jumble and clutter until they move in with a man, he fancied, as the alcohol took effect. He would also know where the bathroom and the bedroom were if the occasion arose. She snuggled up to him as they listened to the music – *Everybody Hurts* by R.E.M. Had she chosen this intentionally? The lyrics were perfect. He was on his own, his days and nights were endlessly tedious, and he hurt deep down inside. Like the song said, he'd had enough, and he needed something…or someone…to hold on to. It was gratifying to know that his own feelings had been translated into a universal truth by a poet, but it never entered his head that Helen might be playing it for herself. Tears were welling up in his eyes as he drained his glass and he stretched out to refill it.

"You've had enough, my darling Clym," she said tenderly. "It's time for bed."

"Time for what?" he asked woozily. "Time for another drink…"

"Come on," she pleaded, and she began to ease him out of the luxurious softness of the cushions. He staggered to his feet and she dragged him unsteadily to the stairway.

"I know where I'm going," he laughed. "I've been here before and I know what you're going to do to me."

Helen too was feeling the effects of the two large scotches she'd consumed, and they stumbled and stuttered their way upstairs where they both collapsed onto the bed. It was a double bed – like Suzie's had been – and, as his mind wandered here and there, he presumed it was for such eventualities as this when fortune smiled on her.

"When were you here before?" she giggled as she removed his jacket and unbuttoned his shirt.

"Does every woman undress a man like this?" he drawled, becoming slightly irritated.

"You mean like this?" she slurred, unzipping his flies and pressing her face into his groin. After a few seconds, she came up for air and removed her glasses. He lay back and waited as she nuzzled him, poked around with her tongue and blew, but nothing was stirring.

"You can't get it up, can you, Mort?" she said, looking up at his face in despair.

"Wouldn't it be better if you took my trousers and underpants off first?"

"When was the last time you slept with a woman?"

"It's never happened to me before. I'm drunk…"

"That's original and I'm not going to ask you if it's me…"

"Why don't you take your clothes off? That'll help."

"All right. We'll get into bed and try again but I'm not optimistic."

She sat up and began to take her jumper off, then she froze.

"You're gay, aren't you?" she screamed, the familiar, scornful sneer appearing on her face.

"What the hell are you on about?" he snarled back. "What's given you that idea? If I was, I wouldn't be here with you, would I?"

"You haven't exactly made any of the running, have you? When did you last have a woman? It all makes sense. No woman, no cry, lady boy…"

"What makes you think I fancy an unpleasant, unattractive, little girl?"

"Go screw yourself then…"

"There you go again with your foul mouth…"

They were both sitting up now and glaring at each other thunderously. She was at the bottom of the bed, and he'd pulled himself to the top, his legs bent at the knees. He moved towards her, and she thought he was going to kiss her but all of a sudden he had his hands around her throat. Thomas Hardy hadn't written it like this. Clym was throttling Eustacia and it felt good, oh so good. He held on, held on, held on and held on. Everybody hurts. Die you foul-mouthed witch! You're all the bloody same and you've tormented me all my life…all my life. As his fingers tightened he saw first Cassandra, then Ariadne, and, finally, when her body went limp, he saw Helen's lifeless face again.

Those bloody stupid coppers, he thought – they hadn't taken his fingerprints or a DNA sample. No one had seen him coming here. He only had to wait for the newly gained warmth in his trousers to cool, then tidy up and leave quietly. He washed everything he'd touched thoroughly, making sure his glass, plate and cutlery were stacked neatly away. It was getting on for ten o'clock as he walked steadily back to the college, sobering up in the cool night air. Most of the houses he passed were in semi-darkness and, apart from a young man distractedly walking his dog, he met no one on his way. When he arrived in the car park it was pitch black; someone had forgotten to set the outside security lights when the clocks went forward, and his car was practically invisible against the night-blurred bushes at the far end. The police must have missed it when they packed up and Wallace also when he locked up. They probably wouldn't have even noticed it, intent as they were at leaving as quickly as they could after their long, arduous day. He thanked God that there was no barrier at the end of the drive. All he had to do was to get out of there unseen and he was safe. For the second time that day he drove home in the dark. It took him less than twenty five minutes.

Part 6

CHAPTER 50

12 April 2005: 5.45am – 7.30am

The heavy overnight rain had slowed to a drizzle when Iris woke at quarter to six. Vic was already up, preparing for his early journey to the city. Since Ariadne was always punctual, there would be slightly more than two hours to get ready, do the deed, and return in time to get changed and go back to the College. She dressed immediately, putting on a black sweater, black slacks and plimsolls, and she placed a black balaclava into the plastic carrier bag she was using to carry her equipment. She'd chosen a black outfit because she assumed that was how assassins dressed. Without washing she went downstairs and made herself a cup of weak, milky tea to settle the butterflies that were flitting around inside her stomach. She had to keep calm to ensure that Vic left promptly; then he wouldn't have the faintest idea what she was planning to do. Her tension eased as she saw the light of his torch as he checked over his wagon outside in the cobbled courtyard.

They lived in a small farmhouse in the foothills, about eight miles from the College, with three enormous barns that had been converted to serve as garages and light-maintenance workshops for his modest fleet of lorries and trucks. He was more than a mere 'lorry driver', as Maureen had sarcastically once described him; he owned a thriving haulage company, made more prosperous in the last few years by a long-term contract with Joe Crossley to transport imported goods from

Peru to the major cities and towns in the area. Most of the larger vehicles had already left to go to the depot in Storbury and, since he was the boss, he allocated himself the smallest articulated lorry and the shortest trip, and he was usually the last to leave.

She fumbled around in her bag to ensure everything was there: rubber gloves and overshoes, darning needles and a phial of curare. There was also a heavy, steel spanner as a fallback if something went wrong. She went over again why she was going to kill Ariadne to satisfy herself that it was the *right, sensible* thing to do and also to check that she hadn't lost her resolve. Then she rehearsed how she was going to do it. This had happened so frequently in the last twenty four hours that everything went smoothly, and this calmed her down even more. At last Vic pulled slowly out of the farmyard gates onto the main road. It would be well after ten before he returned, even later if he went to the café for a second breakfast. There was no one else around and she had about thirty nerve-jangling minutes to endure before she set off. She decided to wash after all and put on deodorant but no perfume or make-up. Obsessively, she paced around in the bathroom and went through everything in her mind one more time. She'd forgotten something: she hadn't yet tried on the balaclava, and she ran downstairs to go through it all again, this time with only her eyes visible. Her face became hot and she hadn't counted on that. To compensate for this she put a small flannel and some wet-wipes into her bag.

"That's it," she said to herself. "I'm going. I can't stay here any longer. I'll have to drive slowly."

She locked the house and went into the smallest barn where their two cars were garaged. She would use Vic's deep burgundy Alfa Romeo in preference to the old Nissan Micra she usually drove, because she'd only been to the college in the Alfa once or twice, and no one would connect it to her. When she got back after killing Ariadne, she'd return to work in the Micra. Everything had been organised so precisely that it didn't seem as if a murder was about to take place. It was more like going for an early morning expedition to the shops. Assuming all went well at the first attempt, she'd booked a holiday in New York, and they were leaving early the next morning. That would ensure she'd be out of the country during the murder investigation. She also persuaded Vic to have his lorry overhauled while they were away and he'd need the Micra later that morning to get back home, but she'd worked that out too. She'd arranged to leave it in a street near the College so that he could pick it up on his way back from the works. She already had the two fobs of keys for the Alfa, and she would conveniently hide Vic's set so that when he came to pick her up that evening, he'd have to use the Micra again.

She arrived at the college shortly before seven. The car park was empty except for the two cars belonging to Steven Wallace and the site technician Paul. She parked behind Wallace's car so that the Alfa couldn't easily be seen from the main building and pushed herself down in the driving seat to await the gruff sound of Ariadne's sports car. As the seconds ticked by, an intense rush of rage welled up inside her as the reasons for her impending, extreme act of violence flooded back into her mind. Ariadne had *ruined* the college in every sense of the word. She was embezzling money with Hugh and Mike, she was planning to make redundancies which would inevitably include her, she was vile to the staff, and she was a hardline, intellectual feminist.

Yet what rankled most was that she did something obscene in a public place, albeit out of sight of prying eyes and ears. This made Iris even more irate. She'd heard her 'doing it' by mischance one morning when she came in early to have a nose around her favourite part of the college, where she'd been happiest, and she still had all the necessary keys. In keeping with her firm belief that a woman's role was to look after the men in their lives, she practised what she preached. She'd looked after 'her Principals' for twenty years, she'd looked after Vic for nearly forty years, and she hadn't regretted any of it. She shouldn't have listened to the noise emanating from Ariadne's office the first time she caught her 'at it', but she couldn't help herself since the racket was very loud and it sounded as if someone was in terrible pain.

It was this that made her decide to kill Ariadne. She wasn't going to let some self-abusing man-hater with her all-women policies spoil everything – but Ariadne hadn't got everything wrong about men. There was Mort Todd, the grubby, cynical, cloth-capped upstart who'd disgusted her the instant she'd clapped eyes on him years ago, and she'd never forgotten his inconsiderate parking – twice. She would try to make it look as if he'd done it. That would be an added bonus, because he'd be a suspect from the outset. He'd known Ariadne long before she was Principal and jealousy would be an obvious motive, more than ever if, as it had been rumoured, he'd had an affair with her. She hit upon the idea of placing some archived course files from 1985 in the store room that would throw further suspicion on Mort, and it would put the police off the scent long enough for them not to consider for one minute that anyone else could be the killer they sought. Who would imagine it could be her in any event?

All that was left was to work out how to do the deed. She recollected seeing a horror film that had frightened and affected her deeply when she was in her early teens. It was called '*The Four Skulls of Jonathan Drake*', in which curare was used in an attempt to do away with the main character but it only succeeded in paralysing him, and the antidote was administered before the poison could take its full effect. This would be the ideal method; it would stop Ariadne in her tracks as well as do away with her. She still needed to locate a small amount of the drug and she knew where to look first. Sure enough there was a tiny supply in the pharmacology cupboard in one of the recently stocked, newly built, forensic science laboratories. It took her three weeks to track it down, and when she did, she had a stroke of luck; the cupboard door hadn't been locked. She was in two minds whether to report this act of negligence but that would have drawn attention to the missing bottle. The final stage was to work out how to use it, and not being a scientist herself, she found the information supplied by the Internet far too technical. In the end, after not too much deliberation, she decided that she would dip the tip of a long, thin, darning needle into the resinous slime and hope that would do the trick. If it was good enough for the South American tribesmen it would do for her.

She had to find a suitable opportunity and she was determined to spy again on Ariadne's early morning activities although she was sickened by the mere thought of it. Each day for two weeks in March, after the college had been opened, she sneaked into the executive suite and hid in the storeroom which she kept unlocked to facilitate her clandestine sleuthing. It transpired that Ariadne went through the same self-gratifying routine on Tuesday and Thursday, but not for the rest of week. She chose a Tuesday, the day of the weekly management meeting and she booked her holiday to start the following day. If Ariadne wasn't there, she'd work something else out when she got back. If she succeeded, she was going to leave Ariadne's body in the most humiliating position possible to reveal to everyone the true nature of the decadent woman she indubitably was. The rest would come out afterwards as the police delved deeper and deeper.

A rasping roar came up the drive and the squeal of brakes announced the arrival of the condemned woman. Iris remained hidden for a few more minutes and then she stealthily scuttled into the deserted building, tapped in yesterday's security code to the executive suite (which was never changed until eight o'clock by the early morning receptionist) and hid in Bernadette's office, locking it behind her, to prepare her weapons. When she knew it was time to act she put on her balaclava, gloves and overshoes and rushed into Ariadne's room, quickly stabbing the ill-fated femme fatale in the neck, and then in the right arm for good measure, using two of her needles. Ariadne didn't seem to register either of them. Iris turned away, not wishing to observe the depravity any longer and quietly tiptoed back to her old office, where she felt more comfortable. She stayed there for three or four more minutes until she heard no sound emanating from across the alcove. She returned to find Ariadne staring blankly at the ceiling, a horrified expression frozen into her motionless face. From her research Iris presumed it would be all over in less than half an hour but she couldn't wait for the curare to stop Ariadne breathing. She was going to do it herself.

"This is *my* college, young lady," she whispered into Ariadne's right ear. "I won't let you destroy it."

She calmly clamped her gloved finger and thumb around Ariadne's nose and placed her other similarly clad hand firmly across the mouth, squeezing the lips together as she did so. When the life went out of those sparkling eyes that had enchanted so many men, she let go and yanked out Ariadne's tongue to make a more grotesque display. Her last act was to steal Ariadne's handbag, which would establish yet another false trail for the police to follow. Finally she locked the door – and the door to Bernadette's office – laughing to herself that no one would dare to disturb Ariadne until twenty five past nine at the earliest.

She drove out quickly but watchfully and she spotted Helen walking up the drive. If that silly girl had seen her, she'd believe it was a man in the car as her face was still covered by her balaclava. No one else had seen her, no one would recognise the car, and no one would expect her to be driving around at that time. No one would suspect *a little, old lady* of anything. She stopped about three miles down the road in a deserted lane near a river where she threw the handbag, the bottle and the needles, one a time, into the fast-flowing stream. She clapped her hands in joy and, now feeling very hungry, she got back into her car and went home to burn her black clothing and the rest of her assassin's costume as soon as she got there.

How could she have known that her husband was at that very moment preparing to play 'Vigilante' with the man from Storbury College in the black Mercedes, the very man she'd introduced as 'Mr Todd' at a summer ball? Mort's memory of his rudeness to Bernadette at the same ball may have been hazy, but he was so drunk that he'd completely forgotten that he spent half an hour chatting to Vic at the bar about a group of elderly secret agents who patrolled narrow country lanes every morning, purposely delaying commuters and making him late for work.

CHAPTER 51

The Arrests and Aftermath

Iris and Vic were packing when they heard the police car sirens coming closer, followed shortly afterwards by blue lights reflecting against the dark sky and the trees beyond their farmhouse. Miller and Harrison allowed Tim to make the arrest as it was he who'd first deduced that it could have been Iris when he suggested that she had a weak alibi. She offered no resistance, asking very calmly how they'd been able to point the finger at her so quickly. 'Once you've ruled out the impossible, whatever remains, however improbable, must be the truth,' was Tim's terse justification, concealing the detectives' collective relief that if she hadn't come clean so willingly they'd have been in a very hard place with nothing more than rocks for comfort – and a great deal more explaining to do to the Chief Constable.

Iris had made two small blunders. First, she had to be the only person other than the caretakers, Bernadette and Ariadne who had a key to the Ariadne's office, having recently left her post as the Principal's Secretary. She was therefore the only person who could have locked the door after committing the murder. Steven Wallace had suggested that Iris might have held on to her keys after changing jobs; sure enough, a quick search of her handbag confirmed this. What clinched it, however, was her misplaced officiousness. She had a notorious reputation as a fierce car park bully, often confronting inconsiderate motorists when the car park was full and ordering them to leave the College and find somewhere else to leave their cars. She'd forgotten that, in her desire to be seen as a paragon of parking virtue, she'd filled in the number plate and the make of Vic's car on one of Wallace's staff car identification forms, so that he could recognise it in the event that she brought it to work and it needed moving. Wallace had remembered that he'd seen Helen walking up the College drive as a dark-coloured car passed her. Her identification of it as an Alfa Romeo by its offset front number plate plus his staff vehicle lists had provided them with the clues they needed to detain Iris before she went on holiday. They took a bemused Vic in too, on suspicion of being an accessory to a serious crime, but really it was to ensure that Iris didn't retract anything until they could get everything down on tape.

To their delight she told them everything. They couldn't shut her up. Not only did she confess to the murder and how she'd done it, she told them about the financial scams that Ariadne and her two henchmen were perpetrating against the funding agency and a multiplicity of local companies. She demanded that they charged Ariadne posthumously for offences against the Equal Opportunities Act by positively discriminating towards women in pursuit of her crusade for *feminist* supremacy over men. Miller wasn't keen to pursue that one, but she notified the Fraud Squad to probe further into Hugh's and Mike's activities. In addition Iris made a formal complaint against the College for keeping a controlled drug in an unlocked cupboard which made Harrison prick up his ears. He was curious where the drug had been sourced, and when she replied that it almost certainly came from Joe Crossley's Peruvian contacts, he became engrossed in her allegations. Finally she wanted Ariadne charged (again posthumously) with lewdness in a public place (or whatever it was called these days) which she regarded as only slightly less detestable than careless parking.

Vic was also very co-operative. On his way to the police station, in a separate car from Iris, he couldn't fathom what had happened, and he mistakenly supposed they were looking into some of his shady dealings where money changed hands without any supporting paperwork. They'd mentioned something about his being an accessory after the fact, but which fact was that? He kept quiet about the 'cash transactions', preferring, again erroneously, to talk about his legitimate contracts. When Joe Crossley's name cropped up again and again under questioning, Harrison leapt up and punched the air. He was looking forward enormously to the rendezvous with his local Member of Parliament the next morning.

At a quarter to midnight they called it a day. They were exhausted but it was the kind of fatigue that made policing worthwhile. They'd solved a murder, discovered a serious fraud, and they had enough evidence to charge Mort and Helen with conspiracy in failing to report a potential suicide. They might also have uncovered some juicy scandal involving a politician, but that would be for the future to decide. Furthermore, as Harrison reminded Miller and Tim when afterwards they were sharing a bottle of cognac in his dimly lit glasshouse of an office on the first floor of the ultra-modern Storbury police headquarters, they'd done it the old way by interrogation, deduction and intuition. Tim added that a large slice of "bloody good fortune" had helped but Harrison merely smiled and took another self-satisfied sip of brandy. Miller let him bask in his accomplishments, confident that this would change the next day when she took over formally as senior investigating officer, and he'd feel the full force of her more up-to-date ways of working. Welcome to the twenty first century she would mention casually as he was scurrying around pulling things together from a variety of electronic sources.

It was two days before Helen's body was found and another squad of detectives was assigned, Miller and Harrison being too busy delving into Joe Crossley's dubious dealings in Peru. Her murder remained unsolved since the new team could find no trace of anyone's presence in the house other than hers – not even her mother's or any of her work colleagues. No one had seen anything remotely suspicious on the night of her death, and everything had seemed normal to her neighbours because she invariably spent each evening by herself with only music for company. All the police had to go on was that she'd come home late and had been strangled. They'd found slight traces of another person's DNA on her body, on the furniture and in her bed, but they could find no match in the national database. She might as well have strangled herself for all they were able to uncover. When Harrison heard about it, he was left with this mystery. Why had two murders taken place in less than twenty four hours involving two people from the College? Moreover the second one had been committed in similar fashion to the first with no physical evidence available, but that was the only link since they already had the first perpetrator locked up. It was then that he dropped the conspiracy charges against Helen and Mort, considering it wouldn't be in anyone's interest to pursue the matter, and he was worried that if Mort brought a charge of false arrest against him, it might take the gloss of his achievements in the 'Storbury Curare Killing'. Unfortunately his newfound reputation became slightly tarnished when the Chief Constable arranged for him to attend a course on following official procedures in a murder investigation as soon as all the dust had settled.

What Miller and Harrison unearthed about Joe Crossley, however, rocked the country. His initial dealing in South American llamas in the north of England as an alternative to sheep farming had made him a tidy fortune. It was when he was approached by a Columbian drug baron that the money started rolling in – all securely tucked away in offshore accounts. He'd used his legitimate trade associations as a front for importing large quantities of cocaine, which he distributed hidden in a variety of other commodities via an unwitting Vic and his haulage company. They also traced numerous consignments to the College which Crossley had also used as a front. If anyone had wanted any drugs, legal or otherwise, they'd have found them there such was the variety that had been supplied and carefully stored, with one unfortunate exception. An inexperienced, young, part-time science teacher had one morning forgotten to lock the 'dangerous medicines' cupboard when she was in a hurry to get to her next class. Crossley was duly arrested and remanded in custody awaiting trial. Senior police officers from Scotland Yard travelled to South America and, together with their Peruvian and Columbian counterparts, they were able to curtail the activities of a large drug ring. Crossley would probably go to prison for twenty five years.

The three detectives who had so cleverly drawn together three separate and diverse crimes were each commended amid clamorous publicity. Miller asked for a transfer to Storbury which was granted straightaway; she headed the elite team there which naturally included Harrison and Tim. The solution to one puzzle eluded Harrison, however. He never did find out why she swept imaginary dust off her thighs. She stopped doing it when she was put in charge, and he never bothered to ask her about it again. The Hulk and Steven Wallace became good friends and two years later they opened a private security company together.

Iris pleaded guilty to murder and was given life imprisonment. She immediately became very unpopular with her fellow inmates up north in Styal Prison who accused her of harassment and constant interference in their affairs. She was transferred to Holloway, and after taking a few weeks to settle in, she is now happily running the place. Vic, who wasn't charged with anything, visits her regularly. He retired from the haulage business to concentrate on his hobby of restoring tractors and light goods vehicles, and he still managed to find time in the mornings to drive one slowly around the outskirts of Storbury.

Hugh Jones was investigated by the funding agency and was found, among a series of other serious discrepancies, to have falsified substantially the numbers of students attending the College and their achievements in order to gain pecuniary advantage. As he predicted, he was dismissed by the College but no charges against him were brought by the police. His solicitor successfully argued that he'd been coerced by Ariadne Hopwood into misrepresenting the figures, and, as she was no longer alive and Hugh hadn't benefitted personally, any grounds for prosecution were likely to be very flimsy. Similarly, Mike Smith was found to have aided and abetted the deception and he was also investigated for infringing the Data Protection Act. He resigned as Marketing Manager in an attempt to mitigate the prospect of harsher punishment. His immediate future didn't improve when his wife discovered his affair with Penny Carlton and obtained an injunction barring him from living at home and having access to his children. Like Hugh, he escaped prosecution, and he hasn't been seen in Storbury since.

Richard Head recovered sufficiently to be able to lead a fairly normal existence, but he resigned his post on leaving hospital and moved quietly out of the area as soon as he could arrange it. Since Mort had also absented himself temporarily from the College after his ordeal, it didn't escape Maureen, Penny, Lucy and Harriet that Ariadne's dream of having an all-female senior management team had ironically been fulfilled. She'd got what she wanted since they were the only ones who survived unscathed.

EPILOGUE

A Few Days Later

When Mort heard about the arrests of three of his former colleagues, he was in the middle of a spell of compassionate leave recovering from the tribulations of the day that had seen the deaths of two women. He hadn't been contacted about Helen's murder, but he expected a visit from the police eventually. He wasn't to know that they'd been snooping around the day after her body was found, asking his neighbours if they'd seen him on the night of the murder, and that they'd already excluded him from their investigation. A light had been on all evening, the neighbours confirmed, and they'd seen his car parked directly outside his house. That's what they thought they saw because Mort didn't get back from Storbury until shortly after ten o'clock but by chance someone drove off as he arrived home, fortuitously leaving him a convenient space for once. They must have assumed that, because of the difficulty in parking on Buchanan Road, the car had been there since early evening, and it stayed there for several days afterwards. Nor was anyone aware that the hall light had been on for most of the evening because it had been timed to come on at dusk. When he unlocked the door that night, he came across a piece of paper on his doormat with something taped to it. It was from Suzie. She'd found his house key in her dressing table drawer and had 'popped round' to post it through the letter box, as she was 'in the area'; she'd also enquired whether, if he still lived there, he 'fancied a drink sometime'. That was all she had written, apart from her name.

"Not another one," he sighed as he removed the key, screwed up the note and went off to bed.

A few days later, he received a phone call from Maureen. They chatted for five minutes about their respective well-being, occasionally reiterating how devastating the two deaths had been until, out of the blue, she asked him to meet her for lunch in Storbury the next day, as she had two 'pretty momentous' things to tell him. Mort agreed reluctantly, not wishing to go back there so soon and he proposed they meet in the Barred Gate, which was on the outskirts and well away from the College. When he pulled up in the small car park, heavy black clouds were gathering, and it was starting to rain heavily. Maureen was standing beside her car holding an umbrella. He noticed straightaway that she was dressed in a smart, brown suit and she was wearing make-up. Her elegant outfit clashed with the harshness of his leather jacket, sweat shirt and jeans.

The pub was empty, as it had been all those years ago when he went there with Ariadne, save for three or four shadowy figures in the tap room. Nothing had changed. There were the same benches against the two side walls and four round polished tables arranged in a horseshoe around the semicircular bar. It was still cluttered with ancient brass ornaments, toby jugs, two or three charity boxes and old newspapers, and the yellowing walls were covered in the same pictures of old Storbury. Mort rapped on the bar and a plump young woman with greasy black hair appeared as if from nowhere, wiping her hands on a towel. He ordered two orange juices and asked for the food menu. She brought up a creased and grubby, laminated sheet of card from under the pile of papers with the words 'Sandwiches: beef, ham or cheese' printed on it. There was nothing else. They both chose beef, and he invited Maureen to sit at a table in the corner on the left hand side of room furthest away from the entrance, the same one that Ariadne had chosen.

"Well," he said when they'd settled down. "What is it you wanted to tell me?"

"It's not like you to get straight to the point," she replied but she wasn't smiling. "Are you feeling OK?"

"I'm fine," he shrugged. "In fact I can't remember when I felt better."

She crossed her legs and smoothed her skirt, after which she calmly informed him officially that she'd been put in temporary charge of the College, and that Barry had taken over from him. He responded halfheartedly that he was content with that as he knew his department was in safe hands.

"I suppose congratulations are in order," he went on. "You must feel pretty pleased with yourself."

"Not at all," she laughed. "It's a poisoned chalice and I don't want to end up like the last incumbent. I'll do it till they find someone else then I'm going back to Student Services for good. Anyway that's not what I've dragged you all the way out here to tell you."

"What about the other lot. Who's covering for them?"

"No-one is. It's bloody chaos."

"*Plus* ça *change*, Maureen. I'm glad I'm well out of it."

She lifted her glass to her lips but didn't drink.

"Mort, why did you choose this place? Have you been here before?"

"Once, about twenty years ago with Ariadne. The funny thing is, it's just as it was then. It must be frozen in time."

"You never told me you went out with her," she said, genuinely surprised. "Did you come here often?"

He resisted the obvious joke and shook his head.

"Is that why you suggested this place?" she went on. "For old times' sake – or are you revisiting the scene of a crime?"

"What crime would that be?" he replied coolly, aware that she was teasing him and his spirits brightened.

When she didn't answer he sensed that there was something wrong and he repeated his opening question.

"What else did you want to tell me? You said you had two things. It must be earth-shattering if you wanted to have lunch with me. What will your husband think?"

"He's left me for a younger model," she murmured, and tears and mascara began slowly to roll down her cheeks. "Some floozy he works with at the bank. You're the only person I could think of to talk to about it."

Mort burst out laughing.

"Me?" he roared, with wide-open eyes. "Mr Has-been!"

"You've been through it all," she sobbed. "Mort, what do I do?"

"Do nothing," he replied, remembering that Ariadne had once asked him a similar question and he'd given her the same answer. "That's what I did. Perhaps he'll go and die on you like Cassandra did on me. Then all your troubles will be over."

They were interrupted by the arrival of the sandwiches. In stark contrast to what they were expecting, the chubby barmaid had brought two large plates on which were piled four large sandwiches, a mixed salad and several thickly cut, home-fried chips. She smiled proudly at them, but she was disappointed that they didn't return her warmth. She asked them if they wanted any condiments and when they both declined, she smiled again and went back to her kitchen, not registering that Maureen was crying.

"This should cheer you up," he said gracelessly as he helped himself to one of his sandwiches.

"You're a mass of contradictions," she said, wiping her eyes with a tissue. "I've always helped you when you've had some emotional crisis or other. God knows how many times. All these years I believed you were a compassionate man but now you're as hard as nails."

He was touched momentarily by her uncharacteristic display of vulnerability. When Cassandra had left him for

Stan, he was in turmoil. He'd felt betrayed, empty, lonely and unloved. He'd derived his confidence and his security from her and, without ever admitting it to himself, he'd floundered around for the last twenty years. Now he was looking at a woman he regarded as his best friend in the same hopeless, wretched state and he couldn't find any words to help her.

"It couldn't have come at a worse time for you, I suppose," he said, trying to be gallant. "Are you sure it's all over or is there any hope of reconciliation?"

"I'll never have him back," she replied bitterly. "How could I look him in the face and see the same man I married. It's deceit. It's a breach of trust. I feel so hopelessly stupid."

"Maybe you understand why I could never find it in me to tell anyone at the college about my break-up," he said, recollecting that he'd never mentioned that his marriage was over – or that his wife was dead – for nearly ten years.

Maureen had admonished him severely for not informing her, amazed that he could have kept such a secret from her for so long. He'd retorted that it was a fine example of how he felt about most of his colleagues and she'd marched off in a huff.

"Do you want to tell me what happened?" he continued. "That's if it's not too difficult."

She was looking sadly at him and nodding slowly.

"He left me a Dear John letter on the mantelpiece. Pathetic isn't it? We've been married for over thirty years. He's moving in with his new woman in the city."

They sat and ate their sandwiches slowly with their fingers. Occasionally they looked at each other but neither could think of anything to say. After a short while she turned to him.

"How did you get through it?" she asked.

"Very painfully at first," he answered, pushing his plate away. "Here's another cliché. I took it one day at a time. It was Christmas 1984 and I got very drunk a lot. Then all at once I snapped out of it. I received a dreadfully condescending letter from Cassandra's mother, which more or less said I'd never been good enough for her daughter. That did the trick."

"Yes," she said, raising a finger. "You changed for a while after that. You smartened yourself up and started to get on with Simon Junkin – and Jeff Shaw. Where have they and all the others gone?"

"How do you remember it all so clearly?"

"I've kept my eye on you. You were very different from everyone else in College in those days. So stiff and distant. You resisted Ariadne too, didn't you?"

She was looking at him intently, even quizzically. He pursed his lips and frowned.

"You want to know if I had an affair with her, don't you?"

She kept on gazing at him.

"Well, there were rumours, and why else would she ask to see you on her first day back at Storbury – directly after her first formal meeting. It looked pretty obvious."

"She once told me she loved me, but I didn't do anything about it. I already had a steady girlfriend – Suzie."

She looked aghast at him.

"I'd forgotten about her! She didn't last long either, did she?"

"A few years. She was my last real relationship but she wasn't important."

He paused, trying to regain his thread.

"If I'd been kinder to Ariadne and not so paranoid, she might be alive today."

"Did you love her? I wouldn't blame you. I saw how men leered at her. And lots of women fancied you too, Mort."

"Those are the words of an evil woman!" he grinned, visibly enjoying himself. "How could I contemplate a relationship with someone who was having it off with my boss, one of my section heads and a local councillor on her self-centred voyage to glory?"

"You're a very deep person, Mort Todd."

"Ah yes," he said gleefully. "Here's another one for you.

She used to pleasure herself dreaming about me. That's how she died, I expect. In ecstasy, thinking about me! That's why she's the second woman I killed."

"Second? Who was the first?"

"Cassandra."

"How?"

"By neglect."

"And Ariadne?"

"Much the same."

"How many more have you killed – Suzie too?"

She was gaping at him in disbelief – or perhaps she was wondering how sane he was. He'd certainly been acting strangely all the time they'd been there.

"Only Helen," he replied with no trace of emotion in his voice. "Inside everyone there's a murderer. It's always there and it comes out suddenly and silently. This time it wasn't…"

"Honestly Mort," she cut in, tilting her head back and tutting. "How did you neglect *her*? You were a model of patience. She was an insufferable, immature, young woman. Not your type at all. Anyway she was found dead at home – you wouldn't have gone there in a million trillion years even if you were plastered. There's no way you could kill anyone. If you'd have been David, Goliath would have killed you. You'd have felt too sorry for him to fire a stone at him."

He wanted to confess to her that he'd strangled Helen in a drunken fit of rage. He had to explain it all to someone, simply to make it real and not some starkly vivid memory from a terrifying nightmare. He had to go to the police but he couldn't, not yet. It would have to remain buried in the dark recesses of his mind a little longer.

"There I've cheered you up already," he said, after a pause. "You've always loved to get at me…"

"Pleasuring herself?" she butted in again.

It had just registered what he'd said about how Ariadne died.

"How do you know she was…?"

"The police told me."

"They kept that out of the papers!"

They were quiet again and she was starting to look disconsolate, wiping her eyes with her finger.

"Eat your lunch," he said, picking up a chip and nibbling it. "You're eating for a college now!"

"I don't want to go back," she murmured. "What have I to go back to? Complete pandemonium, auditors, the police, Ofsted and that's just for starters – and no one to help me. If that place was a hospital most of the patients would be dead or dying! Will you come and help me?"

"I'm never coming back, Maureen," he said resolutely.

"Not even for me?"

He shook his head and she seemed more dejected than he'd ever seen her.

"We've always been good friends…"

"There's a lot you don't know about me. You said so yourself a minute ago. I don't want to harm you."

"Harm me – you? You've many faults Mort, but that's not one of them. You couldn't knock the skin off a rice pudding."

"Working in education stinks, Maureen," he exclaimed, after staring openmouthed at her for a moment. "There's no recognition if you don't walk the walk and talk the talk. Teaching's a great job but you can stick the rest. You never get anywhere if you stay in the classroom. That's why there are so many crap managers. The careerists swallow everything whole and learn the right jargon words and phrases to get themselves promoted away from the real thing. You said it yourself ages ago – 'the bullshitters have finally arrived', and now they're in total control, what with their action plans, performance bloody indicators, quality effing control…You're running a factory, Maureen. There are no human beings in their world. Only data and statistics. I've had enough. I'm resigning."

"Why not be the person to change it. You've done it before and you can do it again."

"Not any more. I don't belong with those braindead, smug, middle-class narcissists I met at Storbury. I never did. I'm going home, back to my roots. I'm putting my house on the market and I'm going to take care of my parents in Leeds."

"What if I asked you to stay…for me?"

"I've told you no. You know nothing about me."

"I know more than you think."

"What are you talking about? You said it yourself. We're just good friends, Maureen."

"We've spent more time together over the years than if we were married."

He tapped nervously on the top of the table and moved around awkwardly on his seat.

"Are you propositioning me?" he said trembling.

"Can we make a go of it? I hope you want to. We can be more than good friends, can't we?"

"I've killed three women…"

"Oh shut up," she snapped. "If that's a put-off it's the worst I've ever heard – or maybe the best!"

"Your husband's just walked out on you and you're planning your next liaison…"

"I said shut up. You're a handsome guy and you're fun to be with until you get into one of your black moods. I've seen the way women look at you. How do you know I wasn't looking too?"

"You were happily married…"

"So were you to all intents and purposes for ten lying years. Look at you now!"

"My parents are in their seventies. They need me."

"I need you too."

"I'm not coming back."

He looked at her with those steel-blue eyes of his.

"Why don't you come with me?"

For a moment she looked uncertain. It was something she hadn't considered.

"I have to go," she said abruptly.

She picked up her umbrella and walked to the door, where she stopped and turned around with a serious look on her face.

"Ring me. Ring me soon. Don't write to me, don't text me and don't, for Christ's sake, email me."

He waited for about five minutes, then he paid for their half-eaten meals and left. As he walked to his car, he lit a cigarette and reflected once again on the vagaries of his life, wondering if there were going to be any more unexpected twists. He'd changed and, it seemed, so had his luck. The rain had stopped and the sun was flickering behind a thin veil of light grey clouds. By the time he started his engine he'd forgotten about turning himself in to the police. After all, Maureen said he hadn't done it – he couldn't have done it, she actually said. It wasn't in him, she said.